Pants On Fire!
A Tale of Friction

Arabella Ark

Pants On Fire! A Tale of Friction is a work of literary fiction. Names, characters, and incidents are the products of the author's imagination and are used fictionally. Any resemblance to actual events, or persons, living or dead, is entirely coincidental.

Other Books by the Author

Doggone

Permissions

Pants On Fire!

Inspired by DW

Believed in by CJ and DG

Take heed lest any man deceive you.
Mark 13

Love is not a plaything···do not write
unless you can do it with a
crystal conscience.
John Keats

Deceiver, dissembler
Your trousers are alight
From what pole or gallows
Shall they dangle in the night?

···What internal serpent
Has lent you his forked tongue?
From what pit of foul deceit
Are all these whoppers sprung?
William Blake

Pants On Fire!
A Tale of Friction

By
Arabella Ark

Part One

Pants On

Waxing Of The Moon

From: Selene Steiner laluna@gmail.com
Date: June 15, 2008
To: Ariane Altar ariane@altarpots.com

Guess who called tonight? Wylie Hymen, our lit teacher from City! I told him to *Google* "The Famous One"...you!

OOO Selene

From: Ariane Altar ariane@altarpots.com
Date: June 15, 2008
To: Selene Steiner laluna@gmail.com

Now how and why would Wylie Hymen call, and how did he get your number, and, my god, how old is he now? Wasn't he old already when he taught us in high school? Is he the one you had a crush on?

From: Selene Steiner laluna@gmail.com
Date: June 16, 2008
To: Ariane Altar ariane@altarpots.com

He hasn't taught in years and is a writer now. When he called, he said he was tracking down old students from City By The Bay, looking through year-books, I guess, trying to reconnect. I got the funny sense he was a little flirty. Anyway, he did an oral history of my mom and her time in Shanghai as a Jewish refugee during the war. You know how many times my mom has hired people to write her story? So, he said he wanted to give the tapes to me, as he's getting old and knows he won't write her story after all this time. I had a crush on the art teacher, until I found out he was sleeping with my mom. Talk about being eclipsed!

From: Ariane Altar ariane@altarpots.com
Date: June 16, 2008
To: Selene Steiner laluna@gmail.com

So, why did Hymen call you instead of your mom?

From: Selene Steiner laluna@gmail.com
Date: June 16, 2008
To: Ariane Altar ariane@altarpots.com

He said he thought she'd probably died, so he started looking for me.

OOO Selene

From: Ariane Altar ariane@altarpots.com
Date: June 16, 2008
To: Selene Steiner laluna@gmail.com
Subject: *Googling* Hymen

I suspect he called you, La Luna, rather than your mom, because he remembered how gorgeous you are!

Wylie Hymen appears to be rather interesting! I *Googled* him. He's an award winning painter, author, and illustrator of children's books, mostly concoctions of moral fables or recreations of historic voyages. From what I have gleaned, most of his stories are about the building of boats from ancient times to the last century and the new worlds they opened—Magellan's *Trinidad*, Captain Cook's *Endeavor*, Columbus' *Santa Maria*, and more. Houghton Mifflin published his latest, *Where's Noah's Ark?* The advance PR says this spring Mr. Hymen is doing a narrative for a video documentary for *National Geographic* in the mountains of Ararat in Turkey based on it. Hymen says about himself,

(he) always got in trouble in school for drawing when he was supposed to be doing his math or geography. Now that he's grown up, nobody seems to mind, so he spends his days in the mountains of Northern California at a place called Chicken Ridge near Indian Springs, places no one has ever heard of, writing, painting, and illustrating books.

I am going to call him. I need to find someone to help me publish the children's stories I've written. I don't know a soul in the field of children's literature. And, voila, you come up with old Mr. Hymen! Let's see if he is willing to help! Thank you, and thank God! Where in the world is Chicken Ridge?

From: Cherry Estrella cherry@starsearch.com
Date: August 8, 2008
To: Ariane Altar ariane@altarpots.com
Subject: This is X rated

Have you gotten the latest news about John Edwards having a mistress, putting her on his campaign payroll, and rolling in the muck? I am wondering if men are actually aliens? What do you think? Have they ever learned to follow basic rules of life on earth, like to play nicely with their friends, to share their toys, to tell the truth, to remember family comes first, and to be nice to girls? Here's a *ha-ha* for you:

> *Apple* announced today that it has developed a breast implant that can store and play music. The *iTit* will cost from $499 to $699, depending on cup and speaker size. This is considered a major social breakthrough, because women are always complaining about men staring at their breasts and not listening to them.

From: Ariane Altar ariane@altarpots.com
Date: August 9, 2008
To: Selene Steiner laluna@gmail.com
Subject: publishing help

Wylie Hymen called this morning (I had called him ages ago and left a message). He remembered me, especially that morning we got the news in his literature class of JFK's assassination. He reminded me that he had to call your mother, because you and I got hysterical and had to be banished to the girls' bathroom until she could pick us up.

We talked for a long time about books. One of the publishers I had sent my books to has published three of Wylie's. Anyway, he is going to come to Berkeley on Monday to help me while I am at mom's house! He said tons of complimentary things about us at City and then about your mom and his desire to write her story. I guess he started to write it thirty years ago when he said he recorded her oral history. He mentioned he had run into you on the U.C. Berkeley campus a few times in later years. You had arranged for them to get together or something.

Pants On Fire!

From: Ariane Altar ariane@altarpots.com
Date: August 9, 2008
To: Wylie Hymen wylie@hymenfables.com
Subject: Ariane Altar's children's stories!

Dear Wylie,

It is awkward to call you by your first name. I feel like I should be saying, "Mister Hymen" like I did in high school.

I want to thank you for the spectacular phone call! You sound wonderful! Little did I know what an interesting life you carved for yourself in the years after City. Wow! I am impressed and embarrassed that I didn't connect the dots that my old teacher was THE Wylie Hymen whose work I have enjoyed for many years.

I am attaching samples from two of my series: the *Mango Tango* series about self-discovery through adventures in nature and the *Bebe Banana* series about learning to become a useful member of the community. You are more than kind to consider meeting in Berkeley at my mother's home. We'll talk about the logistics later, when your computer is up and running! Please plan to have lunch with us.

Gratitude and aloha,
Ariane

From: Selene Steiner laluna@gmail.com
Date: August 23, 2008
To: Ariane Altar ariane@altarpots.com
Subject: Tahoe

Dearest Ariane,

It was great to have you with us at Tahoe last week! Glorious weather, loved our hikes, thanks for all the wine and macadamia chocolates! You spoil us! Rick can't get over how we laughed ourselves onto the floor watching the Olympic volleyball games on TV—I daresay he got a tiny insight into the hysterical idiocy we've shared since City days! Neither of us can get over how happy you made Theia—she's been cranky for months with dad's heart condition and their financial downturn. With your offer to write her life story, she lit up like an electric plant! You know how she loves being the center of attention. Anyway, I think she'll live off this one for a long time.

OOO La Luna Selene

Pants On Fire!

From: Mom ednawolfeson@peoplepc.com
Date: August 29, 2008
To: Ariane Altar ariane@altarpots.com
Subject: Thank you!

Ariane, Emily, Whatever, Whoever,

Thanks for all you did for me. My caregivers were happy to finally meet you. I like that Mr. Hymen. I didn't remember him. He does look like the veritable fox in the hen house. I'll bet he has a lot of old lady friends!

Grrr Your Tiger Mama

From: Wylie Hymen wylie@hymenfables.com
Date August 30, 2008
To: Ariane Altar ariane@altarpots.com
Subject: Beautiful you!

Dear Ariane,

It's hard to describe what seeing you again has meant to me. It may sound odd, but I have never forgotten you and your radiance since my first year of teaching at City. I knew you would make something of yourself: you had that star quality. But, seeing you again, more than forty years later, only confirms my earlier appraisal. You are a beautiful woman, quite unchanged from your glowing sixteen-year-old self, yet so accomplished. When you opened the front door of your mother's house, the breath left my body. I may have even started to pant! Forgive me! And, at the end of the afternoon, when you took my hand so easily in yours, my heart was opened. I am truly touched. One day maybe you'll tell me why you took my hand and told me how warm and comfortable you felt with me. "You are like family," I think you said.

What a career you have had! Pieces of your ceramics in the Victoria and Albert, the Smithsonian, Yixing, Paris, Kyoto, Sydney. After reading your CV, I opened a bottle of wine to toast you! Teaching with residencies at ceramic centers in England, France and Holland, designing for Wedgwood, leading workshops around the world, owning your own gallery in Honolulu, on top of living abroad for so many years: Greece, France, Sweden, Japan, England.

Now my excitement grows. I had long ago given up the hope of writing Theia's story. The whole holocaust experience is daunting and has been fully explored. I could no longer see putting my energy into it. But, your enthusiasm changes everything. To write a book with you would be a joy and an honor!

7

Pants On Fire!

I am Jewish, but, grew up in Chicago, safe, middle class, and American. I was not personally exposed to war or prejudice. But, I have been fascinated by the stories of survivors of the holocaust. Theia was unusual. Oh, she always struck me as unusual for many reasons I am sure we shall discover together and write about, but also because she escaped the horrors of Europe. She was able to mature from an adolescent girl into quite a woman of the world during the war years, living a relatively comfortable life in Shanghai.

I met her at City on parents' night, September 17th, 1963. You might remember Tom Broder, the art teacher? We were standing there waiting to greet parents, and I mentioned I had this extraordinarily pretty girl in my class, Selene Steiner. He said, yes, she was pretty and was taking his art class. "But wait until you see her mother!" he said. And, he was so right. Somehow, I cannot remember why, she greeted me in Mandarin, and her voice and accent made that cacophonous language sound magical. Then she tossed her head, laughed, and said, in her inimitable way, in German this time, "Oh, Mr. Hymen, I hope you'll forgive my little girl, Selene, for becoming so American! Such a cheerleader. I don't understand these things, these American girls!" I found her utterly charming.

Wylie

Letter from Theia to Ariane
with a large box labeled "Shanghai Memorabilia"
September 20, 2008
Berkeley, CA

Dear Ariane,

Vladimir and I have decided to sell our Berkeley home. We are living full time in the retirement community now, which is so convenient, and we don't want to worry about the upkeep of that big old house! The staff here organizes everything beautifully, making our lives much easier. They drive us to the opera and art galleries, restaurants, and the symphony. We don't have to worry about driving at night or parking in the city. It's like the old days in Shanghai when I had my own chauffeur and limousine! Anyway, I have had to pack up all our personal belongings. I found some scrapbooks of those years in Shanghai, some tapes, which may or may not be useful to you as I don't have a cassette player any longer and can't remember what is on them anyway, and some old letters. If you find anything useful, good; if not, just throw it away. We look forward to seeing you at Selene and Rick's wedding.

Love to you always, my darling girl,
Theia

8

From: Ariane Altar ariane@altarpots.com
Date: September 30, 2008
To: Wylie Hymen wylie@hymenfables.com
Subject: my new preoccupation
Photo: My granddaughter

Dear Wylie,

As you can see, my daughter, Ande, had a fine baby girl. I am cleaning, gardening, and generally getting my home back in order after helping her for a month.

I am glad to hear you are getting Theia's tapes transcribed. How do you envision her story? Is it a Jewish refugee story, a Shanghai ghetto story, a story of loss, a communist take-over story, a love story, a story of survival?

I would personally be most interested in crafting a story of hope. Her family, while having to leave Poland and their fortune, did make money once again in Shanghai and did not live in the poverty of the Hongkew ghetto but lived rather in the fashionable French Concession in a home vacated by some repatriating British.

I have always loved names and their meaning. In Greek myth, Theia was the name of the Titan goddess of sight, glitter, and glory, renown for her blue eyes (which our Theia has!). She was the wife of Hyperion and the mother of three children: the sun god, Helios, the moon goddess, Selene, and the dawn goddess, Eos.

Is it common, do you know, Wylie, for Jewish parents to give their children names of Greek gods? I thought Jewish children were named for a deceased relative of the same sex.

Aloha, Ariane

From: Wylie Hymen wylie@hymenfables.com
Date: October 1, 2008
To: Ariane Altar ariane@altarpots.com
Subject: Grandchildren photos

Dear Ariane,

It's a delight seeing the three generations together. What a lovely granddaughter and proud mom. And, what a beautiful name. One of the pleasures of living in Hawai'i was hearing the native language for the first time. What does "Kui'iakealoha" mean? And, what will you call her?

I'll trade you granddaughter photos. Asia is four and Sage is eight going on fourteen, but this photo was taken a year ago. I was often asked after Sage was born what it was like to be a grandfather. It doesn't seem to make much difference, but

9

Pants On Fire!

what's really fun is watching my forty-six year old son grow up and be a parent. Sage and Asia's mom and dad are better at parenting than I was; more purposeful, more focused, and informed about how they are raising the children.

I have not forgotten you. The editor at Roaring Brook will be back from a vacation next week. My editor at Houghton, who is probably the best editor I've ever had and with whom I had hoped to do books forever, informed me last week that she may be changing publishers. Whatever happens, I'll do my best to connect you somehow with someone in publishing before I fly off to Istanbul and Mount Ararat (where we film the location of the *Ark* from October 18th to November 10th).

I had another reunion yesterday. About a month ago, I contacted Roxie Plumm who, I believe, was a friend of your younger sister at City. She told me all about her life as a photo-realism painter of wild and endangered animals after she graduated in 1968. The next thing I know, she arranged a reunion with four other students who were in my Chinese Literature and History class. I'm still thinking about it. We met for lunch on Telegraph Avenue, then we all walked over to City and spent an hour in my old room, followed by a lovely dinner and continued talking into the night. Following my reconnection with you and Selene, it has given me much to reflect on. I'll write you about it or, better yet, tell you about it when next we get together.

No, it was not common for Jews to name their children for Greek gods. But did you notice that my Ukrainian Jewish name could also be Greek? After all, Hymen was the god of marriage. Hymen also became known as the sacred skin of a virgin! I think when my grandfather immigrated, they misspelled Hyman, which in Yiddish means, "man."

All best wishes, "Grandma,"
Wylie

From: Wylie Hymen wylie@hymenfables.com
Date: September 30, 2008
To: Iggy Fumer iggyf@gmail.com
Subject: CASES

Dear Iggy,

Okay, five this month. Four every month until we run out. End of next week should be do-able, after that I am off to film a project in Turkey. If you need help, call Pooky or Roly.

From: Iggy Fumer iggyf@gmail.com
Date: October 1, 2008
To: Wylie Hymen wylie@hymenfables.com
Subject: Re: CASES

Wylie dah-ling.

Can I please get my four cases by the end of next week BEFORE you leave? AND four when you get back to keep me stocked for the rest of season? Okay? Please confirm. Would it be possible for Pooky to send an extra fifth while you're gone? Please let me know ASAP. Don't want to be left in the lurch!

Hugs, Igg

From: Ariane Altar ariane@altarpots.com
Date: October 1, 2008
To: Wylie Hymen wylie@hymenfables.com
Subject: Re: Grandchildren

Dear Wylie,

Your granddaughters are gorgeous: lucky you! Kui'iakealoha means "love that has been consumed as passion." We're calling her "Kui" for short (sounds like a bird's coo-ee) as she coos like a happy little bird.

Thank you for the manuscript advice. I have finished a body of ceramic work and have my kiln firing. Soon I shall focus on some new stories and illustrations. Have a grand time in Turkey. One of my dear friends leaves for Bhutan next week. I envy the travels. I'd be off as well, if it weren't for my empty pocketbook. I continue to see my "ship" on the horizon, probably why I live by the sea, waiting anxiously for it to come in!

Ariane

From: Wylie Hymen wylie@hymenfables.com
Date: October 15, 2008
To: Ariane Altar ariane@altarpots.com
Subject: Updated website

Dear Ariane,

Hymenfables.com is up and running. I had to put a bunch of accolades and other PR stuff on the site, which reminded me of how much fun I've had as a writer.

11

Pants On Fire!

Being on "Good Morning, America" was a particular standout. I've never owned a suit or sports coat in my life. My father was alive then and was mortified at the idea of his son being on national television in a turtleneck or denim work shirt, my normal garb. He had flown to New York from Chicago to be with me for this event. Before I went on the air, he forced his tweed jacket on me, shoulders too tight and cuffs well above my wrists, attempting to cover my old shirt. I felt literally straight jacketed for live TV!

I'm having the same problem with the Roaring Brook editor; I leave messages but don't get called back. I leave for Turkey Saturday, and I feel terrible that I've not been able to do what I promised for your book.

Wylie

From: Wylie Hymen wylie@hymenfables.com
Date: November 6, 2008
To: Dina Cochon dinaRN@iswell.org
Subject: Mount Ararat

Hi, my love,

Oh, how I miss you, my little Pooky. We have had a week of adventure, morning temperatures to twenty degrees, a little snow, and two days trekking before we got above tree line today. It's all too big to write about, but I have made it the whole way without *Diamox*, keeping up pretty well with the young *National Geographic* "mountain goats" (I actually am growing particularly fond of one young fellow named Curt) and our Turkish staff. The food is all wonderful, but I lost my appetite a week ago, even though I am not taking any meds, and have to force myself to eat to fuel the hard trekking.

I am tired and have acquired a cough, but am well satisfied with what I have accomplished, considering my seventy-two years on this planet. I think all the time now that I am only about a week away from seeing you again in our little house in the mountains. Give my love to our kitties, Pearly and Gates. They will be very jealous when I tell them about passing a trekker yesterday, hearing a meow, and seeing a little kitty head sticking up out of his pack. Please call Baron and let him know that all is well.

My love has not dimmed even at this great distance, dear one. How I hope you and Mills have received my postcards and photos of this immense and beautiful place. Two of my exciting and adventurous new friends from *National Geographic* flanking me in some of the photos are Curt Degler and Jill Forthright. How I wish you could have made this journey with me, as we have shared many remarkable journeys. I'll call from the airport.

Know that I think of you in every moment, my love.

Your Wylie, missing you so

From: Wylie Hymen wylie@hymenfables.com
Date: November 20, 2008
To: Ariane Altar ariane@altarpots.com
Subject: Mount Ararat
Photo: Wylie ascending through snow somewhere around 15,000' with guide; another 2,000 feet is the resting place of the *Ark!*

Dear Ariane,

Even though I've been home in Indian Springs over a week, I'm really not "back" yet. I'm sure you know the feeling. I've discovered Turkey, as Bali has always been for me, to be one of those places from which you return but, still, a part of you always remains there.

Then, there's the enormity of the experience; I shall be weeks if not months sorting it all out. What I do know now is that I've had the greatest adventure of a long, adventurous life, and an intensely personal one. Often, on the trail, I thought of a couple passages in Peter Matthiessen's *Snow Leopard*, which I read again after thirty years, before leaving. He wrote something to the effect that mountains, more than the ocean or sky, act as a mirror to one's true being, making the self sharper, tougher, more honest, more real. They open one's spirit to a special emptiness, one without life or sound yet which holds all life and all sound.

So, what did I see in that vast mirror? Well, strange as it may sound, the most profound experience was coming up against what I could not do. For the first time in my life, I found my limit; I actually came up against that infamous wall. I have to say that I enjoyed good health the whole trip – not a single headache, no nausea. But, the morning I headed up toward Ararat's summit, I reached a point about a third of the way beyond which I knew I could not go. Try another day, after a couple more days of acclimatization? Perhaps. But, not that morning, maybe not ever. Then the crew helped this old man out. They brought in their gear by helicopter, and it picked me up to finish the last bit to the summit.

Everyone asks, "What was the best part of the filming?" I'd say looking at the vastness of the landscape from the summit, imagining it as Noah might have seen it, under receding waters, and the miracle of knowing he was spared, relieved his long ordeal was over.

Pants On Fire!

But, in fact, we were there to de-bunk the myth of the *Ark*! There have been numerous searches over the centuries for the *Ark*. *National Geographic* wanted to follow each story and clarify with facts, showing what may or may not have been true.

Lots of fundamentalists and pop mythmakers go in for the *Ark* on the slopes of Mt. Ararat. In 1995, a documentary was made based on the work of two geophysicists. They claim that 10,000 years ago, there was a catastrophic flood of the Black Sea. The Mediterranean broke through the Bosporus and turned what had been the largest body of freshwater on the planet into a brackish, anoxic sea.

But, even if all the ice at the poles and every glacier on the planet melted, there would still not be enough water to get the *Ark* up as high as the summit of Mt. Ararat.

Some geologists believe that quite dramatic, unusually great flooding of rivers in the distant past might have influenced the legends. One of the latest, and quite controversial, hypotheses of this type is the Ryan-Pitman Theory, which argues for a catastrophic deluge about 5600 BCE from the Mediterranean Sea into the Black Sea. This has been the subject of considerable discussion, and a news article from *National Geographic* News reported that the flooding might have been "quite mild."

Perhaps the real story is written in the sky, where the Mesopotamian astrologers first defined the story. There is an astrologic connection to the Flood Myth. Apparently, most of the classical, Biblical mythology consists of literary transcriptions of what the Magi defined in the motions of the constellations.

Amazing meals were prepared on the trek for us: lamb spitted over the fire, eggplant served in more delicious ways than I have eaten in my whole life. The food was fresh, bought locally, until we got above tree line and agriculture. What more can you say about a meal that begins with mint tea, tomato egg-drop soup, then several courses of fresh vegetables, rice pilafs of endless variation, and finishes with pistachio and almond baklava or honeyed dates and succulent dried apricots? All prepared on kerosene stoves amidst a jumble of stainless steel pots in a little tent or, more often, out under the sky. How about waking up every morning to a lilting "Good Morning," and "salaam alaykum" and hot mint tea or aromatic, rich Turkish coffee drenched in sugar to be sipped right there in your sleeping bag?

I think, from what I've seen in the rushes, that the film we shot will be spectacular. If I am immodest, I am well pleased with my narrative. Besides all that, I found beautiful carved miniature boats in an amazing old walled city at the foot of Mount Ararat. One for you, a tiny ark, sits on my window ledge waiting for the day you visit me here. What's next? Several more weeks of filming for the crew. Then the editing. And, for me, sitting in my comfortable cabin on Chicken Ridge, reflecting on this new experience.

My older son, Baron, who was disappointed he couldn't come with me, has asked if I will join him for a trek in Nepal for his fiftieth birthday in 2012. I am honored he thinks I can still keep pace with him!

Wylie

From: Ariane Altar ariane@altarpots.com
Date: November 20, 2008
To: Wylie Hymen wylie@hymenfables.com
Subject: thank you

Dear Wylie,

What a wonderful journey you have had! You are very generous to share it in your writing. My mom is visiting me in Hana for the Thanksgiving holiday. I took the liberty of reading it aloud to her, a little armchair tourism. Ande, Nalu, and the baby arrive later today. We'll have four generations under my roof: mom will meet her new great granddaughter! She and my Marianna were very close. Did I tell you Ande gave the baby Marianna as her middle name? For me, a sharp bite of bittersweet.

Aloha, Ariane

From: Wylie Hymen wylie@hymenfables.com
Date: November 21, 2008
To: Jill Forthright jforthright@ng.org
Subject: Mount Ararat photos

Dear Jill,

Thank you for all the *National Geographic* photos of our expedition to Mount Ararat. Of course, I love all the professional panoramic shots. They are stunning and a wonderful reminder of one of the best trips of my life. I am particularly enamored of the personal, little one of our tent. Your warmth made all the difference to me on the trip between surviving or freezing to death! I'll hold our time within that tent forever in my heart. Stay in touch. If ever in California, let me take care of you in my mountain retreat under a bower of oak leaves and speckled sunlight.

Wylie

From: Wylie Hymen wylie@hymenfables.com
Date: November 21, 2008
To: Curt Degler cdegler@ng.org
Subject: Mount Ararat

Dear Curt,

A note to acknowledge my debt of gratitude to you. I am not sure if I could have made it to the summit of Ararat without your guidance! My legs were great but my lungs were not! I didn't know the effect that altitude would have on my palpitating, septuagenarian heart! It proved a bit more than I could handle. Your support and encouragement were invaluable. Do I owe you my life? Maybe not. Just my devotion! I would trek with you anywhere. Please let me know where you are adventuring next and if I may hitch a ride!

Wylie

From: Ariane Altar ariane@altarpots.com
Date: December 6, 2008
To: Wylie Hymen wylie@hymenfables.com
Subject: ouch and hello

hi wylie
broke right arm
tripped over dog
had surgery
titanium plate and 10 screws
typing left hand
can't drive
nalu took me to the hospital
am doing great as a one armed walking talking adventurer
slightly but only slightly humbled
cannot do art for four to six months while arm heals
i guess it is an opportunity to write

here is an invitation of sorts
i have time and mental energy to conjure a script
would you be interested in coming to hana and camping in my guesthouse after
the holidays to see if we can structure a script about theia
i have a few commitments to honor, but can deal with those if this idea has
relevance for you and if mutual timing works
your thoughts

From: Wylie Hymen wylie@hymenfables.com
Date: December 9, 2008
To: Ariane Altar ariane@altarpots.com
Photo: from Ararat at dawn

Dear Ariane,

Metal plate? You're in for real problems from here on going through airport
security!

But, I have some good news. I decided that our best strategy is to start with
Roaring Brook with whom I am currently working on a book. Besides, I think I
mentioned that my beloved editor at Houghton Mifflin, Erica – I once told her I
wanted her to be my editor for the rest of my life – left. I have no rapport yet with
her replacement; in fact, we've never even talked. After weeks of emails and phone
machine messages, I finally heard from the RB editor, Janet Loughman, this morning, and I told her about you. She would like to see your book and to see some art,
if you're still considering illustrating the book yourself. She wants you to know she
is slow – this from a publisher who has had my manuscript for over two years, and
we're only now beginning the editing process.

If you'd like, we could talk about the next step, your submission. We should
make a phone date. You email me when you are available, and I'll call you. I don't
want you to end up with a big phone bill. Evenings would be best.

Now, about Theia: It seems to be a bad time for arms. Jenn, the woman to
whom I gave the first of Theia's tapes to transcribe, emailed me last week to say she
has a horribly painful case of carpal tunnel and the prognosis is that she will probably not be able to work at a computer ever again, an especially devastating diagnosis, because this is the way she earns her living. I should get the tape back from
her in the next couple of weeks and send it on to you. After you've had a chance to
listen to this first episode in Theia's story, we'll talk, and if you think we ought to
continue, I shall have all the tapes transferred to CD. It's not expensive, and I can
make copies for Selene. In the meantime, I will look for another transcriber.

Hana is an intriguing idea. Sometime after the first of the year, I'm up for a
surgical procedure that could result in some limiting, albeit temporary, side effects.

17

Pants On Fire!

The doctor consultations begin next week. I've known about the possibility for a year and held off doing anything about it until I returned from Turkey. The doctor says NOW! The editing work with Loughman is to start in earnest also in January. Then, a little further in the future, at the end of April, I'm speaking at a literary festival in Massachusetts, and I hope, doing some book signings for *Where's Noah's Ark?* If all goes well, we could think about March, although there is a good chance *NG* will need me at some point to do a voice over for the *Ark* film.

I'd love to have immense amounts of time with you, see your studio, and come home with an Ariane artifact.

Wylie

From: Ariane Altar ariane@altarpots.com
Date: December 13, 2008
To: Wylie Hymen wylie@hymenfables.com
Subject: Re: Lot's of stuff

wow
that photo is a jewel to be contemplated and savored
what good news for me about roaring brook
thank you
i was a bit confused about your editors and publishers
but now i understand
you use different ones for different books
currently houghton
next one roaring brook
sometimes godine
i would like to make the submission to rb
want to coach me
i am around all evenings
what an admission
i ll get text and sample illustrations in mail
congrats on book signing
sorry to hear your transcribers diagnosis
one cd is a perfect way to start the theia project
selene is getting married on valentines day
i hope to be in sf at that time
would you like to plan a meeting
good luck with your health procedure
actually mowed my lawn one-handed this afternoon

got a glowing report from my surgeon on the healing of my arm even got to
watch the metal plate meshing with my bones on a fluoroscope
or some such marvelous imaging machine
i can keyboard again
only wear a *velcro* brace
no cast

From: Wylie Hymen wylie@hymenfables.com
Date: December 14, 2008
To: Dina Cochon dinaRN@iswell.org
Subject: Chicken Ridge Weather Report

Pooky,

Temperature four degrees! And more snow coming tonight. Are you braving
the weather to come and keep me warm? Tickets for the opera at Zellerbach are
reserved for us at the box office.

From: Wylie Hymen wylie@hymenfables.com
Date: December 17, 2008
To: Ariane Altar ariane@altarpots.com

Dear Ariane,

Good news about your arm. Temperatures around here have dropped below
freezing! More snow coming tonight.

Yes, I want to help with your RB submission. I shall call you tomorrow
evening, Thursday, at about 8:00 your time, and we can talk as long as you
like.

I just returned from Berkeley and a remarkable opera at the Zellerbach, *Three
Decembers*, perfect music by Jake Heggie, based on a play by Terrence McNally,
with Frederica von Stade singing the lead; smart libretto, well acted as well as sung,
standing ovation. I want to find the libretto, so I can read it; I think you would like
it, too. Another amazing opera last month, *The Bone Setter's Daughter*, based on
the novel by Amy Tan (which I started to read but couldn't finish); all Asian cast,
stunning stagecraft, evocative score, scary.

Yes, I want to see you in February . . .

I used to regularly suppress wishes, second guessing another's reaction,
worrying if my wishes were appropriate, but, then, somewhere along the way,
about your age, I think, I realized that wishes could never really be inappropriate.
Wishes have been the beginning of many interesting journeys in my life, and, as

19

for another's reaction . . .well, that's part of the surprise and the frisson of risk that comes with expressing wishes aloud. Anyway, I know you'll be coming here for Selene's wedding and to be with your mother. My wish is that you could include some extra time to visit me in the mountains. I would be happy to drive you here and take you back down to Berkeley.

Wylie

From: Ariane Altar ariane@altarpots.com
Date: December 19, 2008
To: Wylie Hymen wylie@hymenfables.com
Subject: how much fun is that snow?
Photo: Confucian Scholars Zhu Xi (1130-1200 AD) and Cheng Hao (1033-1100 AD)

The snows have followed you from Turkey! I hope you have a fire to keep warm! I had to look up the word "frisson." It means a shiver or shudder from excitement or danger. Hmmm. Interesting addition to my vocabulary!

Thank you for a delightful phone conversation and for all your support. Attached are two shots of some of my recent clay wall tablets. These two are 11th century Chinese Confucian scholars. They are smoke fired mixed media clay joined to gilded canvas. I'll send images of the Han dynasty women later as they are on another computer. The only reason I am creating these tablets of men is to balance a show I mounted a few years ago of powerful women. I chose Chinese empresses and concubines. I recreated a lot of clothing with the idea in mind of "donning the robes of power." But, the famous emperors were too bloody for my taste. Finally, I settled on these scholars. I should do poets next.

We haven't spoken at all about religion or spirituality. I am wondering: do you practice Judaism? Believe in God? Celebrate Jewish or Christian holidays: all or none?

Now that I've read a few of your books, I see many *Bible* stories and motifs—Moses leading the Hebrews out of Egypt and the Ten Commandments, Abraham's Sacrifice, Noah and the Flood, to name a few. I am wondering about your interest in and/or belief in these "fables"? Of course, what immediately attracted me were your drawings of boats, since I make them, too; and, as I love the notion of voyages, expeditions, journeys and the courage and willingness to explore the unknown that they imply.

All my work is based in spirit. I create elegant pieces, evocative of a time gone by. I see them as relics—ancient boats, chariots, grave markers, sepulchers, pyramids, ruins, temples, and so on. Twenty-five years ago, I began a continuing series called Vehicles of Transport. I make teapots, vessels, and lidded containers shaped as Chariots, Magic Carpets, Palanquins, Arks and Dhows, Floating Pagodas... It amazed me to read your books and see your interest in history, archeology, anthropology, and myth! Our interests mirror each other! I mean, if you had written of science or math or engineering, we would not be in sync at all, as I am clueless and relatively disinterested, as well as under educated in those arenas!

The important part is my ceramic work gives a feeling of both imaginative flight and serenity, inviting the viewer to contemplate—whether the contemplation is of his navel, or a notion of God and the Divine or the Holy. I want there to be an invitation to communion. Sites of ruins are always quiet. I like that. I also like the high ceilings in Gothic cathedrals that make you want to lift your arms high and wide and reach for God. Isn't it in that empty space contained in the architecture of the cathedral where prayers are born and take wing?

As a child, I was quite devout, being raised Catholic and Baptist simultaneously. At thirteen, my parents divorced, and my faith in God split, too. It was only when I was getting divorced myself at age forty-three, that I found a reunion with God. Actually, it wasn't God at all, but a sense of the holy, the wholly unknowable, and the incredible power of the universe. I think what was reborn in me was a deep and profound reverence and a clear notion of the sacred.

It is amazing to me that I am a seeker of godliness. Godliness. I guess that's a way to put it. Peace. Understanding. Spiritual Peace. Finding the sacred in all things. I work with clay, the most humbling and ancient of materials, building temples of all sorts. I am interested in space and the perameters that define it. I create containers: from 'humble treasures' to shrines. I suppose I am seeking tranquility—perhaps to sit like some monk beneath a pine tree high on some Chinese painted mountain, gazing out to some monastery with a river gorge far below. Me, foreign lands, the sky, musings. I often wonder if souls ever sleep and are tireless. Or, if they need periods of rest. I am pretty sure mine takes naps.

Years ago I put my name on Unity Church's prayer list; strangers pray for me, and I pray for them. When I lived on O'ahu and was going through that hellish divorce, I volunteered at Unity. I answered their phone lines and read *rolodex* prayers aloud to callers on whatever their prayer needs were—prosperity, healing, suicidal impulses, the usual suspects. Don't laugh: you're dealing with a bona fide Dial-A-Prayer junkie.

From: Ariane Altar ariane@altarpots.com
Date: December 20, 2008
To: Wylie Hymen wylie@hymenfables.com
Subject: February

Looking at some airfares and my calendar. I wonder if it would work for you to get together during the week of February 8th? I am not booking anything until I hear what works for you.

21

Pants On Fire!

From: Wylie Hymen wylie@hymenfables.com
Date: December 23, 2008
To: Ariane Altar ariane@altarpots.com
Subject: Re: February
Photo: Camp at summit of Ararat, about 17,000'

Another mountain for you; actually a range, or small part of one anyway. I quickly gave up photographing the mountains, because they are so vast; it's impossible to fit them into the camera.

That week is perfect. I would pick you up on the 9th or 10th and return you to Berkeley on the 13th. We'd have lots of time to talk, linger over good things to eat, take walks (or sit by the fire), and go through the CDs. My usual procedure for interviews is, as we listen to them, I would make either a quick-and-dirty index or more detailed one depending on what's most useful for you.

February often brings a touch of spring. If the ground is not covered with snow, the first wildflowers, Shooting Stars, will be up. The temperatures will be like Tahoe; you should have boots, but I have lots of sweaters and things to keep you warm.

I am doing the Theodore tapes now. You should have them, because Theodore's story provides a little brother's impressions and an interesting counterpoint to Theia's.

I'll share a thumbnail impression with you of my first meeting with Theia. It was on parents' night at City in your senior year: what struck me first when she walked into the gymnasium full of parents was her beauty: she exuded old world glamour. Her hair was brushed in raven waves seemingly content to cradle her head a moment before gently cascading down her back. Her eyes were blue, an arresting blue, a blue so deep I knew at once I wanted to plunge into their depths and drown. How's that for an impression?

As to my religiosity: I have none. I am a complete and devout atheist. My parents observed a few of the high holy days, which was about it for me.

From: Ariane Altar ariane@altarpots.com
Date: December 30, 2008
To: Wylie Hymen wylie@hymenfables.com
Subject: Theia

Listened to the CD. It ended with the cliffhanger: how did they actually leave Warsaw? Something Theia said in the first tape gave me a possible title: *One Step Ahead,* referring to their success in evading capture or death. Remember when the family is sitting at the kitchen table in Warsaw having lunch? Her father quietly tells them to go to the basement? A few moments later, machine gun fire riddles the kitchen walls. When the family re-emerges hours later, her father's sweater hanging on the back of his chair had been ripped apart by the bullets. She said he possessed an uncanny sixth sense that saved them many times.

I am finding one glaring problem: verifying Theia's recounting of the past with historical fact. I am not sure if they jive.

Like you, Theia and Selene are complete atheists despite their Jewish origins. I really want to have a dialogue with you regarding Creation and God and the like. But, not now.

I'll share my impressions of Theia: in her, I encountered my first "woman of the world." She and Vladimir lived such a torrid love affair that, whenever I went to visit Selene, those two were upstairs in the bedroom: Vivaldi, Ravel's *Bolero*, or someone's concerto playing at high volume on the hi-fi, Theia's lingerie scattered on the steps.

I told Vladimir not to call me Emily, as you know was my given name.

"What do you want to be called?" he asked, always bemused. In my impetuous sixteen-year-old way, I answered, "The Woman!" Already Theia had set the mark! I wanted to be just like her. Sophisticated. Worldly. With that certain *je ne sais quoi* and *savoir-faire*. She was always off to a modern dance class, an art show, a piano lesson. She drove a snazzy *Alfa Romeo* sports car, sported dark glasses even at night, and dressed in leopard skin prints. My, my. Heady stuff for me to emulate! But, best of all was her Polish accent, lilting laughter, and artful way of making me feel a little bit foolish as she asked her inevitable, "Oh, really?" question following anything I told her.

Here is some information on the *Final Draft* software I mentioned for screenplays. Do you use a *Mac*? If you do, we can probably share the software, if we decide to write a script about Theia.

Happy New Year!

From: Ariane Altar ariane@altarpots.com
Date: December 30, 2008
To: Ande andeP@gmail.com
Subject: Mom's mainland trip

Dear Ande,

Booked my flights to San Francisco for Selene's wedding. I'm a little worried. We talk every day, and she's already too tense over the details of her Big Day. I am sure she'll become a "bridezilla"! Imagine, right now she doesn't want to invite several of her closest women friends! I had to cheerlead on their behalf—reminding her of how important they were to her when Johnny died or how they helped find her a teaching position, and so on. She is quick to forget the kindnesses people show her! Anyway, I am afraid

Pants On Fire!

somebody's head is going to roll before this wedding comes off. I hope it isn't her mom's or her kids' or Rick's that rolls! I wouldn't want to push her HOT button, that's for sure!

Love Ma

From: Wylie Hymen wylie@hymenfables.com
Date: January 2, 2009
To: Ariane Altar ariane@altarpots.com
Subject: Indian Springs Winter

I had second thoughts about telling you how cold it is here, fearing you might not visit. Nor would you probably want to know that it got down to four degrees a couple mornings before Christmas. But, I have two wood stoves and a fireplace to keep us warm, and you should take heart in the fact that no one, not a single guest, has ever frozen to death while visiting me.

You're going to have to wait for the next episode of Theia's story; the tapes are being copied. What a tale, huh?

I like your suggestion for a title.

I take considerable hope from our grandchildren. I remember a conversation many years ago with my son, when he was certain that it was wrong to bring children into this insane world. Now he has two daughters who give their parents and me immense joy. I had three children by the time I was twenty-eight, starting out in life with not a clue as to how life or anything else, for that matter, was supposed to work.

I'm looking forward to your visit.

From: Ariane Altar ariane@altarpots.com
Date: January 2, 2009
To: Wylie Hymen wylie@hymenfables.com
Subject: that cabin in the snow

That cabin in the snow is very appealing. Quite a switch from our drenching tropical rains this week with mudslides and lawns turned to mud lakes! Do you expect the snow to last?

I cannot figure out from the first tape how Theia's family, who had "nothing" in the Warsaw ghetto where Theia and Teddy were stealing food to feed the family, could suddenly have the means to travel by train out of there to Vienna—and what year was that? then to Trieste where she says they outfitted themselves for the Orient in the finest European traveling attire. Hmm. On top of that, they waited

24

there three months for a ship to take them to Shanghai. But, it was no ordinary ship for refugees like a freighter; it was a luxury liner in the category of a "Queen Mary"! Maybe the other tapes shed more light. I mentioned before how all the accounts she told over the years morphed. So, I am seeking "truth" before committing to write her supposedly "true" story. I want to separate fact from what may be her fictionalized fantasy!

She was young, beautiful, and married a second generation Russian a few years after arriving in Shanghai. A linguist, handsome and brilliant, Ivan spoke fourteen Chinese dialects, Japanese, Russian, Polish, German, and English. He sought work as a Polish diplomat. To succeed, he had to change his name, leave the Russian Orthodox Church, become a Catholic, and apply for Polish citizenship; all of which he did. They moved into a luxurious villa shared with another Russian couple on the outskirts of Shanghai. But when the Japanese invaded Shanghai, the Polish diplomatic mission left. The only work Ivan could find was as a policeman, which upset Theia's social world. Her parents did not approve, and the "Club" to which they belonged wanted to revoke her membership, since they catered only to the professional class. Theia herself detested the new boot polishing, *Harley Davidson* riding persona Ivan had to assume.

The most wrenching personal choice she made was when Mao took over, defeating the Kuomintang in 1947, forcing Chiang Kai-shek onto Taiwan. In November 1948, the American contingent left Shanghai. By March 1949, all foreigners were forced to leave, and the new Chinese communist government took possession of all private businesses. Her husband and his parents decided to return to Saint Petersburg. (One version of her story is Vladivostok, where she claims, Ivan's grandfather was mayor and owner of several hundred acres of land.) Ivan was offered a diplomatic post, land, car, and a high salary by the new Russian communist government. As a linguist, he would be useful to the Soviets. Theia's parents, brother, aunts, and uncles were leaving for the United States and Australia. Fearing they would never see Theia or her infant daughter, Selene, again if she went with Ivan to Stalin's Soviet Union, they begged her to obtain a divorce and emigrate with them to San Francisco, which, of course, she did.

According to her CD, Ivan showed up on her doorstep in Berkeley thirty years later, the first time she saw him again. He had last seen Selene at age two when Theia fled with her from a burning Shanghai. He failed to ask if Selene had survived or what had happened to Theia and her parents after leaving Shanghai. He only spoke about himself, keeping his eyes averted, she said. Ivan had married twice more, once to a willowy Russian woman Theia had trained in competitive swimming at the "Club" in Shanghai, and then to another. He had two grown daughters, each tall, blonde and beautiful like Selene, and he had been living in Lafayette, a suburb of San Francisco only a few miles from Theia's home, for most of those past thirty years! She was dumbfounded that he had not contacted her.

"Don't you want to know what happened to your daughter, to Selene?" she asked. "Don't you want to know if she survived the communists?"

"I am afraid to ask," he said, eyes staring at the floor.

Months later Selene arranged to meet him at his home. She asked to meet his adult daughters, her half-sisters, which he refused. "My daughters know nothing of you," he said, seated in a dark corner of his living room, lap draped in a deep gray blanket. "You are an illegitimate bastard. I will never let them meet you."

Wylie, I really have to question this account. Why? Because when Selene and I were seniors at City, Selene found out her father was living in Lafayette. She met him for lunch. He told her he had been paying child support for her since the day he immigrated. Theia had kept the money secretly and deliberately kept silent about Ivan's whereabouts. Selene was angry at being kept in the dark all the years of her childhood. But, she also found Ivan a rude depressive. He gave her some money, I don't know why, and neither of them pursued further contact.

After I listen to all the tapes, I'll know if Theia and Ivan were actually married and divorced—who knows, maybe they weren't! Maybe Selene was their "love child." And, I wonder, whose story is true?

It is a wonderful relief to me that you are doing all the research and historical background of world events that led to the family fleeing Poland. I am going to rely heavily on you to "fact check" Theia's memory! It is critical to separate fact from fiction, as I have no interest in writing a fictitious, vanity-style, and self-aggrandizing "biography"!

The thing about Theia is that she is so glam, so of another world, both fascinating and irritating, like any vain diva! Kind of a brunette Marlene Dietrich.

Had physical therapy today on my arm; am a bit tired.

From: Ariane Altar ariane@altarpots.com
Date: January 3, 2009
To: Wylie Hymen wylie@hymenfables.com
Subject: UPSET!

Just got off the phone with Selene. Oh dear. I told her I had listened to the first CD you transcribed of her mom's history. The long and short of it is that she has chopped off my head, disowned me as a friend, and told me not to come to her wedding!

I mentioned to you early on that she has some hot buttons. Well, ooops, looks like I pushed one. She accused me of "invading her privacy" by listening to the CD and considering writing her mother's story, even though Theia gave me her explicit approval. Selene and I spoke of it this summer at Tahoe when I was visiting. I don't know what else to say, except to tell you of this sad turn and sudden end. I guess it's two sudden ends: Selene's friendship and our writing project.

I had readied my guesthouse and was listening to the Gaza mess on CNN, musing on the idiocy of human relations small and large. There's generally a hidden agenda to most disagreements, I think. That hidden agenda is often driven by a basic human desire to destroy, which can be as powerful as the desire to create.

Perhaps it's akin to our Kona winds that blow ferociously for ten days a year, clearing lichens and loose branches from the trees, creating havoc, and leaving as suddenly as they arrived, with us to clear away the debris and enjoy a "clean slate" for the twelve months to come. Euripides in *The Bacchae* showed us frenzied maenads, worshippers of Dionysus, ripping up trees and tearing the limbs from deer. (Yes, Wylie, I am putting my pout with Selene on the level of great Greek tragedy!) At any rate, I realized while vacuuming that Selene has always exhibited huge streaks of insecurity and jealousy, her dark side. I suspect that my agreement to write her mother's story must have felt like I was usurping her place as daughter. Perhaps that is what triggered this insane response. Okay. That's all the time Madame Freud has at her disposal today.

I am also thinking about this whole story of fleeing and surviving and want to ask: didn't you mention you knew of other Shanghai refugees' stories? We are free, are we not, to write a fiction arising out of various true experiences, independent of Theia's life? If we write at all, we must decide if we are writing a factual account or a fictional account. Maybe we'll dub ours "Faction"? Or how about "Friction"?

I am currently reading a grand book by Charles Frazier: *13 Moons*. It is based on the removal of the Cherokees from the Indian Nation in North Carolina during Jackson's presidency, and the hero is loosely modeled on the only white man to lead an Indian nation.

From: Wylie Hymen wylie@hymenfables.com
Date: January 9, 2009
To: Ariane Altar ariane@altarpots.com
Subject: Re: UPSET!

I've been away, but my thoughts have turned often to you and Selene. I'm sad about what has happened. So, you got "chopped"; our project got "chopped." It's hard for me to accept that an idea with such intriguing possibilities, one from which much good could come, has raised such rancor and damaged a friendship. And, like you, I've held on to the hope that somehow Selene would call and make it all right again.

I have to admit that when I first read your email and then talked with you, the very first word that came to mind was jealousy. I am not sure, however, that it has to do with you usurping her place as a daughter, but that the agenda is even more hidden than that. I recognize jealousy when I see it, but find it hard to accept in someone else, so I kept my thoughts to myself. I'm going to have to tread carefully through these ramblings, and I'm not certain where I am going with this – how I wish we could talk together in the same room instead of writing. I am not sure I can even express what I'm thinking. These are not judgments, but, as you say, musings; I'm going to let you make your own inferences.

Last summer, there were two telephone conversations: first with Selene and then with you. When I got off the phone with you, and thought about the two conversations, I was taken back forty-four years, realizing, to my surprise, that some things had not changed. Selene was Selene as I remembered her. She was clearly happy to hear from me, quite poised given what a surprise my call must have been. She was deeply touched that I remembered her. She sounded a bit put off, though, when I said I wanted to return Theia's tapes. We talked for maybe twenty minutes. I understand how busy as a teacher of young children she is, especially doing grades, planning a trip to Italy, and contemplating a second marriage. She obviously wanted you and me to get back in touch, because a few days later you called. Nevertheless, Selene was . . . well, guarded.

Your call was a joy, and you were also as I had remembered – brilliantly erudite, out front, funny, bright, winsome, sensuous (I'm struggling, as I do with all our correspondence, to keep this from sounding like a mash note), comfortable, and familiar in that wonderful way that, anyone overhearing our banter, could only assume we were old friends who talk frequently. All of which seemed to belie that fact, as you eventually revealed to me, that you have suffered tragedy so immense and profound that I cannot comprehend it. We met, I learned of your intriguing first incarnation as an actor/director (of which I want to hear more), I read your delightful children's stories, and saw a house full, a museum curated lovingly by your mother, of your fascinating Chinese "antiquities," especially meaningful to me because not only did we both, somewhere along the way, develop an interest in and love for things Chinese, but many of the objects you create happen to be among the favorite things I look for in museum collections.

I am proud of Selene. I take satisfaction, though assume no responsibility, when, especially, my brightest students decide to be teachers. I don't know Selene as well as I would like; I know you better, because I have known you for a very long time (I'm sure that doesn't make any sense, but someday I'll explain, if you like). You have been taking life in big bites, taking scary risks in the way all artists do and which others simply cannot imagine, taking flight, transcending, redefining, creating, satisfying your desires. I came across this comment by John Berger in *About Looking* the other night:

"Art mediates between what is given and what is desired."

I have lived in both worlds and know well how they differ. When Selene looks back now, as we tend to do at this age, is she satisfied with her life? She wanted to be a painter. She is a teacher instead. How does she feel when she compares her life to the deep life in art her friend, Ariane, has had?

I wish I could say I had another story as rich and intimate as Theia's; but hers, I'm afraid, is one of those gifts, which comes along once in a lifetime. Would Theia intervene with Selene on our behalf? What are the risks and possible rewards of pushing ahead and fictionalizing the story? Have we been so chastened that it would no longer be fun?

Even if the Theia/Selene topic has expired, think of all the other topics under the sun we could muse upon. If and when you feel like musing, please muse my way. I'll read with joy and probably even respond with musings of my own!

I want to hear how you went from theater to clay.

Will I see you in February?

Letter from Ariane to Theia Steiner
Sent January 10, 2009

Dear Theia,

It is with great sadness I write. I regret that I shall not be able to write your story as promised.

Selene called about her wedding. I had booked my flights from Hawai'i, when she asked what I planned to do while in the Bay Area. I told her I was there to help her in any way; I also wanted to visit my mother and brother, and that if time allowed, I wanted to meet with Wylie Hymen to discuss collaborating on your story.

She became irate and forbade me to write your story. She told me not to come to her wedding; she never wanted to speak to me again.

I have always loved and admired you, Theia. This book would have been my pleasure to write and a gift of friendship for you.

I hope you understand why I cannot continue your project.

Love, Ariane

From: Ariane Altar ariane@altarpots.com
Date: January 13, 2009
To: Wylie Hymen wylie@hymenfables.com
Subject: Theia

I got two lengthy phone calls, one after the other, from Theia. My letter stunned her. It was news to her. Selene had not mentioned you, the book, or the

29

bridezilla herself kicking me out of her life. Theia could not understand Selene's behavior. And, Theia says she still wants me write her story!

Watched the "Shanghai Ghetto" documentary. It raises more questions than answers for me about Theia, as she was not in the Jewish Ghetto but lived rather in a luxury apartment in the French Concession of the city with six Chinese servants during the war, clearly, this documentary is not related directly to her experience. Her mother's aunt had arranged to rent the fully furnished apartment from a British family who was returning to England for three years of home leave. Theia got off the luxury ocean liner in Shanghai, took a stroll around the Bund area by the river, and then was taken directly by cab to their new eighth floor apartment on Avenue Petain. Her family quickly was invited to join a "Club" where they spent eighty percent of their time socializing with other Europeans, particularly the German speaking Swiss. The "Club" had no Chinese members. Her aunt played tennis there every day; Theia and her mother swam in the pool, and despite having a Chinese cook prepare meals for them at their apartment, ate all their meals at the "Club." There they dressed formally for dinner, the women in long gowns, which their servants would deliver to them, and the evening usually ended in dancing.

Theia laughed about all the faux pas she and her parents made with the servants, who didn't feel these Polish Jews were treating them properly. They were "first class servants" who took pride in working "in a first class home," which meant their employers needed to follow a strict protocol. Her mother, for example, was not allowed in the cook's kitchen. Her only duty was to write the menu for the day. Her father was not allowed to polish his shoes or dust lint from his jacket, for if he did, the Number One Valet lost face. Not an anecdote anticipated from a refugee story!

Mailed my *Bebe Banana* text and illustration samples to Loughman at Roaring Brook today! I have vowed to devote more time to learning new skills. I am going to scout for some classes in illustration, as I would love to draw my own characters. I also want to learn computer animation. I figure I have forty fabulous years to live, and what a lot I want to do!

From: Wylie Hymen wylie@hymenfables.com
Date: January 14, 2009
To: Ariane Altar ariane@altarpots.com
Subject: musings and mountains

What a beautiful mountain; I see you, too, have mountain views and snow! Thank you for the photo of winter snow on Mauna Kea. To think you see it from your kitchen! I remember when I was living in Hawai'i a friend had a bumper sticker that said "Ski Mauna Kea." I thought it was a great joke – I couldn't imagine snow anywhere on the islands – until he explained it really snowed there. I had a similar reaction when a

Pants On Fire!

Moroccan friend told me about the French coming to ski in Morocco – I laughed. But, that's true, too; there's skiing in the High Atlas Mountains, which I crossed driving from Marrakech to Fez, with a ski lift that goes to 3,273 m, the highest in all of Africa.

Good luck on your submission to Roaring Brook; I'm cheering for you.

I would very much like to muse your way. Over the years, I have friends with whom I've shared my musing, but you, dear Ariane, are the first ever to invite me. There soon will be musings on the way, and please do send yours.

From: Ariane Altar ariane@altarpots.com
Date: January 17, 2009
To: Wylie Hymen wylie@hymenfables.com
Subject: Shanghai Jewish info

Huge storm here, almost at hurricane force for two harrowing days and sleep-less, wind howling nights. Today I had to clean up the debris. It was a deep inner time as there was no power, and I would lie in bed by 7:30 p.m. and have lengthy conversations with myself. Amazing what time without any distractions can bring out. I kept thinking of what people like Thomas Jefferson accomplished: work-ing, reading, dining, composing and playing music, writing: all by candlelight (not going to bed by 7:30 like me unless he had the likes of a distraction like Sally Hemmings at hand!).

Watched "The Port of Last Resort: Shanghai", real footage and stories of European Jewish refugees. It is fascinating. Do rent this DVD. It underscores my interest in writing a film. I see five stories intertwining: the established Baghdadi Jews (Kadoories and Sassoons), the more recently established Russian Jews, the Ghetto Jews in Hongkew, the poorest Chinese residents, and a Theia type (a wealthy European Jew living outside the ghetto): how they lived, struggled (or not), and survived (or not).

What particularly intrigues me for today's audience is how international the story of the Shanghai Jewish experience still is! The Baghdadi's and the Russians helping as the European Jews arrived from all economic and career backgrounds... the Japanese occupiers, the Chinese nationals...The refusal of the British and American governments to help...fascinating stuff. Were the refugees ignorant of the plight of their relatives left in Europe? Some, like Theia, say they had no real knowledge of the concentration camps until after the war.

She and her family were unusual Jewish refugees, as they were wealthy and retained privileges through international business connections. Theia claims they had no news in Shanghai of what was happening to Jews in Europe during WWII. By 1942, however, news of the holocaust had reached Shanghai; a Jewish ghetto in Hongkew was established, and refugees poured in. I suspect Theia, as a spoiled daughter of a wealthy businessman, might have kept her pretty head well buried in the sand.

Have you had any thoughts of your own on the Theia/Shanghai story? To tell it, or not to tell it? All silent on the Selene front. I sent an "I'm sorry" note a week ago—not that I have a thing to apologize for! The rest of what I am sending regarding Theia is lengthy. Please peruse and tell me if anything interests you.

Here is some research:

Shanghai developed as a city two hundred years ago. From the beginning, it was a colony or semi-colony. In June 1842, Shanghai was bombarded and occupied by the British ship *Nimigis*. The history of Jewish people immigrating to Shanghai started in 1844.

There were three lots of Jews that immigrated to Shanghai. The first lot arrived around 1844, mainly from Baghdad, Spain, Portugal, and India. They were called Sephardim. There were about seven hundred until 1920. Most of the Sephardim were rich. As Shanghai was 'the Far East trading centre', people came to Shanghai seeking business and development. Most of those people lived near the shopping centre of the city.

Sir Elly Kadoorie (1867-1944) arrived in Shanghai from Bombay in 1880 as an employee of the Sephardic Jewish firm, David Sassoon & Sons. Sir Elly was a philanthropist and member of the wealthy Baghdadian Family having large business interests in the Far East. His family was originally Iraqi from Baghdad, later migrating to India in the mid-eighteenth century.

Within a few years, he had accumulated large sums of money and had gone into business on his own, with companies in both Shanghai and Hong Kong. Over the next two decades, the Kadoorie brothers made their fortunes, achieving success in banking, rubber plantations, electric power utilities, and real estate, even gaining a major share holding in Hong Kong Hotels Limited.

Kadoorie and other members of his family were interned in the Stanley Internment Camp in Hong Kong in January 1942. They were released two months later and allowed to move back to Shanghai. Though son, Lawrence Kadoorie, and his family were later interned in Shanghai's Chapei (now Zhabei) internment camp in 1943, Sir Elly was exempted from internment on medical grounds. He eventually died in Shanghai on August 2, 1944. His grave and that of his wife, Lady Ann, are located in the Song Qing Lin Memorial Park near Hong Qiao Road and are open to visitors. The tombstone of their grave is amongst only four Jewish graves in Shanghai, which remain intact and were not destroyed during the Cultural Revolution.

The second son of the first Jewish Sassoon's family, Elias David Sassoon, entered Shanghai to expand the building market.

Pants On Fire!

Silas Aaron Hardoon (born 1851 Baghdad, Ottoman Iraq – died 1931 Shanghai, China) was a wealthy businessman and well-known public figure in Shanghai in the early 20th century.

Born into a poor Jewish family in Baghdad, his family left for Bombay where he was educated at a charitable school funded by David Sassoon. Hardoon traveled to Shanghai in 1868 and entered the employ of David Sassoon, Sons & Company as a rent collector and watchman. He rose quickly through the ranks of that company, displaying a talent for real estate. He expanded his interests into cotton, becoming a partner in E. D. Sassoon and Company. Shrewd investments, particularly in properties on Shanghai's "Fifth Avenue," Nanking Road, eventually made him one of that city's wealthiest inhabitants. Hardoon was an important figure in the organization of aid and financial support to Shanghai's new Jewish residents. Hardoon was a student of Buddhism, establishing a school for monks at Ai-li Park, his twenty-six-acre estate, and personally financing the printing of Buddhist writings. When he died in 1931, his personal fortune was estimated to be worth $150,000,000.

Hardoon was the king of property on Nanjing Street - the busiest shopping centre in Shanghai, and the Shanghai Exhibition centre was the private park of the Hardoons. Sassoon was the chairman of many Shanghai Jewish financial groups. The Heping Hotel today was their office building. The Shanghai Children's Palace was Kadoori's private home, known then as "Marble Hall."

The Sephardim were respectable Jewish people. They played a very important role in Shanghai's building, religion, social and economic life; they also gave a great deal of help to the Ashkenazim Jews who were kicked out by the Germans during World War II. Forty percent of the staffs of Shanghai Stock Exchange were Sephardic Jews.

The second lot of immigrants was mainly Russian Jews. In the 1906 revolution, many Jews escaped from Russia. Many of them first stayed in Harbin, in the north of China. In 1931, the Japanese occupied the three Northern provinces and tried to build up a Manzhou country. The president of Manzhou Real Way, Zhan Chuan, presented a plan to Japan's Ministry of Foreign Affairs to invite fifty thousand German Jews to Manzhou. Later, when a son of a rich Jewish businessman was kidnapped and killed, seventy percent of those Jews left Harbin for Shanghai. In 1939, there were five thousand Russian Jews in Shanghai. Their economic condition was lower than that of the Sephardim. They mainly worked in restaurants, coffee houses, bakeries, fashion shops, and bookshops. Some were engineers, lawyers, or musicians. In the Thirties, many bus drivers were Jews. A few dealt in drug smuggling and brothels.

Pants On Fire!

The third lot of twenty thousand immigrants was called Ashkenazim. They came from Germany, Austria, Poland, and other European countries from 1933 to 1941, when Hitler came to power. There were more than thirty thousand immigrants, including the twenty thousand from Europe during the Second World War. Those Jews chose to emigrate to Shanghai, because it was the only refuge where there was no need for a visa. With the support of Jews all over the world, and the help of the Chinese people, they survived what they called the "tiger's mouth" during the war.

The first high tide of immigration happened from 1933 to 1934 when several thousand of the most well educated arrived: doctors, musicians, and professors. They mainly lived around Xiafei Street (today's Huaihai Street) where there was a French Concession. They brought a lot of money with them, so they could start businesses immediately.

The second high tide was from August 1938 to August 1939 when ten thousand Jews arrived mainly from Austria and Germany. They escaped very quickly, because of the famous *Kristallnacht*, night of broken glass, 10th November, 1938. In France, a young Polish Jew named Herschel Grasspan, became angry when he heard that his family was forced to move to a wild area of the border between Germany and Poland. He bought a gun, went to the German Embassy to kill the Ambassador. By mistake, he killed a third level secretary, Ernst von Rath.

On hearing the news, Yoseph Goebbels announced spontaneously punishing the Jews. On that night and the second day, at his instigation, a mob of about a thousand robbed and destroyed more than seven thousand Jewish shops, burning and damaging one hundred and ninety one Synagogues.

Two days later, the government officially ordered punishing all Jews. The order was: 1. Make them pay one thousand million marks as a fine for wanting to emigrate, and that proof of payment of the fine had to be shown before approval was granted. 2. They themselves must pay for the damage of their losses, even though insurance had been paid. 3. Announcement of a series of orders that Jewish enterprise became 'alien', so that Jews would be expelled from Germany's economy.

The head of the Gestapo, Himmler, gave an order to catch twenty thousand rich Jews and send them to a concentration camp. In this way, he forced their families to pay ransom for their freedom.

Before the 10th November, 1938, visa offices were full of Jewish applicants; but more and more countries refused to accept Jewish people, with the exception of Palestine and Dominica. The only hope left for the Jews was to go to Shanghai, seven thousand miles away. The public concession of Shanghai was the only place in the world where no visa was needed. The Jews had no time to pack, no chance of arranging a visa, carried very simple

34

parcels, so they could catch the ship from Italy to Shanghai in a hurry. They reached Shanghai after four weeks of hardship.

With help from the Sassoons, Hardoons, Kadoories, the other Jews in Shanghai, and the Shanghai Chinese, receptions were organized. Hardoon's River Building by the Suzhou River was a big reception station. As thousands of Jews gushed into Shanghai, they first went to 'check in' at that reception station. There, a representative of the economic relief committee gave the standard greeting: *'Welcome to Shanghai! From now on, you are not a German, Austrian, Czechoslovakian, or Romanian. You are only Jews. The Jews around the world have already prepared a home for you here.'*

They were arranged according to their economic ability, health condition, and age. Those who had a better economic ability mainly lived around Huaihai Street, Fushou Street, and Nanking Street. Those who had lower economic ability lived in Hongkew District. In the last high-tide in 1939, when a few thousand Jews escaped from Poland as Germany attacked, they only brought one or two suitcases. Most of these Jews lived in that comparatively poor place, 'Hongkew' district, Theia's family being a notable exception.

Jews created miracles in those districts. Many streets became completely renovated along Hongkew, north of Suzhou River. Tangshan, Gongping, Changzhi, Huoshan, and other streets began to look like European streets. Zhoushan Road became the business center called 'Little Vienna'.

Jews built hundreds of enterprises. According to local statistics, in February 1943, three hundred and seven enterprises were forced by the Japanese Army to close and move to the insulation or concentration camp. Those enterprises included sixty-eight fabric stores, fifty coffee houses and restaurants, twenty-six thrift shops, twenty-four groceries, nineteen tailor shops, fourteen book shops, twelve porcelain shops, nine drug stores, nine electrical appliance shops, eight leather shops, seven jewellery shops and sixty one other shops including shoe shops, photo studios, and rubber factories.

Some of the exiled Jews were teachers, editors, reporters, writers, painters, musicians, and sportsmen. They opened schools, organized playing teams, created a moving library. They even started a band and football teams. It is worthwhile to mention that even under such hard conditions, the Jews published tens of newspapers and magazines.

Most of the Jews were religious. After they arrived in Shanghai, they built synagogues. There were four comparatively famous synagogues including Jews Synagogue and Moses Synagogue, which was located at 62 Changyang Road and became the activity centre of Jews during the war. A Russian Jew built Moses Synagogue in 1927; it was one of the four big Jewish synagogues at that time. Today, this small red building is an office of Hongkew district management. On the second floor is a small Jewish museum. The pictures on the wall tell visitors why Jewish people took Shanghai as their second home.

In 1942, the Germans adopted the 'Final Solution' policy. Germans continuously pressured the Japanese to follow their example and finish the Jews in Shanghai. In the Japanese/Russian War of 1904 to 1905, Jacob Schiff, a well-known American Jewish banker and head of Khun, Loeb, and Co. (later becoming Lehman) loaned a large amount of money, over two hundred million dollars, to the Japanese navy. Jewish bankers, the Japanese felt, could be used as bargaining chips. They might use Jews to influence President Roosevelt. Consequently, the Japanese adopted a comparatively 'soft' policy toward the Jews. The Japanese did, however, build the first 'insulation area' in Asia for Jews and guarded it strictly. In February 1943, through Shanghai's broadcasting and newspapers, the Japanese announced that all refugees who had no nationality and lived in Shanghai had to move to the places fixed by the military police for security reasons.

Although the Japanese paid attention to the Nazi's orders, they did not use the word 'Jews' in the bulletin, but everyone knew that it meant Jews. In the following three months, about one thousand Jewish families handed over eight hundred and eleven apartments owned by them, totaling two thousand seven hundred sixty six rooms. Three hundred and seven enterprises were forced to close. All those Jews moved into the insulation area, where the houses were small and dirty.

Once the Jews moved into the insulation area their living conditions deteriorated rapidly. Some had to go begging on the street. Some went to work in Chinese mills. There were seven women registered for prostitution. Some women chose to cohabit to improve their living conditions. There were about ten mothers who sold their own newborn babies. Often it happened that the children of the refugees used to pick up discarded vegetables or fruits in the market. The foreigners in Shanghai never had such hard times before. The 'insulation area' lasted for five hundred sixty one days. At last, it was cancelled, because Nazi Germany lost and surrendered to the Russians. The Japanese army also surrendered without conditions. Between 1939 and 1945, about one thousand five hundred Jews died in Shanghai from poverty, hunger, and disease.

After World War II, the doors opened again for the Jews in the Middle East and Europe. The Jews who lived in Shanghai started to leave for Israel, the United States of America, Canada, Australia, and other countries. In 1948, there were about 10,000 Jews living in Shanghai. But in October 1949, the Chinese government started sending the Jews back.

During the ten years of Cultural Revolution, the Jews went away silently. In 1957, there were only one hundred Jews left in Shanghai. In 1976, there were ten Jews in Shanghai. The last Jew, a lady married to a Chinese, died in 1982. With her death, the one hundred and thirty eight years' history of Jewish community in Shanghai ended.

From: Ariane Altar ariane@altarpots.com
Date: January 17, 2009
To: Wylie Hymen wylie@hymenfables.com

I found an email address for Theia's brother, if you want to contact him.

Mike Medavoy (born in Shanghai in 1941) is one of Hollywood's biggest producers and someone I had hoped to interest in Theia's story...and guess what? He's producing a film called *Shanghai* starring John Cusack, set in 1941, due to come out in October 2009. It is in post-production right now, written by Hossein Amini, who is one of my favorite screenwriters—*Wings of the Dove, Four Feathers. (Do* you imagine he's really that into fowls with those titles? My little joke.) I can't believe I am just a few steps too far behind on this one...the un-syncopated synchronicity of great ideas!

From: Cherry Estrella cherry@starsearch.com
Date: January 18, 2009
To: Ariane Altar ariane@altarpots.com
Subject: Lovemaking Tips for Seniors

Not that you are ready for this guide, but I want to get you all worked up for what the future might hold!

Lovemaking tips for Seniors

1. Wear your glasses. Make sure your partner is actually in the bed.
2. Set timer for three minutes, in case you doze off in the middle.
3. Set the mood with lighting. (Turn them ALL OFF!)
4. Make sure you put 911 on your speed dial before you begin.
5. Write partner's name on your hand in case you can't remember.
6. Keep the *Polygrip* close by so your teeth don't end up under the bed.
7. Have *Tylenol* ready in case you actually complete the act.
8. Make all the noise you want. The neighbors are deaf, too.
9. If it works, call everyone you know with the good news.
10. Don't even think about trying it twice.

(I sent this in large type so you could read it!)

Pants On Fire!

From: Wylie Hymen wylie@hymenfables.com
Date: January 22, 2009
To: Ariane Altar ariane@altarpots.com
Subject: Musing/Surprises

Since reuniting with several students, seeing you last summer, and now with our continuing conversations, some thoughts about those days when we first met have been surfacing regularly. That surprises me; I don't spend a lot of time in the past, and now I'm finding some interesting stuff there. You've welcomed, indeed invited my musings; I feel I have permission to actually write about things, which, before, seemed just too self-indulgent – but in return, you must promise to let me know the instant they become a burden or unwanted. You've reappeared in one of the more intensely introspective moments in my life; more accurately, dear Ariane, you are the cause of it all.

I enjoy the straightforward, candid way you've been with me, so I'll return that in kind. I take delight in one of the prerogatives of being older, the freedom to say what I'm feeling, unguarded, no longer having to worry about being impolite or inappropriate. Speaking your heart, I've learned, is never inappropriate. Tiptoeing around and second-guessing everybody is such a waste of time! I've discovered that at this age a subtle change occurs – I think less of time passed and more of time remaining. A few years before I met you, I had become and remain to this day, fascinated with Brecht and Weill, but only now can feel deeply the metaphor from *September Song:*

"I haven't got time, For the waiting game".

Please excuse my abruptness; it's autumn, and my life is going into early winter, and I do have less time for the waiting game. In truth, ironically, despite my age and illness, I'm enjoying the vivid intensity and poignancy of this time, my russet autumn.

One of things I've been thinking about is that the year I first met you was the beginning of a time of immense change for me. I'm sure you don't need to be reminded of the context of our first meeting, you a teen and me a teacher, the first stirrings of the Sixties: times of exuberance, experimentation, change, and discovery. Having moved to Berkeley from Chicago two weeks before we met, I was too busy starting a new life to comprehend what was happening to me. Today, of course, with nearly half a century of perspective, the magnitude of change I was confronting has become so clear that when people ask me where I grew up, I tell them that I was born and raised in Chicago, but I grew up in Berkeley (read City By The Bay) in the Sixties! Then, too, there's nothing like the assassination of a beloved president to open a new chapter in your life.

Pants On Fire!

It was not a wall I was facing then, not a limit, but rather unimaginable possibilities, which can be even scarier. I see it now as though all my life up until then (I was all of twenty-seven) I had been traveling through a deep, narrow valley, (read a loving, pleasant but bourgeois upbringing, continuing expectations and behavior patterns established in the Forties and Fifties). Throughout our year together as your teacher, the valley began to broaden, imperceptibly, so that after another year or two I could barely make out in the distant haze an immense open space (and you would not have recognized your former teacher). What appeared to be a destination, of course, turned out to be yet another place along the way, whether it was discovering the artist in me, becoming single again, or writing.

On Mount Ararat we were daily reminded of what hikers call a false ridge or summit; it looks like the top, you can see sunlight between the trees, really tired, you are hoping you are there, but when you arrive, there's still another ridge to climb up, and another, and another. And, so it is with life. The way to that place, it turned out, was not a smooth trail. But, I couldn't see that from where I stood, and I was too immature and inexperienced in life to anticipate it. Those ridges, happily, turned out to be interesting new experiences, quite satisfying and fun actually, and stepping stones to the life I enjoy today, but also fraught with dangers, deep, yawning crevasses so wide, I couldn't see the other side, sudden rock slides and avalanches. You, of all people, know that my metaphor speaks of growth and accomplishment, but also of profound emotional upheaval. Like divorce, career change, death, bankruptcy, betrayal.

Here's the real surprise. The strength and resourcefulness I needed to reach those places and beyond, I now realize, came from my students, a few in particular, and one especially, a young woman in my very first class who, as much as I was her teacher, became unwittingly my mentor. Aside from a couple of remarkable women I remember in my six years at the Chicago Art Institute, you were the most intriguing woman I had ever met, and I was enchanted. The moment I saw you standing in the doorway of your mother's house last summer, I realized that, for a very long time, Wylie had been carrying Ariane around in his heart.

From: Ariane Altar ariane@altarpots.com
Date: January 22, 2009
To: Wylie Hymen wylie@hymenfables.com
Subject: Re: Musing/Surprises

Perhaps more surprises from you than musings? I was expecting some response to my Shanghai research bombardment.... and instead? Mmm, the unexpected but sweetest topic: love.

Pants On Fire!

First, thank you for your letter. I agree that candor is the only tack, and I agree about time. I have been in a deep interior space since the Selene crash and a hurricane level storm that blew through here for two days and left Hana without power. I sat and lay in the dark for hours, thinking.

Now to the personal topic you raised: love. (Being flip, which I too often am, forgive me for what I am about to say. Do you remember the female outrage expressed on a "Sex and the City" episode when Burger broke up with Carrie on a *post it* note?)

I think declarations of love are most successfully made in person, not via email!

Forgive me?

Okay, I need some clarification. You mentioned Dina to me as your dear friend and "former" lover. Is she "former"? Are you free and single, or are you involved with her or someone else?

I am not a quick study when it comes to love. Learning about someone over time builds my trust. I like a relationship to evolve. In cooking terms: I want it to simmer, letting the flavours develop ...or... to roast slowly (keeping it rare in the center)! Qualities I admire are honesty, fidelity, honor, intelligence, success, wisdom, and humor. Taking time also allows me to see and understand a sweetheart's decisions and behaviors, the old *actions speak louder than words* adage.

I have had some very great losses in my life, from siblings to parents to lovers to husbands to children to friends. I don't think I am gun-shy or wary. Yet I know I am now very careful in making attachments.

You mentioned age and illness. Illness? Want to elaborate?

Several years ago, I read *The Hite Report: Study of Male Sexuality* by Shere Hite on male love. She interviewed three thousand men. Among her conclusions were, if I remember correctly: men fall in love visually, the actual intensity of that infatuation lasts six weeks, but those six weeks plant the seeds for a lifetime of fidelity.

She also wrote a book on women. Again, if memory serves me, she postulated that women fall in love based on any combination of two of three factors: sex appeal, money and/or power, intelligence. Hence, an unattractive, balding, fat but smart rich guy or world leader might appeal to many women. Conversely, a sexy pauper would need to be very smart to attract a mate!

The Theia situation has been niggling at the back of my daily thoughts. I penned a note. I want to read it to you to get your response. If you'd like to call, I am home today and tomorrow (taking a botanical drawing class on Saturday!)

One little story I want to tell you might reveal the friction between Selene and Theia. Selene was visiting me in Honolulu once, and we were lunching with some of my friends. The topic of names came up. Selene was in rare form. She said, "Oh, my mother nicknamed me La Luna to be a reflection of her brilliance. She said

40

when she had a daughter, she thought, 'O wonderful, all I have to do is clap my hands and call, La Luna, La Luna! Come quickly! You know, the moon has no light of its own, the sun is its source. Get me this, La Luna, get me that!"

To this day, Selene feels eclipsed by her mother and resents her attitude of entitlement.

Oh! Did I mention I got an email from Selene? Here it is.

Thanks for the card and the apology; I appreciate it. I can't tell from the card what your plans are vis a vis the Hymen project related to my mom's story. Let me know.

Thanks, La Luna

From: Wylie Hymen wylie@hymenfables.com
Date: January 23, 2009
To: Ariane Altar ariane@altarpots.com
Subject: Why not Hana?

I need to level with you. I didn't let on how disappointed I was when you told me you wouldn't be here in February; I fully understand your decision, but I was sad nonetheless. You asked about Hana then, and the reason I gave you for not coming was that I'm deep into editing *Where is Noah's Ark?* and putting together all the illustrations and photographs.

Now you've asked about Hana again, and each time it makes me a little sad. You don't know me well enough to know that I never allow my work to interfere with life and friends. There would have to be a more compelling reason for me not to come see you now, and there is . . .

A year ago, I was diagnosed with prostate cancer. Cancer showed up in two out of twelve biopsies, and the chemistry revealed low activity. That's a favorable result, and as my urologist said, "If you're going to have cancer, this is the way to have it." So little activity was detected in fact, and there was little chance of it spreading (the prostate is very isolated) that I was able to strike a bargain with the doctors – let's watch it closely, PSA's every three months, let me get to Turkey in the fall, and when I get back, we can decide on a course of treatment.

Well, I'm back, the PSA rose slightly but not alarmingly, and my wonderful doctor of over thirty years, Mills, said, "Wylie, it's time." I'm under the care of Dr. Doggett, one of the leading prostate specialists in the world – thank god for Medicare, which covers part of the cost – who employs a relatively easy therapy called *TheraSeed*. And that, alas, is what I'll be doing instead of visiting you this spring.

41

Pants On Fire!

In my whole life I have never had any significant contact with doctors and hospitals. I'm not in any way feeling sorry for myself (but, then, I never do). The last couple of weeks have seemed like I'm living in an episode of *House*, without the grumpy doctor. What's like *TV* is all the high-tech machinery I'm getting acquainted with. Two weeks ago I spent a day in an excellent hospital and, since it's a four-hour round trip drive for me, they try to do all they can in one visit. In the morning I had a CAT scan and a tracer injection for the bone scan, which I returned for in the afternoon, and also had an EKG, a chest x-ray, and more blood work. But wait, there's more to come . . .

All of that revealed, happily, that the cancer has not spread. Last Thursday I was injected with a nuclear (radioactive; let's be clear here) tracer with such a short half-life that the material was mixed Wednesday night in Florida, flown to Sacramento, and driven by courier to the hospital Thursday morning in time for my appointment. Its purpose is to find the cancers and make them light up on another scan I had. Now the doctors have a very accurate road map of where to implant rice size seeds of palladium-103 directly into the cancer, all of which takes about an hour, and I can go home as soon as the anaesthesia wears off. The radiation disappears in about ninety days, and I will return for scans periodically to monitor my progress. Dr. Doggett assures me that the chance for serious side effects is less than one percent, and (without me asking; I must be really transparent) I can have sex within a day or two. Dr. Doggett has trained doctors all over Europe in his procedure, and at our last visit, he was headed to China where he is also training doctors.

That's what it takes to keep me from visiting you.

And, yes, I am free and single.

From: Ariane Altar ariane@altarpots.com
Date: January 23, 2009
To: Wylie Hymen wylie@hymenfables.com
Subject: Re: Why not Hana?

I remember you mentioning a little health "something" before you went to Turkey, and I immediately (don't know why) thought prostate. The good news is it sounds like you have incredible care. I am glad for that. But, I am sorry for you facing this health situation.

Do not give a second thought to my beckoning to Hana...the right time will reveal itself.

Besides your health, you must be concerned about work. I hope that it won't be too compromised. Thankfully, the procedures sound non-debilitating. After all, you will glow in the dark and can work all night and save hugely on electric bills!

42

Pants On Fire!

As I have my California ticket, which I have to change tomorrow or lose it, I am thinking of coming in March, around the week of the 22nd. I am a very good Nurse Jane Fuzzy Wuzzy (remember the *Uncle Wiggily* stories?) and would be happy to administer broth and good cheer, if you so desire.

From: Wylie Hymen wylie@hymenfables.com
Date: January 24, 2009
To: Ariane Altar ariane@altarpots.com
Subject: Musing on a potter

When I put down the phone last night after – wow, two hours – there was still so much about you I wanted to know, questions came to mind faster than I could grasp them. Some I don't want to ask on the phone; some so intensely personal you may not want to answer. You fascinate me, and I know writing that gets me in trouble, but I promise to tell you my feelings when you are actually here.

I looked once again at the brochure you gave me filled with your exquisite ceramics, and I wanted at that moment to be in your studio, to watch you work, to put my hands into your paper-laced porcelain clay – I haven't had my hands in clay in sixty years – to watch a pagoda, a teapot, a fortress, palanquin, a dragon-fly, whatever you are doing now, that has taken you beyond them, appear in your hands, watch you tending and taming your fire.

I want to know how you got there. When you visit, and we have all the time our complicated lives allow, I want you to tell me about that journey. I know how hopeless it is to talk about how we create, how we take the first step through that door, but I hope you will try.

I wish now I had taken more time to look at and touch the many pieces in your mother's home that day last summer, but we were getting reacquainted, showing you my illustration techniques, focusing on your engaging children's stories, talking about avenues to getting them published, beginning to think about Theia's film. Besides, I quickly discovered, I can't focus on much else when you are in the room.

I've been thinking of a piece I would like to have, but notice that they date to the Eighties and Nineties. So, what is still available, if I wanted to purchase, specifically, a Fortress or a Temple?

To underscore part of our conversation last night: I have been married twice and have learned I cannot really be in a relationship responsibly and be a creative artist at the same time. I have to be alone to flesh out my books and paintings; sometimes I'll work for thirty-six hours on a drawing with only bathroom or coffee breaks. I don't make good company. My former wives would certainly concur. I have had a ten-year relationship with Dina, never living together, but traveling to many places. I no longer have an intimate relationship

43

with her, but I value her as a friend. She's a bit too hard-nosed New York for my taste, and our sexual compatibility was lack-luster. Forgive my bluntness. I shall share more on this topic when we speak in person. It wasn't Dina's fault; it was mutual.

I suppose I should mention that my first wife, the mother of my children, cheated on me. It not only broke my heart, but also paralyzed my willingness or ability to trust for a very long time. I was bitterly jealous of her lovers. (Jealousy, I admit, has plagued me most of my life.) My second wife left me in order to marry one of my closest friends. They have been together now for over twenty years, living in the house I built.

Your question last night, do I expect to have sex when you visit, caught me off guard; it's a delight how you do that, but I'm not very fast on my feet when I'm taken by surprise. No, as I said, I don't expect to have sex. My only expectations are that you will be comfortable and enjoy yourself in my house, that you will find peace in this quiet solitude in which I live, that we talk through the night exploring all the wondrous subjects that interest us, share lots of good food and wine, and that when you leave, you will want to visit me again someday.

Do I have fantasies about making love with you? All the time now.

From: Ariane Altar ariane@altarpots.com
Date: January 24, 2009
To: Wylie Hymen wylie@hymenfables.com
Subject: Are you inviting me to dance?

Home from a grueling back-road drive after a miserable art class with a drawing "teacher" who admitted she never has gotten a grasp on perspective. Not a good admission! I have unloaded groceries, fed my B&B guests and my pets, had a quick glass of wine and some leftover eggplant/pork dish, and, on my computer, found your invitation to "dance"! I sense that is the mode we are easing into: a bit more perhaps than a two-step, maybe a tango or a swing or a waltz. So many possibilities from polka to cha cha cha. Thank you for your very kind words, your piqued interest, and the rest of which, I am glad to hear your fantasies are alive and well!

I appreciate your approach to having me as a guest in your home. You used the same words I would have chosen had you come here: to "be comfortable and enjoy yourself in my house." Thank you.

I re-booked my ticket for March 24 to April 2. I shall need to spend half the time at my mother's house. Please let me know which part might work best for you for me to visit. I don't want to get my mother all excited over the dates I am to see her. I would like you to choose first, and then I can tell her when I'll be with her.

Pants On Fire!

I sense we could have a very special time. I would truly relish conversation, seeing your work more intimately, taking some walks/hikes, depending on what you feel like after your adventures in the medical community. I haven't been on the Northern California coast since college days. I spent much time in childhood on that coast. I love it—the cold, the fog, the salt spray, the sea lions' roar. I would love to drive it again. I grew up in Fruto, southeast of Indian Springs, before my parents divorced and my mom moved to Berkeley. We used to goof around in little abandoned hill towns like Elk Creek. If you *Google* them, you'll see my childhood turf.

I mailed the letter I read you to Theia this morning. I did not send a copy to Selene. I never did send that earlier letter to her.

As to the pottery, it began in a most unlikely way; like most of my life, it came in through the back door. Most of the things I planned and studied for: acting, directing, theatre, and film got displaced by love, family, uncertainty. I wonder if we ever discover our own true purpose here, our soul path or destiny? Is it all just footfalls on random tracks, some leading to great good and happiness, others to dead ends, as we bumble through our karma? I heard a saying, "If you want to hear God laugh, tell Him your plans!"

Sometimes when I hold a piece of fired pottery under the faucet, I see dozens of webbed crackle lines emerge from under the surface of the glaze. Like life, the piece is far more complex and layered than it first appeared.

One of my dear friends who is an accomplished painter, performance artist, videographer and musician surprised me by saying he's always known his purpose: to help humanity align with holiness. I had been his dear friend for thirty-five years when he told me this! I had been clueless as to this purpose, thinking he was incredibly creative, driven, kind, and ambitious. I had overlooked the spiritual component that was energizing his art altogether.

Do you think we could ever share silence? We seem to have so much to say. I love what you wrote: "that you will find peace in this quiet solitude in which I live." That's quite the world I live in and those words I could mirror back to you from Hana.

The Invitation

It doesn't interest me what you do for a living.
I want to know what you ache for,
And if you dare to dream of meeting your heart's longing.

It doesn't interest me how old you are.
I want to know if you will risk looking like a fool for love, for your dreams,
For the adventure of being alive.

Pants On Fire!

It doesn't interest me what planets are squaring your moon.
I want to know if you have touched the center of your own sorrow.
If you have been opened by life's betrayals
or have become shriveled and closed from fear of further pain.
I want to know if you can sit with pain, mine or your own,
Without moving to hide it, or fade it, or fix it.

I want to know if you can dance with wildness and let the ecstasy fill you
To the tips of your fingers and toes without cautioning us to be careful,
Be realistic, or to remember the limitations of being human.

It doesn't interest me if the story you're telling me is true.
I want to know if you can disappoint another to be true to yourself;
if you can bear the accusation of betrayal and not betray your own soul.

I want to know if you can be faithful and therefore be trustworthy,
I want to know if you can see beauty even when it is not pretty every day
And if you can source your life from its own presence.
I want to know if you can live with failure, yours and mine,
And still stand on the shore of a lake and shout to the silver of the full moon,
YES!"

It doesn't interest me to know where you live or how much money you have.
I want to know if you can get up after a night of grief and despair
And do what needs to be done for the children.

It doesn't interest me who you know or how you came to be here.
I want to know if you will stand in the center of the fire with me
and not shrink back.

It doesn't interest me where or what or with whom you have studied.

I want to know what sustains you from the inside when all else falls away.
I want to know if you can be alone with yourself,
and if you truly like the company
You keep in the empty moments.

Oriah Mountain Dreamer, Native Elder

From: Ariane Altar ariane@altarpots.com
Date: January 26, 2009
To: Wylie Hymen wylie@hymenfables.com
Subject: Theia

The U.S. post did a grand job. Theia called after she and Vladimir had read my letter many times. We spoke for an hour.

She had no idea Selene told me not to write the book and ended our friendship. She was terribly upset, very loving, quite mystified about Selene. She asked me to wait to send Selene a copy of the letter. She wants to digest all the information for a few days first. She is hurt (as I knew she would be, saying she knows Selene is always angry with her, cannot understand why she wouldn't want me to write the story, and remembers our conversations at Tahoe; Selene not saying anything to the contrary then).

Theia absolutely wants her story written. She wants to know why you had contacted Selene about the tapes. I explained that you weren't sure if she was alive! We laughed about that. Anyway, she was very clear that this is HER story, and no one can say to write or not to write it but her. I told her about possibly using her story as the main thread in a film. She loves that idea. She is savvy and wonderful, Wylie. She said she has lots of other tapes to send me, which were recorded by a woman she hired to write her story but who never finished it.

She kept saying, "It is my life, not Selene's! Everyone is talking about me but not to me!" I said I had asked you to wait to contact her until she had received my letter. She said she appreciated that as she doesn't like to be taken by surprise and doesn't want her number given out, even to you.

I miss your voice. I love talking to you. You must be away again.

From: Ariane Altar ariane@altarpots.com
Date: January 29, 2009
To: Cherry Estrella cherry@starsearch.com

You predicted recently, Cherry, that I would have a problem with other women being jealous. I do! A big blow up: Selene, you remember my best friend of forty-six years? Well, she had a bridezilla moment on the eve of her second wedding and has cut me out of her life. It was because of the book I am writing about her mother. Selene got afraid, I think, of my growing too close to her mother, and not, I suspect, because of any revelations researching the book might uncover.

Pants On Fire!

From: Wylie Hymen wylie@hymenfables.com
Date: January 29, 2009
To: Ariane Altar ariane@altarpots.com
Subject: Thank you

Your loving concern and suggestions last night, your being there, hearing your voice, were more comfort to me than you could know. Your very caring and supportive thoughts have brought me encouragement, each reading bringing you closer. I didn't want to let you go. I am sorry for my long absence from email and talks.

If I could have had you close to me by the fire last night, I would have been more truthful. My tears would have made a lie of the confidence I projected over the phone. I am scared, not for my life, but for my way of life, and in that way I know I am spoiled. Seventy-two years of good health have given me the freedom and strength to do virtually anything I've wanted to do. I don't know anyone my age who doesn't have a pacemaker, or isn't minus an organ or two, or doesn't take a fist full of scary pills every morning. That's the real issue for me. It's not the cancer that scares me – beating that is almost a certainty – or the long needle. I'll be unconscious. It's the fear of waking up discovering that Wylie may not have the control over the life he has taken so long for granted. That's especially troubling when I look ahead to magic mountains still to be climbed and the joys and promise of our friendship.

From: Ariane Altar ariane@altarpots.com
Date: January 29, 2009
To: Wylie Hymen wylie@hymenfables.com
Subject: You are welcome

Don't think for a moment that what I am about to say means I envy your position; I don't. Yet I think as you, as any traveler on life's unmarked terrain, when facing a deep personal challenge: it brings us to ourselves, that self without personality, without life's accouterments, the self only we know and who has its unique perception of itself and any notion of relationship to gods or divinity or divine consciousness or lack thereof or fate. In the re-meeting oft brought about by fear, we see so much, learn so much more, like the waters of the Colorado eroding yet deeper into the Grand Canyon of our understanding. While I do not envy your cancer and treatment, I do herald your concerns for life, as you've known it, and the unknowable future.

When I had my arm surgery and anaesthesia, I had no serious side effects. When my former partner, Juan, however, had hip surgery in France after an accident skiing, the anaesthesia changed his personality for six months (a common side effect in some patients, the doctors told me) and caused a defibrillation of his heart, revealing a previously undiagnosed hardening of the arteries. What did all this mean? For the layperson, me, I lost my lover. He became angry, surly, and mean-spirited. I took him to the doctor and asked if he was a heart attack candidate, because I thought his attitude was symptomatic of someone about to burst! And, I was right. We got some corrective medications and yes, six months later his personality was restored. BUT, I had abandoned the lover part of the relationship during that six-month recovery period because of the sudden emotional abuse. It was a high price to pay for needed surgery! I tell you all this, because I am no stranger to surprises that come through the back door when you get treated for one thing and a new problem arises! My role as his Nurse Jane Fuzzy Wuzzy terminated after six weeks of nastiness! So be warned, my fidelity as a nurse has its limitations! (Happily, Juan and I are friends. His accident and our break-up were two years ago.)

I feel reasonably certain that this treatment will be a piece of cake, and you will enjoy a swift recovery and peace of mind.

There is a very beautiful piece of coastline near me where a waterfall drops into a clear, deep, turquoise pool facing the sea. It was my daughter, Marianna's, favorite place. The waves break over the coastal lava and mix salt into the fresh spring water, which bubbles from subterranean lava tubes. On the morning of February 3rd, which is also the anniversary of my daughter, Marianna's, death, I plan to take my golden retrievers there and stand on the green grassy cliffs where the breeze blows onshore and look across the channel to Mauna Kea with her blanket of snow and where below me these wonderful waters mix, all the colors vivid; and I shall send restorative thoughts filled with that beauty your way.

Better, sometimes a few laughs are just what the doctor ordered. Here are some sillies to take the edge off your anxieties!

The Physical

A 75-year old man goes for a physical.

All of his tests come back with normal results and the doctor tells him everything is fine.

He then asks his patient how he is doing mentally and emotionally?

"Are you at peace with God?' he adds.

The patient replies, "God and I are tight. He knows I have poor eyesight, so he's fixed it. When I get up in the middle of the night to go to the bathroom, POOF! The light goes on. When I'm done, POOF! The light goes off."

"WOW! That's incredible!" the doctor says.

A little later in the day, the doctor calls the patient's wife.

"Ethel," he says, "Your husband is doing fine! But, I had to call you as I am in awe of his relationship with God. Is it true that he gets up during the night and POOF! The light goes on in the bathroom, and when he's done, POOF! The light goes off?"

"Oh, my God!" Ethel exclaims. "He's pissing in the refrigerator again!"

Here are some laughs I found online and are things people actually said in court, word for word, taken down and published by court reporters who had the torment of staying calm while these exchanges were taking place.

ATTORNEY: This myasthenia gravis, does it affect your memory at all?
WITNESS: Yes.
ATTORNEY: And in what ways does it affect your memory?
WITNESS: I forget.
ATTORNEY: You forget? Can you give us an example of something you forgot?

ATTORNEY: Now doctor, isn't it true that when a person dies in his sleep, he doesn't know about it until the next morning?
WITNESS: Did you actually pass the bar exam?

ATTORNEY: The youngest son, the twenty-year-old, how old is he?
WITNESS: He's twenty, much like your IQ.

ATTORNEY: Were you present when your picture was taken?
WITNESS: Are you shitting me?

ATTORNEY: So the date of conception (of the baby) was August 8th?
WITNESS: Yes.
ATTORNEY: And what were you doing at that time?
WITNESS: Getting laid

ATTORNEY: She had three children, right?
WITNESS: Yes.
ATTORNEY: How many were boys?
WITNESS: None.
ATTORNEY: Were there any girls?
WITNESS: Your Honor, I think I need a different attorney. Can I get a new attorney?

ATTORNEY: How was your first marriage terminated?
WITNESS: By death.
ATTORNEY: And by whose death was it terminated?
WITNESS: Take a guess.

ATTORNEY: Can you describe the individual?
WITNESS: He was about medium height and had a beard.
ATTORNEY: Was this a male or a female?
WITNESS: Unless the circus was in town, I'm going with male.

ATTORNEY: Doctor, how many of your autopsies have you performed on dead people?
WITNESS: All of them. The live ones put up too much of a fight.

ATTORNEY: ALL your responses MUST be oral, okay?
What school did you go to?
WITNESS: Oral.

ATTORNEY: Do you recall the time that you examined the body?
WITNESS: The autopsy started around 8:30 p.m.
ATTORNEY: And Mr. Denton was dead at the time?
WITNESS: If not, he was by the time I finished.

And the best for last:

ATTORNEY: Doctor, before you performed the autopsy, did you check for a pulse?
WITNESS: No.
ATTORNEY: Did you check for blood pressure?
WITNESS: No.
ATTORNEY: Did you check for breathing?
WITNESS: No.
ATTORNEY: So, then it is possible that the patient was alive when you began the autopsy?
WITNESS: No.
ATTORNEY: How can you be so sure, Doctor?
WITNESS: Because his brain was sitting on my desk in a jar.
ATTORNEY: I see, but could the patient have still been alive, nevertheless?
WITNESS: Yes, it is possible that he could have been alive and practicing law.

51

From: Ariane Altar ariane@altarpots.com
Date: January 29, 2009
To: Wylie Hymen wylie@hymenfables.com
Subject: Ariane's flights

I notice that each of your books is dedicated to a woman: Dina, Colette, Nina, and others. And Dina Cochon took several of the photos you used for your jacket covers. I am coming to you to write Theia's story. But, I am also coming because of our burgeoning friendship. I am not involved with anyone. If you are still involved with Dina or anyone else, please tell me. You must be honest with me.

I have been betrayed in the past, and I would never knowingly be "the other woman"! I know we have spoken of this relationship issue before. I want clarity. In my experience, and I have had it, sketchy love arrangements don't work: "ménage a trois," secret liaisons, and such. I need and would appreciate your complete candor.

If I am to permit love to grow, I need to feel safe and secure in the understanding that I am the one and only focus of attention and desire. I do not believe that is too much to ask, as it is precisely how I would and shall treat you.

Ariane

From: Wylie Hymen wylie@hymenfables.com
Date: January 29, 2009
To: Ariane Altar ariane@altarpots.com

Right now, there is only you, Ariane, on my playing field where my heart is already engaged.

We'll talk soon about how you are getting here. Lots of nice possibilities. I would be happy to pick you up at the airport Tuesday morning and return you to your mother's, especially since it means a couple more days with you.

I had thought on the way back of stopping at the de Young where there will be an exhibit, *The Dragon's Gift: The Sacred Arts of Bhutan*. The announcement shows some of the paintings with a more intense blue than I think I've ever seen in Asian art. Then I noticed that the show actually originated at the Honolulu Academy of Art, and that you might have seen it. Still, who could pass up an exhibit that includes a gilded copper sculpture of the Buddhist saint, Drukpa Kunley, who is described as . . .

The Divine Madman, famous for his unorthodox way of propagating the teachings and for his earthy humor. A highly eccentric figure, he was known to pursue beautiful women and enjoy strong drinks. In Bhutan, he left behind many colorful stories, not to mention progeny. Childless couples may travel to a temple in Punakha to be blessed by a bamboo effigy of Drupka Kunley's *Golden Phallus*.

I think it would be fun to write his biography, and I already have a title: *Fucking Your Way to Nirvana*. But then that seems kind of redundant, doesn't it? I'll call tomorrow evening. Monday I begin my journey.

From: Ariane Altar ariane@altarpots.com
Date: January 31, 2009
To: Wylie Hymen wylie@hymenfables.com
Subject: the woman who lives in the bamboo forest

Dangerous talk, that, of pilgrimages and prayers to a bamboo effigy, to a woman like me, who lives in a bamboo forest! What I don't know about bamboo, please be aware, I am always ready to learn! The Bhutan show took all the resources of the Honolulu Academy and almost cost the new director his job, but wow, it has been heralded as unprecedented...and no, I did not see it, and yes, I would really like to go to it with you. A *Golden Phallus*? Oh my.

I am going to Kaua'i to visit Ande and Kui.

I hope you'll be able to rent *Shanghai Ghetto* and *Port of Last Resort* from *Netflix* before we meet. I'd really like you to see them.

My current thinking of priorities is:

1. Design a legal contract for our collaboration
2. Write a slim book on Theia
3. Write a big film on the larger topic of the Shanghai refugee experience.

I hope your fears have dropped away, and you are actually looking forward to having this procedure done and getting it behind you. I did look at the website you sent. I guess you stay "seeded" forever? Do they dissolve over time? Or, just keep ticking? Have you reconsidered telling your sons that you are planning to have this procedure done before you do it? If I had breast cancer, for example, I know I'd tell Ande as she might also be a candidate, and early detection is vital.

A word about my children: I have come to know over time and experience that speaking of them and my life since their deaths produces an "after-effect." I can (and often have) share a deep conversation, but hours later or surely, by bedtime, I revisit and re-suffer my loss and grief with an intensity that is too painful to invite or to bear. Sometimes, honestly, I don't know if I'll come out alive at the end of it. If I am mum on the topic, it is not because of reticence or lack of interest or understanding, but rather to protect myself. Grief does not go away or get better. I have learned that it is a huge part of me and to compartmentalize it, as best I can, to be able to live.

I changed my name firstly, because I was overwhelmed by grief every time I said it, as it was a million times a day reminder of my children and everyone I'd lost. Secondly, I simply had to have a green card for my future. Our children generally provide us with that entree. Without two of my three, I felt bereft and locked in the past. When I changed my name, it loosened the hold of grief. I had someone new to create and become. Ariane is the French version of Ariadne, which means "most holy" in Cretan Greek. (In Greek mythology, Ariadne was the daughter of King Minos. She fell in love with Theseus and helped him to escape the Labyrinth and the Minotaur, but was later abandoned by him. Eventually, she married the god, Dionysus, who was the god of wine, revelry, fertility, theatre, and dance. Altar, of course, represents a sacred place.) I feel I am growing into both names. I kept my given name, Emily, as a middle name, so my mother wouldn't be too upset! She still cannot get used to the change!

All that being said, my children's deaths propelled me ever farther into mystical queries, dabbling in the occult, in astrology, in Tarot readings. I feel imbued with a desire to penetrate "this veil," and I live in an open state of prayer—not just daily but constant prayer in nearly every waking moment. I long, long in the sense of stretching as far as I possibly can, to reach them. Though I can no longer "see" them in this life, I "feel" them both here and beyond the veil. And that knowledge of life, life of the spirit, hereafter, keeps me, and has kept me, from going insane with grief.

From: Ariane Altar ariane@altarpots.com
Date: February 3, 2009
To: Wylie Hymen wylie@hymenfables.com
Subject: How are you, where are you?

As I haven't heard from you, I am feeling a certain level of anxiety. When you feel like it, do let me know if you are breathing. My granddaughter is beyond adorable. I am enmeshed in a mad love affair with her.

From: Wylie Hymen wylie@hymenfables.com
Date: February 4, 2009
To: Ariane Altar ariane@altarpots.com
Subject: Re: How are you, where are you?

I am fine, really well. I rested in pre-op for an hour talking with a nurse who has been to Turkey and another planning a trek to Cappadocia this fall.

My two doctors, the anaesthesiologist, and the nuclear medicine guy, all came by to visit.

The IV anaesthesia put me out somewhere in the hallway as I was being wheeled to the OR, and I awoke about three hours later feeling like I had to pee really, really, really badly. Oh, that smarts! But, the pain went away almost instantly when they put a nice cocktail into my IV tube.

After the first pee, the nuclear medicine guy came down to scan my urine to see if he needed to recover any palladium-103 seeds I might have passed. I hadn't, but when he placed his *Geiger* counter near my body, it set off quite a racket!

I left the hospital three hours later, having performed that first pee admirably. All the plumbing is working fine.

I have no pain or discomfort and I've not had to take any pain meds, not one *ibuprofen*. I feel so good I have to constantly remind myself that this is a rest day.

From: Wylie Hymen wylie@hymenfables.com
Date: February 5, 2009
To: Ariane Altar ariane@altarpots.com
Subject: How we talk about love

I awoke this morning very early to the welcome tattoo of the rain; the metal roof, like the rest of the house, is meant to bring the outside in. It's sometime after four when I begin thinking about this, and I'm unable to go back to sleep, my mind busy with thoughts begun in a hospital bed, interrupted by the sudden deep sleep of the anaesthesia, then a time for unaccustomed attention to a body and its workings long taken for granted, and long healing naps in the window seat. I'm sitting now in front of the fire needing to continue those thoughts. They are for and about you and me.

I thought about all the things we've talked about, how quickly we've gotten to things some people never get to. I have frequently in my life frightened people away with my openness. But, we have slipped easily and comfortably into talking about anything and everything, no dangling conversations here. Inevitably, we will be ambushed, like that night we talked about our children, the grief it brought you and the sadness with which I was left, both for you and for my daughter, my own Irina's, schizophrenia.

And then there was your rebuke that declarations of love are most successfully made in person. There is always such distance in emails and letters for intimate conversations, and possibilities for things inadvertently not said that should have been said, perhaps signaled by a long silence (which makes silences on the phone tricky). Even the telephone, though we hear one another's voices, doesn't allow, of course, for the body's, especially the eyes', revealing of emotions. Yes, yes, I know all this, so obvious it doesn't need saying, but knowing doesn't help when you feel the need to talk, when there's much that's remained unsaid for so many years.

Then you postponed your trip indefinitely. For how long? I didn't know then. And when would I get to express my feelings in person? You see how tiring my impatience with the waiting game can be, and I'm sorry for that. Then there's the release the doctors want you to sign, but you don't want to read, detailing all the frightening possibilities of what can go wrong in surgery.

I think you know and, if not, I want you to know, that if you were here with me for those times of elation or sadness, I would take your hand at first shyly, tentatively, not yet certain of your response to the intimacy of sudden first touching, and then encircle you with my body, a loving if not lover's embrace, the warmth and closeness soothing the pain, bringing immediacy to feelings of love and caring, eyes and the body making clear what distance makes uncertain.

I sometimes wonder about our inclination toward history, when two people first meet, the delving, explaining, revealing, and catching up with our pasts. While I do it all the time – I seem incapable of being any other way – naturally curious about a new friend's genesis and journeys, I've often thought perhaps it's better to start where we are, anew, unencumbered by our pasts. Of course, we're always marked and shaped by our history, and to ignore the past can lead unwittingly to more perceived insensitivity and hurt than revealing much that has gone before. Hurting, even amidst great caring and love, is always a possibility, especially long distance. It's important that you continue, as we have begun, saying "ouch" loudly and clearly, so I know to kiss the owie.

It meant a lot to me when you wrote about grief, and why you have faith. I do not know such comfort of the spirit and have never understood it. Maybe as I get to know you better, I shall be enlightened!

From: Ariane Altar ariane@altarpots.com
Date: February 5, 2009
To: Wylie Hymen wylie@hymenfables.com
Subject: Gramma opens her wallet and out come the photos of the grandkids
Photo: Ande's partner, Nalu with Kui after breakfast; the ecstatic and enthusiastic one at play. (The baby is the one on the left, in case you wondered; I am on the right.)

Wow! Am I impressed: not only do you know what an owie is, but you also know how to kiss it and make it all better! Any man who can offer that is a man indeed. More when I get home. Glad the recovery is swift.

I had such a wonderful time with Ande, Nalu, and Kui! Kui is doing all the adorable baby things - cooing, grabbing toes, and patty caking. Fabulous!

This evening I saw a glow on the eastern horizon. Was that radioactive you?

Pants On Fire!

From: Wylie Hymen wylie@hymenfables.com
Date: February 6, 2009
To: Ariane Altar ariane@altarpots.com

The photos are delightful: what a beautiful family and sweet, dimpled little girl dumpling! I can see how she enchants you. Don't worry, I enjoy getting photos, especially the way you do them as an easy download on my dial-up modem.

I'm heading for Berkeley Sunday to be with Baron, Barbara, Sage, and Asia before they go off for two weeks to Mexico. Be back Wednesday. Your photos of Kui remind me of when Sage and Asia were that age. I know it's often said, but they do grow up fast and come into their own which, of course, is what we want, with such wonderful surprises along the way.

I lose all sense of time sitting by the fire reading or listening to music. I'm up and around in the morning by six, but I promise not to do that when you're here. I tell my editors in Boston and New York that it's okay to call me early mornings – I prefer it, because then I can be out and around the rest of the day, but they all say the same thing: "I can't bring myself to call anyone that early."

I look forward to our nearly nightly talk.

From: Wylie Hymen wylie@hymenfables.com
Date: February 7, 2009
To: Dina Cochon dinaRN@iswell.org
Subject: the loveseat

Pooky,

I'll be with you on the coast for a couple of days while the loveseat gets reupholstered. See you in the morning, my love.

To: Wylie Hymen wylie@hymenfables.com
Date: February 7, 2009
From: Karen Borders curator@ismuseum.org
Subject: Pillow Book

Dear Wylie,

An intriguing development: Tom Jensen, a major curator known for his unusual exhibitions, has contacted Indian Springs Museum regarding your erotica. He is looking specifically for underground erotic art created by established artists but never publicly shown. He seeks to mount an exhibition of this "underground" erotica in about two years.

Pants On Fire!

The "Pillow Book" drawings you showed me a few years ago when we first got together would suit this show ideally. Tom is gay and apparently discovered some of your early work based on the Japanese Shunga erotic woodblocks in a pawnshop in the Haight Ashbury. As Tom and I have known each other forever, he asked me if I would contact you as a personal favor.

Delving a bit deeper, we found that you also drew many Spring Palace paintings on porcelain shoes and slippers based on Chinese erotic art. Do you have any more of these early works in your personal collection? If so, would you be willing to exhibit them?

I had no idea you ever worked in clay and overglaze. You are full of surprises.

Perhaps you have a list of collectors as well from whom we could borrow works for exhibit. If there is enough, I might convince him to give you a solo show. If you are really nice to me, that is. I look forward to hearing from you.

Fondly,
Karen, Your Foot and Everything Else Fetishist

From: Wylie Hymen wylie@hymenfables.com
Date: February 7, 2009
To: Ariane Altar ariane@altarpots.com
Subject: Night

I wish our late conversations could end with us close by the fire, my arms around you, holding you quietly into the night.

I appreciate your questions about my life of isolation here in the mountains. I actually go to the Bay Area every ten days or so. I like to use UCB's libraries for my research. I love coffee at Peet's or Café Trieste. And, I like to hang out with Baron, if he has any time in the early mornings before work. Not to mention all the museums and cultural events that form a big part of my life.

When I got divorced from wife number two, she bought my share of the home I built on the south side of Indian Springs. I bought two hundred wild mountain acres, part of which was an Indian reservation on Chicken Ridge, sold off by the tribe years before I came along to pay their gambling debts. Building took longer than I planned and cost more than I had. My first winter solo in the new cabin, I nearly froze to death! I had no money for heating stoves, and my fireplace didn't draw right. I had little money for food. I was teaching and receiving royalties from my books, but it really wasn't enough to live on.

I was lucky in the next year that several of my fables were translated into French and Spanish. The unexpected royalties put me back into decent financial standing. I also began selling small drawings and fetishes to a rather eclectic group of collectors, who continue to clamor for this style, a bit like Japanese Shunga, if you are familiar with that woodblock form. It seems there is a market out there for almost anything. I may show you some when you are here. I am never flush, I have never been flush, but a few investments I've made allow me to live in frugal comfort! I sense you are used to being with men who are affluent. I hope I won't be a disappointment to you in this regard.

From: Ariane Altar ariane@altarpots.com
Date: February 7, 2009
To: Wylie Hymen wylie@hymenfables.com
Subject: I'll sit by your fire

Yes, lovely image, sitting by the fire, chatting or not, all pleasant and at peace. Please drive well and have a good trip. The Bay Area always energizes; I know you will feel that rejuvenation. After such a successful surgery, I bet every experience seems a bit new and special. And, I am sure you feel blessed by your good health. Glorious sun here, had book group discussion, then a meeting, and a long walk by the shore. Now to my studio. I think having you as a friend is putting a skip in my step. One day I'll tell you my thoughts on both marijuana and poverty, for me, two distasteful subjects. And Shunga? I had to look it up. Porn! A third distasteful subject! Now I know you are a naughty boy! I am not at all sure I'll be safe with you.

From: Wylie Hymen wylie@hymenfables.com
Date: February 8, 2009
To: Ariane Altar ariane@altarpots.com
Subject: Progress Report

I've returned from my first real outing, a five-hour hike with some rock hopping up into the hills, to a panoramic view of Indian Springs and back, feeling strong and not at all tired. I went with my old friend Darren, a retired professor from U. C. San Diego with whom I also ski and snowshoe.

It was, as always with Darren, not supposed to be that long, but he gets lost all the time. When he says four hours, I factor in an extra hour or two. Darren, by the way, taught geography!

I wanted to write to you of relationships. You have only experienced monogamous relationships; at least that's what you've indicated. I have had two marriages and a few lovers. Over the years I have observed that most people I know—let's just focus on my community of Mendocino, are former hippies, children of the Sixties, of communes and flower children and free love. They never practiced monogamy—it was not a value—and have enjoyed lots of sex with lots of partners, maybe growing addicted to "multiple choice." Drugs, sex, and rock 'n roll! What I am seeing now is that as they are aging, they are in their sixties and seventies and beyond, like us, but they don't feel quite so sexy anymore. They never learned the art of maintaining long-term monogamous relationships or experiencing the depths of intimacy without sex. When the going got rough, they got going!

Today many of these friends are very lonely. They don't have personal safety nets: no intimate partner, shared home, shared financial income, no security, unless they had children, but that still doesn't solve the lack of intimacy problem. And, they are scared. It's scary to be alone when you are old. Yet, they don't have the skills to stay in relationship.

I may go away for a few days while I get a loveseat reupholstered in Fort Bragg. I'll take my cell.

From: Ariane Altar ariane@altarpots.com
Date: February 8, 2009
To: Wylie Hymen wylie@hymenfables.com
Subject: Re: Progress Report

May I call you Mountain Goat? Or perhaps Big Horn Sheep? Or maybe just plain Lucky? Besides the spring in my step, how about the song in my heart? (I promise to avoid such corn from now on out, although I might break that promise!)

Why did I think you went to Berkeley, not the coast? Or, did you go via the coast for a change? You are in Ft. Bragg getting the loveseat fixed?

By the way, I don't know any people like your Mendocino friends. How sad your description is. Due to mental illness (my mother's depression, my sister's suicide) in my family of origin, I avoided recreational drug use and missed out on all those hallucinogens. I kind of like having my eyes wide open, vision un-blurred. I'm part of that monogamous married crowd who believes in honoring a commitment and have only energy for one relationship at a time! Depth, depth, depth! A love relationship is our sacred path to learning the nature of God, is it not? Even for atheists!

You asked about my family, and I forestalled a response. I have written a great deal in the past. I take painful experiences and, to try to gain perspective, turn them into art—through clay or stories. It is raining here, and I am having a grand morning of pineapple and coffee. This morning I wrote something, which I am including here, for your eyes-only.

The Fulcrum

A point of balance. The fulcrum. When I think of my son, Nico, I am overwhelmed by memory of the deepest love I have experienced in my life. My boy was a true Prince of Light. He illuminated all of our lives with his unique beacon of love. Simultaneously, I am overwhelmed by the loss of him, my sorrow and guilt, and unending grief. My mind and heart flood with confusion as I teeter off-balance between conflicting tidal waves of emotion. One moment my heart swells with love and the next ruptures with pain. I totter toward not only his death but also toward my own. Darkness, confusion, and misery surround. To calm this storm, I seek the point of balance between the love and the loss. When I am fortunate, I reach the fulcrum, a point of balance, where I neither go up nor go down. No teeter, no totter. Balance. Stasis. There I try to abide.

From: Wylie Hymen wylie@hymenfables.com
Date: February 12, 2009
To: Ariane Altar ariane@altarpots.com
Subject: Snow leopard sited in Indian Springs
Photo: Gates, my cat, plunging into snowdrift

Once my cat, Gates, overcomes his existential doubts about his place in a winter world, he goes for it. Snow is predicted for the next five days and beyond . . .

"The Fulcrum" touched me deeply. Thank you, dear friend.

I got home from the coast late yesterday with my newly upholstered love seat, but will look over all the contractual information you've sent and will call tonight.

From: Ariane Altar ariane@altarpots.com
Date: February 12, 2009
To: Wylie Hymen wylie@hymenfables.com
Subject: Re: Snow leopard sited in Indian Springs

Glad you got home safely in the diesel monster from Fort Bragg. What a greeting from the Snow Leopard, Gates! I think this sighting might be more rare than one in Nepal. Your snow looks glorious.

From: Wylie Hymen wylie@hymenfables.com
Date: February 13, 2009
To: Ariane Altar ariane@altarpots.com
Subject: Snowy days and nights
Photo: View from the loft, Friday morning

Deep winter, deeper than any I can remember the sixteen years I've been here in the mountains, Sierra deep, black and white days, millions of grays in between, nature imitating Ansel Adams. Snowed through the night, and I awoke this morning in a blizzard, whiteout, yet so quiet all I could hear were the big flakes swirling, ticking against the windows and my own heartbeat. I prize the gift of these days – like German spoken

Pants On Fire!

slowly – leisurely, unhurried, hours passing by the fire, measured only by the turning of pages and the andante of a Dvorak piano quintet (how that Czech could write a tune). Turning on a lamp, suddenly aware that the shadows are becoming darker but the flickering fire more intense, I realize it is evening, the darkening world outside closing to a little circle of firelight and warmth around the stove, and another day has passed in quiet, secret solitude, this one, however, special, because the night will bring your voice, become so dear, and your laughter, so brave for all you have endured.

From: Ariane Altar ariane@altarpots.com
Date: February 14, 2009
To: Wylie Hymen wylie@hymenfables.com
Subject: déjà vu
Photo: my newest Confucian scholar wall portraits in clay/mixed media

A "chicken-skin" deja vu experience: I was having my Sunday breakfast on the lanai, playing solitaire (my meditation) and listening to James McBryde's *Song Yet Sung* on audio. Something in the story triggered an image of you and me working on or just having finished Theia's story and being startled, together, by some piece of international news. In that instant of déjà vu, I understood that we completed this work together long ago, and we are in some kind of time warp to be beginning it now.

I promised to tell you why marijuana is a bit of a hot spot with me. Here goes. I don't have judgments on whether someone should or shouldn't smoke; it is a personal and adult decision. I do have opinions, though! Marijuana ruined my marriage. It changed my husband. He smoked morning, noon, and night and became hedonistic and lazy, debased in his desires. It also led him to an appetite for cocaine. He lost his moral center. I used to tell my children, "If you can find a person whose life is better—richer, happier, more fulfilled—because they are using marijuana, please introduce us. I have never met such a person. If you find him or her, then we can talk about you smoking. Not until then."

Do you worry about the government seizing your land because you allow your friend to grow on it, or is it okay because he has the medical license? I am pretty naïve in the legal department.

Yesterday a couple came to my studio and purchased some work. The husband noticed some portraits in clay I had done of 9th and 10th century Confucian scholars...and he mentioned he had a PhD from Columbia in Chinese History. He's been to China many times, the first time on a Fulbright. Anyway, he is headmaster of St Anne's School in Brooklyn (sounds odd as he is Jewish), which caters to the wealthy and bright, giving no grades and offering a fabulous curriculum. He knew all about the Jewish ghetto, and we had a wonderful conversation. He recommended reading *The Fugu Plan* about the treatment of refugees in Shanghai by the Japanese. I found this description on amazon.com:

Pants On Fire!

The Fugu Plan: The Untold Story Of The Japanese And The Jews During World War II (Hardcover) by Marvin Tokayer and Mary Swartz
Introduction To The Current Edition:
[One] person has come to be the human face of the fugu plan: Chiune Sugihara. From November 1939 to September 1940, Sugihara was officially the Japanese consul in Kovno (or "Kaunas"), Lithuania. . . .Sugihara had been sent to Kovno to gather intelligence about Soviet and German troop movements in the area [and] . . . became one of the crucial players in the fugu plan − a scheme that, by the war's end, would save the lives of thousands of Jews. . . .Sugihara never mentioned his own role in the rescue of the Jewish refugees. . . . "I never knew what happened to the refugees," he said. "I never knew if they got past the Soviet Union, if they actually came to Japan, if they ever found safety. I didn't want to discuss it, because perhaps I had only led them to their death. I was afraid to bring it up." Did he know, I wondered, about the fugu plan? "I only knew about that when you told me. If I had known, it would have been much easier for me. I wouldn't have felt the sole burden of responsibility for issuing the visas." Finally, I asked him the one crucial question: Why did he do it? To the best of anyone's knowledge, before July 1940 Sugihara had never had any personal contact with Jews. Why, then, did he risk his career and possibly his life to save the lives of these refugees?

He looked at me as if he didn't really understand the question. "I just did what we as human beings should do. One of my best teachers . . . once told me: You do the right thing, because it is the right thing. Not for gain. Not for recognition. Just because it is the right thing. The refugees were people who needed my help. I could give help to them. It was the right thing to do. That's all."

In the midst of the horror of 1940, it was the extreme good fortune of thousands of Jewish refugees, and tens of thousands of their descendants, that a rare man such as Sugihara was there when their lives depended on it.

Marvin Tokayer, 2004

From: Wylie Hymen wylie@hymenfables.com
Date: February 16, 2009
To: Ariane Altar ariane@altarpots.com
Subject: Talking

I'm glad you called last night. Your questions were such cause for thought that I'm afraid I talked too much. It's interesting we're both thinking about what the rest of our lives might be like. Next time let's talk about where you'd like to travel. With me.

Pants On Fire!

I actually have a better answer as to why I write what I write. Many of my stories have similar themes – fables about how young people ease into adulthood. My stories often involve youngsters working with and learning from their elders, acquiring skills with which they identify and give them a strong sense of self. I can always tell when a book critic or reader has really read and understood my books; they get beyond the technology, the beautiful ships, maps, explorations, and ancient places to see that these are actually stories about working, about dreaming, about creating, about traveling.

From: Wylie Hymen wylie@hymenfables.com
Date: February 16, 2009
To: Dina Cochon dinaRN@iswell.org

We are meeting Iggy and Co at the train station in Richmond at 3 p.m. tomorrow. I'll leave Chicken Ridge around 9 a.m.; pick you up whenever I get there. Have some coffee ready for me, my love! Should be a fun couple of days! Bring your high-heel slippers for steppin' out in the Big City!

From: Wylie Hymen wylie@hymenfables.com
Date: February 16, 2009
To: Ariane Altar ariane@altarpots.com
Subject: a little humor

A footnote to our discussion about Henry Ford: The four Goldberg brothers, Lowell, Norman, Hiram, and Max, invented and developed the first automobile air-conditioner.

On July 17, 1946, the temperature in Detroit was ninety-seven degrees. The four brothers walked into old man Henry Ford's office and sweet-talked his secretary into telling him that four gentlemen were there with the most exciting innovation in the auto industry since the electric starter. Henry was curious and invited them into his office.

They refused and instead asked that he come out to the parking lot to their car. They persuaded him to get into their car, which was about a hundred and thirty degrees, turned on the air conditioner, and cooled the car off immediately. Old man Ford got very excited and invited them back to the office, where he offered them three million dollars for the patent.

The brothers refused, saying they would settle for two million, but they wanted the recognition by having a label, '*The Goldberg Air-Conditioner*,' emblazoned on the dashboard of each car in which it was installed.

Now old man Ford was more than a little anti-Semitic, and there was no way he was going to put the Goldberg's' name on two million *Fords*. They haggled back and forth for about two hours, and finally agreed on four million and that only their first names would be shown. Consequently, to this day, all *Ford* air conditioners show *"Lo, Norm, Hi, and Max"* on the controls.

Ariane, your Confucian scholars, teas, fortresses, temples, and our talks, have caused me after many years of not seeing them, to rediscover my dusty books of Chinese poetry and open them to once loved poems still marked by little yellowing scraps of torn paper. Last night I found this translation by my teacher, Cyril Birch, of my favorite, Li Po, who seems to speak for you and me.

On the Mountain: Question and Answer

You ask me:
Why do I live
On this green mountain?
I smile
No answer
My heart serene
On flowing water
Peach blow
Quietly going
Far away
Another sky
This is
Another sky
No likeness
To that human world below

Baron and I are heading up to the Sierra for a couple days, he to soar down the mountainside on his snowboard and me to snowshoe some high ridge deep with this new storm's powder. Be back Wednesday. Hope this poem can tide you over till my return.

From: Ariane Altar ariane@altarpots.com
Date: February 16, 2009
To: Wylie Hymen wylie@hymenfables.com
Subject: Musing on things Chinese

Thank you for the poem. I thought Baron was still in Mexico? You Hymens do get around! Have a fabulous time in the snow. Translations are interesting. Here is another version of "Green Mountain"; which do you prefer?

Pants On Fire!

Green Mountain

You ask me why I dwell in the green mountain;
I smile and make no reply for my heart is free of care.
As the peach-blossom flows down stream and is gone into the unknown,
I have a world apart that is not among men.

Li Po

From: Ariane Altar ariane@altarpots.com
Date: February 24, 2009
To: Wylie Hymen wylie@hymenfables.com
Subject: well well well

Dear Snowy,

Well, I just wish you would hurry up and get back...dare I say I miss you? Is that possible? What I do know is that I am patently aware when you are "away" that you are not available for x number of days...no chance of email or conversation...and that alone frustrates silly me!

By the way, Ang Lee's film about Shanghai is out on DVD. It is called *Lust/ Caution*. It's a fascinating love story about betrayal and occupation: bodily occupation as well as the Japanese occupation of Shanghai. It is sexually explicit and mesmerizing!

From: Wylie Hymen wylie@hymenfables.com
Date: February 25, 2009
To: Ariane Altar ariane@altarpots.com
Subject: Blizzards of snow

Baron and family returned from the beaches of the Yucatan and explorations of Tulum, Tikal, and Palenque with the children, thinking it really cool and very California to head immediately for mountains of snow. When the children were young, we used to go skiing in May and early June and a day or two later go swimming at Lake Anza up in Tilden Park. What it's really about is that he's very busy, and this is the last time he'll have to play for a while. We skied in blizzards.

Remember my agony over having damaged his truck? Well, it turns out, the mangled bumper was mangled before I got the truck. Do I live a charmed life or what? All the more now that you have returned to it.

Oh, have you read Wagenstein's *Farewell Shanghai*?

Bonne nuit, dear Ariane

Pants On Fire!

From: Ariane Altar ariane@altarpots.com
Date: February 27, 2009
To: Wylie Hymen wylie@hymenfables.com
Subject: humming

You may be amused to learn that when I first began to write seriously, I took the nom de plume of "Anna Hummer"! I've been whistling a happy tune since our laughter last night. Hope you're humming, too.

Heard this poem last week on the radio. I liked it. I hope you do, too. It's by Tony Hoagland from *Sweet Ruin*.

History of Desire

When you're seventeen, and drunk
on the husky, late-night flavor
of your first girlfriend's voice
along the wires of the telephone
What else to do but steal
your father's El Dorado from the drive,
and cruise out to the park on Driscoll Hill?
Then climb the county water tower
and aerosol her name in spray can orange
a hundred feet above the town?
Because only the letters of that word,
DORIS, next door to yours,
in yard-high, iridescent script,
are amplified enough to tell the world
who's playing lead guitar
in the rock band of your blood.
You don't consider for a moment
the shock in store for you in 10 A.D.,
a decade after Doris, when,
out for a drive on your visit home,
you take the Smallville Road, look up
and see RON LOVES DORIS
still scorched upon the reservoir.
This is how history catches up—
by holding still until you
bump into yourself.
What makes you blush, and shove
the pedal of the Mustang

67

Pants On Fire!

almost through the floor
as if you wanted to spray gravel
across the features of the past,
or accelerate into oblivion?
Are you so out of love that you
can't move fast enough away?
But if desire is acceleration,
experience is circular as any
Indianapolis. We keep coming back
to what we are—each time older,
more freaked out, or less afraid.
And you are older now.
You should stop today.
In the name of Doris, stop.

Thought I'd share a particularly nice comment in my B&B guest book from a couple in their sixties who stayed three nights last week.

Thank you for creating this beautiful, tranquil haven. What a gift for those of us lucky enough to have found our way here. The beautiful landscape, breathtaking views, fabulous food, and gracious hospitality exceeded all our expectations. But, it is you – your special gift, your ability to give of yourself – that makes it unique. Our stay here is a memory we will treasure always. We wish you the best and hope our paths cross again in the near future.

Gratefully yours,
Lee and Cary, Green Bay, Wisconsin

From: Wylie Hymen wylie@hymenfables.com
Date: February 28, 2009
To: Ariane Altar ariane@altarpots.com
Subject: A poem for a poem

What a beautiful tribute. I know it to be true, because I am enjoying the warm hospitality of your heart and the bright melodies of your laughter.

Love Sonnet xlviii

Two happy lovers make one bread,

a single moon drop in the grass.
Walking, they cast two shadows that flow together;
waking, they leave one sun empty in their bed.
Of all the possible truths, they chose the day;
they held it, not with ropes but with an aroma.
They did not shred the peace; they did not shatter words;
their happiness is a transparent tower.
The air and wine accompany the lovers.
The night delights them with its joyous petals.
They have a right to all the carnations.
Two happy lovers, without an ending, with no death,
they are born, they die, many times while they live:
they have the eternal life of the Natural.

Pablo Neruda

From: Ariane Altar ariane@altarpots.com
Date: March 1, 2009
To: Wylie Hymen wylie@hymenfables.com
Subject: new plates at my dinner party!
Photo: upena fish net plates with Cherry and Freddie from Napa Valley eating
coquille St. Jacques

Last night I had some friends over for dinner. I liked the table so much, I took a photo. I made the plates this week (if you can't tell, upena is a fishnet design) and used flowers and leaves from the garden everywhere. Great night. Maybe you'll come next time?

From: Wylie Hymen wylie@hymenfables.com
Date: March 2, 2009
To: Ariane Altar ariane@altarpots.com
Subject: Let's talk

Wow, you are really something, coquille St. Jacques, the ocean in the distance, on your new upena plates, made just for the occasion. I do wish I could have been there.

I rented *Lust/Caution*, by the way. Whew! I have never seen such detailed sex scenes! I think they were real. My god! I had to watch it twice!

Pants On Fire!

From: Ariane Altar ariane@altarpots.com
Date: March 4, 2009
To: Wylie Hymen wylie@hymenfables.com
Subject: Re: Let's talk

Thank you for your note. It means a lot, as you are on my mind. I am on Kaua'i, and then going to O'ahu for the wake of my son's friend, who died, then back to Hana.

I'm glad you saw *Lust/Caution*. The Japanese military occupying Shanghai; the Japanese head of interrogation occupying the Chinese loyalist girl's body through rape and domination. The scene that is seared into my mind's eye is when the Japanese lover, warned of an imminent ambush, skitters down the staircase from the diamond dealer's, where he has chosen a ring for her, like the terrified rat that he is! Deception: how I loathe it! The Chinese paramour who saved his life is brave and truer to her heart than her politics! Betrayal: ugh! Now you know another of my "hot spots"!

From: Lucas Dmitri lucas@unityworld.org
Date: March 5, 2009
To: Ariane Altar Ariane@altarpots.com
Subject: Metanoia

Well, Lent started. It's a church season with such mixed feelings for me. I hate it, which is strange for a clergyman to admit! But, it gives me a chance to describe and talk about repentance, a word that's loaded. Here's a little piece I wrote about it. Now please try to ignore the institutional religious, "Jesus" stuff; I remind you that it's written for a worshipping congregation. My audience is at times spiritually adept but not as spiritually independent as I consider you to be. My followers are still stuck in religious structure, which I am trying to broaden bit by bit.

One fall as a kid, many years ago now, I recall finding a big juicy striped caterpillar on a stick. I ran into the house yelling for my mother. "Look at this, look at this!" She rummaged through a drawer until she found an old *Skippy* peanut butter jar. She told me to get a hammer and a big nail from the garage and pound some holes in the lid. Then I remember stuffing some leaves into the jar with the caterpillar on a stick. My mother told me to watch, because it would change. I had no idea what she meant. I put in on the windowsill, and it became a routine for me to take a look at it every morning. It wasn't long before it wove itself into a cocoon. Then came the long wait until the spring. She kept telling me to be patient.

Finally, it happened; I came yelling and running into the kitchen, "Look! Look!" A monarch butterfly experienced metamorphosis. What a thrill for this young boy. At my mother's urging, I took it to school that day for "show and tell" before letting it go in the afternoon.

As metamorphosis is for butterflies, "metanoia" is for humans. It's an experience each of us can have. The extraordinary spiritual experience of being "changed."

May I suggest, Ariane, that you described this so well with your words about how you found a way to re-enter life after the grief you experienced within your tragedies and trauma surrounding your children dying?

Lent gives us a time to experience this. It's a time to step away from the normal habits of life. We can change something immediate or make it long term as we renew the search for a spiritual focus. We can reflect and experience what it means to repent. Some of us have the word, "repent" etched in our memories. You may recall the way some preacher used to shout the word, almost spitting it out at you. "Repent! Or go to hell!"

In the ancient language of New Testament Greek, the word for repentance is "metanoia." It describes what happened to people when they met Jesus. A change of mind, a reorientation happened. It gives us a glimpse into the fundamental transformation of outlook, of a person's vision of the world and the self, describing a new way of loving others and God.

Repentance is necessary and valuable. It brings about change of mind and heart. Can you be open to the experience of "metanoia" this Lent. Can I? It's about a transformation of our minds and hearts; letting go of those parts of living that separate us from Love. May we experience Lent together!

One of the prayer concerns someone brought was about a twenty-year-old sophomore in college who ended his life. During the time of sharing, I talked about the way in which depression and mental illness need to be taken seriously; otherwise, they can become terminal illnesses.

Afterwards, some who struggle with depression came to talk. A man whose brother was blown up in an industrial accident told me my talk made sense. A wise old nurse who used to head up the nursing staff at the local hospital was grateful that I didn't hide or deny the reality of depression or give simple answers full of inadequacy and manipulation.

My brother happened to be in worship. He has a place not far from here. He came up for communion, so crippled he can barely walk. He has a condition called hemochromatosis, a condition where he had too much iron in his blood and rusted out. It basically ate away his ankles maybe twenty years ago. He's the only person I know who has had six ankles. The original two and then two operations on both ankles. He's five years older than I am. I call him the kindest man I have ever met, and, in some

Pants On Fire!

ways, he is. Theologically, he never made it out of conservative fundamentalism, which makes conversation tiresome. Still he's my older brother, and I do love him.

Anyway, I set up communion after blessing the elements, and let the laity serve and greet. I stood back and focused on people as they came forward. It's quite humbling to watch and to experience. Today I could feel my heart go all smooshy when I watched him hobble up, sincere and fragile in his aging body.

I drove to Brainerd about twenty miles in my old ratty *Trailblazer* that is dying a slow death; it uses antifreeze as if it was a blood transfusion to keep going. Skied what – maybe three plus miles on "skate skis," a fast and somewhat esoteric brand of cross-country skiing. I feel better today as I throw off this cold. At a full sweat afterwards at fifteen degrees, I duck into the men's bathroom, which has warm water in the sink. Strip down, take a sponge bath that's enough so I don't get too chilled afterwards and head for the movies. I wanted to see what Mickey Rourke did to receive a nomination. I want to think about the movie some, but his character struck me with some vulnerability as, I too, am an aging man who still wants to be physical.

Lucas

From: Ariane Altar ariane@altarpots.com
Date: March 5, 2009
To: Lucas Dmitri lucas@unityworld.org
Subject: Re: Metanoia

I am on O'ahu for the wake of my son's childhood friend, Davin, who committed suicide last week, leaving behind a wife and two year old daughter, his parents, grandparents, and five siblings. He was our neighbor during my twenty-eight years on O'ahu. A darling and talented young man of twenty-nine.

There is a feeling of shared or assumed guilt when a suicide occurs. I know that none of Nico's inner circle of friends went unscathed by his death. All slipped into some form of depression lasting two years or longer. Davin is the first of those friends to die. It is particularly heartbreaking for me to see such sorrow perpetuated.

For me to go, to speak, to greet, to grieve, and to see them all: a torment beyond words. His mother said to me on the phone, "Now I know how you feel" to which I protested, "I don't ever want anyone to lose a child or to feel what I feel!"

So, I am looking for words, and I may just plagiarize a bit of your sermon, if you don't mind, as I think it will give solace where it is sorely needed.

I remember your brother from Northwestern days when he became engaged. How wonderful you love him so much. And, yes, how interesting these aging

72

bodies are. I was baking cookies the other day and a seven year old, Hawai'ian boy was visiting. "Auntie," he said, pointing to my cheek, "What's that?" "What's what?" I asked. "That line." I thought for a minute and then realized, "Oh, that is a wrinkle. It's what skin does when it gets old."

"But, Auntie, why are there so many of them?"

I actually love it. Not advancing toward the end of life, but rather being comfortable and happy in my own wrinkled skin! I feel I have earned each wrinkle with laughter and heartache, and they are mine, and I love them.

Thank you again, Lucas. Your sermon means a lot to me. The eulogy I wrote follows.

Aloha.

I am here as your friend and former neighbor. As many of you know, my children grew up with Davin and the Castro kids. What you may not know is that two of my beloved children are now dead. And, sweet, sweet Davin is dead. All beautiful young people. All suicides.

I have no answers. I have no solution for the grief and the loss. I can only share the love in my heart each and every moment for you, for my friends and family, and for my children in life and beyond.

I have no answer today for myself or for the Castro family. This kind of pain is a pain beyond comprehension. To ask why it happened, as if there is punishment or purpose, doesn't make any sense. All I know is that with the strength of our capacity to trust in hope and compassion, to imagine that holiness cries with us, to know the support we can offer by our presence and our care is important. By accepting the support we can receive from others, then we can be the carriers of love and grace.

I offer you, Castro family members, and you, fellow grievers, my strength and my experience of loss, the loss of my dearly beloved children, so that you will learn that you can be your best and most loving self for your friends and neighbors and family right now and always, despite the pain.

A headstone in Ireland reads, "Death leaves a heartache no one can heal, love leaves a memory no one can steal." The television show, *The Wonder Years*, broadcast, "Memory is a way of holding onto the things you love, the things you are, the things you never want to lose."

"When you are sorrowful look again in your heart," writes Kahlil Gibran, "and you shall see that in truth you are weeping for that which has been your delight."

"The deep pain that is felt at the death of every friendly soul," says Arthur Schopenhauer, "arises from the feeling that there is in every individual something which is inexpressible, peculiar to him alone, and is, therefore, absolutely and irretrievably lost."

There are things that we don't want to happen but have to accept, things we don't want to know but have to learn, and people we can't live without but have to let go.

For me, Winston Churchill and Judy Crowley gave the best advice: 'If you're going through hell··· keep going! Every evening turn your worries over to God. He's going to be up all night anyway···"

Someone known only as Peter said what I wish to say to Davin now:

"As long as I can, I will look at this world for both of us. As long as I can, I will laugh with the birds, I will sing with the flowers, I will pray to the stars, for both of us."

From: Ariane Altar ariane@altarpots.com
Date: March 7, 2009
To: Wylie Hymen wylie@hymenfables.com
Subject: thought you might be interested...

As we both have lived with teenaged daughters who've suffered forms of mental illness, I thought you might like to read *Hurry Down Sunshine: A Father's Memoir of Love and Madness* by Michael Greenberg.

"On July 5, 1995, my daughter was struck mad. She was fifteen, and her crack-up marked a turning point in both our lives ... I wanted to grab her and bring her back, but there was no turning back. Suddenly every point of connection between us had vanished."

From: Lucas Dmitri lucas@unityworld.org
Date: March 8, 2009
To: Ariane Altar ariane@altarpots.com
Subject: a meditation

Ariane,

Thinking of you and how you change or sometimes lose yourself when you enter a new relationship.

It takes us a while to see where we are. It takes us even longer to see who we are. Therefore, the most subversive invitation you could ever accept is the invitation to awaken to whom you are and not to whom you are when you are with someone else. Just you. Your soul.

When your soul awakens, you begin to truly inherit your life. You discard the kingdom of surfaces, repetitive talk, and role-playing to slip deeper into the true adventure of who you are and who you are called to become. The greatest friend of the soul is the unknown. Yet, we are afraid of the unknown because it lies outside our vision and our control.

Now you are willing to put yourself in the way of change. You want your work to become an expression of your gift. You want your God to be wild and to call you to where your destiny awaits.

When you begin to sense that your imagination is the place where you are most divine—and not your love relationships, you feel called to clean out of your mind all the shabby trappings of thought. You begin to become true to yourself. As Shakespeare says in "Hamlet":

To thine own self be true, then as surely as night follows day, thou canst to no man be false.

The journey shows you that from this inner dedication you can reconstruct your own values and action. You develop from your own self-compassion compassion for others. More naked now than ever, you begin to feel truly alive. You begin to trust the music of your own soul; you have inherited treasure that no one will ever be able to take from you.

From: Ariane Altar ariane@altarpots.com
Date: March 10, 2009
To: Wylie Hymen wylie@hymenfables.com
Subject: *Ancient Voyages* and Hubble

Your book, *Ancient Voyages*, arrived. Wowie, zowie, fantastic! You are writing about explorations to places that fascinate me and hold such power. I am over the top with excitement to read on, having just finished looking at all the drawings and reading the section on the Greeks. When I worked in Athens at the Greek National Theatre, I spent several nights inside Agamemnon's palace at Mycenae where I was rehearsing *Electra* from the *Oresteia* for performance at Epidauros. I also went to Troy, Pergamon, and Ephesus. Most of my wall pieces are inspired by cuneiforms, hieroglyphics, and calligraphy. You can see the connections. Know that I am thrilled to have your book!

Thank you for the Hubble photos as well: absolutely fantastic images; mind expanding, to say the least.

Finally have some sun, and today becomes gardening day. A kiln is cooling. Birds are singing. Life is grand.

Have you seen the Canadian film board's *Black Robe* about the first French Jesuits in Huron territory? The questions the isolated and tortured priest asks about

God and faith are powerfully put. It is beautifully photographed. I just watched *Burden of Dreams*, a documentary about Werner Herzog and the filming of *Fitzcarraldo*—both are riveting. They filmed four years in the Amazon, two thousand five hundred miles from the nearest town!

Have you ever gone to Israel? Egypt?

From: Dina Cochon dinaRN@iswell.org
Date: March 10, 2010
To: Wylie Hymen wylie@hymenfables.com

Need to get to San Francisco tomorrow to ship our product from a new location as we discussed. BUT my clutch has gone out and can't be fixed right away. Called Iggy about a delay, but he is being pissy as his usual drama queen (with a capital Q) self and wants his order "NOW, NOW, NOW, Dah-ling". Please, please, please save me: pick me up in the morning, okay? Call when you get this.

Pooky

From: Wylie Hymen wylie@hymenfables.com
Date: March 10, 2009
To: Ariane Altar ariane@altarpots.com
Subject: Lots

I came home to a delightful message on my phone this afternoon. You like *Ancient Voyages*? Well, I had a lot of fun researching and writing all those pieces. I think I mentioned that I wrote that book while living in Honolulu in Manoa. I was teaching at the East West Center at UH and got hired to write a series on *Human Culture*.

I have been to Egypt, the realization of a childhood dream. I have not been to Israel.

I remember the *Black Robe*, memories of very beautiful, dark images; will look for *Burden of Dreams*.

Not only will I tell you about the snow, but also I have an extra pair of snowshoes and, maybe, if there's snow and time, I'll take you out. An immense full moon is lighting my house tonight, and I wish you were here to share it with me.

From: Wylie Hymen wylie@hymenfables.com
Date: Wed, March 11, 2009
To: Iggy Fumer iggyf@gmail.com
Subject: 2nd package

Pants On Fire!

Dear Iggy,

Both packages went out today. I will be able to send you four cases in April and four more in May.

From: Lucas Dmitri lucas@unityworld.org
Date: March 14, 2009
To: Ariane Altar ariane@altarpots.com
Subject: I'm being sent to the tropics!

A surprising development: one of our ministers on Maui just suffered a massive heart attack. I have been asked to postpone my retirement and "minister to his flock" until a proper search has been conducted for his replacement. I am delighted to come; Christine is not thrilled, as she cannot come with me due to her teaching commitment. We'll have to see how it goes and if we can afford a few trips for her when school is out. I'll send logistics later. I am trusting that you'll help me out with Hawai'ian customs, words, and places!

From: Wylie Hymen wylie@hymenfables.com
Date: March 14, 2009
To: Ariane Altar ariane@altarpots.com
Subject: Night

Have I ever told you what a joy it is for me to sit by the light of the fire, to hear your voice and your stories, to speak what is in our hearts, and have you all to myself for hours into the night?

From: Ariane Altar ariane@altarpots.com
Date: Mar 14, 2009
To: Wylie Hymen wylie@hymenfables.com
Subject: Re: Night

You at your fireside and me on my lauhala mat chats are lovely indeed. It's a no brainer that your fireside seat is far cozier than my floor! I shall be glad to spend time at your house, even if the snows have melted, and spring is blazing forth!

In the event you subscribe to Netflix, would you be willing to rent the Kristen Scott Thomas film *I've Loved You So Long* for us to watch? If not, I can bring it. Please let me know.

Ah, off to steel cut oats and pineapple...breakfast bliss.

Pants On Fire!

From: Iggy Fumer iggyf@gmail.com
Sat, March 14, 2009
To: Wylie Hymen wylie@hymenfables.com
Subject: Re: 2nd package

Hello dah-ling.

I got shipment information for one package to Ron. Did the other go out as well?

Love and hugs, Iggy

From: Ariane Altar ariane@altarpots.com
Date: March 19, 2009
To: Wylie Hymen wylie@hymenfables.com
Subject: Babies

Congratulations on birthing your "baby," *Where's Noah's Ark?*
Photo for you of the babies closest to my heart, Ande and Kui.
Got my kiln loaded and firing. Table is set for tonight's dinner gala. Need I add that I wish you could join us? (I write all this in case the way, still, to a man's heart is through his stomach?) Here's the menu:
curried corn chowder (just finished making it and it is divine – topped with minced herbs, green onions, avocado, and diced cucumbers)
mahi mahi and shrimp risotto cooked with coconut milk and white wine
blackened red and orange peppers
bok choy wilted in sesame oil
homemade banana bread topped with vanilla ice cream and strawberries soaked in grand marnier, hot fudge option

From: Ariane Altar ariane@altarpots.com
Date: March 21, 2009
To: Wylie Hymen wylie@hymenfables.com
Subject: Theia document idea

That may be one of my all time favorite phone calls. Great. Just great. Thank you! I am sorry to hear more details about your daughter's schizophrenia. I do hope you continue your efforts to reach her. It's been two years, did you say, since you've seen or talked to her? What sadness. I am sorry, too, that she has anger issues on top of dysfunction. Do your sons see her?
Please tweak the attached letter to Theia any way you like.

From: Wylie Hymen wylie@hymenfables.com
Date: March 22, 2009
To: Ariane Altar ariane@altarpots.com
Subject: Just in time for your visit
Photo: snow on cabin Sunday morning

It's still snowing. But, it is supposed to clear tonight and be sunny all week. I like your letter as is.

Last minute instructions. Since you are wanting to travel with as little as possible, I have lots of warm, wooly sweaters, expedition weight underwear, extra parkas and caps, small Ariane-sized boots, all the heavy stuff you will need. I take it as my personal responsibility to keep you warm – whatever it takes.

From: Ariane Altar ariane@altarpots.com
Date: March 22, 2009
To: Wylie Hymen wylie@hymenfables.com
Subject: Fairyland

It looks like your cabin is set in a fairyland!

Here is another draft of the Theia agreement for your approval and changes. When you are finished, I'll print three copies so we can each have a signed one, hopefully, when we leave Theia's house on Tuesday.

I think my humming may be turning to song.

From: Wylie Hymen wylie@hymenfables.com
Date: March 22, 2009
To: Ariane Altar ariane@altarpots.com

I just printed three copies.

You won't need to bring your snowshoes, mukluks, and dog sled; the snow is almost gone.

From: Ariane Altar ariane@altarpots.com
Date: March 22, 2009
To: Wylie Hymen wylie@hymenfables.com

Okay, no snow, no mukluks, but will you still promise to keep me warm?

I am glad you printed the letter of agreement, because my printer just died. I am packed, bills paid, and dogs ready for the beach. Much excitement! I don't go to the Hana airport until five tonight. There are lawns to mow and much to put in order before then. When do you leave? How cold will it be at Point Reyes and San Raphael? *Polarite* or light wool?

○

From: Ariane Altar ariane@altarpots.com
Date: Saturday, March 28, 2009
To: Mom ednawolfeson@peoplepc.com
Subject: up in the wild blue yonder

Dear Mom,

Made it to Wylie's and should be seeing you in the Bay Area in a few days. Hope you are doing well.

Wylie is just great and enthusiastic about having me here and starting the work on Theia's story. I saw her in San Raphael before Wylie picked me up at the bus station. Boy, is she still smarting over Selene's behavior! Nonetheless, she wants me to write her story, and I left her with legal contracts for ownership of copyright. I was adamant that I would not type a single word without a signed contract from her! Theia asked about you and was happy to hear you're still living at home and not in a nursing home! She and Vladimir now live in a posh retirement community. She remembered teaching English as a second language with you at City, saying she loved it when you picked her up in the *Model A*!

The drive up to Wylie's was four hours of freeway tedium, and then one hour on two lane twisting roads leading far away from the coast. I somehow always thought Mendocino County was all coast! We bumped inland to a tiny, neglected farm town called Indian Springs. It looked pretty deserted, paint peeling off abandoned turn of the century wooden storefronts (I was awaiting tumbleweeds and harmonica music), and a few mangy dogs roamed lethargically down the center of town. The obligatory casino that seems to be part of the Native American landscape today was there, but it was some plastic tent structure that looked flimsy and uninviting.

Wylie was very excited, acting as tour guide, clearly in love with this off the beaten track Dead End where he has spent thirty-five years! We parked and strolled to the Farmer's Market, which was a public park where some leftover hippies in some kind of time warp were hanging out in one corner with macramé creations laid on the ground. I call it ground, but it was more like a scraggly patch of grass, unkempt, unwatered, unfertilized, rivaling in decrepitude the mangy coats of the aforementioned dogs. Two trucks parked side by side on the other diagonal corner offered vegetables set in baskets on their tailgates. Besides the vendors (three), there might have been eight shoppers at this "Market"! We bought a tomato, a potato, and a zucchini from one vendor for, would you believe, eight "organic" — the magic label here, dollars! I gasped, but Wylie forked over the dough. From the other highway robber, we purchased some onions and garlic. Wylie was thoroughly delighted with the whole scene and showed no embarrassment at how dismal it was, and I, good guest that I am, refrained from comment.

Then we drove to his home. He turned on Diana Ross and sang along, karaoke style, telling me it was his theme song, something to the effect of:

Long ago, far away···Remember?
Life is just a memory···Remember?
Life is never as it seems···

It took about twenty-five minutes to get there from Indian Springs on an old, dirt-logging road. Since logging died out in the Sixties, you can imagine that the road was pretty rugged and about two feet deep in alpine dust, pine needles, blown out tires, discarded bottles and cans; general *Styrofoam* and plastic detritus hopelessly clutching the jumble of manzanita branches at its edge. Little dirt driveways intermittently led off the road, all barred by metal gates and chains. I asked Wylie if anyone lived up those roads, and he said it was mostly *dropout* country.

Many bumps and jolts later, we arrived at a locked yellow metal gate. Wylie punched in a pass code, and the gate swung open, powered by a solar battery, as there is no conventional electricity in these remote parts. A few hundred yards later, there was a long wooden privacy fence followed by yet another dirt driveway. Wylie pulled in and announced we had arrived at Chicken Ridge. I opened my door, was assaulted by the dust we'd churned up, and stepping out, sank ankle deep in the same said alpine dust. I immediately suffered a coughing and sneezing fit—you know my lungs!

We walked through a pine, oak, and madrone forest to his cabin. No walkway or stone path, no outdoor lights. This place in the rain must be a muddy hell. And forget a nighttime arrival. Okay, Ariane, I told myself, suspend judgment.

The cabin itself is a lovely design, all glass on the southern view exposure, high ceilings with a small, open sleeping loft at one end and a massive stone fireplace at the other. Great restaurant gas range in the kitchen, and oh boy, is it orderly! All the spices in matching jars with labels clearly printed, spotless stainless steel pots and pans hanging from a rack, a full, walk-in pantry behind. Wylie wondered if his anal compulsive orderliness put me off: not in the least! He proudly showed me his bread making area, his *Kitchen Aid* machine, and told me his plan to make us brioche, Madeleine's, and olive bread during my stay. His shelves are lined with cookbooks and tiny antique boats, sources of inspiration for his kids' boat building stories. Actually, one tiny ark was a gift for me from his trip to Turkey. Luckily, he is not proprietary and is letting me use my high energy to cook most of our meals.

He set me up in his guest room off the study. To my surprise and delight, one wall of bookshelves is filled with theatre books! He loves drama and travels to New York and the Bay Area regularly to see plays. I feel like I am in hog heaven! As you know, I had to get rid of most of my theatre books as Hawai'i's humidity and bugs reeked havoc on them—between the mildew, mold, and silverfish, my books were ruined; every trace of my studies for Berkeley's PhD in theatre arts gone. I am enjoying pouring through his collection. We are comparing notes on productions seen over the years. He is equally delighted to learn of my work with the Greek National Theatre. I've shared in detail how I directed Euripides' *The Bacchae* and rehearsed for the *Oresteia* when I played Electra at Epidauros. I realize it is a lengthy trip down memory lane, yet we are living vicariously off each other's pasts.

Outside stands a forty-foot container. It houses his paintings, drawings, and illustrations and acts as his studio during the fall and spring, as winters are too cold, and summers are too hot! Does this mean he is a seasonal painter? I have not had a chance yet to peruse its contents. There are a couple of sheds on site as well for gardening tools, I suppose, and stacks of wood for his stoves.

He takes an arsenal of pills every day. His prostate condition is improving. He gets daily calls from either his nurse or doctor checking up on him. He says the pain is going away. I think the nightly peeing is the most annoying. He has to climb down a metal ladder in the dark from the sleeping loft to get to the john.

It's pretty chilly for me, even inside. I am bundled in wool socks and *Polarite* vest over thermal underwear. There is nothing for me to do here. It smells a bit of must and cat piss. There's nowhere to exercise or breathe deeply. Well, I guess I can read, write, cook, clean, talk, and sleep, which I do. But, I certainly could never sculpt here. (Not that Wylie has suggested we co-habit! But, I am thinking ahead!) First of all, this area is tinder dry, and there is a very real fire hazard year round— usually from lightning. There would be no possibility of propane firings. Second, Wylie uses solar batteries for power, which could never generate enough juice to fire an electric kiln. Worse, he is on dial-up for the computer. Trying to do my work or anything else on the web is tedious and really out of the question. (I guess I am very spoiled by the modern conveniences like high speed *Internet* to which most of us have grown accustomed, even in parts as remote as Hana!)

There is no garden to tend. Wylie says he has potted plants to tend, but I haven't seen any. And, outside, oh my gosh. There are bears, coyotes, skunks, foxes, poison oak, and rattlesnakes! You can't take a walk without carrying your cell phone, pepper spray, and a big club! He has a book on critter prints and scat, which I carry on our walks while I try to identify poop! I am now an expert on raccoon, skunk, squirrel, mole, deer, rabbit, and coyote scat! A fresh pile of steaming shit filled with berries lay in our path this morning. Before I could look in my book, Wylie grabbed my arm, turned me around, and starting high tailing it back to the house. It was fresh bear scat! The berries are the give away.

You remember my sad and fevered history with poison oak. It is growing everywhere here. I am particularly skittish when his cats go in and out and then sleep in the beds, fearing that I'll catch it from their fur. I think what I'm saying is that I am neither relaxed nor enchanted by this locale. I think "under-whelmed" is the operative word?

All these observations and complaints being voiced, I must say, Wylie is a real gem. He is funny and entertaining. I don't think there's ever a pause in our conversations. It feels very natural to be with him 24/7.

Don't hesitate to call if you need me. See you soon

And, Lots of Love, Ariane

Part Two

Fire!

Full Moon

From: ariane^^^75.23.154.208@serve.com
Date: Mon, March 30, 2009
To: Wylie Hymen wylie@hymenfables.com
Subject: Thank you for keeping me warm

A poem for you, Wylie, to thank you for keeping me warm as promised at your mountain retreat, for rekindling poetry in my heart, and for stroking, oh the stroking, my loins, bare and hot on your deck under the late winter's afternoon sun. You deserve kudos as a host. I should hang a banner from your chimney, a toast, proclaiming,

"MY PANTS ARE OFF TO YOU!"

Now, when the waters are pressing mightily

Now, when the waters are pressing mightily
on the walls of the dams,
now, when the white storks, returning
are transformed in the middle of the firmament
into fleets of jet planes,
we will feel again how strong are the ribs
and how vigorous is the warm air in the lungs
and how much daring is needed to love on the exposed plain,
when the dangers are arched above,
and how much love is required
to fill all the empty vessels
and the watches that stopped telling time,
and how much breath,

Pants On Fire!

a whirlwind of breath,
to sing the small song of spring.

Yehuda Amichai
translated from the Hebrew by Leon Wieseltier

From: Ariane Altar ariane@altarpots.com
Date: April 3, 2009
To: Cherry Estrella cherry@starsearch.com
Subject: Big News!

As you know, after visiting you in Napa at the wineries, I met my writing partner, Wylie Hymen. All went well with the preliminary discussions of the Theia story...but there's a bonus. What kind of a bonus? A love bonus! I have fallen Big Time for Wylie!

It feels a little kinky as I told you, because he was my high school lit teacher! But, that was forty-six years ago! He's leaving shortly for New York to launch his new book, *Where's Noah's Ark?*, and then I hope to get him to Hawai'i. He was a fellow at the East West Center in the Eighties or Nineties, speaks fluent German and Mandarin, is a Chinese scholar, has published over thirty books, is currently working both as a writer, illustrator, and painter. I am in awe! He just returned from trekking in Turkey with a *National Geographic* crew to film and narrate the story of the search for Noah's ark. What energy and charisma! When my mom re-met him last summer, she said, "Well, if ever I've seen a fox in a hen house···!" I don't know about that, but what he lacks in looks, he makes up for with charm and vitality. If you are interested in seeing some of his books, go to his website.

You know I never do this, share intimacies about a lover, but this is so good, I want you to read it! You'll see why this darling, romantic man makes me happy! (He actually recites poetry to me from memory). Attached is the note I received this morning with a poem by Stephen Spender.

Ariane,
Dreams of you.
   I fell asleep early last night in a wild, blustery storm, tired and happy, warmed by memories of our days and nights together, burying my face in your scent on my pillow.

Daybreak

At dawn she lay with her profile at that angle
Which, when she sleeps, seems the carved face of an angel.

88

Pants On Fire!

Her hair a harp, the hand of a breeze follows
And plays, against the white cloud of the pillows.
Then, in a flush of a rose, she awoke, and her eyes that opened
Swam in blue through her rose flesh that dawned.
From her dew of lips, the drop of one word
Fell like the first of fountains: murmured
'Darling', upon my ears the song of the first bird.
'My dream becomes my dream,' she said, 'come true
I waken from you to my dream of you.'
The audacity of her sleep. Our dreams
Poured into each other's arms, like streams.

Stephen Spender

From: Ariane Altar ariane@altarpots.com
Date: April 5, 2009
To: Wylie Hymen wylie@hymenfables.com
Subject: Re: Dreams of you

On arriving home, I was exhausted, and fell into my wonderful bed before ten last night after loving up my dear animals. Even this morning I still feel delightfully "spent." The Spender poem is beautiful.

Much to do here with gardens overgrown and unpacking...but I am going to have some coffee and oatmeal and take my time to return to life without you.

You. Ah, you. I am without words; my heart is full.

All night you have been with me in both deep and fitful sleep. Memories of you placing a pillow beneath my hips, of the slow descent of you into the well of me. My hips lifting in the impossible task of union, of touching what cannot be touched, yet seeking ...still... and passionately. (And how now am I ever to sleep alone?)

You mentioned drawing. Images of you drawing came to me in the night. It must be like conjuring. From nothing, from the blank canvas or paper, your hand creates a line...and another, and another. I would like to sit invisibly and watch you draw. It must be magic.

I did not know until I saw your studio that you not only illustrate but you also paint, magnificently. I am in awe of your many talents. And not to tell me you worked in clay early on? I loved the Japanese pillows and small fetishes! The over-glazes are exquisite!

Here is a small poem for you. I wish it were mine, as I want to write for you. But, today mr cummings must suffice. It captures some of the emotion I felt in our cocooning.

Pants On Fire!

i thank You God for most this amazing
day: for the leaping greenly spirits of trees
and a blue true dream of sky; and for everything
which is natural which is infinite which is yes

(i who have died am alive again today,
and this is the sun's birthday; this is the birth
day of life and love and wings: and of the gay
great happening illimitably earth)

how should tasting touching hearing seeing
breathing any—lifted from the no
of all nothing—human merely being
doubt unimaginable You?

(now the ears of my ears awake and
now the eyes of my eyes are opened)

e e cummings

From: Cherry Estrella cherry@starsearch.com
Date: Apr 5, 2009
To: Ariane Altar ariane@altarpots.com
Subject: Re: Big News!

Congratulations! Very impressive guy! I wondered why you had dropped off the map. By the way, has he been married? Check his story, please. You always fall for the romantic, promise you the moon, intellectual type. I don't want to dampen your fire, but I want to remind you to be careful. Your friend here has picked you up a few too many times from dating nutcases!

From: Ariane Altar ariane@altarpots.com
Date: April 6, 2009
To: Cherry Estrella cherry@starsearch.com
Subject: Re: Re: Big News!

Yes, married twice; three adult kids, two granddaughters. I first met him when I was sixteen! I didn't drop off the map; I just entered a special cocoon. He's quite oddball in appearance. Please don't be taken aback when you see him! You know

90

the old adage: don't judge a book by its cover! He is an absent minded professor type: scruffy beard, balding, holes in well-worn clothes, and an enormous schnozzle! Remember the *Mr. Potato Head* toy? Well, that's Wylie! Ukrainian Jew from Chicago. Only child. Funny, chunky little body with skinny legs, but quite fit for seventy-three and just pulsing with vitality! I feel like I've known him for years. Doesn't appear to suffer from the usual Jewish neuroses! Not like people I've met on the *Internet* at all.

But, I think I am nuts. I haven't heard from him. After the intensity we shared, complete silence. I feel insecure and foolish. I wish I didn't! Maybe the affair was just a mirage. You know how I can delude myself about love.

From: Ariane Altar ariane@altarpots.com
Date: April 7, 2009
To: Wylie Hymen wylie@hymenfables.com
Subject: how silence from you affects my heart

e e cummings says it best, Wylie, so I'll rely on him:

···or if your wish be to close me, i and
my life will shut very beautifully, suddenly,
as when the heart of this flower imagines
the snow carefully everywhere descending

From: Wylie Hymen wylie@hymenfables.com
Date: April 7, 2009
To: Ariane Altar ariane@altarpots.com
Subject: Which is infinite which is yes

I have printed "memories of you" to have with me wherever I go, to be read with coffee at Cafe Trieste, to be read again up in the spring green of Tilden Park while Sage and Asia run up the hill and roll, hands at sides, shrieking all the way down, collapsing in a giggling heap at the bottom (a little trick Gramps showed them from his childhood), again in the quiet of the night when these grandchildren are asleep, again in the dawn, and again tonight, touching what cannot be touched (you far away) but seeking (recalling, imagining, grown more vivid by your presence in my life, the feel, the incense, and delicious flavors of your body) . . . seeking ways to be with you. I've sorted out my calendar for June and July, I want to begin exploring the possibilities of a visit, depending on how much time you have for me.

Pants On Fire!

Quietly

Lying here quietly beside you,
My cheek against your firm, quiet thighs,
The calm music of Boccherini
Washing over us in the quiet,
As the sun leaves the housetops and goes
Out over the Pacific, quiet –
So quiet the sun moves beyond us,
So quiet as the sun always goes,
So quiet, our bodies, worn with the
Times and penances of love, our
Brains curled, quiet in their shells, dormant,
Our hearts slow, quiet, reliable
In their interlocking rhythms, the pulse
In your thigh caressing my cheek. Quiet.

Kenneth Rexroth

From Ariane's journal
April 7, 2009

Poems for Wylie
1.
Calendars

Times
Markings of possible dates
To meet, to be, to embrace
To live
I asked how could I sleep without you, now that I have, now that I know
You ask the impossible of me by distance, by silences, by this unwanted
separation
You ask me to trust
When all I want is want
Wanting to begin
Wanting to have
Wanting to yield
Wanting to be with you

92

Wanting to seize our day, our opportunity, our destiny, if we have one
Time
Impossibly stretched
Moving so slowly
Time
By myself
Time
Unmarked
With you

2.
Free

I felt so free
Like a kindergartener soaring on a swing
Laughing at the sky
Happy in your delight
No thoughts of my now Rubenesque belly
Which housed three children
No thoughts of my lined face and creped neck
No thoughts of ochre tinted teeth crowding forward
As if to see a little more of the world
Before it's all over
No self-consciousness at all
Holding you, kissing you, caressing the short hair on your head
Soft the same length and silver as your beard
Holding you, kissing you, blue eyes peering into purple
Holding you, kissing you, penetrated so deeply by your fullness
Repeating, repeating, repeating
The joy
As if we were Old Masters
And we are

3.
Six Nights

A full moon overhead seeps grey light into the foggy sky
Palms silhouetted in mist rim the front lawn
It is the sixth night since we loved on the rollaway
Across the Pacific
Time prized, measured by your embrace

It is the sixth day apart
Time now measured by visits to the *Internet*
Waiting for your words to remember your touch
The day slipping away
Email
None
Worse than the telephone that doesn't ring

From: Ariane Altar ariane@altarpots.com
Date: April 9, 2009
To: Wylie Hymen wylie@hymenfables.com
Subject: your letter

Your drawing came today. How glorious. It takes me right back to your table and mornings and Peet's coffee and, best, you. You are right: our relationship is "seamless"! There are no snags, no crags, no hard edges, and no misgivings. Absolutely, joyously seamless!

Did your neighbor, Roly, ever find his money? I was pretty shocked to hear him talk about the *UPS* and *FedEx* drivers knowing he ships dope and stealing his money. Are you sure what he is doing is legal? I know Mendocino County is a big growing place for dope (as is Hawai'i). But, I actually know nothing about it, and none of my friends smoke, at least that I know of! I hope you're not in danger by associating with him or being his neighbor. Maybe there is no danger, and I am just naïve.

So much rain here. I am wet, the pets are wet, and the studio is wet. Nonetheless, I am working. Making pots with fish net themes and the Chinese carp we call koi.

I so look forward to hearing your voice.

I wanted to start my day just a "little bit better" by calling you to tell you how happy you make me, but your line is busy. Do you realize how much we talk without mentioning our subject, Theia? She is actually the reason I want you to stay longer when you come: my intention is to have finished the oral history CD's in May and have an outline. When you are here in June, after the initial weeks of play and pleasure, might we do some Theia work? (By the way, I have not heard a word from her and no Letter of Agreement. Looks like I'll be ordering *Final Draft* soon and writing the film script instead!)

Quiches are baked, book reviews read, passages underlined for my book group meeting, only the lanai tiles are left to be washed and chairs placed. Morning doves are cooing like a brass band harkening a beautiful day to be.

Pants On Fire!

From: Wylie Hymen wylie@hymenfables.com
Date: April 10, 2009
To: Ariane Altar ariane@altarpots.com
Subject: Musings of a septuagenarian

It was to be a "septuagenarian going on thirty,
or, maybe, twenty," but then I realized that
at no time in my life have I known a love like yours
or felt so sensual, so free, and then there are yearnings,
the insistent, tingling yearnings that awoke me at five this morning, wanting you,
and wanting to tell you things
which have only just come to mind.
I am aware now of a particular way I am with you,
little private moments that are actually new to me,
those moments when I come upon you in our bed,
by candle light or the soft gray of dawn,
kneeling above you to see your body, head to toes,
each time seeing you anew, running my hands
softly over your body, each time feeling you anew.
What I gather up in those special moments,
are fleeting impressions of you, of a beautiful,
mature woman, lapis eyes fixed on mine,
soft, fine hair, spilling across the pillow,
running from under your arm, and your breasts,
that lovely curve into your waist, and around
the fullness of your hips. You are not, by the way,
one of Peter-Paul's blowzy women (once my adolescent fantasy)
I see lying there so soft and lovely;
no, the body that so delights me is an odalisque,
perhaps the graces of Titian or Ingres, surely
Manet's *Olympia*. And, yes, you mentioned
your neck – creped? I hadn't noticed – for me
a warm, snug hollow to nuzzle, a quiet place to be
in the peace after our lovemaking,
listening to the calming sounds
of your heart and breath.
You are clearly a woman who has enjoyed
loving and being loved, often, with ardor,
and passion, and abandon (three or four times
a day, I think you told me). And yet, I've learned
that all lovers come to one another

95

as virgins. Everything we do makes me feel
I'm learning to love and be loved as never before,
now the one wanting, hoping to please you,
while delighting in your presence, and
the pleasure your body, sweet Ariane,
brings to mine.

Notes in Ariane's journal:
April 10, 2009

Ravished

I simply must remember the first night of lovemaking with Wylie. One word swims through memory's veins: ravish. Ravishing. Ravished. Ravishment. He ravished me as every woman imagines being ravished. He was my Errol Flynn, swashbuckling, saber drawn Captain Blood of the pirate film, our ship heaving on the high seas, escaping all pursuers, me Olivia de Havilland in bondage, hoop skirts lifted by the alchemy of a pirate's lust, lying on the sea-slicked deck, ravenous for the forbidden fruit, decimated by the treasure trove of desire.

It was late, after eleven perhaps. Flickers of starlight filtered through the sky-light above the sleeping loft, far fainter than the single white candle burning near the mattress. I had slipped out of my deep blue silk nightgown before lying down. Wylie embraced me there on the navy cotton duvet, his unclothed skin powdery soft and sweetly delectable, like the first lick of a marshmallow coveted by a child, but as firm to the touch as the maroon trunks of the dark madrones outside the windows. And so the intimacies of love began.

We had slept together the night before, chaste as brother and sister; our bodies spooned against each other, heads turned away, with no chance kisses to interrupt the comfort of our virginal sleep. There was no fondling, no excitation. I think we slumbered like babies, blissful in our innocence. I suppose it was the respect Wylie afforded me that night, honoring my wish to share his bed and not his body that wooed me. On the next night, this first night of love I am remember-ing, I was ready to open my heart and entwine my limbs to mingle my essence with his.

He had told me on my first evening at his cabin that he was impotent. That he had been plagued by this flaccid curse since his first divorce. Nothing he tried, ther-apy, *Viagra*, women, masturbation had cured it. "Oh my god!" I thought! "How can I love a man who can't love me sexually? Well, we'll become good friends and writing partners and forget about a possible love match."

Wylie excused himself from bed and went downstairs to pee, at least, that is what I presumed, since he had to pee several times a night after the "seeding" of his prostate. I lay enjoying the quiet and the night and the warmth of being embraced by a lovely and kindly man.

Then I heard his light steps echoing on the metal stair tread, and soon his smiling face appeared at the floor level of the loft. The next thing I made out in the darkness was a marvel, an astounding marvel to behold. I wasn't sure if I was dreaming. Time stopped and resumed in slow, viscous, liquid motion. I saw pointing, no, looming toward me a deep purplish, reddish, glistening erection. Not any erection. The largest, thickest, longest erection I had seen in my sixty-two years of life on this planet. My god, it was gorgeous. En-gorgeous? Ha, ha! It was luscious! It pricked (ha, ha again!) my unconscious, opening the lid on all the forbidden sexual fantasies of a lifetime. The deep purple throbbing color could have belonged to a Nubian slave, the sons of Ham, a desert sheik, a Hindu Raj, a Polynesian warrior, an Easter Island bird dancer, Geronimo, Blackbeard, even the genii imprisoned in Aladdin's magical lamp.

I could no longer see Wylie's face in the shadow of the night. I could only see this gleaming missile. I managed to whisper, "Is this for me?" And, he whispered back, "It's a gift." Yes, it was a gift, a rare and desirable gift. What a gift it was.

It fit me. Like a glove? Let me just say that huge and shining monster of pleasure pressed on every nerve on every cell of every wall of my interior and ignited a raw carnality in me I had known I surely possessed but had never experienced. It launched me into subliminal seas where I navigated, explored, conquered new realms of bliss, eliciting exotic juices, composing new songs, arias to joy, rare odes sung to the wildness of our flight toward heaven, and arriving there, to whisper thanks for this blessed voyage into God's good ear. And I slowly, slowly floated back down on pillowed clouds to the mountains, on gentle breezes to the cabin, on Wylie's adoring words to the mattress, where we dined on each other, slowly gaining sustenance to resume anew our night sailing on his engorged barque of love.

I didn't know if I was dreaming or waking. Could it be Wylie, impotent Wylie? Whose erection came to me? Whose erection took me in the dark of night? I didn't know. I didn't care. I was lustily satisfied beyond satisfaction yet hungry, thirsty for more, gaining moment by moment, movement by movement, a never ending appetite for this kind of intimacy, this soaring ecstasy, peaking, peaking again and again, as high and breathtaking as a view of the Himalayas, Everest and Anapurna beckoning in the distance, luring my exhausted footfall forward.

My memory of his touch, of that first night, triggers my body to shudder. I quiver, I tremble, and I thrill in pulsating waves of anticipation as I remember his touch. His fingers were doubly blessed. As artist's fingers, they traced patterns of delight and desire on my nipples and breasts, dribbling honey onto my skin, his tongue licking it clean. As writer's fingers, they described worlds of pleasure to my tingling clitoris and unfolding labia, writing words of love and tenderness in whipping cream and letting them melt over the warmth of my belly. Wetted by

97

his tongue's paint or dipped in ink dripping from the tip of his penis, ten talented, blessed fingers jangled my nerves, vibrated, enticed me to open and yield, until I begged for the masterstrokes of his magic wand. There I lay like a newly baptized acolyte singing grace, in tongues unknown, for my supper.

From: Wylie Hymen wylie@hymenfables.com
Date: April 11, 2009
To: Ariane Altar ariane@altarpots.com
Subject: Five-part French Holocaust documentary, *Shoah*

Something I forgot to mention . . . sorry I was so inattentive last night, but my thoughts kept drifting to the image of me rubbing my lips so gently on your nipples, nibbling, feeling them grow harder when I touched them lightly with the tip of my tongue . . . and you urging me to bite, bite harder. I did get a copy of *Shoah*, the complete text of the film, but it is not indexed. I'm going through page by page to see if Theia shows up. I had kind of blocked from my mind the whole Theia oral history chapter of my life. Okay, that's out of the way, I can go back to fantasies of pushing my tongue hungrily into your luscious pussy.

Bon Appetit!

From: Ariane Altar ariane@altarpots.com
Date: April 15, 2009
To: Wylie Hymen wylie@hymenfables.com
Subject: you and memory

Please tell me about us. I am forgetting. Not forgetting, how could I? Rather, I realize that my senses were overwhelmed and cannot report back to me now details I so want to know. My eyes, for example, were often closed as I was enfolded deeper and deeper into our cocoon of love and sensation. And, now I have no clear visual memory. So, tell me, Wylie, tell me about us. I remember one evening, the second I think, or was it the first? sitting in your chair by the hearth and suddenly you were kissing me. Where did you come from? I have the sense you sat or knelt before me. How did you come to kiss me? Why then, in that moment and in that way? Tell me, Wylie, my darling, Wylie, tell me about us. I want to know. There is so much time to be apart; I want to fill it with as much sweetness of you as I can. Please tell me what you know, what you remember. I have no visual memory of your arms, your legs, your chest, your back. I know your face, your head, your neck, your hands, your feet, your toes, and your skin, your explosive, inflatable *"Hindenburg"* of love. Yes, those I know and can see, and they make me glad.

But, the rest? Even the nights are a blur. The first night I remember the peace of sleeping with you, me dressed in a whisper of sapphire silk. The second night I remember as well, naked and alive in your embraces; the sapphire gown cast from the loft, descending like a blue heron to nest in folds on the floor below. But, the third and fourth nights? Oh, tell me, please, Wylie, tell me about those nights. I want to know, to remember.

Our last night I do remember clearly: every kiss, every motion, every breath, every conversation. That was spectacular. My mother's lumpy old living room rollaway became a dhow of romantic transport. The previous nights I was simply so stunned and overwhelmed that I need you to remind me of what we did, what we said, how it was.

From: Wylie Hymen wylie@hymenfables.com
Date: April 16, 2009
To: Ariane Altar ariane@altarpots.com
Subject: Re: you and memory

I will help you remember.

When I first saw you at the bus terminal, I was struck, much more than I had remembered, by how beautiful and animated you were. From the very first moments I was enjoying you, happy you were there – I felt blessed – there with me on a magical ride through the countryside, the breakfast in Point Reyes of home fries and omelettes, shielding you from the wind as we stood on my favorite beach, looking at the long coastline assaulted by cresting rows of white water waves, the joy of getting reacquainted, the excitement of being close to you. We talked and laughed, and it was so easy, the two of us.

I, too, felt like a kid on a swing, or running against the wind, but I was mindful. One of your last emails revealed some justifiable hesitancy, second thoughts about what you were doing. It had dawned on you that you were traveling great distances to spend a lot of time with someone you didn't really know in an isolated, unfamiliar place. You sounded a little scared on the phone.

I had promised to make you comfortable, and you told me in many gentle, endearing ways what that meant: Please, Wylie, not too fast. I'm a little afraid. Yes, let's hold hands. Yes, yes put your arm around me; hold me against the wind from the sea. Slowly, slowly, let's be friends. All the time I thought, if we weren't to become lovers, I wanted this lovely woman as a friend for all the rest of my life.

I was happy being friends, that evening by the fire (though I wanted to be closer to you, to touch you and feel the warmth of your body, and those blue eyes were always just a little too far away). If we had nothing more than that day and evening together, it would remain until the end of my days one of my most cherished memories.

You were saying in the flickering glow of the fire that you really needed to protect your heart and your feelings, that you had had in your life too much of loss and grief, that you didn't want to lose someone again. That you needed to be certain.

I did not offer a response; I am not one to speak of certainty. It seemed you wanted to sleep as a guest, alone, and I thought once again of your comfort, of building a fire, warming your room, leaving you a lot of space to think and consider.

But, then you touched my arm and looked up at me for the first time in that enchanting way that you do, and you said no, you did not want to sleep alone, and would I, could we, just sleep together? I kissed you, tentatively at first, the way I would kiss a young girl, the young girl, young Emily, who had once been my student, and you kissed me back as a woman, the way Emily now grown Ariane kisses.

What I remember after that is you in your blue silk gown, climbing up into the loft with me, holding you close in my bed, spooning, my arm cradling your head, burying my face in your hair, breathing you in, placing little kisses on your neck, and shoulders, and arms, moving my hand down into the curve of your hips and waist to spread my fingers over the soft roundness of you under silken azure folds.

Until tonight, dear Ariane

From: Ariane Altar ariane@altarpots.com
Date: April 16, 2009
To: Wylie Hymen wylie@hymenfables.com
Subject: Re: Re: You and memory

Oh, thank you. I needed that. My musings are of a thirsty woman, for I am like a traveler stranded in the desert, thirsting for your words: a sip, oh, just a sip... and then another.

Thank you for a wonderful conversation last night. I want to underscore my happiness for your success with *Where's Noah's Ark?* It must be immensely heartening to receive fine reviews and a second printing!

Just thought of a tiny, insignificant piece of info: when I met you in September of 1963, I was 16. When I re-met you in August of 2008, I was 61. Nice inversion, eh?

I think it is grand that we have lived quite differently and come together at this time. What a conversation about trust and its breach, and what direction that has taken each of us, since we each experienced infidelity in our marriages.

Sometimes I think about "themes" or "patterns of events" in my life. I have noted two significant ones on the very negative side of things: betrayal and abandonment. Because of them, I have also asked why? And wondered if I have, in some unconscious way, contributed to them? I think about a "soul path" a lot, if we have one. But, I don't have any clues. Do you?

I am particularly enamored of your chest right now: wanting to lay my head on it, wanting it above me as you enter me, wanting the rise and fall of your breath. Actually, I am also quite enamored of your nose, fantasizing about tender ways to rub it with mine, to travel its length, to breathe you in. Might there exist such a thing as a Nasal Phallus?

Perhaps we have been narwhals in another life, rubbing our narwhal "noses" as we played in the sea? I love that you love rubbing noses and inhaling me as I inhale you. It is so sensual. I finally understand why Hawai'ians and Eskimos rub noses! I feel I touch your essence in those moments; you warm me from the inside out. Maybe rubbing our narwhal noses creates friction, like rubbing two sticks together will ignite a fire?

Noses

My nose wants to rub against your nose.
My nose wants to stroke back and forth the sides of your nose.
My nose wants to inhale your exhalations.
My nose loves you.
Your nose is naughty.
Your nose lengthens
As a narwhal
And delights not only my face

From: Wylie Hymen wylie@hymenfables.com
Date: April 16, 2009
To: Ariane Altar ariane@altarpots.com
Subject: Musings on an old body (mine)

Your email and our conversation last night sent me to bed with a big smile on my face, an occasional chuckle, and this morning, out loud laughter that startled the cats. Several of the many things I love about you are your frank observations, considerate, but always so real and on the mark.

I am not surprised nor in the least offended that you are unable to remember my body. It is, after all, a body embarking on its eighth decade of life, grown a bit paunchy and, here and there, lumpy. Certainly no one would mistake it for anything other than what it is. I do have powerful legs which have carried me quite effortlessly, if I do say so, to the corners of the globe with nary an ache nor complaint. And, once, at an outdoor fair, a woman whom I thought was admiring my *Birkenstocks*, exclaimed, "You have beautiful feet." Dina once told me, in a rare mean mood, that my arms were too spindly and my shoulders too slight for the rest of my body. Still, I'm happy with it or, at least, quite used to it – even with the recent addition of 139 palladium seeds, each emitting 1.65 millicuries.

I, on the other hand, can recall numerous details of you – your hair, the color of wheat in the sun; your eyes – lapis in candle and moonlight, cerulean in the day – your mouth, when I cover it with mine excites your mischievous tongue, your breasts, so neatly filling my cupped hands when I put my arm around you in the night heat, your smooth, lovely legs which part to invite me into the mysteries of you and then grasp me tighter and tighter, pulling me closer, so that I shall never leave, your little toes that curl up tightly in our lovemaking (did you know that?). Parts of you I can recall vividly daydreaming, on my morning walk, or those dreamy moments falling asleep and awakening; all of this and, still, Ariane is greater, so much greater than the sum of her parts.

What amuses and delights me is the one part of my body you do remember, a part of me that has never elicited much comment. I have to say that I am very impressed with and proud of him myself, but not for the reason you might think. It's not the usual guy thing; he was never, as far as I can remember, my *raison d'etre*. I certainly never felt he was anything to brag about (he's really tiny except when he's around you). As you know, we had a falling out years ago. I was angry that he was never there for me when I needed him and, despite our years of therapy together, he was never forthcoming about what was bothering him. As you know, also, we've become buddies again.

No, it's not about size. What I do like about him is the pleasure he brings you – it pleases me that you refer to him as a "gift," for that is how I offer him to you – the soft murmurings, songs to our love he coaxes to your lips, the surprise in your eyes and the little gasps when he enters into the unfolding petals of your rose, stopping to rest deep inside you, still, bathing in your hot nectar, alert to your pulse and gentle inner movements, to be drawn deeper and deeper, and still deeper to your very core, where I can feel my spent balls, still quivering, nestle snugly against your soft fur. And you have named him, an honorable name. Golden Phallus. Alive and aglow for you, Ariane, who live beside the bamboo forest. It was not a dream.

Yes, Ariane, it really did happen, and I shall always remember.

From: Ariane Altar ariane@altarpots.com
Date: April 16, 2009
To: Wylie Hymen wylie@hymenfables.com
Subject: tonight

I am overwhelmed and delighted simultaneously. I do remember your body, silly: I just didn't scrutinize it! I think it is perfectly marvelous. It's clever, too, as it fits mine so well! You are right, I did name your member the *Golden Phallus*. It sounds like a mighty steed, doesn't it, like out of a knightly jousting match played before a queen? Or like a religious search for the Holy Grail: a chalice (phallus, chalice, who knows?) I think I also called it the *Hindenburg*! You'll have to decide whether I meant it for its size or for its explosive force!

From: Iggy Fumer iggyf@gmail.com
Date: April 17, 2009
To: Wylie Hymen wylie@hymenfables.com, Dina Cochon dinaRN@iswell.org
Subject: OH MY GOD my order!

Wylie and Pooky Dah-ling – I just realized you are leaving tomorrow. How is that possible with your product being worked on right now? OY. Let me know if anything is possible or must it all wait for shipment until you return.

Well, Pooky Dah-ling, Almost Birthday Girl! You'll be here soon, the toast of the town, and we'll do nothing but thea-ta, thea-ta, thea-ta! New York City awaits!

Thanks, Luv.

LOVE YOU madly, Iggy

From: Wylie Hymen wylie@hymenfables.com
Date: April 17, 2009
To: Iggy Fumer iggyf@gmail.com

I (no qpotrophe) m writing on Pooky's computer qnd eveything on the ksubo-qrd is scrqbled;
Well lat you no when stofff is qvqilqble,

Lov Wylie

From: Ariane Altar ariane@altarpots.com
Date: April 18, 2009
To: Wylie Hymen wylie@hymenfables.com
Subject: Quite Sulky Over Being Unfairly Left

You are heading to New York without me!
Warning: Do not leave me behind again: I do not give second chances.

Pants On Fire!

Here's my favorite Italian restaurant in the city: Sandro's, 306 East 81st Street
Here are theatre and film recommendations, if you get time to do any fun stuff.
I don't know what you can get tickets for?

Poet William Butler Yeats: twenty-six plays are being staged along with readings at the Irish Repertory Theater.

Mary Stuart: Rivals: Harriet Walter as Elizabeth I and Janet McTeer as Mary,
Queen of Scots, in Friedrich Schiller's 1800 play about politics and power

The Norman Conquests: *Living Together: Unrequited Lust in Triplicate.*

Il Divo (2008): "I don't believe in chance, I believe in the will of God." That
credo, spoken in a dry, dispassionate voice, drops more than once from the
mouth of Giulio Andreotti, the scandal-ridden seven-time Italian prime minister, in this flamboyant biographical fantasy.

From: Wylie Hymen wylie@hymenfables.com
Date: April 18, 2009
To: Ariane Altar ariane@altarpots.com
Subject: My body (Part II)

I think it's unfair to go away, not being able to see you for another couple of
months, and leave you with an incomplete image of me. In my usual way, I was
being modest and self-deprecating yesterday. I want to refresh your memory of the
part of me you don't remember: my chest and upper body.

I have immense biceps, which, when you tap on them, ring like hardened
steel, and very prominent abs rippling down to my powerful thighs which
some have likened to the legs of a draught horse. My shoulders are about
forty inches across supporting my head mightily like a marble plinth (which
is also why you can't remember my neck) and, the last time I measured, my
upper arms were about twenty-six inches around. People stop in awe of me
on the street, and I am often mistaken for Arnold Schwarzenegger. It's hard
finding clothes to fit, but the upside is that, even in rowdy Indian Springs, no
one ever wants to pick a fight with me. (Of course, the Golden Phallus is a
local landmark.)

I hope this helps you remember me throughout this long period being apart.

From: Ariane Altar ariane@altarpots.com
Date: April 18, 2009
To: Wylie Hymen wylie@hymenfables.com

You know, I think I saw you years ago; it must have been in Florence. Some old artist, Michael somebody? had sculpted you from a chunk of marble hanging around his studio. I was rather taken by the thing. Even though many years have passed, I recognized you by your body right away. It hasn't aged at all! Actually, I was confused at first, because I called out, "David!" and when you didn't respond, I corrected my mistake, and, in more hushed tones, called, "Da-Veed", and as you still didn't respond, then "Wy-leeeeeeee", and as you turned, I couldn't help myself, I began caressing those sinewy muscles you described so aptly. And I hope to continue caressing them for the rest of my days and nights and afternoons and mornings and dawns and sunsets.

I slept for three hours after your call. I dreamt Selene apologized, and I told her she was a jerk and could never make up for my absence at her wedding. I dreamt of my platters being copied by University of Hawai'i students and sold at high prices. But, mainly I dreamt of our cocoon and its expansion, knowing the chrysalis growing inside is gorgeous; but hesitant to stretch its wings, because by doing so, the cocoon, the wonderful cocoon, would be broken. For now, it lies still and warm, awaiting your words, your beautiful words, awaiting your successes, awaiting for your arms, awaiting opening by you when next we meet.

From: Ariane Altar ariane@altarpots.com
Date: April 19, 2009
To: Wylie Hymen wylie@hymenfables.com
Subject: lost memories!

I have lost or erased the "memories of you" email I sent when I got back from Chicken Ridge. I know you won't be home for a long time, but when you do get there, I would like to ask you to forward a copy to me. I like to know what I have said and, in the wondrous event our feelings for each other grow, be able to look back and see how that miracle happened.

I started listening to Theia's CD's today. I am starting with 5A and B when she arrived in Shanghai. After the long ship voyage there and stops in many exotic ports of call, she commented that she was used to "not understanding languages." But, her father insisted she learn both Chinese and English, because "you must speak the language of the land where you eat their bread." Within a few months,

Pants On Fire!

Theia and her brother could speak enough English to communicate with their servants and later with their young friends at the "Club." Ted was enrolled in a British school, and his English improved rapidly. Their understanding of Chinese was much slower as each servant came from a different region: one spoke Cantonese, one Mandarin, and so on.

Her first impression of Shanghai was the congestion: too many people, cars, buses, streetcars, and rickshaws. Shouts of "Hey ho! Hey ho!" rang in cacophony with beeping, clanging horns along the Bund, the beautiful boulevard lined with impressive European buildings and flanking the Huangpu river. Down every side street was a major accident. She couldn't distinguish the men from the women; all the coolies looked the same to her: same nose, same eyes, same brown hair. There were multitudes of human beings. "I had never seen so many people massed like that in Europe," she said.

Her uncle had paid the Chinese authority the fee for each family member to enter the city; no passports or visas were required. The Japanese authority did not take over until two years after Theia's arrival. (Note: you'd best double-check these dates.)

Her father worked as an engineer in Shanghai for an American company, earning two hundred dollars a month. Their living expenses for the month totaled twenty-five dollars, and that included rent, food, servants, clothing, utilities, car, and entertainment! There was a cinema across the street from the "Club." She and her friends watched lots of French films there. Theia loved the silk fabrics and even though tailors came to their apartment once a week to make new clothes, she began designing dresses. Her designs were so stylish, she said, that Madame Chiang Kai-shek came to call on her!

Theia's first love was choreography. She obtained the use of a consular ballroom and began giving lessons in modern dance. "I organized several soirees and called them Moonlight Follies. Two of the Soong girls, Madame Chiang Kai-shek's sisters, were very enthusiastic about my modern dance techniques. I was interpreting music, emotions, and colors; something very, very different from the Chinese Opera and from the ballet lessons they had taken. They read Chinese poetry, had it translated, and we made dance performances. "I don't think any refugee led the life I did!" she laughed.

"Then the Japanese came, overnight, and that finished all our fancy dreams. My father was wiped out financially. All his merchandise was stored in warehouses, which were suddenly occupied by the Japanese army. 'I'll make money again,' he said and in one hour was creating a new enterprise. He became a leather merchant and earned fees teaching tanning techniques he had learned as a boy in Poland to the Chinese."

It is interesting to me, Wylie, that neither the Chinese nor the Japanese had prejudice toward the Jews. Theia related that after the Japanese took over Shanghai, all foreigners had to wear armbands. The Jews wore blue and white; the Poles, red and white. All the Jews were told to move to a slum, Hongkew, which quickly became the new Jewish Ghetto. But, Theia's father refused to go there and had the family identify themselves as Poles, wearing red and white armbands. The Jewish community hated him for that choice.

Theia describes the military occupation as one of "little, little men, little bastards who barked. If you heard barking, you knew they were serious and to pay attention. One day my car was stopped on a bridge. The Japanese officer pointed his bayonet at my chauffeur and barked at us to get out of the car and to bow to him. My driver did and begged me to do the same. But, I would not bow to a Japanese! I sat in the car very erect and did not move. The officer pushed his bayonet through the window and barked and barked at me. Then he pulled me out of the car and told me to bow. I would not. He turned his bayonet around and hit me on the back of my head with the butt until I lowered my face a few inches. I had some swelling when we got home, but my father said the officer had been gentle with me as he could have knocked me out. And that really was the only incident that frightened me in the whole war."

Lucky lady, if you ask me! Amazing! I am fascinated by her remark, "My life was totally isolated from Chinese life except for the food. I might as well have been living in Europe."

Thank you for your wake-me-up call. I am glad you called; it stops the "disconnect" that time and distance create. Have you ever felt at odds with your actions/intentions in life and your inner impulse/inspiration? I feel I have glimpsed, no, not just glimpsed, tasted you and what time with you feels like...and nothing I do now, while all the things I do are good and satisfying, measures up to the sublime pleasures of discovering you and being with you.

A Sunday poem just for you:

Wylie Wylie Wylie
Walking without you
Or are you with me
A blind phantom
A somnambulist
Dreaming my dream
Eyes shut seeing nothing
Accompanying my mind and heart
The distant waterfall around the corner high and white
Amid the green ravines
Brisk breeze off the sea not felt in the shelter of my house
Bird song, bird symphony, bird cacophony
So many morning birds busy with lives I cannot see
My two goldens racing around the curves

Pants On Fire!

One's tail high and arced like the plume on Hector's helmet
The other's stubbed and wagging
Both peeing and sniffing
Peering over cliffs to the spewing sea below
Oblivious of cars, slow on a Sunday morning
The new bridge almost complete, concrete fresh gray
My winding stretch of highway
Slick from the night's rain and strewn with fallen mango leaves
All greens and shadows
So much to show and share
With only your specter striding beside me
When will you
Dear darling beloved you
Walk with me?

April 20th
Tumescence in Perpetuity!

Languid morning
A return to bed
Alone and lazy
Memories of our union
Return with me
Under our sheets
Where they root
Uncovering desire

Trembling, my womb calls
To you
Why such carnal greed
Its softness wonders
Why this turbulence
Its juices beg
Why does your image
Alone
Spark
Ripples
Repeating the call
A river floods
Crossing the sea
To you

Pants On Fire!

From: Wylie Hymen wylie@hymenfables.com
Date: April 22, 2009
To: Ariane Altar ariane@altarpots.com
Subject: Re: Theia

I've forgotten so much of Theia's oral history. It was forty years ago when I recorded it! I remember, though, what she described as the immediate effects of the Japanese occupation. There was a six p.m. curfew imposed on the city. Theia's family was forced to move to a crumby apartment with neighbors from lower economic and social backgrounds, who argued a lot and hung their laundry in the hallways. Her mother had never learned how to cook; their servants fled to the countryside; the Japanese military took over the "Club;" there was no electricity; and the life she'd enjoyed "slowed down."

I enjoyed hearing your sleepy, bed-warmed voice today. Thank you for the dear poems; I wanted to hold you while you were reading them to me. I am sorry to be an ocean and a continent away.

Postcard from Wylie to Ariane
Mistress and Maid c. 1666-67 Johannes Vermeer
The Frick Collection, NY

Dear Ariane,
Art is so much a part of who we are individually
And together that it
Seems strange to be
Here without you—

From: Ariane Altar ariane@altarpots.com
Date: April 24, 2009
To: Wylie Hymen wylie@hymenfables.com
Subject: Your workshop at R.I.S.D.

Dear Wylie of the Early Morning Rising,

I want to wish you well with your workshop! If you are anything near as fascinating, magnetic, informative, and helpful as you were with me at my mother's house in August, showing your illustration techniques, you'll be a smash hit. I can't wait to hear how it goes.

Your Biggest Fan

From: Wylie Hymen wylie@hymenfables.com
Date: April 26, 2009
To: Ariane Altar ariane@altarpots.com
Subject: I miss you

I've written on so many computers the last few days I'm not sure what I'm doing, hoping this actually gets sent, hoping you know how much I miss you and how often I think about you. Strangely, the distance between us has brought you into sharper focus, all that I enjoy about you clearer, the memories of you more vivid.

The conference came off well; my section was well attended—about twenty-five adults, teenagers, and little kids, and everyone had lots of intelligent and interesting questions. But, my Rhode Island School of Design experience was unsettling, as I do not use a computer to create my images. To the students, I was a complete dinosaur. I'll tell you all about it on the phone, because I probably won't have email in New York.

Tomorrow is Houghton in the morning, lunch with David Godine, and then an afternoon train to New York City.

As always, no matter where I am, you are in my thoughts and my heart.

From: Cherry Estrella cherry@starsearch.com
Date: April 27, 2009
To: Ariane Altar Ariane@altarpots.com
Subject: too funny to pass up

World News

A woman is in custody, accused of breaching a court order banning her from being noisy during sex. Neighbors complained of hearing Caroline Cartwright, 48, moaning and groaning and her bed banging against the wall at her Washington home.

Earlier this month she was given a four-year court order banning her from making excessive noise anywhere in England. But, she appeared in court on Monday, charged with three breaches in just ten days. She will remain in custody until 5 May.

Cartwright was convicted of five breaches of a noise abatement notice on 17 April and fined £515. But, Magistrates' Court heard police arrested her on 18 April, on 22 April and again on 26 April, after reports from neighbors she was flouting the ban with her husband, Steve. Prosecutor Claire Ward said neighbors complained to police about early morning noises including shouting and groaning coming from the Cartwrights' home. Cartwright elected to be tried by jury and the case will be transferred to Newcastle Crown Court at a later date.

Pants On Fire!

From: Ariane Altar ariane@altarpots.com
Date: April 29, 2009
To: Wylie Hymen wylie@hymenfables.com
Subject: since I've spilled the beans about love...

Thank you for calling me from the Brooklyn Museum. It was delicious. Hearing your voice, time with you, your adventures, the lobster, the sailing, the theatre, your conference. Mmm. All good. Ah-ha! You ate at Sandro's! That was a nice way to thank your gay friends for hosting you and arranging theatre tickets.

I really cannot believe you are traveling without me and torturing me, a former actress, by going to plays in the Big Apple!

Since I spilled the beans on the phone by not censuring my poem and voicing the incandescent love I feel for you, ahem, I thought I would just go all out and give you the written version. Plus, a few more.

Do consider "going west, young man"...I hear there is a mighty perty hula girly swayin' under the palms and star encrusted skies...a waitin' fer ya···

1.
Languor

Morning stasis
Lingers to mid-morning
Hovers through afternoon
Retreats with a sigh in evening
Returns fiery in predawn sun
Roasting as I doze
Basting with desire and uncertainty
Something happened
And I love Wylie
But, we are apart

2.
Adrift

Unable to move forward
Bathing in memories
Resurfacing periodically to face the day
Not knowing the now
Imagining a future
Floating softly

Pants On Fire!

Sleeping dreaming
Loss of momentum
Languorous
Curling around
Ever closer
My heart

3.
Being sixty-two amazes me

I am a
Juvenile at heart
Traversing uncertainties of first love
Lost in the giddiness of desire and longing
A suffering adolescent still
Despite a long marriage
A cruel divorce
Love affairs
Breakups
Relationships
Live-ins
Long distances
Losses gains
Three children
Two gone
First grandchild
Joy of rebirth
Here I am
Fumbling
In love
Sweet sixteen
Again

From: Ariane Altar ariane@altarpots.com
Date: April 29, 2009
To: Wylie Hymen wylie@hymenfables.com
Subject: satisfaction

You know the lyric, "I can't get no ... satisfaction"? Well, your phone call
did two contradictory things. On the one hand, it totally satisfied my desire to hear
your voice and your adventures and to be with you for a while, even if short and

at a distance. BUT on the other, it rekindled my desire for you and has left me tumescent.

What have I done while wallowing in this uncomfortable sensual state? I took my dogs for a rough-water swim and walk at Hamoa beach, ran errands, drove, hardly able to contain my turbulent self, and on return home, sat in the sun eating chocolate mint ice cream! Small moments of pure pleasure within the larger scope of desire, heat, and dissatisfaction! By the time you read this, it will be very old news and not noteworthy at all. Your offer to pet my tush is welcome, the sooner the better.

Regards, Miss Turbulent Tumescence

Postcard from Wylie to Ariane
April 30, 2009
Brooklyn, NY
Girl with Apple, William Glackens, 1909-10

Thinking about and missing you, dear Ariane

Postcard from Wylie to Ariane
May 1, 2009
Brooklyn, NY
Oarsmen Rowing on the Yerres, 1877, Gustav Caillebotte

Dear Ariane,

Surprise! The Brooklyn Museum has the most interesting collection, more beautifully displayed than any other museum I've been in a long time. Who knew? The reason I've seen only a few Caillebotte's over the years is that most are in private collections.

Take care, my love, and know that you are always in my heart.

Wylie

Postcard from Wylie to Ariane
Sunday, May 3, 2009
NYC, NY
Flint 707, color photograph, 1973 Jack Stewart

Now familiar, welcome friends, tears, flowing freely with the cello and first movement themes of a Schubert quintet, evoking loving moments and conversations with Ariane, deliciously vivid still.

Pants On Fire!

From: Ariane Altar ariane@altarpots.com
Date: May 1, 2009
To: Wylie Hymen wylie@hymenfables.com
Subject: Two poems by Britain's new poet laureate, Carol Ann Duffy

Valentine

Not a red rose or a satin heart.
I give you an onion.
It is a moon wrapped in brown paper.
It promises light
like the careful undressing of love.
Here
It will blind you with tears
like a lover.
It will make your reflection
a wobbling photo of grief.
I am trying to be truthful.
Not a cute card or a kissogram.
I give you an onion.
Its fierce kiss will stay on your lips,
possessive and faithful
as we are,
for as long as we are.
Take it.
Its platinum loops shrink to a wedding ring,
if you like.
Lethal.
Its scent will cling to your fingers,
cling to your knife.

Words, Wide Night

Somewhere on the other side of this wide night
and the distance between us, I am thinking of you.
The room is turning slowly away from the moon.
This is pleasurable. Or shall I cross that out and say
it is sad? In one of the tenses I sing
an impossible song of desire that you cannot hear.
La lala la. See? I close my eyes and imagine the dark hills I would have to
cross

to reach you. For I am in love with you
and this is what it is like or what it is like in words.

From: Ariane Altar ariane@altarpots.com
Date: May 7, 2009
To: Wylie Hymen wylie@hymenfables.com
Subject: a lovely surprise today

An amazing synchronicity happened today. I finished a present for you,
packed it, and took it to the post office. A package was waiting there for me...
from you! I feel like we embraced! So! It is *Where's Noah's Ark?* With the
inscription: "For so many reasons..." Hmmm. Is this going to be a challenge for
me to discover them? Or will you whisper them to me, slowly and carefully, one
by one?

From: Iggy Fumer iggyf@gmail.com
Date: May 8, 2009
To: Wylie@hymenfables.com, Dina Cochon dinaRN@iswell.org
Subject: MISSING CASES

Wylie dah-ling,

Did you get my messages from yesterday? I received two EMPTY boxes. We
must talk!

Love you, Iggy

From: Dina Cochon dinaRN@iswell.org
Date: May 9, 2009
To: Iggy Fumer iggyf@gmail.com
Subject: Many thanks

You did a mah-velous job of hosting us. The company was the best, the plays
superb! Wylie's choice of Schiller and dinner after at Sandro's was nothing short
of brilliant! I don't know where he gets these grand plans!

Do you have the book on the Impressionists I got at the Brooklyn Museum?
I can't find it.

115

Pants On Fire!

From: Wylie Hymen wylie@hymenfables.com
Date: May 9, 2009
To: Ariane Altar ariane@altarpots.com
Subject: A surprise and bouquet of Camas and Buttercups for Ariane

I wasn't prepared for the exquisite object I found when I got home from the post office and opened the box. I'm sure that if I had seen it among all the other pieces in your studio, I would have chosen it. Thank you. I move this ceramic Chinese Scholar's Cloak around, so it can be with me wherever I am. I can't stop touching it. I miss you.

Drawing of Chinese Scholar's Cloak vase and letter

When I look at your Chinese Cloak (which I do several times a day) I hold and touch it and think about how your lithe, delicate, strong hands shaped the clay, now firmly, now gently, and I like to recall how those same hands, which I held and kissed, brushed sensually over my skin and lovingly caressed my body.

From: Ariane Altar ariane@altarpots.com
Date: May 10, 2009
To: Wylie Hymen wylie@hymenfables.com
Subject: softly tonight

Absolutely exhausted from a friend's beautiful wedding and Mother's Day weekend. Ande, Kui, and I arrived home in Hana! She got a lullaby, and I fixed salmon.... I look forward to speaking with you between bites (hmmm, food or you? It's like the "which came first" riddle: the chicken or the egg?)

Tonight I want a love poem from you. A poem as soft as the way I danced on the breezeway earlier, gently holding my granddaughter to lull her to sleep. A poem as soft as the way I stroked my Goldie's fur to calm his fierce excitement on being let into the living room at night. A poem as soft as the way I cooed to coax my cat, Beauty, to join me on the couch, where I played with my daughter's clutching chirping baby. They are all asleep. Now, it is I who needs the dancing, the holding, the lulling. It is I who wants the stroking, calming, cooing. Only from you. Write, Wylie, o please, write me a love poem to put me to sleep...to read when I cannot fall asleep without you. I wish I were in your arms tonight.

From: Wylie Hymen wylie@hymenfables.com
Date: May 12, 2009
To: Ariane Altar ariane@altarpots.com
Subject: a song and test results

As to my health: the clinic reports my PSA is 2.0 down from 6+ and will drop below 1.0 this summer. They say the prostate cancer is gone!

You asked about Roly, one of my land partners, who happens to be a born-again guy. He got a license to grow and sell medical marijuana (when it was legalized for some growers in California). He is able to support his five children and enjoy a country lifestyle. Just about everybody in Mendocino County is involved in some aspect of the marijuana trade.

And speaking of Mendocino, I realize that we've missed an important date on the calendar. Friends in Mendocino embroidered a sampler hanging in my bathroom that proclaims:

Hurray, hurray, it's the first of May,
Outdoor fucking begins today!

A song for Ariane from the "Song of Songs"

With one flash of your eyes, you excite me,
One jewel on your neck stirs my heart
O my sister, my lover.
Your love, more than wine, is enticing,
Your fragrance is finer than spices,
My sister, my lover.
Your lips, sweet with nectar, invite me
To honey and milk on your tongue,
O my sister, my lover.
And even your clothing is fragrant
As wind from the Lebanon mountains,
My sister, my lover.

From: Ariane Altar ariane@altarpots.com
Date: May 12, 2009
To: Wylie Hymen wylie@hymenfables.com
Subject: Re: a song and test results

Thank you, dear Wylie, for singing to me and for such a beautiful song. Could you sing a little louder, though, and closer, much closer to my ear, so I could hear you better and feel your warm breath, and compliment you, thank you in person for your wonderful singing?

Your health: what good news! You are cancer free! Sounds like *Theraseed* really worked. Do you still have to take those little pills each morning or is that over?

Have you been reading about the new $294 million wing of the Chicago Art Institute? Want to go see it together? It would be such fun to see where you studied art. I haven't been there since my freshman year at Northwestern! Chicago is your hometown, so let's go!

From: Wylie Hymen wylie@hymenfables.com
Date: May 16, 2009
To: Ariane Altar ariane@altarpots.com
Subject: I am sorry; no travel for us yet

This photo was taken by Roly, who stepped out on his front deck yesterday morning to find their dog, Sienna, just hanging out with her bear friend.

I enjoyed our romp on the phone this morning. You are a fire starter, you know!

If I could somehow put into words how much I've been looking forward to seeing you, perhaps as soon as a week or two, then you'd understand how oddly conflicted and disappointed I am over some very exciting news from my editor, Erica, this morning. I have been summoned back to New York, this time for a meeting at the Turkish Consulate with Dr. Patton, who led earlier expeditions as an archeological excavator, to present him with a signed copy of *Where's Noah's Ark?* HM will also be arranging book signings while I'm there, including, possibly, at my old hangout, the Brooklyn Museum.

Just a couple of days ago, before this news broke, I had received an invitation from the curator at the New York Hall of Science to do some presentations with kids there the next time I was in New York; little did she realize I'd be there again so soon. There's also a possibility for the Boston Children's Museum.

I called *NG* to see if they are ready for me to do the *Ark* voice over yet, as I would like to accomplish as much as possible while on this trip.

My sadness about all this, of course, is that I was a keystroke away from arranging a flight to you later this month. The details of the trip are still to be worked out, but the certainty is that it will be at least three or four days and maybe as long as a week right in the middle of the time I had planned to be with you. This happened once to me a long time ago, when a book took over my life for almost a year, but I've told both Loughman and Erica that I will not be available the last two weeks of June and the first week in July. At least I can be there to administer back, shoulder, and neck rubs, after you've cooked a zillion meals for your visiting family. I don't care if the next invitation comes from Noah or the pharaoh himself, nothing will interfere with my visit next month.

I'm wanting very much to hear your voice tonight.

From: Ariane Altar ariane@altarpots.com
Date: May 16, 2009
To: Wylie Hymen wylie@hymenfables.com
Subject: bear country!

Wow! Proof positive that your food isn't safe hung in trees when camping! That bear doesn't seem worried about the branch "bearing" (ha-ha) his weight! Wonder if it dumped him?

I loved our call, too. It set me up for the whole day, which has been very productive aside from me yelling at Goldie like a madwoman at the beach when he wouldn't come (I promise not to do that to you...yell like a madwoman, if you don't...ahem...come!)

Why I Want To Sleep With You

Sleeping with you
Relieves all the lost nights
Where sorrow and loneliness presided
And returns me to cradled bliss
In the deepest way
Of innocence recovered

This profound comfort
And dreamless sleep
Nestled along your torso
No separation of skins
Breathing as one
Soothes nourishes restores
As we dream
In a chrysalis
Of our own

Why I Want To Sleep With You II

I want to sleep with you because
I don't
Sleep
You wake in me
Desire
I lay
In the dark
Back against your chest
Anticipating your touch
Yes, your fingers curl around my breast
Your breath travels down my spine
From shoulder to hip
A warming moon
Turns me
Your lips find my belly
And below
Your tongue ignites my sighs
I want to sleep with you because
I don't
Sleep
I tremble
Rediscovering the pathways of love
Its terrain varied and foreign in its newness
Taking us up steep trails littered perhaps with psychic burdens
And down into dark gorges gouged by times with others
Or forcing us
Drenched in sweat
To hack our way through lush jungle overgrowth of tangled emotions
Or to cross parched deserts of past loneliness and loss and age
Toward that shifting mirage
Where -we hope- ecstasy and rebirth lie
And, persevering
We arrive at an oasis
Where our thirst is quenched
By clear waters
From a new well of love

From: Ariane Altar ariane@altarpots.com
Date: May 20, 2009
To: Wylie Hymen wylie@hymenfables.com
Subject: Theia

Thought you might like to see photos of my guesthouse today. I did several flower arrangements using heady blooms from my garden. Then I listened for hours to Theia's description of the luxury boat trip from Trieste to Aden to Bombay, to Ceylon, to Manila, to Hong Kong, all the way to Papeete and back, finally to their destination, Shanghai. Not a description of the boat trip itself (except that it wasn't the style in which most refugees traveled) but her fascination with what she was exposed to for the first time in her eighteen year old life: being picked up in Bombay by a business associate of her father's in the longest, blackest limousine she'd ever seen. Being told by the associate not to give anything to the beggars all around them or they would belong to her for life. Admiring the saris and gold bracelets of her Indian hostess, only to have them delivered in a package to her later in the day, having unwittingly obliged the hostess, by Indian custom, to gift them to her. While there, she saw her first Hindu and Buddhist shrines.

Do you remember her description of seeing her first stone Buddha? Being Jewish she was familiar with the religions of the West, but she was unfamiliar with those of the East. She was very surprised by the reverence of the Buddhists. The hundreds of people praying to a stone amazed her.

Her father refused to ride in a rickshaw, saying it offended his democratic principles to be pulled in a cart by another man as though that man was a beast of burden. But, Theia, her mother, and brother rode in the rickshaw, which Theia loved, a diva even then, while her father walked beside them. Oh, and the poverty of the Chinese. Yet, her surprise that the little white houses dotting the green mountains of Hong Kong, which looked European, were actually lived in by Chinese!

From: Wylie Hymen wylie@hymenfables.com
Date: May 22, 2009
To: Ariane Altar ariane@altarpots.com
Subject: Spring Awakening

Imagining Ariane on a Spring Morning
The windows of the loft are open now,
to spring, to the night and first light of dawn,
to whispers high up in the firs, and pines,

and on the black wings of ravens.
In my awakening, eyes still closed,
you are here with me, dear Ariane,
our bodies curving, pressing together,
your hands lightly caressing here and there
(wake, Wylie, wake and come play with me).
You fill my senses with your soft breathing
and early morning murmurs of love,
so sweet among the birdsongs, and
a mingling of flavors and scents,
the perfume of your skin, redolent of
carpets of wildflowers, spring green, and
the musky incense of the forest floor.
Your lips brush my ears, my neck, your
nipples move playfully on my back.
A time of imaginings, delicious feelings,
your soft belly and little frizzly bush,
still dewy from last night's lovemaking,
warm, and tickly against my bum.
Suddenly, your hand slips down from my chest,
brushing over my nipples, down, down,
until your fingers weave into my kinky hair,
firmly taking all of me in your gently tightening hand.
When you arch your leg over my hip
I feel the full wetness of you, open, beckoning,
a new freshet of sweet honey on my back.
Oh, Ariane, it is time, and I turn,
placing my mouth on yours,
tongues touching, exploring, tasting.
Oh, Ariane, it is time. Take me
in your arms and tightly between your thighs,
draw me deep into the wondrous journey
to the very heart of you, and sing, sing in our dawn,
sing me your little song of spring awakening.

W.

Pants On Fire!

From: Ariane Altar ariane@altarpots.com
Date: May 22, 2009
To: Wylie Hymen wylie@hymenfables.com
Subject: Re: Spring Awakening and Pillow Talk

O Wylie, How lovely. Thank you. How about an aria? Or is that reserved for summer? Darling, Darling Wylie, (in whose ear I wish to whisper the sweetest words of love), under my pillow is a small collection of your cards and endearments to me. During the day, if I lay down to rest, I slip my hand under the pillow and just rest it on top of your cards. That way, a little bit of you comes to be with me.

From: Wylie Hymen wylie@hymenfables.com
Sent: May 22, 2009
To: Bill Partridge shipcraftsmen@verizon.net

Dear Bill,

I was in your wonderful shop a few weeks ago during the Newburyport Literary Festival. I mentioned I had a kit of Noah's Ark for sale. I'd like to send it to you on consignment, caring not about what I get for it; more that it gets to someone who would like to build it. I'll let you decide how much to ask for it. I bought it in '96 and, I think, paid $175 for it, but have no idea what it's worth today. It is plank on frame. Let me know if you are interested, and I'll *UPS* it to you.

I look forward to another visit sometime soon. Since I have friends there, I'm sure to get back in the next couple of years.

All best wishes, Wylie

From: Wylie Hymen wylie@hymenfables.com
Date: May 24, 2009
To: Ariane Altar ariane@altarpots.com
Subject: New Yawk and Bahston

I have an itinerary for this sudden return to the east coast. Friday take a red-eye to Boston. Book signings over the weekend, and long visit with the Godines. Tuesday, train to New York. Meeting with Patton Wednesday, with signings scheduled throughout the week. Will come home next weekend, probably the seventh of June. I'll call soon.

Pants On Fire!

From: Ariane Altar ariane@altarpots.com
Date: May 24, 2009
To: Wylie Hymen wylie@hymenfables.com
Subject: your news

Am I not invited? I said, No Second Chances!

From: Erica Reading erica@hmhco.com
Date: May 24, 2009
To: Wylie Hymen wylie@hymenfables.com

Houghton is putting you up in New York for the signing with Dr. Patton; it makes no difference to us if you bring your partner along.

Letter and Drawing from Wylie to Ariane
May 26, 2009
Indian Springs, CA
Drawing of heliconias in jug

If I were with you now—it is dusk—I would draw you to me, cover your face, and neck, and shoulders with kisses, and your mouth with mine, until nothing remained of the world, and at the end of a trail of our clothes, lying at your side, brush my lips on the little nubbins rising from your perfect breasts, and the smooth softness of your belly until, with my face pressed into your tawny curls, I would seek with my tongue deep, deep into the unfolding petals of your dusky blossoming the salty, sweet nectar that will nourish me and bring to your lips little cries, your song to the evening of our loving, until the dark wraps us in peace and sleep.

From: Ariane Altar ariane@altarpots.com
Date: May 29, 2009
To: Wylie Hymen wylie@hymenfables.com
Subject: your exquisite drawing

Your beautiful rendering and love letter came today. That is the most remarkable thank you I have ever received! How wonderful! I have placed the card upright on my nightstand, where I can enjoy it before I sleep and when I wake. At this moment I am writing, you are flying to New York or Boston. All the best at *National Geographic*.

Pants On Fire!

From: Wylie Hymen wylie@hymenfables.com
Date: May 26, 2009
To: Ariane Altar ariane@altarpots.com
Subject: Another itinerary

I am coming to you soon, dear Ariane, arriving United June 23rd at noon.

From: Karen Borders curator@ismuseum.org
Date: Monday, June 7, 2009
To: Wylie Hymen wylie@hymenfables.com
Subject: us

Dear Wylie,

Indian Springs Museum is honored you have consented to join our community lecture and exhibition program this summer. The schedule of events will be forthcoming.

On a personal note, listening to me adore you must be getting old, but I can't help it. I adore you. So there. Thanks for the private view of your Chinese porcelain slipper. If the shoe fits···I'd like to put it on.

Karen

From: Wylie Hymen wylie@hymenfables.com
Sent: Monday, June 7, 2009
To: Karen Borders curator@ismuseum.org
Subject: Re: us

August works best for me to participate in your lecture program.

I am profoundly touched by the care and tenderness with which you've expressed your feelings for me. My porcelain slipper is just the tip of the proverbial iceberg. Lots more in the darkest recesses of my closets.

I got home last night after midnight and will soon be leaving again. I would like more time to read over and think about what you've written. Let's just say for now that I don't think there's as much difference between how you and I feel toward one another as you may think. The difference stems from my hesitancy to express how I feel about you. I'm perfectly capable of expressing my feelings, but experience has taught me to be more circumspect about what I say and how I say it.

It's clear that I needn't worry about expressing myself to someone as aware of feelings and as capable of expressing them as you are, but rather than write, which always seems to cause misunderstandings, I want us to get together soon. I'll be gone until this weekend. Then I'll call to arrange a time and place.

Letter From Wylie to Ariane
June 8, 2009
San Francisco, CA
Drawing of pot with ivy

For Ariane

Madrigal (Anon. 17c.)

My love in her attire doth show her wit
It doth well become her
For every season she hath dressing fit,
For winter, spring, and summer
No beauty she doth miss
When all her robes are on:
But, beauty's self she is when all her robes are gone.

From: Ariane Altar ariane@altarpots.com
Date: June 15, 2009
To: Cherry Estrella cherry@starsearch.com
Subject: Paranoia or Instinct?

Hi! Need some backup and female expertise here! Hope you can shed some insight! Wylie has gone off on a second trip to New York in a month without me! The reason for the trip is a book signing and to do a voice over for his *National Geographic* film, I think. But, he's going to lots of plays again—which really hurts, since you know my career was in theater and film. He says he's visiting two gay friends who used to live near Indian Springs and who have season tickets to everything. Okay, okay. But, I haven't heard from him in ages···and I feel paranoid. His ex-girlfriend is a theater buff and a mutual friend of these Big Apple gay guys. Do you think SHE is on the trip? Should I ask? I am so shaken up; I am like a little kid with butterflies in my tummy and jangled nerves, totally insecure.

Let me know, Cherry, what the stars whisper in your ear about Wylie!

From: Cherry Estrella cherry@starsearch.com
Date: June 15, 2009
To: Ariane Altar ariane@altarpots.com
Subject: Re: Paranoia or Instinct?

I think it is important not to bring last night's garbage to tonight's dinner. Please forget your paranoia. But, I also think trusting your instincts is vital. Consequently, I am no help at all. I do think you can ask if she is traveling with him. I checked your charts, which show clear communication between the two of you, so ask!

From: Ariane Altar ariane@altarpots.com
Date: June 15, 2009
To: Wylie Hymen wylie@hymenfables.com
Subject: silence

Any reason for the all quiet?

From: Wylie Hymen wylie@hymenfables.com
Date: June 16, 2009
To: Ariane Altar ariane@altarpots.com
Subject: Re: silence

Just moving around a lot. Getting ready for my trip A WEEK FROM TODAY to see you. May I call this evening? Or would you rather call when you have a few moments free of family? Seven days: count them.

From: Ariane Altar ariane@altarpots.com
Date: June 16, 2009
To: Wylie Hymen wylie@hymenfables.com
Subject: Re: re: silence

Seven days, Wylie? Oh my! Thank you for letting me know you are okay! I am prone to worry! Night is not good for a call as everyone is here dining and yakking. Calling early morning here is great, anytime after six a.m., if that works for you.

It is a fine visit thus far. My brother's children are delightful, and I love having them here! The girls are staying in the guesthouse and Jackie in my office bedroom. They are cheery and helpful. I adore them. Today they took a surfing lesson. It was magical. Little Kui and Ande make my heart sing.

Pants On Fire!

From: Wylie Hymen wylie@hymenfables.com
Date: June 19, 2009
To: Ariane Altar ariane@altarpots.com
Subject: your family

What fun! What an exquisite grandmother and aunt you are!
I am glad you trust me enough to ask about Dina. As I told you, she is not on this trip. Dina and I are just very good friends at this point in time. Not to worry, my love!

From: Wylie Hymen wylie@hymenfables.com
Date: July 8, 2009
To: Ariane Altar ariane@altarpots.com
Subject: The road to your heart

Ariane, Ariane,

I want to say your beautiful name over and over. Ariane. My love.
Sitting on the plane, trying to control my tears, I thought of the Hana Highway. How that twisting and tortuous drive up and down cliff faces, in and out of ravines, from dappled sun to bamboo shade, on and on for seemingly hours, led me as though on a sacred journey to a place far removed from the busy worlds of New York and Boston and California where I have just been, to you, to your home, to your creativity, to your heart, to your bed, and, at last, to us. The moments of us, our selves merging as our bodies so sublimely did in that rarified capsule of time together.
What can I say about Hana—not the tiny town but rather its sixty-mile coast-line—that hasn't been said before by the early sojourners like Georgia O'Keefe and writers like James Michener and many a travel guru? I feel like I have fallen in love not just with a unique woman, you, but also with a very special place. Have I found my Eve, I wonder, in her innocent state, in the garden? Oh yes. What a gar-den I found you in! Eden before the apple, before the snake? Alright, perhaps not Eden, but rather, I'll call it our quiet inner sanctuary, which nourished and afforded our retreat into the sacred space of love. The place Adam and Eve vacated, you cultivate, my dearest.
Greens, greener than any others: did you tell me the Hawai'ian language has more than sixty names for green? Sunlight that is yellow, unlike the blue/gray light

128

of my northern clime, warming a floral rainbow before my eyes in that tropical splendor. The moistness of your skin maintained by the gentle humidity in the air.

Again a question: did you tell me Hana is the third wettest spot on earth? The thunder of the nightly downpours on your metal roof makes me a believer and will always form the remembered drumbeat of our nocturnal sojourns. Seeing my first "night bow" as it arced across the constellations in silvered shades of violet and navy, lit by the moon shining on the rain falling outside your bedroom window the only night we took our eyes off each other for a few seconds even to peer at another landscape.

The different roads which have brought us together—mine a dusty climb into the Native American territory at Chicken Ridge, dry, colors of earth, yellowing leaves and vermillion madrones, incendiary in summer yet mainly California cool; yours to Hana green, wet, and warm, a dizzying roller coaster ride into the heart of old Hawai'i but which is also simply at the end of the world. (You worried that the ride would make me nauseous. I only felt giddy and awed by the magnificence of the sea and cliffs; I had no idea the coast would be as wild, remote, and unspoiled as it is.) I drove slowly, zigzagging around cliff edges, past dozens of tumbling waterfalls and vegetation cascading from above offering me an unfiltered view of nature as it must have been in the beginning of time. Then you, you took me deep into Hana's dark rain forests, showed me her exuberant flora, ran with me on her black sand beaches where once airborne lava descended to solidify into sharp and fantastic shapes washed only marginally softer by the edges of the sea.

My cabin rustic; your home elegant. My art kept in a dark container; yours in a sunlit, open air gallery adjacent to your home and studio. In each of our separate worlds, the commonality we share of art, poetry, literature, film, and where all things Chinese and ancient perch on display for our pleasure.

Being with you, Ariane, in your lush and fragrant gardens, in your lush and fragrant arms, I can understand now why you chose such a remote landscape to nurse your heart. Not having known your children, I feel in an odd way that I "met" them in the plentiful photos on loving display in your home. I now have a modest understanding of your loss and silvered grief, and how the greenery surrounding you and the foam flecked sea of cobalt below with the sapphire sky sparkling above could replenish, if anything could—and I hope my love can, your spirit.

You are right about Hana attracting unique (should I say what I really think? motley!) visitors. After seeing the transients hitching barefoot along the road, dreadlocks akimbo, like wanna be hippies born too late to partake in the freedom and bliss of that generation, I sense that perhaps they seek the western most frontier to blaze a free and new life. Then you told me many work on local organic farms for a few months thereby indulging their vision of playing Adam or Eve in Paradise before moving on. I am glad I met many of your friends who seem to make up the weft of the community. I see the transients and tourists as part of the warp on the island's loom while the Hawai'ians dance through the locals, visitors, kama'aina and mali-hini like a magic shuttle connecting and creating a rich pattern.

Don't think me ungrateful, but I hated sharing you with your friends! I would have preferred spending every moment lost, and found again, in your arms.

I am hating this flight. It is going in the wrong direction.

Wylie

From: Ariane Altar ariane@altarpots.com
Date: July 8, 2009
To: Wylie Hymen wylie@hymenfables.com
Subject: you have flown away

Are you as deliriously exhausted as I? I am glad you came, Wylie. Thank you for taking the time and for showering all your attention on me! How I basked in your light! Our photo at Red Sand Beach is already framed and on my bed table. You will find below my journal entry.

For Wylie:

Our Nights
It is the moon, perfect in its purity, which paints the ceiling of our nights an unexpected blue. A rumpled sheet lays quietly. Above us, flung upon the bleached lunar surface, the shadow of a rabbit, the Chinese say sleeps there.

I wake to your weight hovering above me. I know it is you by the silvered glint of your beard, though this glimpse is captured through lids only partially opened. I close these lids and sink back into the reverie of sleep.

I see behind their black curtain a horizon suffused with color. I watch this inner landscape. It is not the moon, which blinds me here, rather, it is a setting sun emblazoned in scarlet flames. It feels as though I, too, am suffused by its colors, its yellow-tongued rays licking the canvas of my waking dream.

But, it is you. It is your tongue and your light that rouse me. My eyes now pressed shut not only by the vision but also by the pleasure you give. You caress my eyes with your lips, lips slightly opened, whispering, as though to gild the lashes of my rapture with the deckled edges of your golden poetry. The *Golden Phallus* has wakened as well; it penetrates the vermillion wetlands of the dream. The pressure of your touch ebbs. I open my eyes. But, I close them again swiftly in the ecstatic onrush of your thrusts.

The crimson of your ardor heats my loins, melting my body into a pool of hot liquid, pulsating, like the molten lava in a cratered landscape. Heated beyond the boiling point, steaming, you erupt and release random explosions upon the surface of my sleep, the carnelian colors of my inner sun vaporizing into another pink dawn under the drowsy eye of this, our ancient moon.

From: Wylie Hymen wylie@hymenfables.com
Date: July 10, 2009
To: Ariane Altar ariane@altarpots.com
Subject: Immense joy

Until I find the words and a few quiet moments to express the delight of our days together, I'll paraphrase Gertrude, about what I have discovered about you . . . (I loved your recommendation of *Gertrude Bell: Queen of the Desert, Shaper of Nations*: I had never heard of her, and now I learn from biographer Regina Howell that, among other triumphs, Gertrude was responsible for uniting Iraq!)

In truth the real basis of Gertrude's

I would substitute your name here

nature is her capacity for deep emotion. Great joys came into her life, and also great sorrows. How could it be otherwise, with a temperament so avid of experience?

I would like to think she wrote this next part about us instead of her paramour:

Life seized us and inspired us with a mad sense of revelry. The humming wind and the teeming earth shouted Life! Life! as we rode. Life! Life! the bountiful, the magnificent! Age was far from us – death far; we had left him enthroned in his barren mountains, with ghostly cities and outworn faiths to bear him company. For us the wide plain and the limitless world, for us the beauty and the freshness of the morning!

You are always in my heart and my thoughts, dear Ariane. I am filled with your love and mine.

Pants On Fire!

From: Ariane Altar ariane@altarpots.com
Date: July 11, 2009
To: Wylie Hymen wylie@hymenfables.com

Dearest Wylie, My Darling Sweetheart, Finest Man, Dear Friend,

Today has been filled with downpours and studio cleaning. All pots washed, pedestals rearranged, and my work looking grand. The grass has been doing its fair share of growing and needs mowing again. Thank you for your efforts on the lawn front while you were here! You gave me a nice break. I took note (but failed to thank you!) that you thoroughly cleaned my stove! It was helpful and thoughtful. Just like you!

I also vacuumed and tidied yesterday; my house is in order. Seven quiches baked for guests. I feel I have rested at night enough to have my normal energy back, at least it should be by tomorrow.

Despite this whirlwind of work, I have been thinking of you and of our time together: splendid; that's one very fine word for it! Delightful. That's another. Surprising and sweetly satisfying. Three more. I love your vitality and energy and enthusiasm and curiosity and thoughtfulness. Five more. To mention only the tip of you. To say I feel blessed to know you and be loved by you is the greatest of understatements. I feel privileged to love you! And love you, I do! Luckily my memory is better than all the *Sony* and *Nikon* and *Canon* and *Casio* cameras on the market...so I have thousands of images of you and us to sort and savor at any given moment. The images are of such happiness and beauty and lust and love and pleasure and pure fun that they should keep me busy for a long time!

I cannot wait to spank you again.

Letter from Wylie To Ariane
July 13, 2009
North Bay, CA
Turquoise vase drawing with seedpods
On Knowing Enchantment

For you, dear Ariane,

I tried to be stoic at our farewell, fighting back the tears to look deeper into your blue eyes, until, suddenly, you were gone. Then, no longer able to be brave, I sought out a quiet corner of the airport's garden to weep, not so much from sadness as released from the emotions built up, tears for having to leave you, our joys freshened by your scent still on my body, tears for all the years we might have had; tears from realizing I love you even more than I knew, love so profound, more than I have ever known, tears from not

132

knowing when I would hold you again—if ever! I, too, am visited by those terrible fears of loss.

But, then came tears of joy, recalling our adventures, how we romped, and laughed, shared our joys and sorrows, talked of "cabbages and kings", and played and loved. Oh, Ariane, how we loved, our bodies and souls now quiet, now moving as one, my lips moving over your sweet body as I bent to kiss you again, and again, and again—so I dream it will always be—

I am remembering the little bird that awakened us each morning with a song celebrating our love, me turning once again to enter the sweet depths of your body and our ecstasy.

> sunset dinners
> soft rain
> poems and stories and kissing of toes
> Ariane *mit Schlagsahne* Oh yum!
> And going to sleep each night warm against your body
> Mai tai's and pillow fights
> Splashing in deep pools of dark water
> Fingertips touching

When I sent you *Where's Noah's Ark?* inscribed "For Ariane, for so many reasons," you asked if, some day, I would tell you the reasons. I intended to and that might have been possible then, but now the reasons are myriad and my task, if not impossible, will take many, many quiet nights together, holding you in my arms, beginning under the autumn moon and continuing throughout our lives together.

To begin: you have graced my life with the delight of your presence, dear Ariane, with your beauty (in every possible meaning of the word), your playfulness and laughter, your passion for life, your art. You have honored me with your trust and your love, and allowed me to know for the first time in my long life, the joys of enchantment.

From: Ariane Altar ariane@altarpots.com
Date: July 14, 2009
To: Wylie Hymen wylie@hymenfables.com
Subject: Re: On knowing enchantment

Your words, your feelings, fill me. Thank you. My lips are quiet and smiling without speech, my heart continues to fill. All, because you touch me.You touch me in all the right places and beyond, leading me ever onward into the unexpected, the unknown pleasures of spirit and unfettered force of what we choose to create in our lives as lovers, artists, writers, journeyers, dancing a rapturous jig upon the sheer crust of this magical, molten, and mysterious planet.

The day here is filled with sunshine. I woke at three a.m. feeling the full effects of the shingles vaccine: chills, diarrhea, oh yuck! I took a hot shower, read, and tried to return to sleep, without success. At midday, I feel better.

I know you must be rediscovering the comfort of being back in your own home.

A poem (unfinished) for you

July 15
Midsummer Song

You asked me in May to sing my little song of spring dawning
It is time, Ariane; it is time, you said
Take me in your arms and tightly between your thighs
I sang my little song for you
In the summer sun of late June
I sang again for you
Under the full moon of early July
And in the garden
Not once was it time
Not twice was it time
But, always, our time became always
My song
Became eternal
So oft sung
And at what pitch
And with what delight
A melody carrying
Our days of summer

Now my song turns inward, silent
You away but never gone
Conversations dancing in my mind
How I yearn to sing aloud again,
To hear your baritone beneath my high notes,
A duet, my love
Looking into your sunlit eyes
Lying alive in the garden's dappled light

Pants On Fire!

Our glow outshining the afternoon
My little song
Silencing the birds

From: Wylie Hymen wylie@hymenfables.com
Date: July 16, 2009
To: Ariane Altar ariane@altarpots.com

I awoke this morning in a delicious, drowsy, voluptuous dream and a sensation so alive that I actually felt you roll over, your breasts brushing over my chest and your head tucked under my chin, your hand gently on my cheek, and I buried my face in your hair, breathing in the sweet morning scents of your body, our bodies, redolent with a rapturous night of love . . .and then I found your poem of midsummer song. Oh, Ariane, suddenly September seems far away.

From: Ariane Altar ariane@altarpots.com
Date: July 16, 2009
To: Wylie Hymen wylie@hymenfables.com
Subject: missing you

Today was rich, so rich...in your dream related in an email...in the post came your watercolor: a delicious snapshot in memory and tenderness of our time. Yet even blessed by this richness of love, I miss you and want you and don't know how to contain or compartmentalize the missing. I thought surely you would call tonight. (I called you earlier when I received your beautiful watercolor and letter.) But, it is now too late...and I am left full of love and longing...and the ever present desire to touch, to speak, to kiss, to inhale, to share time and space and bodies with you.

Never let go of that fiery sadness called desire.

Patti Smith

I have been musing about work...what project to begin (I mentioned this yesterday re ceramics or writing)...but mostly I was thinking about the space you take now in my heart and mind. A lot. Instead of my mental space filling with forms or glazes or words or phrases (good rhyme, eh?), it fills with you. Now the gentle hum of Wylie, happy Wylie, fills the background of my thoughts. You are happy, you know. Your joie de vie shows.

Anyway, my musing went twirling around the notion of loss of creativity (if there is) due to complete absorption with love. I was considering whether we'd be able to concentrate on our work if we tried to live together for periods of time or eons or forever.

135

I think I'm going to go make a salad and drink some white wine and get blotto and go to sleep.

From: Ariane Altar ariane@altarpots.com
Date: July 19, 2009
To: Wylie Hymen wylie@hymenfables.com

Here is a report on the lasting effects of euphoria (induced by both your presence or absence in my life):

Thursday, July 16th

Your email upon waking and your letter in early afternoon produced sublime euphoria lasting uninterrupted until 7 p.m. when sorrow set in with a prolonged longing to speak and touch

Friday, July 17th

Your call at 9 a.m. Euphoric state lasted until 12:30 p.m. when missing kicked its nasty way into my heart creating a bruise. By 3:30 p.m. the bruising of the heart subsided (particularly because I sold a pricey teapot) enabling me to think happily of your journey to Yosemite and you enjoying a pleasant time among friends.

Saturday, July 18th

Awakened in night by full body sweats despite pouring rains outside, then third migraine in a row and upset digestion. Another fast is in order, starting Wednesday as friends from Beijing are coming to dinner Tuesday.

Did a mini Tarot reading and researched our growth years. Fascinating. Plan to make copies for you. Right now we both just happen to be (it's all numbers and this is pure synchronicity) having a 9 year, which is the Hermit (very inward, completing old business). On our birthdays, we each happen to enter a Wheel of Fortune year (10) signaling great prosperity and creativity and change. Yours also involves the 7, the Charioteer, which is the stable tree by the rushing river. Great career success and travel and moving homes. Mine involves 19, the Sun, which is creative partnership.

What did I do today? Lots of furniture rearranging! I totally cleaned the guest bedroom, except the closets, and rearranged the bed and bureau. I moved the desk and a table to the laundry room, which is now my office (except I can't get the wireless system working for the *Internet* there). I made lentil soup for dinner; eating it is next. Did I tell you I love you and think of you all the time? I do, Wylie, love you.

Sunday, July 19th

Awoke to sunny skies and no headache, hurray! Also awoke missing you beside me. Missing our morning glory. Our timeless, endless, never wilting morning glory. Mid afternoon finds me still cleaning and sorting. No business. Gorgeous day.

I am signing off. If I am very lucky, you will call after your long journey.

Pants On Fire!

Oh oh oh, *Miss Marple* is on PBS Mystery Theatre, and I need you to snuggle close, smooch, and enjoy a good mystery.

Your secret admirer

From: Ariane Altar ariane@altarpots.com
Date: July 20, 2009
To: Wylie Hymen wylie@hymenfables.com
Subject: a true love story!

The honeymooners, Dave and Carmen, renting the guesthouse told me their story.

They met seventeen years ago when Carmen visited California as an exchange student from Madrid. They got engaged but their relationship fizzled out after Carmen went back to Spain, and a love letter Dave wrote went astray.

Carmen had moved; his letter went unanswered. Determined to trace his lost love, he wrote her another letter and sent it via her mother's villa in Spain. That love letter was put on the mantelpiece, unopened, and forgotten. Sometime and somehow, it slipped down the back of the fireplace. Workmen carrying out renovations on the villa ten years later discovered the letter and passed it on.

Carmen had never married. She rang Dave a few days later.

By then, Dave had moved. Fortunately, he had kept his old phone number. "When I got the letter, I didn't phone Dave right away, because I was so nervous. I nearly didn't phone him at all. I kept picking up the phone then putting it down again, but I knew I had to make the call." They decided to meet in Paris where she was living a few days later. Within minutes of seeing each other at the airport, they were kissing.

Carmen described their wedding as the pinnacle of an "amazing" love story. "I never got married and now I've married the man I have always loved," she said.

Their story inspires me to ask all my guests, as they are generally honeymooners or celebrating an anniversary, how they met. Each story is unique. I'll call them *Woo Woo!* I absolutely love the sound of the word "woo." Doesn't it sound like a train whistle and a lover's sigh at the same time! Just have to say it once again: *Woo Woo!*

Pants On Fire!

From: Wylie Hymen wylie@hymenfables.com
Date: July 21, 2009
To: Ariane Altar ariane@altarpots.com
Subject: Morning

Our talk last night brought you alive to me this morning. I awoke in the gray dawn to your head close to mine on the pillow and listened a while to your soft breathing before turning to touch my lips so lightly to your cheeks and sleepy eyes and the tip of your nose, and then to press them onto yours, little kisses at the corners of your mouth, to awaken you gently, inhaling the bed and love-warmed fragrances of your hair and body and mine. Our tongues touched, and I moved my hand down over your breasts and soft belly (you shivered) and slid my fingers between your parted legs, gently opening the petals of your flowerbed, dipping into the hot moistness still fresh from our lovemaking sometime in the dark of last night. I held you there quietly, feeling the first stirrings of your body and arousal, the tingly fur of your pussy in the palm of my hand . . .Good morning, my sweet Ariane, I whisper, I love you.

Letter and Painting From Wylie To Ariane
July 21, 2009
Indian Springs, CA
Painting Of Turquoise Temple

Our Temple of the Earth and Sky

Of all the beautiful pieces I saw upon entering the magical, bright, airy space of your studio, it was the Blue-Green Temple that called to me. Then, as I visited the temple each of those delirious, delicious days together, at different times, in different lights, and we became closer, and our experiences of one another became deeper, more and more, the colors took on meaning. The green of the Hana hills. The first misty lemon gray light of morning tinting our bodies, awakening, aroused. Dark clouds that brought rain tickling our nakedness. Pink-gray clouds shrouding the mountain. Frothy, white surf where we played, and splashed, and laughed giggly as children. The wet green of the waterfall rocks where you slipped, twisting your ankle. I caught you, remember?, as you began to free-fall toward the blue pool below, and you clung to me, breathless. Floating cottony clouds, like the ones we named, lying together, hands touching, looking up into the sky. Then, when the temple arrived in Indian Springs, you came with it.

Now it reflects the changing California sky, from the hazy gray of dawn to purple dusk and the pink alpine glow of evening. That first night your temple was here, and I was missing you, remembering our glorious days together, I thought I heard sounds coming from our temple. Placing my ear against its cool porcelain, I heard, somewhere in the distance, softly but distinctly, the beating of two hearts, and from deep in some bright, sun-lit chamber your laughter, and the lilting, trilling, soft chirring songs of love and ecstasy you sang to me when I covered your body with mine.

From: Ariane Altar ariane@altarpots.com
Date: July 23, 2009
To: Wylie Hymen wylie@hymenfables.com
Subject: Re: Morning

Meeeeeeeeoooooooooooowwwwwwwwwwwwwwwwww! The sound of a happy pussycat! I, too, awoke to you...missing you in our bed. I must have felt your hand, because I experienced a shiver of early morning pleasure. (You are the only man I've ever met who makes me shudder, shudder in anticipation of pleasure, shudder just because you excite me!)

By the way, that hand did save me when I slipped on the rocks above the blue pool! Clear evidence of what I have told you: Hana is not for sissies! Beautiful though it is, it is not a safe *Disneyland*. Accidents do happen!

Tonight friends are coming for a Mexican dinner right at the time of the eclipse. We'll see if the sky goes dark, and the birds fall silent.

I love you, Wylie. And, remember, I am a greedy woman: I want you all to myself.

From: Wylie Hymen wylie@hymenfables.com
Date: July 23, 2009
To: Ariane Altar ariane@altarpots.com
Subject: Trust

I feel very privileged to have had the conversation we just had. Thank you for sharing your deepest concerns and taking me into your confidence. It's one of the many things I love about you.

I am not with Dina. I have told you this. I feel it is indiscreet to mention her. I am asking for your trust in this matter.

Pants On Fire!

From: Ariane Altar ariane@altarpots.com
Date: July 23, 2009
To: Wylie Hymen wylie@hymenfables.com
Subject: Re: Trust

Just when we hung up, I got a call that my mom is in Kaiser emergency with
pulmonary trouble. I'll know more after she's evaluated.
Heard this poem on NPR today:

Fault

In the airport bar, I tell my mother not to worry.
No one ever tripped and fell into the San Andreas
Fault. But as she dabs at her dry eyes, I remember
those old movies where the earth does open.
There's always one blonde entomologist, four
deceitful explorers, and a pilot who's good-looking
but not smart enough to take off his leather jacket
in the jungle.
Still, he and Dr. Cutie Bug are the only ones
who survive the spectacular quake because
they spent their time making plans to go back
to the Mid-West and live near his parents
While the others wanted to steal the gold and ivory
then move to Los Angeles where they would rarely
call their mothers and almost never fly home
and when they did for only a few days at a time.

Ronald Koertge

From: Wylie Hymen wylie@hymenfables.com
Date: July 23, 2009
To: Ariane Altar ariane@altarpots.com
Subject: Images of Indian village life two thousand years ago from the Gatha Saptasati

Ancient poems

When her friends ask her why
saffron blossoms stuck to her breast
she brushed them away, only to reveal

140

bite marks of her lover, left and right

Your hairs rise up when you're kissed
and your goose bumps break out.
Quit feigning sleep
and I'll do it the way you like.

She let him come in,
sharing her cool room at noon,
for even a shadow seeks refuge,
and under a body's a good place.

Dear, dear Ariane,

I so look forward to our evening talks; I sit with you, usually now on the summer warmed deck suspended out over the valley, in the quiet dark under stars, the hours go by like minutes, and still I want more of your stories and your laughter to take me into the night.

Then I go to sleep, missing your touch, and your lips and fingertips just lightly fluttering over my body, your fragrance – the smell of you, and the way you take me hungrily into your mouth. I want to wrap my arms around you and nuzzle the soft hairs on the back of your neck, to begin a long, slow trail of kisses and little nibbles and licks down the length of you, to your toes, until you first bid me, then draw me ravenously to you, urging me to go deeper, deeper, still deeper.

From: Ariane Altar ariane@altarpots.com
Date: July 24, 2009
To: Wylie Hymen wylie@hymenfables.com

Poems for you on a rainy July day in Hana

1.
How I would like to float with you
Upon an eternal sea
Blue
Two yellow hibiscus
Petals like wings
Floating and fluttering
Delicate beauties
Timeless in the sun

2.

An afternoon nap with giggles
An involuntary chuckle
Rumbles from my throat
I lay in reverie this afternoon
Remembering how you
Like a master chef
Stirred me
Deliciously
Making me apologize yet again
For coming
I am on the rise
Oh yes, I am coming yet again, Wylie
And you, naughty you
Beat our love batter to a stiff froth
And then slowly our peaks collapsed
And we laughed and gasped and clasped
Offering our huzzahs to the almighty's oven
And steamy eyed thanks to each other

Dearest Wylie,

I am amazed that you didn't write the ancient poems you sent as they sound like us! There indeed is a score for love being eternal, even if the lovers change over the centuries! (We'll have to work a bit on our personal immortality!)

Did I mention that in the eons I was married, I never experienced loving, never once the kind of loving you freely give me?

How are you? I loved our conversation and did not want it to end either. I spent a good deal of time on the phone with my mom and later with her caregiver and doctors. She'll be in the hospital a while longer. She has a lot of fluid in her lungs from congestive heart failure. We ordered a hospital bed for her at home as well as more oxygen. I looked at flights to come as soon as tomorrow, which are available but which I am resisting. Cassandra, the caregiver, said she sees a recovery rather than a decline. I almost called you to see if I came now if you would be willing to join me in Berkeley? But, I decided, at least for today, not to come. I have so many arrangements to make here, that I really don't want to leave now unless it truly is a grave situation.

Pants On Fire!

From: Wylie Hymen wylie@hymenfables.com
Date: July 24, 2009
To: Ariane Altar ariane@altarpots.com
Subject: A found poem for you

This immediately brought back our rainy mornings –

It Is Marvellous ...

It is marvellous to wake up together
At the same minute; marvellous to hear
The rain begin suddenly all over the roof,
To feel the air clear
As if electricity had passed through it
From a black mesh of wires in the sky.
All over the roof the rain hisses,
And below, the light falling of kisses.

An electrical storm is coming or moving away;
It is the prickling air that wakes us up.
If lightning struck the house now, it would run
From the four blue china balls on top
Down the roof and down the rods all around us,
And we imagine dreamily
How the whole house caught in a bird-cage of lightning
Would be quite delightful rather than frightening;

And from the same simplified point of view
Of night and lying flat on one's back
All things might change equally easily,
Since always to warn us there must be these black
Electrical wires dangling. Without surprise
The world might change to something quite different,
As the air changes or the lightning comes without our blinking,
Change as our kisses are changing without our thinking.

                                        Elizabeth Bishop

I will be in Berkeley anytime you're there, to support you, to help you, to love
you. Please, dear Ariane – work on new pieces, work in the kitchen, and now this with

Pants On Fire!

your mom and all the stresses of a hurried trip – you need your strength and a clear head, and I'm not sure this is the time to be fasting. Take good care of yourself my love.

Musings on Dear, Dear Ariane

Whenever I think of you, which is
most of my waking moments, I'm frustrated
that this writer can't find words to describe
the depth of the feelings and sensations
that come to mind and imagination (and,
worse, I'm tongue-tied on the phone).
How can I describe the sensation of your hands
dancing, flickering, exploring my body,
each time as though it were all so new to you?
And that look in your eyes, that naughty
twinkling, which says I love you, darling Wylie,
now fuck me harder, deeper, deeper, there!
There's my spot, stay here with me.
Or the subtle differences in your scent,
and the fruity, salty flavors of your body,
when we first make love in the morning, and
again, later, when I take you suddenly,
from behind on the bed in your office, and then
again, in the evening when I surprise you on the chaise,
your body now redolent of the sun, and a day lived in,
and how many delirious encounters of sex,
until my body smells of yours.
Or how do I describe that feeling, you stretched out
below me, that moment, lowering myself
down onto, into you, slowly, just the tip,
made so exquisitely tender by your lips and tongue,
I can feel the unfolding petals of your pink liquid lily,
open and then fold back around me, so softly.
And it is all I can do, to hold that moment,
wanting to hold that quiet moment looking into your eyes,
and feeling the little shudders, pulses and vibrations of your body,
until I can hold it no longer, and must thrust as violently and deeply as I can
to hear you gasp and feel your nails digging deliciously,
painfully into my back, your legs and feet gripping me tighter
and tighter, your breath coming into mine,
your little ostinato coming faster and faster,

until we are moving as one, breathing as one,
coming as one, being as one.
What I think I know, my love, is that
you and I reach out to each other with
a language more ancient than words. It's as though,
throughout our lives, we have been learning a language
which, perhaps, long ago disappeared. Now,
you and I are the only ones remaining who speak it,
and the wonder is that we have found one another.

From: Ariane Altar ariane@altarpots.com
Date: July 27, 2009
To: Wylie Hymen wylie@hymenfables.com

Darling Linguist of the Lost Tongue!

Your writing is just exactly what I was thinking on the drive today – only the
reverse: how you pleasure me and the joy I take in the gift of you, all of you. I was
thinking of our carnality and feeling a bit in awe of it, as it is only our bodies, after
all, yet it allows the expression of our souls, allows an intermingling leading to
ecstasy and the out-of-body experience we crave (whether through religious experience or intoxicants or this love).

Just home from acupuncture and a long walk. All is good. And you? Fun in
Mendocino? The music?

On one of last night's topics: I am not sure I agree that the older people get,
the more sensitive to others they have learned to be. My observation is that they
get more entrenched in their behavior patterns, both good and bad, and are far less
flexible. You, my darling, seem to be the Grand Exception! I love you, and I love
you in my life, and I, too, want to sleep together every night. Every night. Are we
going to? That's the big question. I think the ball is now in your court.

From: Wylie Hymen wylie@hymenfables.com
Date: July 28, 2009
To: Ariane Altar ariane@altarpots.com

Picked up the loveseat on my way back from the coast. Pussycat heaven: a soft
chair, a warm fire, and not a dog in sight. If you come visit me this winter, we'll
sit here all cozy, your head on my shoulder and my arm around you, by a crackling
fire listening to the snow ticking against the windows.

Pants On Fire!

From: Ariane Altar ariane@altarpots.com
Date: July 28, 2009
To: Wylie Hymen wylie@hymenfables.com

Your love seat is a great shape! The new upholstery shows it off. Why not share our love there and everywhere?

A honeymoon couple rode a Harley up the drive and bought a box. I photographed them with the view, asked a bit about their love story, and told them I would include it in my *Woo Woo* book as a chapter called "Hanging Out on the Harley"!

My mom has worsened and is very ill, but still says not to come.

July 28th
Something From the Night For You

As I switched off the last light,
The house fell into darkness.
Yet a silver light slid into the bedroom
From the window facing west.
It was still raining out, but tapering
And large drops hit the banana leaves
Making overloud plops
Disturbing the night's silence.
It came from the moon, the light
The half moon
Reclining above the black slope of the hill.
It looked so very sad, the moon.
The round portion lingering above the horizon
The sliced top, slightly higher on the right
Looked like a sleeper ready to lie back in bed.
I have never thought the moon looked sad.
But, tonight
It was slowly descending
To lie down
Upon the hill
Alone

I sleep alone
And I miss you
One of my tears drops

Pants On Fire!

Quietly
Without a plop
Without fanfare
For I am stoic in your absence
Though my heart aches
I see
Through the wet sky
That the moon
Just before disappearing
Brightens from its shadowy silver to yellow
My eye is caught by a beacon
From the south
Ah, yes
The old lighthouse on the far shore

July 29th

This morning I wanted you
I wanted the cool roar in my ears
Of galaxies passing by
Pulsating with light and touch and speed
Traveling masterfully together through time and space
Avoiding meteorites and asteroids
Soaring ever higher
Spiraling further
Encased in our rocket ship of pleasure
A jet stream
Of love
Criss-crossing the universe

I am imagining you painting, hot in the Indian Springs' sun, dark strokes of green coating your door and windows. But, perhaps it is not your house but me you are painting! I, too, am painting...varnishing the mango, easy work but not particularly pleased with the results, mango now too red and in hot competition with the more subdued and tasteful travertine on the counters. Interior design star I am not. Glorious day here. I long for a nap under our avocado tree, head on your naked chest, your breathing as regular and gentle as the breeze.

Pants On Fire!

From: Wylie Hymen wylie@hymenfables.com
Date: July 31, 2009
To: Ariane Altar ariane@altarpots.com
Subject: Morning poems

Two for Ariane, from ancient India

No one else knows how
to do it that way.
One moment she gives a massage,
the next you're in heaven.

O moon-faced lady,
because of your big eyes
the night had twice as many hours.
And I used all of them.

And one from old Wylie

I lay dreamy at dawn
savoring all the times we made love.
And then I wondered,
why did I waste all the minutes in between.

From: Ariane Altar ariane@altarpots.com
Date: July 31, 2009
To: Wylie Hymen wylie@hymenfables.com

Yes, Wylie, I agree. Let's go to bed and hibernate through the rest of your hot summer, except I won't be sleeping. I'll be fooling around with you and your delectable appendages!

I just booked A MONTH in California! I don't need to be at my mom's till her birthday on the 18th, and I am sure she will be happy to have both of us stay with her.

Quite a day here: Three cars came up the drive, and I sold three pieces! Then a designer called and bought a very expensive wall tablet and ordered one more! I created the piece as a vertical, but the designer's client wants it mounted horizontally which should look great. It's part of a series called *Blind River.*

Did I tell you about my blind side? I have been ambushed by life so often— events I "didn't see coming" that I realized a while ago that I must be blind, at least emotionally. I don't see the world or people as a realist might. My sister, Laura, claims I see the world as I want to see it, as I wish it would be. She's accused me of being a *Pollyanna* since we were kids. Rose tinted glasses and all that. Mildly delusional. Trusting.

In any case, I began work and continue work on a series about blinds—whether blindness or shades, which look pleated, literally like louvers. After Nico died, in Ravello, I bought a tiny tile of the Saint Lucia, who holds a platter of eyeballs representing inner sight. I have it hung at the entry to my studio. Each time I enter, it reminds me of my blindness and to pray for insight.

From: Wylie Hymen wylie@hymenfables.com
Date: August 2, 2009
To: Fran Krok franorg@mind.net
Subject: Re: When can I see you?

My first thought after receiving your email, Frannie dear, was to meet in San Francisco with a fantastic Ming Court Arts exhibit at the Asian, four women impressionists at the Legion, and acres of Chihuly glass at the de Young. But, quickly I realized that we will have little time, that I would like to be with you without the distractions of the city, that quiet and seclusion and intimacy are really what I'd like.

I can't speak to how you arrange it, but I've thought somewhere like Dunsmuir or Mount Shasta City we could spend the night, or perhaps some little place you know over your way; wherever, I'd just be happy to see you again.

Your schedule works for me. I may be in Yosemite for a weeklong hike in the high country the last week of August. I have guests from Paris the weekend 9-10. Otherwise, August is open. We've lots to talk about.

The thunderstorm that passed through here last week while I was away and the over two thousand lightening strikes that hit the county knocked out my communications. There were numerous strikes on the telephone lines. Not only has phone service been erratic, but also my modem was fried. All this to say nothing of the hundreds of fires in Mendocino County alone, one just a few miles away, and the smoke so thick we drive in daylight with our lights on, peering ahead as though in a thick fog. Instead of returning to my cabin, I'm sitting at the Headlands Coffee House in Fort Bragg awaiting my computer's repair.

From: Wylie Hymen wylie@hymenfables.com
Date: August 2, 2009
To: Ariane Altar ariane@altarpots.com
Subject: Oodles of fun

Baron and family arrived safely. We're having oodles of fun. The grand girls slept out on the deck in their sleeping bags, giggling into the night. There have been walks and a visit to the horse-powered organic farm. I've gotten out old family photographs for them to see their grandfather at all his awkward stages in life; more giggling (I'm going to scan a couple and email them, then you can have a good laugh, too). And, we've been taking turns at your favorite game, *Boggle.*

But, alas, we'll not talk tonight. We got to talking about how school starts in three weeks and agreed they should stay another night. We're packing a big picnic and heading for the North Fork of the Eel, about ten miles north of here, to spend the day splashing and staying cool.

We'll have as long a talk as we want tomorrow evening. I'm excited about your California plans and itinerary. We have lots to dream about. It's wonderful how your work is selling. Don't forget that I love you.

Somewhere in this photo, Chicago 1942, is a little boy who, in sixty-six years, will become your lover. Until tomorrow.

From: Ariane Altar ariane@altarpots.com
Date: August 3, 2009
To: Wylie Hymen wylie@hymenfables.com

I recognized you immediately! You are the little boy center stage in the white shirt and *V-neck* sweater. I would have loved you at ten, except that at that time, I was only a month old!

Last night the old lung problem reared its painful head, and I am too ill to visit Ande. I am staying home this week. How I wish you were holding me in your arms and telling me to get better. I want you to stroke my forehead and my back, my sore, sore back. I am resting, doing absolutely nothing today, which is sheer torment in itself. But, I must remain still. Drink lots of tea. My lung problem comes on suddenly, taking me by surprise with its virulence.

Losing Julia by Jonathan Hull is a wonderful read, full of love, loss, war, aging, and art. Just finished it and have been bawling my head off!

From: Wylie Hymen wylie@hymenfables.com
Date: August 3, 2009
To: Ariane Altar ariane@altarpots.com

We have returned from a lovely day at the river; everyone is exhausted; the children and parents have crashed. I will not be far behind. I'll call just as soon as I can tomorrow, wanting to find out how you are feeling. Take care of yourself and, though I know it's hard for you, get lots of rest.

When you come, what's important to me is that you are comfortable and enjoy our first nights together. I suggest that we stay at the King George, which serves

High Tea in the afternoon. Got tickets for the King Tut exhibit at the de Young. I'm assuming we'll be able to get out of bed and get to the museum by two, since we probably have to check out by eleven. There is much to see!

> Lords of the Samurai
> Photographic Memories
> Great Works from the Museum's Collection
> China: 5,000 Years of Tradition and Innovation
> Korea: Treasures Past and Present
> Special Exhibition Tour: Lords of the Samurai
> India and Its Neighbors: Beliefs Made Visible
> Japan: Land of Contrasts

The room will be on my card. We can arrive late, having gone to a restaurant, especially as you may be hungry by the time you get off the plane.

From: Ariane Altar ariane@altarpots.com
Date: August 4, 2009
To: Wylie Hymen wylie@hymenfables.com

You are the master of knowledge when it comes to art exhibitions! Let's see them all! Besides the art itself, what I love is the "back story" for great works of art: I want to know how the artist came to feel what he expresses in his painting or the poet came to understand in the working of his heart. To learn that Beethoven was deaf when he composed the Ninth Symphony is astonishing!

Writing a friend, Beethoven said,

> How can I, a musician, say to people "I am deaf!"? I shall, if I can, defy this fate, even though there will be times when I shall be the unhappiest of God's creatures ... I live only in music ....

Or, to learn that Claude Monet, the great impressionist painter, was almost blind and needed eye surgery when he painted his twelve most famous paintings of water lilies. He could barely see! Perhaps he had no concept of "impressionism" and thought he was painting realistically, for he was painting what he saw, after all!

One of the most tragic back-stories belongs to Camille Claudel, the sculptress and sister of the poet, Paul Claudel. Around 1884, she started working in Rodin's workshop. She became a source of inspiration to Rodin, his model, his confidante, and lover. She made most of the maquettes in Rodin's studio. He fell madly in love with her and then became jealous of her talent. He stole her commissions and helped to have her incarcerated in an insane asylum! Her early work is similar to Rodin's in spirit, but shows an imagination and lyricism quite her own, particularly in the famous *Bronze Waltz* (1893). The *Mature Age* (1900), interpreted as a powerful allegory of her break with Rodin, has one figure, The Implorer, which was produced as an edition of its own. It has also been interpreted as a powerful representation of change and purpose in the human condition. Though she destroyed much of her artwork, about ninety statues, sketches, and drawings survive.

Look at Gustav Klimt: a married Catholic in turn of the century Vienna said to have fathered fourteen children with his muses. He conveniently dressed in a cassock, so he could make love to his models without undressing.

Should I go on to mention Picasso and his relationships?

Thanks for your expertise and the list of exhibitions. Shall we go to Epidauros this summer to see Helen Mirren in *Phedre*? I can still speak a little Greek! First performed in 1677, this play by Jean Racine, translated by the late Poet Laureate Ted Hughes, at the National Theatre, is traveling to Epidauros in July. They say Mirren, cast perfectly as the queen, believes her absent husband, Theseus, to be dead. She is consumed by lust for her young stepson, Hippolytus. There are two standout speeches - her mad fantasy about helping Hippolytus find his way out of the Minotaur's labyrinth and later her deranged imaginings about his love for the captive princess, Aricia. "I stink of incest and deceit," Phedre spits, as she lurches towards her doom. I enjoyed reading Ted Hughes' muscular translation. Through his words, you can almost hear the rumble of the gods meddling.

From: Wylie Hymen wylie@hymenfables.com
Date: August 5, 2009
To: Ariane Altar ariane@altarpots.com
Subject: Awakening in love

Your lover, hidden among the oaks and pines, is hungry for your touch, your kisses, wanting only your forest to hide him, craving only your sweet embrace.

Ancient verses copied for your morning:

It is the fortunate who live
in the mountains
where bamboo always hides lovers
and music of brooks babbles on.

They found each other at the same moment,
both with their eyes half afire.
So that no one could have said
which looked first, or was hungrier.

A flock of green parrots
falls from the sky
like a necklace of emeralds.
But, she's not looking, nor is he.

From: Ariane Altar ariane@altarpots.com
Date: August 5, 2009
To: Wylie Hymen wylie@hymenfables.com
Subject: Re: Awakening in love

You are wonderful in the morning, Wylie! That is when I see those "half hungry" eyes of glittering amethyst, but then I see them again at coffee, again at lunch, at tea, and dinner, dessert and nightcap, on to dawn amid the fire of sunrise. I like the verses a lot. For some reason, I am up early, hoping to sleep again soon.

From: Wylie Hymen wylie@hymenfables.com
Date: August 5, 2009
To: Ariane Altar ariane@altarpots.com
Subject: drawing I made of Roly's House

The green of the frame is almost an exact match for the window trim and the metal roof. He just completed his "root cellar" and is having a celebratory gathering. This drawing will be my gift.

From: Ariane Altar ariane@altarpots.com
Date: August 5, 2009
To: Wylie Hymen wylie@hymenfables.com
Subject: you amaze me anew

O Wylie! What a fabulous rendering! Roly is very lucky to have you as a friend! I can't believe the detail, especially the leaves! It is wonderful! Are you certain the new building is a "root cellar" and not some hideout for his dope plants?

Pants On Fire!

Mouse! arrived. What a darling book! I had forgotten you mentioned sending it! It is wonderful! Thank you! I know how much fun it will be to "read" to Kui! Reading a wordless picture book is the best!

From: Wylie Hymen wylie@hymenfables.com
Date: August 6, 2009
To: Ariane Altar ariane@altarpots.com

Sierra musings as I head off to Yosemite for the week

You will be with me, dear Ariane,
over snowy mountain passes
and along white water rivers
in my thoughts and my heart.

From: Dina Cochon dinaRN@iswell.org
Date: August 6, 2009
To: Baron Hymen baron@classiccompany.com
Subject: my car

Hey, Baron,

The girls are growing fast! Glad you could spend some summer days with us playing at the river. Have some concerns about leaving my car parked on the street in Berkeley while we are in Yosemite. Any chance of leaving it at your workplace? Let me know as we leave tomorrow morning.

Dina

From: Ariane Altar ariane@altarpots.com
Date: August 6, 2009
To: Wylie Hymen wylie@hymenfables.com
Subject: tonight?

Around seven my time, Lucas is coming by to help me load a dead barbecue and other paraphernalia into my truck for a dump run tomorrow. He is staying for a quick bowl of lentil soup and then will be on his way back to his new church. If you are not too tired, may we speak after that? Or will you wake me in the morning?

From: Ariane Altar ariane@altarpots.com
Date: August 6, 2009
To: Wylie Hymen wylie@hymenfables.com
Subject: a mistake?

Did I get your dates wrong? Are you gone already? You don't answer either phone.

From: Wylie Hymen wylie@hymenfables.com
Date: August 7, 2009
To: Ariane Altar ariane@altarpots.com
Subject: On the move

I went over to see Roly last night to talk about taking care of the kitties and the house, got invited to dinner, and ended up staying much too late to call. I'm heading down to Berkeley today to make a run on the library, provision the trip, and get some things I need. I will try to call before you go to Kaua'i.

I awoke yesterday morning to a two hour show of lightning and thunder I've experienced only a very few times in my life. Spectacular, and the rain came hard, lessening the chance of wild fires. Pearly and Gates dove under the comforter and didn't venture out until several hours after the storm had ended.

From: Ariane Altar ariane@altarpots.com
Date: August 12, 2009
To: Wylie Hymen wylie@hymenfables.com
Subject: Where are you, my darling

Are you still in the wilderness? I am wondering if the little girls have survived? I am imagining you in high country, camping (you are camping, aren't you?).

I am just home tonight from Kaua'i. I thought of you often, salvation thoughts, actually, strange as that may sound. Ande and Nalu are having relationship bumps. I listened and listened some more, and tried to give encouragement and support. All heavy and loading my heart. I thought of my happiness in loving you and what we each have described in our relationship as "seamless" and wish that ease for them, but it is not their fortune thus far. I wonder if our ease comes with lots of experience or just the gods being kind to us?

Pants On Fire!

From: Wylie Hymen wylie@hymenfables.com
Date: August 13, 2009
To: Ariane Altar ariane@altarpots.com
Subject: Re: Where are you, my darling

Yes, I've returned to the hubbub of the big city, I'm in Berkeley earlier than planned. Asia and Sage had many exciting adventures – including meeting bears – summer stories to delight their friends. I thought of you at every Sierra glade and glacial lake, and when, often, I would lie down in wildflower-carpeted meadows, my head on my pack, to watch the changing clouds, imagining you at my side.

From: Dina Cochon dinaRN@iswell.org
Date: August 13, 2009
To: Baron Hymen baron@classiccompany.com

Hi, Guys,

Sorry I couldn't stay longer and forced your dad to leave early. I am not much of a camper. Between the bugs and the altitude, I was miserable. I did take some photos, even of the bears. I hope when you get them, this City Girl will be a bit redeemed in your eyes.

From: Wylie Hymen wylie@hymenfables.com
Date: August 14, 2009
To: Ariane Altar ariane@altarpots.com

Thoughts of you, dear Ariane:

Lovers on the Nile

When she welcomes me
Arms open wide
I feel as some traveler returning
From the far land of Punt.
All things change; the mind, the senses,
Into perfume rich and strange.
And when she parts her lips to kiss
My head is light, I am drunk without beer.

Love Poems of Ancient Egypt, translated by Ezra Pound

Pants On Fire!

If I were with you now
my dear, sweet Ariane,
we would sit on the chaise,
your back against my chest,
your troubled heart beating
as one with mine, embracing you
with my arms and my love,
my hands softly on your breasts,
and I would take up into my body
all your pains and fears, until
your head dropped back
lightly against mine
and you slipped into a
deep and peaceful sleep.

From: Ariane Altar ariane@altarpots.com
Date: August 14, 2009
To: Wylie Hymen wylie@hymenfables.com
Photo: Your *Golden Deer* Alive in my Living Room, Waiting for You, Capturing the Light

Hurray! You are back! I can't wait to hear all about it. I am thinking of how lucky we are to have come together this year! Together in such splendor not just once but twice and about to have a third opportunity of time suspended deliciously to allow our love to play. How I want time to race when we are apart and to dawdle ever so slowly when we are together.

I have written a poem to thank you for your most precious gift: the painting of the *Golden Deer* which now hangs above my mantle.

Creator of the *Golden Deer*

Gilder of my heart
Your arrow has pierced my hide
Releasing sweet nectar
Straight from my heart
It flows in a continuous stream
Back to you
To your hand that drew the deer
To your arm that released the arrow
To your kiss that drew me to you

Pants On Fire!

Had you presented a diamond
Cut with a thousand facets
Capturing the light
Each more brilliant than the next
You could not have dazzled me more
Than with the gleam of this *Golden Deer*

So dear a treasure
Drawn by your hand long ago
Presented to me now
A symbol of your love
Like a diamond
Forever

Wylie, if ever you need to show the *Golden Deer* in an exhibition or retrospective, you know you may! I hope you won't grow tired of me waxing on about your gift! I look at the deer and the arrow and think how well it suits us: the moments you ask me to wait while you prepare, those wonderful moments before you return to our nest, those moments of anticipation and desire before you launch your beautiful self into me. Yes, the deer and the arrow, Ariane and Wylie.

In the legend of *Rama and Sita*, the deer is actually a symbol of the monster king's trickery. The deer lured Sita to leave the protective circle, and when the arrow pierced its hide, the monster king stole Sita away to be his unwilling bride. But, I don't want to see the deer that way! In my usual blind way, I want to see it as Sita did: the most beautiful creature she had ever seen.

I am thinking of what was happening in my life in 1993 when you created and gilded the *Golden Deer*. I was living on O'ahu, raising my children, and doing quite well as an independent artist. Ande was a junior in high school. I took her with me that spring to New York where I was having a teapot exhibit at the American Craft Museum, just across the street from the Museum of Modern Art. We saw Bruce Springsteen in a second hand shop in Soho, bought her a prom outfit at Bergdorf Goodman, stayed at the Waldorf Astoria, visited the United Nations. Marianna was extremely ill with anorexia/bulimia, hospitalized in Arizona. I flew back and forth. A nightmare I hoped would end, praying for her return to health and normalcy. Due to her illness, I cancelled a major museum exhibition, setting my career back about five years. Nico was in middle school, a national body board champion, feeling his oats, the joy and light of my life.

Pants On Fire!

From: Wylie Hymen wylie@hymenfables.com
Date: August 16, 2009
To: Ariane Altar ariane@altarpots.com

Morning memories

Awake in the muted morning light of Hana,
my tush warm against yours and
the heat of your body radiating toward mine,
I roll over to you and bury my nose
in the soft down on the back of your neck
and dot your shoulders with tiny kisses,
my hand sliding into the dank
secret place between your cheeks,
until you awaken and sleepily turn toward me.
And rising up on one elbow, hovering over you now,
I place my lips on yours, rubbing gently until
your lips open and our tongues touch,
becoming rigid, insistently, exploring our mouths,
I inhale your shivering breath and
rub the side of your nose with mine.
Fully on top of you now, locked in our kisses and
your ankles wrapped tightly around mine,
I can feel your nipples hardening, reaching
out toward me, bringing a shock of surprise
like lightening, pulsing through my body
to my toes.
You spread my legs with yours until
my balls and soft penis drop between
the silky petals of your dusky lips, a rose,
and into its magic, deep, glistening pool.
Now I'm compelled to break free from our embrace,
dear Ariane, to rub my face over your breasts,
to gently mouthe your nipples,
to breathe in and savor your fragrance,
sliding down over your firm, Rubenesque belly,
to press my lips and tongue thirstily into your pool,
and rest there, my face and beard wet with you,
your salty-sweet nectar flowing into my mouth.

From: Ariane Altar ariane@altarpots.com
Date: August 16, 2009
To: Wylie Hymen wylie@hymenfables.com
Subject: synchronicity once again!

Just as I got off the phone leaving you many kisses of X rating, as I was desirous of kissing you and expressing love in a thousand happy ways this sunny quiet Sunday, I looked at the computer, and there was penned your beautiful morning lovemaking to me. Oh, let's make love in just that way! Let's play and play! Let's be hard and soft and teasing and inviting and restful and joyful!

I told my mom you were picking me up at the airport, and would it be all right for you to stay with me at her house. And yes, yes, yes she would be very happy to have you there!

Heather and Joe, Cherry and Freddie, and some other friends were admiring of the *Golden Deer* at my dinner party the other night. Cherry felt, as I do, that it would look splendid with a larger frame. They enjoyed meeting you last visit and said they hope to see you soon!

The Truth

I do not consider modesty
I stand simply naked before you
Old-ish
Unconcerned about skin and wrinkles, sags and cellulite
Irrelevant to the mysteries
Within and without
We pilot chartless
Waters deep
Skies vast
Navigating
On wingless limbs
Launching into the unknown
Where love beckons

From: Ariane Altar ariane@altarpots.com
Date: August 16, 2009
To: Ande andeP@gmail.com

Dear Ande,

Today I was cleaning closets when I came upon a manila envelope. Inside were several black and white photographs Marianna had taken of herself in 1997 during a bulimic binge. I had completely forgotten about them, as they disturbed me so much at the time. In one of the photographs, she posed lying in a coffin holding some white lilies. There was a brief note. She told me the pictures were mine to do with as I pleased. If I wanted to write the story of her struggle, I could. The note really surprised me, because she was such a private person.

What do you think I should do?

Love, MA

From: Ande andeP@gmail.com
Date: August 17, 2009
To: Ariane Altar ariane@altarpots.com

moms,

you've got to do it. write her story.

luvs, ande

From: Wylie Hymen wylie@hymenfables.com
Date: August 18, 2009
To: Ariane Altar ariane@altarpots.com
Subject: more ancient poems

Love Not Far From the River

He's so lonesome
he touches the leaf with soft down,
rubs it all over his body
as if it were her soft cheek or breast.

When the lady's on top
her hair's a splendid curtain, swaying,
Her earrings dangle, her necklace shakes.
And she's busy, a bee on a lotus-stalk.

Here is Wylie's interpretation!

Bee on a Lotus-Stalk

When the bee becomes greedy,
There is no action he withholds.
He makes love to those buds and wet petals.
You'd think he had studied our love poems.
Fantasies of you this morning, dear Ariane –
your Wylie bee buzzing about, alighting
on the here and there of you, lightly,
nuzzling, caressing, little licks and glancing kisses,
my eye lashes flitting,
arousing you to giggles, shudders and shivers,
circling now closer and closer above your body,
around your knees, your soft delta of fur,
your hips and navel and, when you open to me,
the delicate, warm insides of your thighs,
until, impatient for your pleasure, and
your hands on the back of my head,
you press me hard between your legs,
my tongue hungrily parting your soft petals,
plunging, seeking, deeper and deeper the
rich, nourishing sweetness of you.

From: Ariane Altar ariane@altarpots.com
Date: August 18, 2009
To: Wylie Hymen wylie@hymenfables.com

Me as a bud or petal on your glorious lotus stalk? You as a bee pollinating my
petals? You make me laugh.

I am thinking of you preparing a vegan feast for friends and wishing I were in
the loft awaiting your ascent tonight. I wouldn't promise to be quiet, but I would
make an effort at muting my song for your ears only.

Today has been stellar. Worked on Marianna's story, which I am calling *Close
to the Bone* on and off all day. I also finished loading my kiln, which is now firing.
And, I laid out three new teapots! Some clients came. I made two small sales, had
my photo as the artist taken, and gave a tour of the flower gardens. The very good
news is I clinched the commission for my wall tablet! I'll drive to the airport later
this week to ship it out!

Sun was brilliant all day. I finally had a little time to enjoy a dear memory of
you by lying in the afternoon shade of the avocado tree. Oh yes. We had a FINE
time there. I like making love outdoors, my skin naked, your hands caressing, your
lips caressing, and the breeze caressing as it wraps us both in perfumed warmth.

Yes. That was a lovely spot, perched astride on that grassy knoll. Mmm. Let's repeat that many, many more times.

You mentioned that you re-read my emails. I am glad you do. They are tiny records of my love for you. I want to communicate all you are to me. But it is less; it is always less than reality, with words. May they be the "leaf with soft down" brushing over your memory, reminding you of me while we are apart.

Tell me. Art is supposed to reveal Truth, right? When I was an actress, I searched for the key to each character's soul. To portray another, I had to "find their truth" and so express aspects of character that would ring true to myself and to the audience. But, as an actress, I was well hidden behind the playwright's words. Emily, as I was then known, was not revealed; she hid behind the mask of the character.

As an artist in clay, I create all sorts of forms, glazed in all sorts of colors and patterns. Certainly, the pieces reveal my interest in antiquities, but the pieces do not tell the public anything personal about me: the color of my eyes, what food I eat, and so on.

But writing. That is truth telling, even when the writing is fiction, isn't it? You are a writer. Doesn't the author stand naked on the page before his reader? Yes, he is telling a story, but is he not also showing more of himself than any other artist in any other media?

Okay, I know you have painted self-portraits, so I realize I am wrong, going overboard! Yes, yes, "a picture is worth a thousand words!"

It occurs to me, though, that if you ever printed the poems I have written for you or read them to anyone, I would feel violated. Our sacred space would no longer be sacred. My words, my expressions of love and longing might sound tawdry and cheap to a stranger's ear. I couldn't bear either the exposure or the humiliation. Imagine, if some hacker got hold of our emails. I am sure they wouldn't have any understanding of what we have gone through to enjoy the love we share. They would probably think we were just, as some British crudely say, *"a couple of slutty, old farts!"* I suppose there is a very fine line between the sacred and the profane, depending on your point of view and level of experience.

In *The Invitation* I sent you by Oriah Mountain Dreamer, she asks her lover if he is willing "to stand in the center of the fire" with her.

You know we are there, together, Wylie. And, that is beautiful. But, boy, I am telling you now, I would really be burned up if you ever made what is private public!

P.S. I fell onto the rocks on a steep slope picking pineapples today and bruised my tailbone!

Pants On Fire!

From: Wylie Hymen wylie@hymenfables.com
Date: August 19, 2009
To: Ariane Altar ariane@altarpots.com
Subject: Dr. Wylie's Prescription

Here's how I would treat your tailbone owie:
First, I'd lift your skirt and lay you on your tummy across the bed or the chaise. Then, I'd pull your panties down around your ankles and begin applying gentle kisses and soft rubs with my face all around the hurt, now and then pushing my tongue deep into the warm cleft between your cheeks until the hurt went away. Or, you just weren't noticing it anymore.

From: Ariane Altar ariane@altarpots.com
Date: August 19, 2009
To: Wylie Hymen wylie@hymenfables.com
Subject: Re: Dr. Wylie's Prescription

How did I find such a naughty boy? Perhaps the question is, how did I find such a good doctor? The owie is bad enough that I cannot sit on a chair comfortably, nor can I lie down comfortably. Your suggested position might be the only viable one.
Here is a poem I have written about Marianna.

Close To The Bone

My daughter died
Bones shattered
Formless puddle
Melting
Color raspberry
Jell-O
The concrete
Unforgiving

She tried
Fourteen times
To die
I told her
She wasn't
Very good
At it

Pants On Fire!

Then she took
The leap
Twenty-three stories
Landing
Feet first
Startling
Tourists
Bathing
Poolside
In Waikiki sun

Ironic
My daughter
The jogger, the runner, the cross-country champion
Marathon finisher
Feet shattered
Unfinished
She
Shrunk
Eighty-two pounds
Bulimic
Perfection
Melting
Noonday heat

How can I
Tell
Her story
I don't
Understand
How can I
Tell
Her story
Cramps
My womb
How can I
Tell
Relief
Felt
Each time
She failed

Pants On Fire!

To die
How can I
How can I
How can I
Stymied
How can I
Magnitude
How can I
Stop

How can I
Intake breath
Who failed
Help
Save her
Who failed
Help
Hold her
How can I
Help
Live
Long
Hours
Dark
Insomnia
Her loss
Help
Extinguish
My heart

Marianna first born
Blonde lavender lovely
Delivered
Past midnight
November 29th
First anniversary
November 29th
My sister
Dead
Her birthday, too
A suicide

Pants On Fire!

Two
Her birthday
Same
November 29th
Name her Melinda, my mother said
Name her Melinda, my father said
Melinda, my sister, I said
Good Lord No
Bad luck
Bad luck
Nothing
But

Marianna
Played
Name
Played
Across
My lips
Natural smile
Sweet sigh
Mouth relaxed
Happy
Marianna

She weighed
Eight pounds four ounces
Whisked
Away
Hospital rules
No baby
Until morning
She weighed eighty-two pounds
Taken
Away
Coroner's rules
No visit
Till mourning

All the mornings
Of her

Pants On Fire!

Twenty-nine years
Came and went
Happy
Sad
Family
Broken
Nothing
Normal
All mornings
Mixed
Angry
Sad
Brother crying
Sister crying
Mother crying
Father playing
Taken
Away
Mad

Seeking
My daughter
Enlightenment
Seeking
Release
Marianna seeking
Escape from the
Hurt
Questions
Help
What is life
No answer
Help
How to live
No answer
Help
What is death
Velvet, velvet delicious
He said
What
She found

Pants On Fire!

Who
Death
Who
Her lover
But
Held him
At bay
Until

O shock
My son
My boy
Died
Help
Her brother
Dead
Help
Is he cold
Help
Is he scared
Help
O Mom, O Mom
His blanket, his blanket
I must take it
There
Where

To find him
To cover
To lay down beside
No more food
No more water
Soon
To disappear
How to die
How to die
Ask Death
Who
Her seducer
Who
Come

Pants On Fire!

Stay
Who
Death
Her lover
At bay
No longer

No baby
Until morning
The hospital said

No baby
Until

The hospital

No baby
No baby

Until
Mourning
I

From: Wylie Hymen wylie@hymenfables.com
Date: August 19, 2009
To: Ariane Altar ariane@altarpots.com

Oh, Ariane.

I'm not sure I can remember reading anything as raw. Honest. But, then, I've never known anyone like you before. It is inappropriate for me to write about it, only cherish it as part of you, and hope I deserve this gift of your soul, where I can discover more of you with each reading.

Close to the Bone is now an indelible part of me. The poem has made me weep. I hope writing it has helped lessen your pain and your grief. Your feelings of frustration and responsibility for Nico and Marianna's loss, while understandable, are misplaced. It was not your fault. You did everything you could to help them. You made their lives possible and filled their lives with all the light and good within you. You are a kind, loving, giving, and gentle person. All people about you have been made better by you. Know that others love you as you love

170

them. I wish I knew how to absolve you from all the hurt you feel. I want to warm you in the glow of the happiness and contentment you deserve. Take solace in the wonder of your granddaughter. Enjoy each day, and each of our days together, for the miracle in it.

Yes, I have read the narrative you sent by post, so different from the poem. The first part of the narrative is strong emotionally, but I think you might need to fill in some holes to make it a fuller book of who-where-what-why-how: what is the context and who are your readers? Parts two and three are, sadly, weaker and need some heft—perhaps more research and reporting, not just on your personal experience but rather nationally, with a broader spectrum of anorexic patients' experiences and clinical programs. I think, too, your spiritual bent in the third part smacks of sentimental new age gobbledygook, which doesn't hold any appeal for this reader. I don't want to offend. These are just some thoughts.

I am reading *Interpreter of Maladies*, and the contrast is interesting, stunning. Lahiri's understated coolness works well for a few of the stories, but doesn't work for me when the characters are suffering; muting and understating pain seems untrue to the story.

What you read to me is raw and intense, raging with a mother's disbelief and confusion. The death of a child, my god, two children and a sister is more pain than I can imagine, requiring more support and understanding than, I fear, I'm capable of giving you; but I will try dear Ariane. I will try. It is what in German is called *treuewerk*. Your choice of words, the tone, each phrase, the unguarded, unconstrained, bluntness of your writing is true to the story, artless. Perhaps you will bring what you've done and read it to me. I would take it as a most precious gift. If all goes according to plan, I expect to have you all to myself again tomorrow night.

P.S. I just came across a note I wrote to myself, probably when I was there with you. I can't remember the context, but I recall telling you about my liking for Japanese Haniwa period terracotta horses – more stylized and primitive than Chinese – and thought you might be interested, too. We'll look for them at the Asian when you're here. I do usually manage to get my life in order now and then; hopefully it doesn't always take this long.

I'll call from the east coast when I'm settled and know my agenda with *NG*. I am looking forward to doing this voice over and seeing the Ark; and I am regretting the loss of precious time with you. I am sorry this came up right when you are preparing for Kui's first birthday luau. You know I would carry you with me if I could.

I love you, W.

From: Ariane Altar ariane@altarpots.com
Date: August 22, 2009
To: Wylie Hymen wylie@hymenfables.com
Subject: in case I can reach you via email

I am so missing you. I have to reach out to you. Touch, touch, touch! I love our conversations, but hanging up is becoming ever more problematic and painful! Do not disconnect! How I wish you were with me, and I was with you, and we were in each other's good company and arms! Now, remind me, why was it you didn't invite me on this trip? Oh, my fault—that's right! I had to stay home as I have a granddaughter's first birthday luau coming up!

My tailbone is still exceptionally sore from my fall on the rocks.

Your second *Mouse* present about making the paper boat came for Kui, and I love it. I wish you could be with me for the luau. I know you would relish it. I want you meet my family and friends. Your trip to the east coast is really bad timing. It marks the THIRD trip without me! You are forcing me to eat my words, "No Second Chances!"

Lucas' daughter is beginning a relationship with a Brazilian windsurfer and asked me for this list. I thought you might like to see it as well. Clarissa Pinkola Estes is a Jungian marriage counselor who wrote *Women Who Run With the Wolves* a few years ago. She made the list of twelve elements for a harmonious and healthy relationship and gave it to her three daughters when they were choosing mates.

1. When choosing a mate, act blind. Close your eyes. See with your inner eye: their kindness, their loyalty, their insight, and their devotion. See their ability to be independent
   See what you "feel" of them. See their ability to care for you.
2. Do they have the ability to learn? Are they curious?
3. Are they willing to be both strong and sensitive, tough, and fragile, flexible, and substantial like a tree in the wind?
4. When you hurt them, do they feel pain? Do they show it? And when they hurt you, do they perceive your pain and are they sorry?
5. Choose someone who has his or her own inner life (religion, meditation, art, hobbies).
6. Choose someone who has similar passions in life to your own.
7. Choose someone who has similar values for child rearing and family relations
8. Are they compassionate? Are they a good listener? Do they give you equal time?

9. Choose someone who can laugh at themselves and stop an argument in mid-sentence.
10. Choose someone who is able to overlook certain faults and characteristics.
11. Be friends, not just lovers.
12. Choose someone who makes your world bigger, not smaller.

From: Wylie Hymen wylie@hymenfables.com
To: Fran Kroc franorg@mind.net
Sent: Sunday, August 24, 2009
Subject: Re: A visit

Okay, Frannie, just you. No Tim (whew). I'll make you corn bread in the morning. I return from the east coast September first. Your arrival on the third is perfect. Take Hwy. I5 to Williams, which would probably be faster since you'll be able to make good time all the way down. Williams is about four hours from Indian Springs. I'll meet you around three at Dos Rios Bridge, and we can travel together from there.

I can't wait. It's been far too long.

From: Ariane Altar ariane@altarpots.com
Date: August 25, 2009
To: Wylie Hymen wylie@hymenfables.com
Subject: I love you

Thank you for your lovely call. I miss you, and it was wonderful to hear from you.

Some craziness here: my guests had a screaming fight...then went silent and didn't open a door or window all day. I got very scared, thinking they might have died. Finally, I knocked at their door with much trepidation. Fortunately, after a nervous while, the woman emerged and said her partner was feeling ill. Yikes. I guess they are okay but weird as hell. No one has ever stayed here for days without emerging! No beach, no sight seeing, no noise except the fight. I panicked.

I looked at photos of you today: at my mother's house after I stayed with you in March. We look very happy. Nice. I also looked at pictures from Hana. I love you, Wylie. I keep thinking of this "ferocious" love I've begun to experience. It is a hunger, a desire to consume time and distance, a need to gnaw upon your sweet and comforting flesh (puts a new spin on "comfort food"!) I am feeling carnal and feline with this newfound ferociousness. I don't know what it means.

I hope you have access to a computer and get this note. It's a love letter, despite the screwy content! I love you, I love you, I miss you, I love you. At least I have your *Golden Deer* to keep me company!

It may be cuckoo to consider the holidays when they are so far off, but I have inquiries already for my B&B. We briefly spoke about you coming to Hana for your birthday, Thanksgiving, and hopefully the holidays through New Year's. Would this be a real consideration and possibility for you? I usually have Ande and family here for Thanksgiving and Christmas. Then they go to Nalu's parents' for New Year's. I am going to check her plans...and if they want to come, I won't rent the guesthouse to anyone over the holidays. Would you like to bring Baron, Barbara, and the grand girls? My guesthouse could accommodate everyone comfortably. They would have a ball here on the lawns, in the pools and waterfalls, don't you agree? Let me know.

From: Ariane Altar ariane@altarpots.com
Date: August 30, 2009
To: Wylie Hymen wylie@hymenfables.com
Subject: Missed your call!

Darling Man I miss so much!

When you called this morning, I was on the phone organizing flowers for some leis I want to make for the luau. Had I known it was you, I would have taken the call! I tried to call you back, but your pay phone wouldn't accept incoming calls. Boo. I was glad to hear your voice, though. It is really nice to have your books and art here: I can visit you through them when I get lonely!

I went online to see if there is any PR out yet on *Where Is Noah's Ark?* which looks fascinating. (Personally, I would want a nice warm Ariane in my bed after a long day of film work. She would help me relax and unwind after all that stress of becoming a celebrity.)

I love the Chinese chop you dip in red ink to sign the drawings you've done for me. I magnified it, cut it out, and impressed it in clay to reproduce it in relief in the center of each plate I am making for you.

The missing has gotten tedious. I wish you were home. No, what I wish is that you were with me. Then we would be together and talk and be and goof around. I don't like being apart at all. It is not what I want. Grouchy, eh? I am tired. And worried. Awful news: there is a huge brush fire threatening Ande's house on Kaua'i. She's okay but evacuating...not enough fire trucks to save homes...helicopters had to stop at dusk···the hills are still burning wildly. I told her to leave right now with the baby and get over to Nalu's folks' house where they'll be safe, which is far away from flames and smoke.

From: Wylie Hymen wylie@hymenfables.com
Date: September 2, 2009
To: Ariane Altar ariane@altarpots.com
Subject: An ancient Egyptian poem for Ariane

The swallow sings "Dawn,

Whither fadeth the dawn?"
So fades my happy night
My love in the bed beside me.
The whole world shines
I wish we could go on sleeping together,
Like this, to the end of eternity.

From: Ariane Altar ariane@altarpots.com
Date: September 3, 2009
To: Wylie Hymen wylie@hymenfables.com
Subject: the birthday baby

Kui just loves the *Boat* book featuring Mouse. I have "read" it a dozen times already! Her favorite page is the big splashing wave! Thank you for your thoughtfulness and generosity! A little girl and her Gramma appreciate you so much! We had two hours alone this morning, just Kui and me, to savor her special day. We lounged in my bed and read books, my kind of baby. I feel blessed. We have a special relationship; I can see she really loves me, clinging to me amid the hordes of clamoring cousins, aunties, and uncles.

It's wild and fun here: a bit unbelievable preparing for her luau. I'll tell more when we speak. Just imagine over fifty men, women, and children engaged all day in the hot sun in various activities: planting trees, digging the imu, cutting kiawe wood, building a huge log fire to heat the rocks which will cook the pigs. That's only the first bit. Imagine a fifty-foot long open-air kitchen where dozens of people are preparing lunch, then dinner for the family and helpers. Kids circling everywhere skateboarding, bike riding, shooting baskets, rough housing.

The constant noise of engines revving, people coming and going, bringing more helpers or supplies, trucks delivering restaurant size refrigerators, not one or two but several, platform stages for the bands, truck loads of six foot tall heliconias and gingers to decorate the tent poles and tables. The whooshing sound of giant propane venturi burners heating woks and chafing dishes. Not for the luau to come but rather to feed all the workers and family who are there each day. How do they stir the chili or stew or chow fun in such gigantic woks? With garden shovels, of course!

Pants On Fire!

Taro, banana, and sweet potato harvesting, smoking wild venison, cleaning and de-boning fresh fish, crab, and sea urchins...laughter...and these are just the preparation stages for the food at Kui's birthday luau on Saturday! Her Hawai'ian grandparents planted gardens to grow the food for this party the week she was born. Her aunties and uncles raised the pigs, caught the fish, hunted the deer, and more. Ande and her partners printed fabric and sewed special clothing for the family to wear. Her artist friends painted paper tablecloths. Classmates from Punahou came from their lives around the globe to enjoy this unique reunion. Girlfriends gathered forest flowers to make haku head leis for the family as well as for the dinner tables. Others wove palm frond baskets and filled them with jars of honey Nalu had collected from his hives, placing in each basket a young taro plant, a sweet potato, sea salt, and other symbols of this generous Hawai'ian way of life to give as thanks to all who had helped. Imagine a celebration a year in the making.

I made dinner for fifty thousand by myself today. Fortunately, some of the hordes brought dishes as well. I made smoked venison lasagna, chocolate birthday cake (along with a trillion cupcakes) with marshmallow cream frosting. I have cooked, cleaned, and baked for ten hours straight, driven twice to the airport to pick up Ande's friends. My swollen legs tell the story!

I mean it when I say I wish you were here. It is a unique experience.

From: Wylie Hymen wylie@hymenfables.com
Date: September 4, 2009
To: Ariane Altar ariane@altarpots.com
Subject: Counting

There are now only eleven days until I see you again. Soon I will be counting the hours until I can hold you in my arms and feel your body against mine.

From: Ariane Altar ariane@altarpots.com
Date: September 4, 2009
To: Wylie Hymen wylie@hymenfables.com
Subject: Theia

We need to talk about Theia and the Shanghai book/film project. I haven't heard from her. Has she contacted you? If not, I find it both bizarre and insulting. I suppose it has to do with her age and desire to keep Selene close. Selene has always included Theia and Vladimir at family dinners, holidays, and special occasions, even though she resents her. (I know my mom isn't willing to alienate my sister, Laura, even though they have a painfully antagonistic relationship.)

I didn't listen to all the CD's you had made of the family's oral history after Selene cut me off. I question myself for being willing to give up a year of my life and income to write a book about someone who at core is a narcissistic diva, a survivor, yes, but spoiled and pampered as well. I am not sure if her memories are true or self-aggrandizing. My mother says the public loves to read about selfish people and to write the story, despite Selene's protests and Theia's foot dragging.

I find it remarkable that Theia, who suffered little, wants her story told, but Vladimir, who suffered much, is mum. He watched Nazi soldiers gun down every one of his relatives as they waited in lines beside the train tracks outside of Zagreb to be taken to concentration camps. He was fifteen. In the mayhem, he managed to tumble and roll away unnoticed. He has no desire to revisit that past.

I do not have the desire to write about her life at this time, but later, when my emotions have settled down, I might. I hope you understand.

She has come to mind, since I'll soon be in the Bay Area, and we'd have time to meet with her, if that is your wish.

From: Wylie Hymen wylie@hymenfables.com
Date: September 4, 2009
To: Ariane Altar ariane@altarpots.com
Subject: Re: Theia

About Theia: no, I've never heard a word from her, either. I have not done any writing or formal research yet. I do have some old Shanghai maps and photos. I'm going to leave the decision to proceed or not with you. It was your heart that got a beating; I'll leave the decision to continue up to you.

I love the plates and you, my dear Ariane, for all your beautiful gifts.

From: Fran Krok franorg@mind.net
Date: September 5, 2009
To: Wylie Hymen wylie@hymenfables.com
Subject: us

Thanks, Wylie. Just like old times. The sketch is flattering, too.

Frannie

Pants On Fire!

From: Wylie Hymen wylie@hymenfables.com
Date: September 6, 2009
To: Ariane Altar ariane@altarpots.com
Subject: morning

> This morning, at dawn, a delicious dream
> of you, sweet Ariane, so real.
> You had pulled down the covers
> and were sitting on top of me,
> settling down, slowly, gently,
> your tush resting on my thighs.
> You raised and lowered yourself
> the full length of me,
> and when you bent over to kiss me,
> your breasts danced on my chest.
> I felt your soft hair on my face,
> and I awakened aroused and hard,
> to your lips touching mine,
> whispering my name.

From: Iggy Fumer iggyf@gmail.com
Date: September 6, 2009
To: Dina Cochon dinaRN@iswell.org

Dah-ling,

Loved loved loved seeing you again and so soon! Brilliant you could come along to hear Wylie tape. Don't take offense, now, (you know I'm always "straight" with you, ha!) but you are putting on some pudge around the middle! Even Michael, who never looks at women, noticed. Thanks for bringing our order in person.

Kisses, Iggy

From: Ariane Altar ariane@altarpots.com
Date: September 7, 2009
To: Wylie Hymen wylie@hymenfables.com
Subject: luau!
Photo: The family; nine pigs "a roasting"; Nalu's friends' tattoos; Kui eating her first sweet: a birthday cupcake; Ande, the happy Mommy; 1,500 guests under a full moon

178

Pants On Fire!

I had the most enchanting experience: I was sitting in the backseat of Ande's car next to Kui as we drove to the beach house on Kaua'i this morning. I looked at her and didn't say a word. She looked at me. Our quiet gaze lasted around seven full minutes. Slowly, during those moments a smile opened on her face, and on mine, and we enjoyed one another in perfect love and bliss and calm. It was wonderful and entirely unexpected!

The dogs went crazy with love when I got back, too. I played ball with them and gave them hugs and some kalua pig. Goldie mouthed my arm a hundred times and jumped all over me.

I am happy we'll be together in a few days. I thought about you on the long drive to Hana, as I can't wait to be in your arms again!

From: Wylie Hymen wylie@hymenfables.com
Date: September 8, 2009
To: Ariane Altar ariane@altarpots.com
Subject: Welcome home

My heart is filled with the joys and wonders of you. Your photos are such fun. I see once again why you're in love with Kui.

There's an old saying attributed to Bismarck: there are two things people should never see – the making of laws and sausage. I might have to add: pig preparation for a luau.

I think the most ghastly thing I ever witnessed were preparations for a very wealthy man's funeral feast on the Indonesian island of Sulawesi. The children chased squealing pigs through the village and made great sport of sticking them repeatedly and then killing them with daggers. Then came a moment in the ceremony when men with machete-like knives lined up twenty water buffalo and simultaneously, as if on some silent signal, slit their throats. It all happened so fast I didn't have a chance to turn away.

As the animals writhed in their death agony, the villagers scurried around with ceremonial cups collecting the blood spurting everywhere. The buffalo were butchered, and the hunks of meat passed out to the villagers; the whole thing so expertly done that the buffalo were reduced to piles of bones in about ten minutes. I did not partake of the feast that day and came seriously close to becoming a vegetarian.

Enjoy your morning and the little pleasures of returning home. I can see you there with your coffee on the lanai in a kimono open to that lovely place between your breasts I long to rest my head (the one I liked slipping off of your shoulders as I opened my robe, so I could hold you to me fully naked), looking out over the ocean, the dogs frisking about with their chewed up tennis balls, your kitty, Beauty, scowling his "how dare you abandon me" scowl, the perfume of a million blossoms and you on the morning breezes.

From: Wylie Hymen wylie@hymenfables.com
Date: September 11, 2009
To: Ariane Altar ariane@altarpots.com
Subject: *Firebird*

I was going to surprise you, but I can't. I got tickets for an early birthday present for us to see Stravinsky's *Firebird,* which is being restaged by the San Francisco Ballet with Chagall's costumes and Diaghalev's original choreography. I'm telling you now, because you must pack some formal attire! I'll fill you in on the story, as we are going to see the ballet day after tomorrow!

Until tomorrow when you, my own firebird, fly to my arms.

The hero, Prince Ivan, enters a magical realm of the Immortal, wherein lie magical objects and creatures of Kashchei. While wandering in the gardens, Prince Ivan sees and chases the Firebird. Once caught, she begs for her life. In exchange for freedom, she agrees to assist Ivan.

Next, Prince Ivan sees thirteen princesses, and he falls in love. Ivan asks Kashchei's permission to marry one of the princesses, but they quarrel. Kashchei sends his magical creatures after Ivan. The Firebird, true to her pledge, intervenes; bewitching the creatures and making them dance an elaborate, energetic dance, called the "Infernal Dance." The creatures and Kashchei soon fall asleep. When Kashchei awakens, he is bewitched by the Firebird, who forces him to dance.

Then she tells Ivan the secret to Kashchei's immortality: his soul is contained inside an enormous, magical egg. Ivan destroys the egg. With Kashchei dead and his spell broken, the magical creatures and the palace disappear. All of the beings, including Ivan's princess, awaken and celebrate their victory.

From: Ariane Altar ariane@altarpots.com
Date: September 12, 2009
To: Wylie Hymen wylie@hymenfables.com
Subject: excitement rises!

What splendid dusk and dawn conversations. Oh, the freedom to say, to SING: I love you, Wylie! My suitcases are open on the bed, mostly filled. Notice the use of plural: suitcases! I have packed your Japanese cotton yukata robe.

Pants On Fire!

Our worlds are very different at this moment. I am glad time is shrinking, and I'll soon be in your arms. Driving my car is nigh impossible, because the vibrations from the rough road rock me like your erotic joystick. The arousal only makes me frustrated and wanting, wanting, wanting to be with you immediately! I can hardly bear the waiting. Had a massage this evening...delicious...but also had a meltdown: when I get all that body work, the missing of Nico and Marianna floods me and the sorrow grows unbearable. I wear a coat of armor most of the time, my body stiff to protect my vulnerability. When I am made malleable by a massage, those repressed feelings surface and seem to gulp at the air on being exposed.

Hope you are home, happy, and safe from bears and snakes and mountain lions.

See you in how many hours?

Your Firebird, Your Firefly

◑

From: Wylie Hymen wylie@hymenfables.com
Date: October 16, 2009
To: Ariane Altar ariane@altarpots.com
Subject: Happy Birthday, Muse!

Speaking of Keats and *Bright Star:*

I cry your mercy - pity - love! - aye, love!
Merciful love that tantalizes not,
One-thoughted, never-wandering, guileless love,
Unmasked, and being seen - without a blot!
O! let me have thee whole, - all - all - be mine!
That shape, that fairness, that sweet minor zest
Of love your kiss - those hands, those eyes divine,
That warm, white, lucent, million-pleasured breast,
Yourself - your soul - in pity give me all
Withhold no atom's atom or I die.

Ancient words of love from Petronius for my beloved Ariane on her birthday:

Pants On Fire!

Let it always be like this,
Just like this,
A never-ending festival,
Lying with you, mouth to mouth,
Nothing to do,
In this there is, there has been,
And there will be,
For a long time to come,
Nothing but delight,
Never diminishing,
Always just beginning.

Ah, my Love,
You have flown back to the islands; gone from me, my arms, my kisses, but never from my heart. I feel you inside me, pulsing as my very blood itself. You are deeply rooted in me now. A month. Our month of seamless bliss.

From: Ariane Altar ariane@altarpots.com
Date: October 16, 2009
To: Wylie Hymen wylie@hymenfables.com
Subject: Keats and Brawne

I guess *Bright Star* is "our" movie, as it really was our first date! *Firebird* was beyond description, the score still thunders in my ears. It is midnight, and I'll sleep on freshly laundered sheets and remember our thirty nights together. Do you know Fannie Brawne never told her husband or children that she had once been the inspiration for Keats, his muse and his love?

Letter from Wylie to Ariane
October 17, 2009
San Francisco, CA
Filled with autumn oak leaves

Forevermore, dear Ariane
Autumn will stir in my heart
Delightful memories of
Our Indian Springs days

From: Ariane Altar ariane@altarpots.com
Date: October 18, 2009
To: Cherry Estrella cherry@starsearch.com
Subject: Wylie's new art

Cherry, I want to share a few words about my time with Wylie and his art.

When we got to his place at Chicken Ridge a few weeks ago, he surprised me. He had told me with the onset of his cancer that he wanted to stop writing, as books take so long, start to finish, and he didn't know if he had two or three years left to see a new one born. What he wanted to do was spend more time painting and drawing. Well, la de da. What a surprise awaited me at his cabin.

I think I told you its southern flank is a two-story wall of glass, making the house full of light, even when the oaks framing the windows are in leaf. When we walked in, it seemed kind of shaded and gloomy. I thought he had put sheets or curtains across the glass. I asked what that was all about, and doing his squeaky little giggle, he said, "Look."

They weren't sheets or curtains. They were huge parchment papers and on them, nude figures were lightly outlined in graphite. The bodies were female, sensuously and erotically posed, and absolutely gorgeous. One reminiscent of Matisse's *Nude at the Mirror*, another of *Nude Reflected*, 1937.

"Recognize them?" he asked. And, when I shook my head, he said, "They're you!"

"Me? But, I'm not that beautiful. I mean, my breasts are smaller, and my hips are larger···"

"Oh, shush! I've drawn you over and over. I know every inch of your body. I drew these figures with my eyes closed. I'm sure I've told you over and over that I trace you in my dreams when you're not here." He slipped his hands beneath my arms and cupped my breasts, breathing on my neck and pecking me lightly with his lips. I couldn't move. I could only stand there and stare.

Some of the figures were almost twenty feet tall. They were bathing, drying, sleeping, thinking···all sorts of positions. But, the weird thing was the faces were blank.

"Wylie, why didn't you draw my face? My hair? You write so much about my eyes and my hair, but you haven't drawn them."

"Darling, darling···these are just the beginning. Sketches. They'll get fleshed out in the end. You'll see."

I love these sketches, but I am mortified at the thought that one day he might exhibit them! Remember how shocked Georgia O'Keefe was to find her lover Steiglitz exhibiting nude photographs of her before the art world of New York?

Pants On Fire!

Maybe I'll be long dead and won't have to worry about it! At least the nudes he's painting have better figures than mine!

Ariane the Naked

From: Ariane Altar ariane@altarpots.com
Date: October 18, 2009
To: Mom ednawolfeson@peoplepc.com
Subject: photos of your 88th birthday and more
Photo: Uh-oh, black water waste problem: Call the insurance company!; Your 88th birthday breakfast at Yvonne's; Cherry and me with you in Napa Valley; You, wasting good chocolate on a chipmunk at Muir Woods; Birthday dinner: you, 88 and me, 63!; The lovers, Wylie Hymen and yours truly

Dear Mom,

Here are sweet pictures from my visit, from your sewage spill to our birthdays to the lovers camped out on the rollaway in your living room! Thank you for having us. For all the conversations and games. You did indeed earn the *Scrabble* Queen crown!

Did I tell you, Wylie let me watch him paint in his funky Matson container "studio"? It was almost pitch black inside (not even solar lighting there), but he didn't seem to care. He's developing some new phosphorescent paints that glow in the dark. He is quite ingenious. It was fun watching his luminous brush touch the parchment and see new torso lines emerge from the gloam. He says his new work is illumined by his mind's eye anyway. There is more than a touch of me in his work. He is experimenting by coating both parchment and canvas with a thin porcelain slip, clay artist's influence, you see, which he hopes will enhance the pigments and reflect light back to the eye.

Loads of love, Ariane

From: Mom ednawolfeson@peoplepc.com
Date: October 18, 2009
To: Ariane Altar ariane@altarpots.com
Subject: Re: photos of your 88th birthday and more

Emily, er, Ariane, gall dang it, Can't get used to that stupid new name of yours

184

Pants On Fire!

Like some of the pictures, but you make me look like an old hag with that new lipstick and hairdo. You should just let me be. Anyway, that Wylie sure has piercing eyes. And purple. Yuck. What man has purple eyes? The way he stares gives me the willies. My caregiver is better at giving me a bath than you are. You hurt me, squeezing so hard when you lift me. I've got the bruises—purple as well to prove it! So there!

Your Tiger Mama Grrr

From: Wylie Hymen wylie@hymenfables.com
Date: October 18, 2009
To: Ariane Altar ariane@altarpots.com

My Lover, Sweet As A Rose

You come to me laden with scents.
I know it is you next to me in the dark of night,
even before I reach out to touch you,
before I roll over to embrace your body with mine,
I am embraced by the sweet sachet of you,
dear Ariane, fragrances, still on your soft skin,
a rainbow of sensuous, fleshy blooms
you have gathered so lovingly in the day,
and brought to the house held to your breasts,
 – Oh, how I envy them – and the plants and leaves
that have brushed against your face and bare arms and legs,
and the newly mown grasses that have tickled your toes,
and perhaps – how I love this image – perfumed
all the parts of you I love so as you lay out naked
under the rain or the hot sun which brings out
the spiciness I breathe in hungrily and seek out with my tongue.
And when I do move close up against you,
and inhale your breath, fruity from the berries
and dark chocolate I fed you from my lips,
I place my hand between your thighs,
releasing to my delight, the rosy incense,
of your dusky bud as it opens to me
in the first light of morning.

Pants On Fire!

From: Ariane Altar ariane@altarpots.com
Date: October 18, 2009
To: Wylie Hymen wylie@hymenfables.com
Subject: a few photos from our month together and back home
Photos: Stinson Beach and book browsing at Point Reyes; Investigating "scat" and footprints on Chicken Ridge; baking brioche; christening our new Persian carpet; my early birthday dinner in Berkeley; you sketching me in my birthday suit!

Your devotion unhinges me. It was a glorious month!

I have to admit, something remains unsettled in me, and I only dare to mention it now. This morning I woke up and rolled over and reached everywhere for you, then held you tightly in my imagination and again in my memory. I got up and thought, "It's okay. I can handle being apart." But it's not true.

Just days ago we were together in your dining room. I asked if you were still in touch with Dina. You replied, "She's in love with me." I was startled by that response. I remember looking at you for a long time. What did that mean, to say, immediately and casually, that she IS in love with you? And, there you were, sitting with me. Then you added, "She knows you are here." That also surprised me. Then, you said that you had always accepted in your friendship that the other was free to pursue other relationships. And, then, I said, "I could not live that way." And, you said, "I am not in love with her. I am in love with you."

I cannot help but think that she would be in great pain if she understood the love, passion, and understanding we share. The very thought of her pain unsettles me. I do not know what you confide in her. I know you consider her "just a friend." But, let me be clear: I would not appreciate details of my life with you being shared or discussed. My love for you, which you call a gift, is our private business.

That night I also made clear, I want the kind of love where anything less than living and sharing life together would be impossible. I don't want a long-distance affair with you. Love for me is not a choice. It is a snare. Once I am caught, it takes possession, perhaps of us both. Caught, life alone is no longer an option.

How helpless we are, like netted birds, when we are caught by desire!

Belva Plain

I remember your tears. I remember your long silence. I remember your words. "Oh, Ariane. I don't know if I can be that person." I responded, thinking you were thinking of finite time left to live and your illness, "Let's not put the cancer into our equation." Then we went to bed.

But, is it the cancer that keeps you from me? Or is it someone else? I must know.

From: Dina Cochon dinaRN@iswell.org
Date October 18, 2009
To: Wylie Hymen wylie@hymenfables.com

Remember: dinner is at 7 tonight. Don't be late!

From: Wylie Hymen wylie@hymenfables.com
Date: October 18, 2009
To: Ariane Altar ariane@altarpots.com
Subject: In a rush

I looked at my calendar and discovered I'm volunteering for the pledge drive at our NPR station today. That's three hours away, dinner this evening with friends, and then home late. Sadly, I'm in the wilds all day out of cell phone reach, but I'll call tomorrow. Where is the piece about *Hana Cows* you promised to send me? Your photos are a delight; what wonderful memories they evoke.

From: Ariane Altar ariane@altarpots.com
Date: October 18, 2009
To: Wylie Hymen wylie@hymenfables.com

You know by now writing is my way of coming to grips with loss, how I have failed, and the joys lost to me now. I wish sometimes there was a roadmap for living, and all I had to do to be happy was to follow it.

Hana Cows
2007
Marking Time, Waiting For My Kids to Come Back

There was a cow in the field below the house bellowing. She bellowed, and she bellowed, and she bellowed. She bellowed all morning. Deep. Resonant. Prolonged.

I watched her plod next to the fence lines, first the south edge next to the highway, then west up the ravine, then north uphill toward my place, then a sharp turn east down the side of the driveway and back to the highway.

Checking. Re-treading the edges of her known world. Looking. Calling. It made me sad to hear her. I know just how she feels. I started crying.

I'd found her calf on the highway near my driveway the previous evening. It was lying with its head on the roadway and its body on the incline uphill. I couldn't figure out what had happened. It looked dead. The fence wasn't damaged. I supposed it had run downhill and taken a tumble and flipped over the fence and broken its neck. I got some fluorescent orange cones to put by its head, so the tourists wouldn't run over it as they drove around the curve. As I walked up to the calf, its soft, big eye blinked. Oh God, it was alive. I thought it was dead. It was alive, but it couldn't move.

I play solitaire. Every morning. I call it my meditation. It is really my waiting. I watch DVDs at night. I also channel surf. Sometimes I watch "Judge Judy" and "Oprah" at four in the afternoon, switching from one to the other during commercial breaks. I am waiting. Just waiting.

I don't bellow anymore like the cow, but I am wet inside; I never stop weeping. I weep quietly, on the inside. I weep in my womb, in my heart, in my breasts, in my memories. I keep waiting for my children to come back. I expect them. Momentarily.

The house is beautiful, clean, beds made, flowers on the tables and in every room. I bake lots of breads and cookies. The lawns are mown, the breezeway power washed. I am waiting. I am waiting for them to come home, home to this beautiful house, to this lawn perfect for all sorts of games—badminton, croquet, boule, horse shoes—games now stored in the garage, to this jungle for hide and seek, to these hills for somersaults, to this large property, to this large heart with separate and adjoining rooms for each of them.

I rent their would-be rooms for bed and breakfast guests. I feed the guests the baked goods. I make the guests' beds. I arrange the guests' flowers. I greet the guests as family, which they are not.

I am sixty. Sixty. I have twenty, thirty, or even forty more years to be here. Without them. My children.

My real life was when I was their mom, those sweet, crazy, hard, so hard, and happy years. Nico was my baby. He was twenty-one when he died. My baby, my baby boy. The boy I had begged for, dreamt of. He was beautiful. Marianna followed him, dying two years later, searching her broken heart for him. She died at twenty-nine. My first-born.

I keep thinking I shall wake up, and they will be alive and bringing their families home to see me, and there will be a lot of us, and the house will be full and messy and happy, and we'll have lots and lots of meals. I love to cook. And I love to cook for the people I love. And the people I love are my kids. My three kids. And two of them are dead. And they were so beautiful. And I loved them so much. And I couldn't save them. And I couldn't stop them from dying.

Pants On Fire!

I really do keep waiting for it to end. It. The grief. The loss. The horror. I lied. When I said I don't bellow anymore, I lied. I do. Bellow. Sometimes I'll see a star, and think it's Marianna. I talk to her and beg her to come back, and I tell her how much I love her, and I wish she could feel it. I wish she could know it. And sometimes I yell, I just yell. "Nico! Come back! Where did you go? Where are youuuu? Please, please come back to me! Mom loves you! I love you, Nico!"

Marianna took some black and white photographs, which looked like something out of a 1940's film *noir*. The photos were of her breasts beneath some black lace. They were round and small and absolutely perfect. She was looking for beauty. Seeing beauty was the latest assignment in her senior photography class. She told me it was easy, because everyday of her life I had pointed out beauty, created art, and celebrated beautiful ways of doing everyday tasks.

"Thank you, Mom, thank you for showing me beauty," she said and gave me a light hug. I was touched, and I was particularly gratified she had found beauty in herself.

As an eight month old balanced on my left hip, she went with me on ritual tours of the gardens. We would find whatever flowers were in bloom—I remember the peach colored roses were our favorite—and we would smell them and name them and gently touch their petals. We would watch the sky change color at sunset and whisper about each changing hue: watch the brilliant golds soften to coral, tangerines turn to scarlets and streaked blood orange, to descend with darkness into deeply lush and lavender, plummy purples and drowsy navy blues. We hoped to see some "Jesus' rays" and catch the elusive green flash.

She was beautiful to the end. Even at eighty-two pounds. Translucent. Radiant. The famous Boogie smile, the smile that lit up the corridors at school. The body that could dance frenetically all night, the delicate frame, the chiseled feminine face. Mistaken by autograph hounds outside the Tate Museum in London for Nicole Kidman. The aura of a superstar. Reddish gold hair cascading in curling spirals down her back, loose dress skirting soft ballet slippers, laughing. So alluring you wanted to reach out to touch her, but hesitant, fearful of breaking her, like a figurine of rare and delicate porcelain.

And break she did, dropping twenty-three floors off the Prince Hotel in Waikiki onto the swimming deck below. She landed standing straight up, all the bones in her feet—her runner's feet—shattering on impact. Then her body tipped backwards to lie flat on the terrazzo deck next to a chaise, as though she were just catching a few more rays of the noonday sun.

A change of pace. I know that was morose. I have penned a few new poems for you.

Pants On Fire!

1.
What Happens When I Miss You

I sort of fall apart
Slowly
It happens slowly
I begin to disintegrate
Quietly
Without notice
An absence
Yes
Something is absent
But I am not sure what
Or where
And I continue as before
Though sensing that
More is falling away
I feel heavier
Instead of lighter
From the loss
I discover
It's not just
My body dissolving
Little drops of acid eat
My mind as well
Deterioration without movement
O
I realize it is my heart
Stretching away from my body
Painful
As it reaches
Back in time distance space
For you

2.
Lovers in the Wind

Wylie Blowing As Wind

I would like to be the wind,
so that when you are far away, Ariane,

Pants On Fire!

I could travel over oceans,
find you walking along the seashore,
your sweet body warm and salty in the sun,
then playfully tousle your golden hair,
and caress your neck, shoulders, breasts,
and the firm softness of your thighs
with my breath.

Ariane Feeling the Wind

I long to lie
Unclothed
In the open air
Legs askew, Wylie,
Letting your gentle breezes
Travel the intricacies of my contours
Meandering from toe tips
Across shins and thighs
Discovering the down drafts
Which lead to deep crevasses
Updrafts leading to twin peaks
Your winds eddying and lingering
Upon my lips

From: Wylie Hymen wylie@hymenfables.com
Date: October 22, 2009
To: Ariane Altar ariane@altarpots.com

With my love by the fire

Sitting by the fire into the night,
Outside the wind whispering in the trees,
You came to me from the dark,
Into the flickering light, your face
up close to mine, looking deep
into my eyes, deep into the soul of me
that loves you more than I can say.
I took your head into my hands,
thrilled by your soft, fine hair
on the back of my arms,

191

nuzzled my face warm against your neck,
brushed your nose and lips with mine,
and placed my lips so gently onto yours,
holding you, my hands moving slowly
up and down your body, so familiar
yet always so new, taking in deeply
your warm breath, our hearts beating together,
and I fell asleep there, a peaceful sleep,
there with you in my arms, and later,
awakening from my dream of you,
still making love in the deep, slow way we do.
You sang your purring song of love to me,
and I whispered your name over and over,
Ariane, dear, dear Ariane, softly,
outside the wind whispering in the trees,
sitting by the fire into the night.

From: Ariane Altar ariane@altarpots.com
Date: October 22, 2009
To: Wylie Hymen wylie@hymenfables.com

O my love,

You took me there, with you by the fire, and as I read your words, I felt each touch and heard each soft word...until my purring drowned out all other sound. Thank you for bringing me back to us and away from my daily Hana concerns. Thank you for your beautiful night of love and your poem.

Cherry from Napa sent me a book on reverse aging. I read about fifty pages last night. What is the single most important key to good health—more than food or exercise? Love! Does this key mean we have a handhold on eternity?

She is also doing astrological charts for my whole family and me. I'll see what's in the stars!

From: Wylie Hymen wylie@hymenfables.com
Date: October 23, 2009
To: Ariane Altar ariane@altarpots.com

Dawn Love

Dawn has come, pink, orange, and blue streaks

Pants On Fire!

against a turbulent graphite sky, and
you are here now, asleep, lying beside me,
my chest against your back,
my arm around your shoulder,
my hand cupping your breast,
my knees tucked in behind yours,
and my face exploring the silky strands of your hair,
breathing in the earthy incense of your scalp.
I wonder if you are asleep, you are so quiet, but
I am unable to wait any longer – aroused by
the touch and fragrances of your body – so I return
to spoon again, this time slipping gently into you
from behind, between your swollen vulva,
(I like that word; I think it sounds sexy, nasty even),
teasing, just the hot tip and ridge barely entering, until
you reach back, grab my butt with insistent hands,
and pull me greedily deeper, deeper into you,
where I will rest, not moving, teasing again, feeling
your little tightening caresses, searching for your spot,
humming along with your sighs and purrs of pleasure,
your nipples growing hard under my hands.
I pinch them suddenly to make your whole body shudder.
And when your warm nectar floods out over me,
moistening my thighs and wetting dark spots into the sheets,
I realize you, you naughty little girl, were having wet fantasies,
or perhaps you were not asleep at all,
but impishly anticipating my return,
drawing up your knees tightly against your breasts,
presenting, guiding me where you want me to be,
welcoming me through the unfolding petals of your dusky rose
toward the delightfully sweet cavern within.
        Naughty! Naughty! And such naughtiness, little girl, surely
you must agree, such lasciviousness calls for punishment,
a spanking at the very least, but first,
I will fuck you harder and with such force as
I have never fucked you before, furiously,
my dick and my balls driving into you,
my body pounding, hammering against your tender, pillowy ass,
ramming deeper and deeper, harder and harder, until
you call out my name over and over, demand
that I thrust even more fiercely, cry out in ecstasy,

Pants On Fire!

our voices a lovers' duet: I love you Ariane. I love you Wylie.
I love you, I love you being in me, Wylie; I love being in you, Ariane.
Can you feel me, Ariane? Yes, right there, Wylie, that's my spot.
And then, when I am certain you have been punished enough,
when I am spent and you can come no more,
I will spank you, stinging slaps, leaving the fiery imprint
of my hand on your soft, pale tush. Marks, not of anger,
or violence, but of the intense love and the passion
to which you move me. (It is my new discovery with you,
being able to lose control, to fly unfettered with you,
on wondrous journeys unlike any I have ever known,
confident you will guide me to your pleasure
and away from any pain).
　　　When I turn you over, gently now – don't fear,
my love, you have taken your punishment well
(I saw you grinning the whole time,
your delicious I've-been fucked smile
that makes me want to fuck you again),
I will kiss the damp, satiny inside of your thighs
and press my face into your dewy fur
redolent with our sex, and from there
trace a path of little kisses over your belly,
(stopping to dip my tongue into your belly button),
between and upon your breasts, your neck,
and behind each ear, and run
just the tip of my tongue between your lips.
And so I will stay there, in that deep kiss,
just as when we find one another in the dark night,
murmuring testaments of my love for you,
over and over and over again.
　　　But rest now, my love, I leave our bed and
you so beautiful there, sprawled in a tangle of sheets,
to return soon with black French coffee in gleaming white cups,
a single rose bud, buttery, warm brioche with sweet marmalade,
to feed you tart, crimson strawberries from my lips.

From: Ariane Altar ariane@altarpots.com
Date: October 23, 2009
To: Wylie Hymen wylie@hymenfables.com
Subject: Re: Dawn love

Pants On Fire!

Oh my god. You transport me there, completely there, with you through your words vivid, conveying our times together and more, your desire, your love, your intensity. Your poems are reverberating and creating an immense love and thrill in me that you have written them and that you have written them to me and that they are true and real and oh my. O, what a time in our lives. Are we blessed. My god, to adore you and to have you love me and to receive such poems...there is such a fullness, a richness. This is not the naive and idealistic love of a Keats. This is our love. Our well seasoned, well aged, absolutely mature, and delicious love. The best of the best. I thank you, Wylie, for this beautiful testament, which makes me happy, makes me laugh, makes me squeal, makes me miss you even more. I love you, Darling. (Ouch! Did you just spank me?)

You won't believe this, I don't believe this: I just cut off all my hair. Yep. Just did a shaggy rag just below my ears. I do things like this now and again. The crazies grab hold of me, and there's no stopping them. I hope you'll recognize me. I hope you'll still love me. It's not that it is too short; it isn't; it's just choppy!

Last night's supper with girlfriends was great. We laughed a lot. The corn/carrot soup I made was yummy, the spinach salad makings I laid out on the counter, so everyone could build their own: bacon, artichoke hearts, marinated cranberries, honeyed walnuts, onions, red peppers, tomatoes, lettuce, spinach and a choice of dressings, followed by an apple tart for dessert. Heather's car battery was dead when she wanted to leave. I brought up my truck and used jumper cables to get her car started.

I have been thinking about you and realize I have not met your tummy button. I have not explored it. Big mistake. In fact, I wouldn't even recognize it! I must correct that next time we meet.

Hope you are having fun with your family. Travel safely. I wish you were en route to me.

From: Dina Cochon dinaRN@iswell.org
Date: October 25, 2009
To: Baron Hymen baron@classiccompany.com

Let's meet at the Academy of Sciences in the morning. It is stupid for us to drive to Berkeley and then back to SF. Maybe brunch after, if your girls can sit still, that is?

From: Ariane Altar ariane@altarpots.com
Date: October 25, 2009
To: Wylie Hymen wylie@hymenfables.com
Subject: packages and photos

Pants On Fire!

Two packages should arrive this week for you. Be on the lookout when you get back. When you look at the photos, notice how clean the studio is! I worked all day as a charwoman. Three cars came up the drive, and I made a fortune! A couple from New Jersey came in a chauffeured limo! They bought two pieces with a taro motif.

Then some of Ande and Nico's friends surprised me with a visit. They were excited to see my Hana home and studio. I cried on and off afterwards, as it is always such a reminder of loss when I see old friends from my former life. Memories awakened make it hard, hard, hard. After the visit, I got a call from Nico's best friend's mother. It was wonderful to hear from her, and we laughed a lot. But, she called because she had gone to Ande's grandfather's funeral and wanted to talk about the past. I traveled down memory lane with her and got stuck in the usual places of love and longing for my dear children and fell into the deep well of tears and fury over their deaths.

I hope your grand girls are a joy. I hope to meet them soon. Have you told Baron and Barbara they are invited here? I bet the science academy was wonderful. What did you like best? I've called, but your message service picks up on first ring. I am frustrated and missing you. Your cell never seems to work when you are traveling, which is when it is SUPPOSED to work!

From: Wylie Hymen wylie@hymenfables.com
Date: October 27, 2009
To: Ariane Altar ariane@altarpots.com
Subject: You, dear Ariane

What I think about when I think about you:

Long ago when you were a girl, and that first time last year
when you took my hand in yours, so trusting and loving,
and the way you always take my hand now
wherever we are, and when you say grace and pray for us,
expressing thanks for our being together, for our love,
(with a warmth and sincerity I've not known before,
so that I can honestly partake of your faith and belief),
before beginning meals always prepared with care and,
like you, always a surprise of fragrances and flavors.
And again when you take my hand in the night and
place it on your breast or between your legs.
The directness of the way you fix your shimmering blue eyes on mine,
move your face close, and bring my whole body alive,
touching my lips and cheeks softly with yours.
Your curiosity about the world, and bright intellect,

196

Pants On Fire!

and the lively way you talk about books (I want to read
them all, so that I can share the experiences with you)
and describe art and films you've enjoyed.
Watching films together, your head on my shoulder, and
you hold me tighter and understand why I cry
at the sadness and happiness of characters I've come to believe in.
Looking at art together as if through each other's eyes.
Your whole sense of the world, and the sacredness of life,
the way you've made art and beauty so much of you.
Your easy laughter and gaiety and the way you make me laugh.
Talking with you about everything imaginable (and many things not)
through candle-lit dinners, dropping our napkins and
leaving the table suddenly to make love into the night.
Coffee and croissants on the lanai in our robes on
warm Hana mornings, fresh from making love.
Making delicious treats together in your kitchen and mine;
How well we work together.

Your giggles when I put my hand up under your robe
and wiggle my fingers between your legs, surprised and delighted
that you are always wet, always wanting and open for me,
laughing as I lick your nectar succulently from each finger.
Your playfulness and rollicking sense of fun.
How you enjoy helping me to make decisions,
make them your own, and make the decision making such fun.
Like choosing our magic carpet from Persia for my living room.
Your temples and teapots and your blues and greens, from cerulean to chartreuse,
and all the beautiful objects you make with your hands,
which I honor, kissing your fingers and palms,
wondering at the creativity in those lithe little hands
that play upon my body as they do your clay.
How you've welcomed me into your heart, and
how comfortable we are together and how
we're never apart, even after months of being apart.
How you embrace and love life and me.
The way you help me be more understanding of
the weaknesses and foibles of others.
That I love you more than I have ever loved before.
Your creative uses for whipped cream.
Your poems and how they express the spirit, tempo,
and the spirituality of our love.

Pants On Fire!

Splashing in the surf with you, enjoying from behind
the tightness of your bikini on your sweet little ass.
Entering from behind, holding you tight to me,
with my hands on the curves of your hips, my goldenrod
blooming in your backyard sun.
Watching you dress and undress, aware of
your delight knowing I'm watching you, and
the unselfconscious way you come, sometimes
like the trickling waterfalls you have taken me to,
sharing with me your beautiful world of rock and water.
The music of the way you say my name,
and your songs of our pleasure.
The joy you take in a life struck by such unimaginable tragedy,
and the joy you give to me.

And more, so much more my love, new thoughts to add each day, soon making necessary a whole new list.

From: Ariane Altar ariane@altarpots.com
Date: October 27, 2009
To: Wylie Hymen wylie@hymenfables.com
Subject: thank you, my sweet

I would be overwhelmed and embarrassed by your poem, but I feel the same way and have the same list about you, you beautiful, wonderful friend and man and sweetest love. I love you and only wish to be with you.

I realize I have never officially invited you to play in my studio. You are cordially invited, kind sir, to join me in my studio at any time to play with clay! Would you love it? I love to teach (just basics of forming and joining) and then you are launched into your own special realm of mud and architecture! I would love to see what your beautiful hands would shape...and most of all, it would be such fun to have your energy beside mine, playing and shaping! Can't you come to me after Matthew leaves and stay for months?

From: Wylie Hymen wylie@hymenfables.com
Date: October 27, 2009
To: Ariane Altar ariane@altarpots.com
Subject: Winter

It is nearly noon and only forty-three degrees. I have noted in my journal – - First day of winter. There has been a fire going all night and the house is warm, especially the loft, where I imagine taking you hand in hand, removing your clothes, slipping your panties down your lovely legs, and taking you under the comforter with me to celebrate this clear, crisp day with endless caressing.

From: Ariane Altar ariane@altarpots.com
Date: October 28, 2009
To: Wylie Hymen wylie@hymenfables.com
Subject: Re: Winter

Our minds are traveling similar paths...was having coffee when you wrote and imagining you here and wondering if I would want to break away to work or if work would be an abandoned path.

You better start eating lots of turmeric! I grow turmeric *(olena* in Hawai'ian, a type of ginger) in my garden.

World News
Curry spice 'kills cancer cells'
An extract found in the bright yellow curry spice turmeric can kill off cancer cells, scientists have shown. The chemical - curcumin - has long been thought to have healing powers and is already being tested as a treatment for arthritis and dementia.

Dr. Sharon McKenna and her team found that curcumin started to kill cancer cells within 24 hours. The cells also began to digest themselves, after the curcumin triggered lethal cell death signals. Dr. McKenna said: "Scientists have known for a long time that natural compounds have the potential to treat faulty cells that have become cancerous and we suspected that curcumin might have therapeutic value."

I also read there's a coyote alert: watch out for those critters in your back acres, Wylie! Don't be going out under a full moon!

Here's what Ariane and Wylie sound like on Withdrawal:

Yakk, yakk, yakkety yakk, silence, sigh, yakk, yakk, yakkety yakk, sigh, email, email, email deluge, yakk, yakk.

I hang up or sign off, my tail between my legs (wishing, ardently wishing, it was your tail between my legs) and go about my dailies. Loving you, missing you, wanting you. Now repeat that phrase as a mantra for the rest of the day and night.

I am missing you, wanting you, hating that you are at the doctor's, and I cannot call. I am working in my studio and have hours ahead of me. This is my afternoon chocolate and love break.

Pants On Fire!

On Waking

On waking you are in my arms
close by in the warmth of the bed
Together we see the sudden light on the yellow root strands
cascading from the monkey pod
beyond our bedroom window
as the sun enters our world
And I love you
But, you are not really here in my arms or bed
And I want you to be

From Wylie To Ariane
A Card, A Box Of Freshly Baked Madeleines, A Bag of Italian Coffee Beans
Sent October 24, 2009
North Bay, CA

For Ariane

(Your Wylie has been in a baking orgy)
Some magic Madeleines
Which I hope will bring you
La Recherché du Temps Perdu

From: Ariane Altar ariane@altarpots.com
Date: November 3, 2009
To: Wylie Hymen wylie@hymenfables.com

Madeleines and Italian roast! How divine! Now the only thing I need are your
fingers to feed me, your lips to kiss me, your arms around me...in other words, I
love the sweets, but I want to devour the baker.

From: Wylie Hymen wylie@hymenfables.com
Date: November 4, 2009
To: Ariane Altar ariane@altarpots.com
Subject: My baking orgy continues unabated

Recipe for Tassajara Cream Scones (serves 2)

After baking slowly: Wylie is sitting up in bed awaiting your return from the kitchen, his Lotus Root stiff and hard and, by now, really throbbing. Facing him, gently, you lower your Jade Gate until his Lotus Root has traveled the full length of your Heavenly Path at the same time feeding him pieces of warm scone from your lips. He will also want honey to sweeten the scones and your pokey little nipples.

An alternative: Although my China Root will still be hard, I don't think the scones will be very good several hours later, so here's my suggestion:

Buttermilk-Cinnamonmanomian (I have a hard time with that word)
Coffee Cake
Serving suggestion: This works as well as the scones, except that we'll be thrashing about all day in sheets sprinkled with crumbs and crunchies. And though it won't be needed for the coffee cake, don't forget to bring the honey.

From: Ariane Altar ariane@altarpots.com
Date: November 4, 2009
To: Wylie Hymen wylie@hymenfables.com
Subject: Re: Baking orgy

A new twist to breakfast in bed! You have me chortling with laughter this morning! Chortling because your lotus root is my favorite ingredient (but hard to find at this time of year) and grasping because it is what I want to hold forever. Laughing because it is all fun and naughty and nice and, oh do I miss you! Pokey little nipples? Best for dripping honey...and melted butter...only if they go down, down, down to baste that gorgeous lotus root as it goes in and out of my very hot oven!

Thanks for the recipe! You may have to come (!) teach a master class in how to bake breakfast "rolls" in bed!

From: Wylie Hymen wylie@hymenfables.com
Date: November 6, 2009
To: Ariane Altar ariane@altarpots.com
Subject: Loughman

Loughman called about my manuscript edit. I think I've just broken my personal record for time on the phone – four and a half hours! (of course, with you, it's different: four and a half hours of phone sex is not enough!) But, we did take a lunch break somewhere in the middle. All went well, however I have lots of homework.

Pants On Fire!

She is worried as the *National Geographic* people are very detail oriented, and Loughman is keen to make this joint book/film venture a success.

From: Ariane Altar ariane@altarpots.com
Date: November 8, 2009
To: Wylie Hymen wylie@hymenfables.com
Photos: Patched pot and flowers: garden gingers, a sexy pink heliconia, and furry pinks

Somehow, despite all our wonderful communication, Poet of my Heart, I do not know where you are.i If you have gone to the Bay Area or just Indian Springs or missing in action on Chicken Ridge...? Which brings me to this thought: if something untoward were to happen to either of us, we wouldn't find out, because NO ONE knows we are connected and love each other! If you ever get concerned about me, please feel free to call or email Ande. I'm sorry I cannot remember if you told me your plans. I love you (wherever you are).

Unsettled

You don't answer
You are gone
Perhaps
Why don't I know
Where I can't guess

All my thoughts long to
Come alive in conversation with you
Over two thousand watery miles separate us
And three time zones
Yet my psyche is tethered
To your mast, its beacon
Which should shine bright
Obscured for me
By distance and time
Where are you?
Change, all the changes swirling around me
Drenching me in their unknowns
Baffled by the mysterious energy
Keeping me in limbo
Not knowing

Pants On Fire!

A stranger, a healer, stays in my guesthouse
Asks me of my dark side
Tells me I manifest it as outer reality
Why don't I believe her?

The ill fortune that took my childhood, my children,
Marriage, inheritance, first career
Suggesting I am
Responsible for those losses
Why don't I believe her?

I feel imminent change
Like a wind about to howl
I need you, Wylie, to hold on to,
To anchor me,
So I am not swept into a storm
Of my making
My life

I want to run away. Let's go to London, okay? Freddie and Cherry have invited us to join them in Cornwall this spring. They also have a flat in London. I lived there for eight years, and I know my way around and can fill in any gaps as your tour guide! There are two must do events: first, see the new Ashmolean; and second, the Mocteczuma show at the British Museum.

With a magnificent new building and inspiring displays, the 17th century Ashmolean Museum of Art and Archaeology in Oxford has been transformed into one of the world's great cultural jewels. The £61m renovation features thirty-nine new galleries, including four temporary exhibition galleries, a new education centre, conservation studios, and a rooftop restaurant.

Juan sent me a link to his fiancée's website. It is really good, particularly the life-size, *papier-mâché* giraffes she makes! You'll see what I mean when you go there. She is a theater director and puppetry maker. She created a show about, would you believe, the ark! I sent Juan our regrets that we won't attend his wedding, since you do not want to go. I am pleased he wanted us there.

Here's a link to my temple the Smithsonian recently acquired for its ceramics collection. It's the pinkish "Sunset Temple" you may have seen in my studio.

Point Reyes, eh? I feel much better now having heard your voice. By the way, do you realize that we just spent a month together in Berkeley and never once visited Baron or your granddaughters? I really hope I get to meet them the next time I'm there.

Wylie, the time has come: you must venture into the twenty-first century and hook up to the *Internet* via satellite. *Starband* is the best. Come on, Mr. Jurassic Park!

My head cold is terrible. Long talk with my brother about my dead sister, Melinda: a good talk but intense and very sad; I learned some new details.

I think about what goodness you bring into my life each time we speak or are together. Many times in the day, I close my eyes and place myself in your arms, where I am held close and comforted. I adore you. I can feel your strength clearly. You have no idea how good you feel to me, even at this distance.

From: Baron Hymen baron@classiccompany.com
Date: November 9, 2009
To: Ariane Altar ariane@altarpots.com
Subject: Important numbers

I'm at Baron's struggling with his Wifi connection and hope this gets to you. I've left important phone numbers for you to have on your answering machine: my neighbor, Roly's; my son, Baron's. No point in giving you Irina's or Matthew's. Regarding *Starband*, I don't know if I want to enter the twenty-first century! Being a fossil feels pretty good. Little girls and craziness reside here; I'll call at our usual time tomorrow night.

From: Cherry Estrella cherry@starsearch.com
Date: November 9, 2009
To: Ariane Altar ariane@altarpots.com
Subject: a story I have been following for months in the London Times

When this story first came out, it just shocked me. I couldn't believe anyone could legitimately complain about what goes on in his or her neighbors' house. Well, this is the third time this couple has been taken to court.

World News
Court hears couple's sex sessions
A ten-minute recording of Karen Cartwright and her husband Steve having sex was played in court. The couple's nightly sex sessions were said to have ruined the lives of neighbors.

Karen and Steve Cartwright's lovemaking was described as "murder" and "unnatural." Mrs. Cartwright, 48, is appealing a conviction for breaching a previous noise abatement ruling. She argues she has a right to "respect for her private and family life."

Specialist equipment installed in Miss O'Connor's flat by Sunderland City Council recorded noise levels of between thirty to forty decibels, with the highest being forty-seven decibels.

Unemployed, Mrs. Cartwright said she was unable to control the noise she made during sex. "After I got the Noise Abatement Notice I tried to control it. I even tried to use a pillow over my face to try and lessen the noise. I did not understand why people asked me to be quiet, because to me it is normal."

The case continues.

From: Wylie Hymen wylie@hymenfables.com
Date: November 11, 2009
To: Ariane Altar ariane@altarpots.com
Subject: A Geography Of Love

Last night, I felt somewhere deep inside a little bite of disappointment – you will not be here as soon as I hoped and dreamed. But, this morning I chide myself: "You are such a spoiled little boy, Wylie, you have Ariane in your life, and even from afar she delights and brings such happiness, and joy as you have never before known."

You are never far away, dear Ariane, but always close, here in my heart, and my love for you, far from being diminished by the geography of our lives, transcends all time and distance.

From: Ariane Altar ariane@altarpots.com
Date: November 11, 2009
To: Wylie Hymen wylie@hymenfables.com

It is the most crystalline day: clear bright sky, slightly cooler because our tropical "winter" is beginning, birdsong, and views of the Big Island across the channel.

I awoke to the sound of a rat gnawing wires in the attic crawl space above my bed. I padded barefoot in the morning rain to the garage for the ladder, filled a bait box with some tantalizing to rats, I hope, peanut butter and bacon, and climbed to the attic to place the black menace strategically to lure the vermin to their doom. (Ironically, Magellan's crew on the *Trinidad* gambled their wages to eat rats in the starvation days aboard ship. Rats have something

205

in their blood that actually staves off scurvy. The rat eating gamblers from the crew survived. What saved the officers was quince jelly, although they didn't know it, as they were getting vitamin c from eating it. But, yours truly is not on a long sea voyage, and rats won't grace my dining table: a hefty dose of *Warfin* for them!)

From: Wylie Hymen wylie@hymenfables.com
Date: November 12, 2009
To: Ariane Altar ariane@altarpots.com

Were you here, dear Ariane, I would make love to you in the dappled light of the morning sun you can see in this photo of autumn taken outside my living room window.

NG is slow. There may be too many editors on the *Where is Noah's Ark?* film! From what they've sent me to view, it could use a little tweaking, but it's mostly there.

I love you and woke up this morning missing you terribly.

From: Ariane Altar ariane@altarpots.com
Date: November 15, 2009
To: Wylie Hymen wylie@hymenfables.com

How beautiful the golden trees! Yes, let's love in the dappled morning sun! It is too early for sun here, but the birds are babbling.

I awoke again with the realization that despite our hours on the phone, we still don't talk about everything! I wanted to discuss *Longitude* by Dava Sobel with you. Such an adventure to create the horologe! Could we add it to our list of topics? I am also glad you enjoy listening while driving.

Well, little boy, it's time for me to ask: what do you want for your birthday? I have been thinking about it for days. Please tell me. I know what I'd like to give you, but I might not be there to do it! I really want to fly to you for your B-day and Thanksgiving. Would that work for you and be FUN? Shall I surprise you? Jump out of a cake at your party with a smile and a breathy rendition of "Happy Birthday"?

Hope your day of drawing is going well. I look forward to seeing your creations! I have just unloaded my bisque firing which, unlike the last, is perfect! I have some good pieces, so I am happy. Working on clay pedestals today.

Did I tell you my mother's toilet and bathtub downstairs backed up again, exactly like they did when we were there? Her caregiver was showing the apartment and came up to tell Mom the problem was back! The *Roto Router Company* came back and fixed it. At least, the sewage backup didn't damage the new repairs!

Thank you as always for your call and the sharing of your heart: its sweetness, its fullness, its melancholia, its hope, and desire.

I love the *Ark* drawing you sent. I think the addition of receding cloud shadows is gorgeous and adds to the feeling of relief and hope signifying that moment the *Ark* was safely grounded atop Mount Ararat high above the floodwaters!

From: Wylie Hymen wylie@hymenfables.com
Date: November 15, 2009
To: Ariane Altar ariane@altarpots.com

Sadness Turned To Joy

Yesterday, I awoke to a sadness,
instantly recognized as an old friend,
come to me now and then over the years,
but this sadness so intense and insistent I had to flee
to my healing forest and soft whispers of wind
high above in the tops of the firs and pines,
breathy murmurs like those first words of love
with which we greet one another
upon awakening, my arms around you,
your head cradled on my shoulder,
our breathing speeding with arousal
and anticipation of the morning's first loving.
Stumbling along the path, surprised,
jolted, confused: what is this?
And from where does this come?
I am so happy, and still
there is this sadness so deep,
even the first sun in a week of clouds,
streaming gloriously through the trees
cannot dispel, all with a suddenness
that forces the breath from my lungs,
brings me to my knees in the soft duff,
unable to go on, my familiar trail now
a Monet of liquid greens and browns,
my chin dropped to my chest, my body shaking
in a posture of pain going all the way back to childhood.

Days? weeks? will pass before I know why, what,
but I do know that if you were with me,
and I could wrap you in my arms,
feel your head on my chest,
and the reassuring beat of your heart
finding its rhythm and tempo with mine,
that I could have faced up to this better.
I repeated your name, dear Ariane,
over and over to the trees and birds,
wanting you here to comfort me,
to touch the back of my head, soothing me
in the ways you have learned to do
from your lives as a mother and lover.
And if only that were true,
my heart would have instantly lightened.
So I called you and then there you were,
your sweet, laughing voice comes from afar,
and in an instant I felt your arms reaching for me,
wrapping me in your mantle of warmth and love.
You kissed my face, my wet cheeks, and
with the tip of your tongue took
from the corners of my eyes, my tears,
and with them all troubling thoughts.
Not that I any longer need proof,
my sweet, but proof just the same,
how our hearts have become so entwined,
and we have become one.

From: Wylie Hymen wylie@hymenfables.com
Date: November 15, 2009
To: Matthew doc@iswellness.com

Dear Matthew,

Knowing how easily you get car sick, I think it best to meet on the coast at Dina's. Don't even try to drive the mountain roads to my place. I'll arrive mid-morning. Looking forward to seeing you!

Dad

Pants On Fire!

From: Ariane Altar ariane@altarpots.com
Date: November 17, 2009
To: Wylie Hymen wylie@hymenfables.com
Subject: Has Matthew really got a muzzle on you?

Your answer machine isn't picking up. I hope all is right with you and the world. I know my suffering from your silence is all for a good and just cause: your long sought reunion with Matthew. But, that won't stop me from moaning about not being with you!

Cherry is teaching astrology and Tarot readings in Hana this week and is staying in the guesthouse. My firing was good; one more bisque then the glazing begins. I have so many lids I cannot figure out which lid goes to which pot. That puzzle will keep me busy for a while.

God, I miss you. This silence is awful. Matthew better be being really, really nice to you, or he'll have me to contend with! All this misery for his benefit! Okay, I'm through moaning.

The Ballad of the Jilted Maiden

Honey, honey, honey
O I miss my honey

Matthew beckoned
And I reckon
Wylie's being held by him
O
Wylie's being held by him

From: Ariane Altar ariane@altarpots.com
Date: November 19, 2009
To: Wylie Hymen wylie@hymenfables.com
Subject: blah-zeah

I find our absences stretching into a territory of misery. I won't allow myself to be miserable from love sickness or wallow in my ever-deepening sadness. To avoid feeling pain, I go numb. I am officially, well, almost, officially, numb. A zombie. A love zombie. I feel myself getting very blasé...able to go without calling, go without writing, go without crying, go without desire...just bumbling forward, pushing thoughts of you from my mind as they well up from my heart and loins. My soul is feeling crippled.

It is crazy, because this is a full time for you: reconnecting with Matthew, seeing old friends, going to art events and concerts, being in the swing of life. I am glad for you. Trust me on this. In my small world, I am accomplishing a lot: in the studio, in my gardens, home, and office. All is good. But, what I crave is the succor: the marrow, the guts, the us.

I am in love with you, and I do not enjoy the moments apart. I want to be alive and growing in the "us." Patience. I know. Patience. But, I am done with patience, I am in the now, and I want you, now in my life, in my heart, in our homes, in our work (maybe this, too, will happen). I think this qualifies as a love letter, Wylie. I hope you receive it that way. I love you. It's greed, my darling, pure greed, raising its head, mouth gaping. I love you, and I miss you, and I want you. You are divine. Kisses everywhere and deeper.

By the way, where do you store the precious *Golden Phallus* when your family is there? Oh, what a naughty girl I am! Naughty, naughty! I ought to be spanked!

From: wylie@hymenfables.com
Date: November 20, 2009
To: Ariane Altar ariane@altarpots.com
Subject: Re: blah-zeah

I'm feeling our distance, too. Life is a little scattered right now and will continue to be until Matthew and Beth's return for Thanksgiving. I know you want to join us. I wish you could, but not this time. The whole reunion is too sensitive and complicated to add my new lover to the mix. I'll be in Berkeley until early Monday morning when I have two doctor's appointments. We'll be back "together" by phone Monday evening, but please know that I love you more than I can say and that you are in my heart and thoughts every waking moment and in my dreams.

Believing

Never think I leave you
from any desire to go.
Never believe I live so far away
except from necessity.
After weeks of separation,
still you are alive my heart
your fragrance and softness
rich in my memory,

and I love you more
each passing day.

From: Ariane Altar ariane@altarpots.com
Date: November 20, 2009
To: Wylie Hymen wylie@hymenfables.com
Subject: Matthew mystery

Why did Matthew decide to return for Thanksgiving? You haven't seen him in seventeen years, he comes for four days, and then flies back to Chicago only to return the very next week for Thanksgiving? I don't get it. It's very nice, but I don't get it. I was hoping to be with you for your birthday on the 24th and to share Thanksgiving. This turnaround is a bit of a puzzler. I can't tell you how disappointed I am for us. Isn't there room for me at the table? In Hawai'i, everyone is welcome. Not being welcome feels very foreign to me. Is there no *aloha* on Chicken Ridge?

From: Ariane Altar ariane@altarpots.com
Date: November 21, 2009
To: Wylie Hymen wylie@hymenfables.com
Subject: take me away

I want to talk to you about a couple of ideas – one about travel, the other about spirituality and karma. I do hope we'll have a chance to speak, to touch soon.

Whenever it is not monsoon season or too hot, let's go to India, okay? I probably have enough free miles. April? I love you. I promise not to bring a suitcase. I'll wear the same thing every day and nothing at night. Okay? I'll carry a toothbrush and camera and water. Simple: you and me and the basics. Please. Let's go away. Together. Soon. Very soon. Please. I wish you were here. Every minute. There is lust in my loins. The sun is shining, the air is cool, the gardens inviting. It should be our day to love each other outdoors. I wish you would call or write.

From: Ariane Altar ariane@altarpots.com
Date: November 24, 2009
To: Wylie Hymen wylie@hymenfables.com
Subject: Your Birthday!

The sun's rosy aura is lighting your birthday dawn. The birds are loudly singing, clueless of the tune of Happy Birthday, but singing full heartedly nonetheless. The gardens are beautifully lit by the rising sun, just as last night they were quiet

211

and regal in the light of the half moon. And the stars. Ah, last night the stars were brilliant, reminding me to remember them in the day, to remember the smallness of our planet in the larger firmament, to remember the smallness of our temporal concerns in the scope of eternity.

What matters? Well, to start with, birthday cakes with fluffy pink frosting! You are going to get pampered on your special day: let's see, I was thinking of starting from the top. Let's get you in the shower. I would like to shampoo your glorious head with lots of bubbly foam, and let the lather slide down your neck (oh, being careful to keep the soap from your eyes) and gently wash your shoulders and arms and arm pits...oooh...now the work gets much Harder as there is much more to clean after I finish your navel. O, the work, the hard, hard work at the groin. Yes, I am groaning at the groin, rubbing, scrubbing, more bubbles please. O, will I ever get it clean? It is taking so long, despite my best effort.

I guess I better get down on my knees for this job. Scrub, scrub scrub, rub-a-dub-dub get the buns, yes, get those buns rub-a-dub sparkly shiny clean. Can we just forget the legs and feet and toes-ies? Because I am very engaged, bubbles blowing from my lips, here at this junction of your legs. Can you guess what I found there? A great big birthday party blower! What fun to blow and hear it squeal! I cannot abandon it to sink any lower! I'll have fun blowing it all morning! HAPPY BIRTHDAY, BIG BOY! Time to make a wish···Oh? Got your wish already? Well, here's one to grow on!

From: Wylie Hymen wylie@hymenfables.com
Date: November 25, 2009
To: Ariane Altar ariane@altarpots.com
Subject: Urgent!

CALL MY CELL

From: Ariane Altar ariane@altarpots.com
Date: November 25, 2009
To: Wylie Hymen wylie@hymenfables.com
Subject: Re: Urgent!

A biopsy? In the hospital on your birthday? I am frantic. I was weeping profusely during our talk. I am in shock: it is a beautiful warm sunny morning. I have chills. I put on a Polarite vest and am drinking hot coffee to stop shaking. I am now doing my usual-in-a-crisis: Praying. Meditating. Sending you golden light. Loving you. That's what I've been doing since we spoke: praying, meditating, sending you light, and loving you.

Pants On Fire!

Hope when you get this you are feeling all right. What a way to spend your birthday! In the hospital! An emergency biopsy! Poor you!

I have been reading online about biopsies. It sounds major: groin lymph biopsies need a drain in the leg afterwards (do you have one?), and they snatch lots of flesh, clearly related to Shylock, these surgeons! I also understand that they read the biopsy while you are under, in case they need to take even more of you...? But, in that case, you don't have to wait days or weeks for a pathology report...?

From: Wylie Hymen wylie@hymenfables.com
Date: November 26, 2009
To: Ariane Altar ariane@altarpots.com
Subject: I'm okay

Awoke feeling fine this morning, emerging from sedation, my head and heart filled with delightful, delicious images of you, dear Ariane. Assuming you worked late in the studio last night, I'm not calling you now as I leave the hospital, but I'll call as soon as I get home. Got a chorus of Happy Birthday sung by the nursing staff. Awoke from surgery groggy but up and away in about an hour feeling surprisingly good. I get the results of the biopsy next Wednesday. No stitches, no drain; the surgeon super-glued me back together.

From: Ariane Altar ariane@altarpots.com
Date: November 26, 2009
To: Wylie Hymen wylie@hymenfables.com
Subject: Want to invite Matthew and Beth to Maui?

Did Matthew take you to the hospital and stay the night? Who brought you home?

Thank you for the photo of you with Matthew and Beth! I cannot see any family resemblance in Matthew nor are his eyes lilac like yours. But, he's handsome! Nonetheless, they look like wonderful, happy, healthy people, and they look like they are a lot of fun as well.

I remain disappointed not to be with you on your birthday or to share Thanksgiving. I understand it is family time for you, but I get to say I don't like it, and I want to be included! I most definitely want to meet your sons, and I want you to meet my daughter.

For your birthday surprise and for our happiness, I am giving you 40,000 award miles on United to come see me when you're well enough.

Have a wonderful, loving, happy Thanksgiving, Wylie.

Pants On Fire!

From: Wylie Hymen wylie@hymenfables.com
Date: November 27, 2009
To: Ariane Altar ariane@altarpots.com
Subject: Thanksgiving morning

I take Matthew and Beth to the airport tomorrow, and I will be home the following day. Forgive me for not calling; I am really unable to make any sense now,
maybe this musing will help, but I look forward to talking, and hearing your reassuring voice take me into the night.

I have always had much to be thankful for –
my life of art, my children, this magical, peaceful place,
caring friends, those I love, those who love me,
a strong body, really, too many things to count –
and now there is one more, you dear Ariane.
I am thankful for your presence in my life,
and for how you have welcomed me into yours,
for the gift of your thoughts and feelings,
and immense talents, and the joy of your art
which you share so unguardedly with me;
for listening, for your wisdom and compassion,
for taking my head to your breast and gathering me up
tenderly, reassuringly in my times of fear, sadness,
or just uncomprehending the unknown territory,
the new land of aging I encounter every day.
I am thankful for every morning I have awakened
to the touch of your hand and the warm embrace
of your body, your lips on mine, your blue eyes
inviting, welcoming me to share with you
delirious hours of pleasure exploring our bodies together.
I am thankful, even now when I can't be with you,
for the vivid memories of when I have been,
laughing, frolicking like little kids in the pounding surf
(for with you, dear Ariane, I am enjoying again the innocence
and abandon of childhood) walking hand in hand on the beach
and everywhere we are together, always together,
our thoughts and dreams, said and unsaid,
melding into a single vision of a life of loving
and caring, and beauty.

Pants On Fire!

From: Ariane Altar ariane@altarpots.com
Date: November 27, 2009
To: Wylie Hymen wylie@hymenfables.com
Subject: Re: Thanksgiving morning

You have made me cry – cry those tears of joy and melancholia – on this
Thanksgiving dawn. May I echo those words back to you? They shape the song
in my heart as well. Below are some Thanksgiving poems by e e cummings for
you.

love is a place

love is a place
& through this place of
love move
(with brightness of peace)
all places
yes is a world
& in this world of
yes live
(skillfully curled)
all worlds

i carry your heart with me (i carry it in
my heart) i am never without it (anywhere
i go you go, my dear; and whatever is done
by only me is your doing, my darling)
i fear
no fate (for you are my fate, my sweet) i want
no world (for beautiful you are my world, my true)
and it's you are whatever a moon has always meant
and whatever a sun will always sing is you
here is the deepest secret nobody knows
(here is the root of the root and the bud of the bud
and the sky of the sky of a tree called life; which grows
higher than the soul can hope or mind can hide)
and this is the wonder that's keeping the stars apart
i carry your heart (i carry it in my heart)

Pants On Fire!

From: Wylie Hymen wylie@hymenfables.com
Date: November 29, 2009
To: Ariane Altar ariane@altarpots.com
Subject: nudes
Photos: Sketches of Ariane in Blue; Ariane Bathing

Here are two snapshots of parts of two nudes I've been literally fleshing out since I returned from the hospital. Note there are no brush strokes or lines. Your figure is composed of tiny words, a love poem I wrote for you in many shades of blue···not stylized like Matisse's blue figures, but using blue in a sensuous way to convey language and shape all in one. This word as substitute for line really interests me. You understand I write on the parchment what I want to do to your delicious body with my lips, my fingers, my Alabaster Man, hard just for you···

As you have generously gifted me with your ceramics (I cherish the Chinese chop dinner plates and servers you sent), these sketches evolving into paintings of you are my gift in return. I suspect we are guilty of mixing up all the arts in our love collaborative. Tell me what you think. I've not been this happy or focused in years. I loved painting lessons as a child at the Chicago Art Institute, and that happiness is reborn in me now through you.

Knowing and Unknowing

Sometime in my young life I concluded that
knowing is always better than unknowing.
Never mind that age has revealed knowing
to be unattainable or, at least, a phantom of the mind,
eager to bring order and resolution where there is none.
Knowing is a balanced, comforting place to be; and
Unknowing, is for me a chaotic, frustrating confusing place.
But, now I have discovered a nether place, an untenable void,
a terrifying chasm between unknowing and knowing.
These last few days have been just that sort of place.
And for the first time in my life I am frightened.
I feel as though I am soon to go on trial – for my life.
Awaiting on Wednesday the verdict of
the judge, my good, compassionate surgeon,
and a jury of faceless pathologists who have
been analyzing a piece of my body to determine my fate.
Still, I am sustained by the loving presence,
boisterous good humor, and laughter of my children,

an inherent, until now largely unchallenged, cheerful optimism,
the knowledge that I have had a purposeful, good life,
but most of all, my dear, dear Ariane,
by knowing that I will soon be with you, and
by your love, thousands of miles away,
yet so present and warm in my heart.

Your Wylie Always

From: Ariane Altar ariane@altarpots.com
Date: November 29, 2009
To: Ande andeP@gmail.com, Juan Silver jsilver@gmail.com, Mom ednawolfe-son@peoplepc.com, Wylie Hymen wylie@hymenfables.com Cherry Estrella cherry@starsearch.com
Subject: sad news!

A tragedy: Carter and Jean Lincoln were swept away in torrential rains! Everyone in Hana is in shock. I was near them at the time of the accident, also driving home in that downpour from a dinner party. I was following another guest's taillights, because all I could see in the headlights were chocolate rain and rushing streams!

The Honolulu Advertiser
Missing Maui couple illustrates deadly force of flash floods
The apparent deaths of a Häna couple believed to have been swept away while crossing an East Maui streambed on Thanksgiving night are a grim reminder of the potentially deadly force behind Hawai'i's swift and sudden flash floods. At least a dozen other people have died in flash flood-related incidents in Hawai'i since 2000.
Maui officials said Häna residents Carter and Jean Lincoln, both seventy-five, likely perished on their drive home after enjoying Thanksgiving dinner at the Hotel Häna-Maui. Their battered 2004 *Ford* sport utility vehicle was found Saturday about 200 yards downstream from their home. Maui Fire Department officials said water levels in the stream reached twelve feet or higher on Thanksgiving, when Häna was hit with two inches of rain in an hour.
The islands' steep topography and miles-long stream systems provide an efficient pipeline to send large volumes of rainwater from mountaintops downstream to sea level at high speed. For those at lower elevations, there often is little warning.

From: Ariane Altar ariane@altarpots.com
Date: November 29, 2009
To: Wylie Hymen wylie@hymenfables.com
Subject: fear and cancer

You have entered the netherworld of cancer. My heart breaks for you. If there is any thing of value I have gained from the illnesses and losses of my children it is this:

fear, doubt, and worry are poisons to the soul.

We have many bridges to cross, and right now you and I know nothing, absolutely nothing about what the medical world may discover. I say enjoy your good health and feel blissful in these moments of ignorance! You and I might prove to have very separate notions of the medical field and one's own body and sense of security and correct course of action. Just know I am here to love and support you in whatever does or doesn't come to be.

Piece of news: Juan called me; his wedding is off, and he has returned to England. I think he discovered his fiancée has financial ties and maybe more with another man.

From: Matthew doc@iswellness.com
Date: November 30, 2009
To: Wylie Hymen wylie@hymenfables.com

Good to reconnect and have some time together on the coast. Sorry we couldn't be with you for your birthday or Thanksgiving. Too much jammed into one trip, you understand. Hope you can make it one day to see the new clinic. Be well on your solo trip to Hawai'i.

Matthew

From: Dina Cochon dinaRN@iswell.org
Date: November 30, 2009
To: Iggy Fumer iggyf@gmail.com
Subject: Thanksgiving

Dah-ling Igg and Michael,

It was grand to share Thanksgiving yet another year with you and our friends on the Mendocino coast. Is it our twelfth annual feast? We are glad you made the trip! It seems to be a week of reunions, as Matthew visited us earlier this month. Of course, we were happy to bring your holiday order of ten cases, as you saved us the effort of shipping (avoiding those pesky and unreliable *FedEx* drivers)! The business you have brought us over the years we are truly thankful for, as it is paying Wylie's horrendous prostate bills and allowing us to travel when we can. Cheers!

Pooky

From: Wylie Hymen wylie@hymenfables.com
Date: December 1, 2009
To: Ariane Altar ariane@altarpots.com

Morning

I awoke before dawn (cold: twenty six degrees)
Happily free of the cares of the last few days.
Your head was on my shoulder, snuggled under my chin,
My face buried in your hair all tousled from sleep,
Your arm lay across my chest, and under your leg
Stretched over mine, your little bush
Tickled my thigh, still wet from sometime
In the night, when I entered you slowly, gently,
And lay there, quiet, cushioned by your breasts and
Soft belly, my lips on yours, quiet, not wanting to
Disturb your sleepy, whispery breaths
Quickening to little sighs and whimpers of arousal,
Until I felt you swelling, grasping me, your body
Shuddering, wriggling beneath me, your
Eyes wide and sparkly in the moonlight, and
We fell into that drunken, tender state of lovers
Having just loved, each to the fullest, slipping into
Sleep again until, in the bright morning,
Your hand finds me, and we begin anew
Celebrating our love.

Pants On Fire!

From: Ariane Altar ariane@altarpots.com
Date: December 4, 2009
To: Wylie Hymen wylie@hymenfables.com

You know I am deep in the realm of Gramma-dom; I have almost forgotten computers, cell phones, and message machines! I took the Adorable One to the aquarium today and had one of the best times ever. The monk seal did all sorts of cute things for our pleasure, the large groupers and sharks scared Kui, but she found the jellyfish fascinating. Gramma hit the aquarium trinket shop and came away with some rubber bath toys to remind her of her aquatic adventure. It's the zoo tomorrow!

Just ordered Kui's Christmas present: an antique replica of a *Model A*, a child's pedal car called "Brum". I think the Chinese manufacturer meant, "Vroooom"! I am going with Ande for Kui's fifteen-month check up in Honolulu. This kid is a jokester already.

You are out, perhaps with Roly or perhaps you are just not answering. I want you to know how I regret not being with you at this time, if only to hold your hand, as you get the biopsy results in the morning. Please call no matter what. This is such an important time (of course, all the time is important time!). May all goodness be upon you today. Drive safely, think happy thoughts, know you are beloved, and hold me in your heart.

Monday, o Monday, how divine. But, I do not understand why you've changed your dates and need to leave before Christmas?

I have dutifully done as you requested: you are booked to return to San Francisco on December 16th.

I am disappointed you won't stay with me over the holiday, especially when I am paying for this flight! How ungrateful you are! There are excellent oncologists and cancer clinics here. You could refill your little pill prescriptions and anything else you need on Maui.

I am miffed.

From: Wylie Hymen wylie@hymenfables.com
Date: December 5, 2009
To: Ariane Altar ariane@altarpots.com
Subject: I will be there

Winter Winds Cold and Blea

Winter winds cold and blea
Chilly blows o'er the lea:
Wander not out to me,
Jenny (Ariane) so fair,
Wait in thy cottage free.
I will be there

Pants On Fire!

Wait in thy cushioned chair
Wi'thy white bosom bare.
Kisses are sweetest there:
Leave it for me.
Free from the chilly air
I will meet thee.
How sweet can courting prove,
How can I kiss my love
Muffled in hat and glove
From the chill air?
Quaking beneath the grove,
What love is there!
Lay by thy woolen vest,
Drape no cloak o'er thy breast:
Where my hand oft has pressed,
Pin nothing there:
Where my head droops to rest,
Leave its bed bare.

John Clare (1793-1864)

●

Postcard From Wylie To Ariane
December 17, 2009
North Bay, CA
The Kiss, Klimt

This morning leaving Hana—comforting, teary-eyed memories of our December sojourn into deeper communion, images of you, dear Ariane, lying beside me, hand in mine, naked on rose petaled sheets, our bodies bathed in Hana breezes, talking, sipping dark coffee from Italian flowered cups, my face nestled in your soft bush, and we laugh, your voice soothing my thoughts away from the fears and dark foreboding of what lurks, threatening me, and more of these times together from within my body feeling now, only the pleasures of your loving caresses—the mind tingling pleasure from watching, feeling, you sit, slide, atop my tall and swollen lotus root, sinking back to lay your head between my feet, I feel the soft brushing of your hair across my arches, as your hips raise and lower, now toward the ceiling, now toward the floor, and I can think of nothing, nothing, only aware of the dazzling sensations coursing

221

from the tip of my shaft through the top of my skull, carrying me out into the heavens like a shooting star in a vast Milky Way of our own creation, these memories will carry me through this winter of uncertainty and, most surely, despair.

From: Ariane Altar ariane@altarpots.com
Date: December 17, 2009
To: Cherry Estrella cherry@starsearch.com, Mom ednawolfeson@peoplepc.com, Ande andeP@gmail.com
Subject: terminal cancer

Well, Wylie has come and gone. We "happy campers" got some hideous news. He has a rare form of non-Hodgkin's lymphoma called Mantle Cell Lymphoma. Deadly. Only 15,000 people have had it. They have tried all the nasty treatments but basically haven't found a cure for it. It's been a scream-y, weepy night. Of course, I'll stand with him through all this. But, you know, there's part of me that just wants to say screw it and run away. I don't want death around me again. Sometimes I get tired of being "strong." I don't want to be in situations where I HAVE to be strong! I can't bear the "knowledge" (whatever that means) that cancer is hanging over us like some ghoulish specter.

From: Ariane Altar ariane@altarpots.com
Date: December 17, 2009
To: Wylie Hymen wylie@hymenfables.com
Photos: Hana in December, the windswept cliffs we walked above Kawaloa, Alau Island, Lehoula beach, and our bed of roses

When I was going through divorce, I was in a state of shock, then grief. It really helped me to understand that there are five levels of emotion associated with loss. They don't appear in any specific order, and they often surface over and over. It helped to know it was "normal" to feel the ways I did. As you are facing your changing health and perhaps its loss, you may also feel some grief, particularly if you lose any of the freedom you have always experienced. I am sending you this info with love.

U.S. National Library of Medicine:

People who are grieving may have crying spells, some trouble sleeping, and lack of productivity at work. Grief is a reaction to a major loss. It is most often an unhappy and painful emotion. There can be five stages of grief. These reactions might not occur in a specific order, and can (at times) occur together. Not everyone experiences all of these emotions:

Denial, disbelief, numbness
Anger, blaming others
Bargaining (for instance "If I am cured of this cancer, I will never smoke
again.")
Depressed mood, sadness, and crying
Acceptance, coming to terms

From: Wylie Hymen wylie@hymenfables.com
Date: December 20, 2009
To: Ariane Altar ariane@altarpots.com

since feeling is first
who pays any attention
to the syntax of things
will never wholly kiss you;
wholly to be the fool
while Spring is in the world
my blood approves
and kisses are a better fate
than wisdom
lady i swear by all flowers. Don't cry
– the best gesture of my brain is less than
your eyelids' flutter which says
we are for each other: then
laugh, leaning back in my arms
for life's not a paragraph
And death i think is no parenthesis

e e cummings

From: Ariane Altar ariane@altarpots.com
Date: December 20, 2009
To: Wylie Hymen wylie@hymenfables.com
Subject: our days

It is quiet and lonely without you. I hope your conversations with Baron
have been good and that you were able to talk about your cancer and the new
lymphoma. I hope he is supportive. By the way, I've meant to ask if the little pills
you take every morning are for the cancer, or the prostate, or something else?

What do you want me to do about the box of memorabilia Theia sent? I haven't opened it. Do you want it? I can hold it for you or trash it, as I doubt she'll ever get back to us about writing her story, which I am less and less inclined to write.

I may go to a Christmas party with Cherry and Freddie who are in town tonight. Freddie seems kind of down. Cherry hasn't said anything. Maybe it's just a passing mood. We had a huge thunder and lightning storm last night. It's scary to venture out at night in the rains after what happened last month to Carter and Jean! Come back to me.

Expéditeur: Wylie Hymen wylie@hymenfables.com
Date: Sat, 20 Dec 2009
Destinataire: Raf Haloui raf@haloui.com
Objet: Dina's Birthday

Chers Joelle et Raf,

We are planning to take another trip before Dina has to find a new job. What we would like best would be to spend the week of Dina's birthday in France with you. It is a long way off, but it is also a long distance to travel, so we must plan ahead! Dina's birthday is Sunday, April 22. We could arrive after traveling from Venice and Milano through Provence to Toulouse. We could stay until April 29, and then we would have to take a flight to London and return to California by May 1st.

Would our visit mesh with your plans to be in France? In order to get a good fare, we need to know very soon. It would be wonderful to see you in the spring! Please let us know what you think of this plan.

With our very best wishes and gros bisoux, W&D

From: Raf Haloui raf@haloui.com
Date: Thursday, December 21, 2009
To: Wylie Hymen wylie@hymenfables.com
Subject: Re: Dina's Birthday

We are always very happy to have some news from you. Unfortunately, we can't know yet the date of our staying in France. We can't plan anything about meeting you or not. We can know our plans only a few days before. Try to have a nice trip, and if we plan to be in France at this time, we'll be happy to meet you.

Raf

Pants On Fire!

From: Wylie Hymen wylie@hymenfables.com
Date: December 24, 2009
To: Ariane Altar ariane@altarpots.com
Subject: A poem for my love on Christmas Eve

You are in my heart, dear Ariane, always, and forever.

A Red, Red Rose

O my luv's like a red, red rose,
That's newly sprung in June,
O my luv's like the melodie
That's sweetly played in tune.
As fair art thou, my bonnie lass,
So deep in luv am I;
And I will luv thee still, my dear,
Till a' the seas gang dry.
Till a' the seas gang dry, my dear,
And the rocks melt with the sun;
O I will luve thee still, my dear,
When the sands o' life shall run.
And fare thee weel, my only luve,
And fare thee weel awhile!
And I will come again, my luve,
Though it were ten thousand mile.

                                                            Robert Burns

From: Ariane Altar ariane@altarpots.com
Date: Sunday, December 27, 2009
To: Laura Wolfeson lauraw@yahoo.com
Cc: Mom ednawolfeson@peoplepc.com
Subject: your efforts

Dear Laura,

I am glad you came to spend some time with Mom. It is important at this final
stage in her life. Trust me, I understand the challenges. I hope you can appreciate
each other and feel the love you share, despite the years of dysfunction and discord!
I think your suggestions for Mom's safety and care are very practical and valuable:
a safer bed, table, trapeze, and so on. I know you have spent your career studying

geriatric care. I hope you can leave her house on a positive note. I wish you well on your trip back to Johannesburg. Lucky you, going around the world in eighty days!

Ariane

From: Laura Wolfeson lauraw@yahoo.com
Date: December 27, 2009
To: Ariane Altar ariane@altarpots.com
Subject: Re: your efforts

Dear Ariane,

After incredibly abusive treatment from our mother, I can hardly say my experiences trying to keep her safe helped to heal old wounds. Instead, she managed to inflict many more. You asked me to check on her and prepare Thanksgiving dinner for her, so she wouldn't be alone. I flew all the way from South Africa when I got your email on Monday night, arrived Wednesday, cooked for ten, and served turkey at three the next afternoon.

When I arrived, I found her breathing labored, her lower extremities swollen, her lack of strength preventing her from repositioning herself even in bed, her body covered in cuts and bruises from frequent falls, and the arrival of her care givers irregular at best, with many meals left in a refrigerator she could not reach. I felt I could not abandon her.

I have stayed six weeks to organize things around here. Finally, her caregivers understand she cannot be left alone. A nurses' aide from Eritrea will stay at night. A hospital bed was ordered.

But, our dear, sweet mother, Ha Ha, said she wanted me to leave as soon as possible; I was driving her crazy. Me? Driving her crazy? She was driving me crazy! She always has. When I left this afternoon, she said she was sorry. She is the meanest woman I have ever met. And infirmity makes her worse. I only left because I was asked to leave. I did not abandon her. I hope she can find some peace. She better start looking, because she doesn't have long to live.

I think you are a real shit for telling me to come when you know she hates me. She's always loved you best. You never can see the truth.

May we all find peace in the New Year, Ha Ha.

Laura

From: Mom ednawolfeson@peoplepc.com
Date: December 28, 2009
To: Ariane Altar ariane@altarpots.com
Subject: Laura

Dear Emily, I mean, "Ariane,"

Your sister left me at the hospital over Christmas! What an ordeal! She called 911, and the fire department carried me out of here and down all those brick steps on a gurney, four big handsome men. I told her not to call, because it would cost me a thousand dollars that Medicare doesn't cover. But, she went ahead and did it anyway. She never listens. The big boss. Did I tell you, she's fatter than ever? That girl. Anyway, she makes me so nervous, I thought I was having a heart attack. At the hospital, I heard her bossing the staff so loudly, they called security! Then social workers came and wouldn't let me go home if she was going to be there. They filed a report, would you believe, for elder abuse! I don't know what to think of that girl. She is generous on the one hand and angry on the other. She completely took over my house, insulted my caregivers, and held me in a reign of terror.

I am home now; Cassandra finally picked me up from the hospital and brought me home. Laura is packed and gone. I am so relieved. And it is all your fault. You should never have asked her to visit me. I told you I'd given up on her a long time ago. You're a bad, bad girl.

Grrr Your Not So Ferocious and Very Tired Tiger Mama

From: Ariane Altar ariane@altarpots.com
Date: December 28, 2009
To: Wylie Hymen wylie@hymenfables.com
Subject: a poem for you this morning
Photos: Christmas eve on Kaua'i: all of us paddle boarding at sunset; Kui
Christmas morning climbing into *Vroom* car; Ande and Nalu bottling honey
(Nalu knows a thing or two about bees!); Gramma with her Christmas stollen
ready for baking!

December 28th
The Way I Want to Live

The Way I Want to Live
Is with you

Pants On Fire!

In the moment
In every moment
Awakening to crushed rose petals
Clinging pungently to our dawning skin
Sipping aromatic espresso forte in the new day's light
Looking at you
Looking into you
Through your eyes
Your nostrils
Your lips
Your flesh
Gaining entrance
To the realm of spirit
To catch the scent of eternity
To reach to touch to grasp
If only for this moment we share
But which I want to stretch
To stretch as a canvas
Painting our love and longing
A canvas that has no bounds
Wider than the known universe
And deeper
A hologram
Infinitely stretching in all dimensions
Filled with color and shape
Forms amorphous and real
Finite and abstract
A reflection of sweetness
Cut by swaths of bitter
But
Enchanting
Sublime
To hold you in my arms, Wylie
To breathe your kisses
To be succored
Allows my soul to rest
Gives meaning
To our being
In human form
How can I thank you for loving me
And opening your heart to receive my love

Pants On Fire!

You are my jewel
Shining
In the darkness of night
Eyes sparkling like molten amethyst stars
Whose light reaches us
After they have long burnt out
We who have no sense of that elapsed time
Bask in their enchanting light
Dreaming
Content
Deluded
None the less

From: Wylie Hymen wylie@hymenfables.com
Date: December 28, 2009
To: Ariane Altar ariane@altarpots.com

Journeys

        Our journeys began each morning,
with the sun's slanting rays golden on the mountain,
the distant swash of the surf, birdsong, and
awakening to your sparkling, laughing eyes
fixed on mine, the delicate touch of your hands
on my face, beckoning, whispering my name.
        I touched my lips to yours,
we kissed for an eternity, and began
the most delightful journey of all.
Later, after we had loved and loved again,
I reluctantly left you sprawled
in the rumpled sheets, your arms
flung across the bed, your legs apart,
so wickedly winsome still
dotted with the rose petals I collected at dawn,
to sprinkle over your body, calculated to
make you giggle in that way I so love,
returning with coffee and sweet fruit,
an offering, my lips to yours, to our sweet intimacy.
        Soon, reluctantly, you will coax me away from our bed,
and take me out onto your beautiful island . . .

Pants On Fire!

Forgive me if it was not the scenery I was attending to
(though I thrilled to the spirit of discovery and adventure
with which you shared the glories of your world with me).
The waterfalls, deep pools, vistas to the sea, and grasslands
stretching to the foothills, the volcanic mountain itself
had become but a setting for our love and our days together.
Instead, I am intent on the foreground,
on the woman who walks before me,
(and those lovely hips she frets about),
dropping back when the trail widens to take my hand,
arms and shoulders touching mine,
our faces close so that I could inhale
the saltiness of your sun-warmed skin,
as you name for me the trees, and flowers, the birds,
the grasses underfoot and the plants
brushing and tickling my bare legs along the way.
        We travel the earth unaware of passing time,
the boundaries of past and present blurring,
together down steep, meandering paths,
to the green headlands and the precipice,
the end of one world and the beginning of another,
where once you stood, a spot now sacred to you, above crags of black lava
unyielding under the crashing, foaming waves,
to send your precious daughter's ashes on the winds,
to the sea, bidding her god speed and, at last,
peace.
        I have a new sense of time now, my love,
no longer infinite as it once seemed,
stretching out forever beyond all care and thought,
but bounded; my life no less predictable than before and yet,
strangely, more certain in its uncertainty. Still,
I dream, and hope, and love, and play,
promising that will always be my way, but
with a changed perspective, a sharper one in which
I see, and hear, and feel only what is close up,
in time and space, the sensual, the present, now.
My field of view has narrowed, foreshortened,
focused only on what is essential,
writing, drawing, and painting, starry nights,
the frost on the tips of the pine needles,
the rose of cinnabar opening outside our window,

230

Pants On Fire!

and especially on you, Ariane, my lover and friend.

   I am a camera, collecting and hoarding images, hoping,
with such clarity and vividness that they will never fade,
snapshots of your smile, the way your body moves,
how it trembles, and flutters and shudders under mine,
how it sits in a blue chair in quiet repose,
how the azure of your eyes changes with the sky,
and the growing intensity of our love making,
and the color of your skin with each hour of the day,
how the sea breeze swirls your flaxen hair about your face
(just like when you make love to me astride, hips galloping, slowing as you
bend over to press your lips against mine, and then canter toward the highlands
of our love).

   I listen in a different way, intently as always for meaning,
and because your voice so delights me, but now
because I want always be able to hear your voice,
especially your laughter, I hold on to each word
a moment longer. The sounds, the nuances, how
your voice gently breaks in that way of a child's voice,
will fade, of course but only after I have made them mine
to hold on to forever.

   And the song I once quoted to you? The words
taken on new meaning over the last few weeks,
touching me deeply now, heavy hearted to tears,
and become a gentle reminder; it is November, and
I haven't got time for the waiting game.

   I want to enjoy every moment of this life,
not put off the dreams and the joys, especially the joys.
These precious days, dear Ariane,
I spend with you.

From: Ariane Altar ariane@altarpots.com
Date: December 31, 2009
To: Wylie Hymen wylie@hymenfables.com

   My, my, my. I couldn't get past the second verse without being blinded. My
reading prescription is outdated and, between the crying and the desperation to
read, it has been hard going. But, now I have finished. Your words. Isn't it amazing how honest emotion can come to life even on the page? You have done it well.

Thank you for these reflections of our combined experience. I cherish them...and you, darling, dearest you.

You make me chuckle: the unexpected package, wow! espresso forte!, the Klimt (how did he capture us so well?), the words...I just sat in my truck at the post office and chuckled. Dear, sweet you. I am over the moon about you, as they say, Wylie. I am also pleased about the happiness Matthew brings by coming back into your life.

This morning I awoke remembering it is the last day of 2009. The year you leapt into my life and heart bringing such joy, pleasure, fun, happiness, friendship, and love. It is also the year my oldest friend, Selene, vanished. A year of blissfully becoming a grandmother, beginning my monthly treks to Kaua'i where I learned more about the Hawai'ian family and community, and savored a sweet mother/daughter year with Ande.

2010 heralds the Chinese Year of the White Tiger. I wish a very happy new year for us all.

From: Wylie Hymen wylie@hymenfables.com
Date: January 1, 2010
To: Ariane Altar Ariane@altarpots.com

You were delightful last night, sniffles and all.

Thoughts along the road today: I know that over the years I've become more thoughtful and surely more aware, and while I don't think I am insensitive, I'd always felt there's something lacking in me, holes in my consciousness where there ought to be feelings, feelings I appreciated in others – empathy, or acceptance, or communion – but didn't feel, feelings I wished I could have, feelings which would make me more complete, a better companion, or lover, or friend. Until you came into my life, Ariane, and helped me to find what I had always been wanting. You are the strongest, most compassionate, most loving person I have ever known, and when I first met you I was in awe of your power, your ability to love wholly and unconditionally. I wondered in those early days before you invited me to be your lover, whether you would find me worthy of that love.

But, in a marvelous turn of events, dear Ariane, you have become my mentor, my guide through the intricacies of the heart and the emotions. You have shown me a way of loving, a boundless, deeper, more open love, freer of inhibitions than I have ever known, opening me to welcome and embrace emotions and feelings that had never visited me before. When I've been judgmental (old stuff I struggle to overcome), you gently guide me toward compassion, and a kinder way to see others. When I am uncomprehending, you help me not just to comprehend but, by example, to find my own way toward understanding and acceptance. My love, I'm stumbling around here trying to find words I don't know to express feelings I don't know how to express.

Simply, your love has brought me immense joy as the you of you graces my life beyond measure.

From: Ariane Altar ariane@altarpots.com
Date: January 3, 2010
To: Wylie Hymen wylie@hymenfables.com
Subject: Fwd: Karen Borders sent you a message on *Facebook*

I just got the message below from someone I don't know. Is she a friend of yours? How in the world would this person put my name and yours together?

Date: December 31, 2009
To: Ariane Altar ariane@altarpots.com
Subject: Karen Borders sent you a message on *Facebook*...

"Are you Ariane of the lovely pottery, Wylie from Indian Springs' friend?"

Who is she?

Woke thinking of you returning home. Saw an image of a tree digger boring a hole into the earth with its screw-like mechanism...and thought of the mud and moisture and deep soft earth...and the delicious feeling of returning home and putting your feet like roots into your own soil, onto your floors, on your carpet...and the replenishment traveling through the earth of your home through the soles of your feet, up through your legs, swelling into your torso to your heart where at last you would feel the peace and deep comfort of "being at home".

Center yourself. The world, people, emotions, events, adventures, health issues, past present and future have been bombarding you of late, and now it seems is your time to regroup and calm down and restore your balance and self with all the new stimuli. I hope you can rest, my darling; nap. Go softly into yourself, curl around yourself like a kitty cat, purr and snooze, and replenish yourself with yourself. Take a cue from Pearly and Gates. I think that is what "coming home" feels like.

In the event you have to have chemo or radiation, I think we should do it together. I'll organize a house sitter on my end and fly over. I found these places we might rent in Berkeley. I don't think you'd get proper rest at Baron's or my mom's. I can cook and minister to all your needs in a nest of our own. Our rest nest.

Pants On Fire!

I hate not being with you when you get the bone marrow done next week and again when you get the results. I am sorry, my darling. It is such a busy time for me. But, I know you feel reassured having your son, Dr. Matthew, fly down to hear the news with you.

From: Wylie Hymen wylie@hymenfables.com
Date: January 4, 2010
To: Ariane Altar ariane@altarpots.com
Subject: a morning memory

A Morning Memory

Late morning. We have been making love
and talking in a light rain since dawn,
and you have gotten up from the bed,
leaving me sitting there aglow,
your scent strong on my beard and face,
and the spicy flavors of your body still
rich on my tongue, and I want more,
my love, I want you again.
So searching the house, I find you,
standing barefoot at the window in the kitchen,
radiant, beautiful in your white gown.
I surprise you, wrapping my arms around your waist,
my hands enjoying the roundness of your sweet belly,
rubbing my lips and face on your shoulders,
and the downy hairs on the back of your neck,
and then, taking your hands in mine,
I lead you back through the house
to our bedroom, you giggling all the way,
because I am hard, poking out
through the front of my robe.
Standing at the edge of the bed I hold you,
and when I slide my hands up under your gown,
up your willowy legs,
the folds of cotton billowing over my arm,
you take me between your thighs,
kissing me and looking into my eyes
that long, deep way that you do.
And when I lay you back on the bed,

234

you wrap your legs tightly around my waist,
making me one with you, and we lie silent,
because you have taken my breath away, and
because I am unable to find words
to express the ecstasy of that moment,
and how enthralled I am in your love,
my dear Ariane.

From: Cherry Estrella cherry@starsearch.com
Date: January 4, 2010
To: Ariane Altar ariane@altarpots.com
Subject: should we ladies offer them proof positive?

World News
    The G-spot 'doesn't appear to exist', say researchers. The elusive erogenous zone said to exist in some women may be a myth. Their study in the "Journal of Sexual Medicine" is the biggest yet, involving 1,800 women. The King's College London team believes the G-spot may be a figment of women's imagination, encouraged by magazines and sex therapists.
    "It is rather irresponsible to claim the existence of an entity that has never been proven and pressurize women and men, too." The Gräfenberg Spot, or G-Spot, was named in honor of the German gynecologist Ernst Gräfenberg who described it over 50 years ago and is said to sit in the front wall of the vagina some 2-5 cm up.

From: Wylie Hymen wylie@hymenfables.com
Date: January 16, 2010
To: Ariane Altar ariane@altarpots.com
Subject: Night and Two Hearts

Night

In just a few moments,
sitting in the dark,
warm by the flickering fire,
I will call you knowing that
at the first sound of your voice
and laughter, all cares and

any sadness that have visited me
in the day will disappear
in the sweet embrace of your love.

Two hearts

Oh, Ariane,
I awoke to your heart beating,
returned, clear and strong,
a joyful sound I've been missing.
For days and weeks now, that beat,
which lives in me, the cadence,
counterpoint, and rhythm of my days,
has been all but stifled by fear and
the specter of sickness and death.
But now it has returned to me,
beating once again in time with mine,
counting, not the years I have left,
but the seconds and minutes until
I will be in your arms again.

From: Wylie Hymen wylie@hymenfables.com
Date: Jan 22, 2010
To: Ariane Altar ariane@altarpots.com
Subject: Just flat out bragging

Just look at this news from my editor!

Hi Wylie!

You might have already heard but we got official notification yesterday of
our 2010 Notables and *Where's Noah's Ark?* was on the list! Congratulations!
Erica

From Wylie to Ariane
Date: January 22, 2010
Letter and Drawing of Ariane's hands at rest, Drawing of Ariane's breasts

My Love,

Inspired as always by your hands—how they feel upon my skin, how they
create such temples of beauty, I sat in my window seat and sketched them for you

today. My only wish is that your firm but delicate touch will stroke me all the days—and nights, I have left.

You are my muse, you know. I am seriously drawing again. Nudes. I am keeping most of them here for my pleasure and am only sending you this line drawing of your hands and another of your precious breasts. I draw you from my mind's eye, over and over. I turn you over. I sketch your tush from every perspective. I hover like a lover above you and sketch your face in rapture, then your breasts, and on to your precious mound below. I may start to add color. But, what I ask, what is the color of nectar?

Your Hands

When your hands go out,
love, toward mine,
what do they bring me flying?
Why did they stop
at my mouth, suddenly,
why do I recognize them
as if then, before,
I had touched them,
as if before they existed
they had passed over
my forehead, my waist?
Their softness came
flying over time,
over the sea, over the smoke,
over the spring,
and when you placed
your hands on my chest,
I recognized those golden
dove wings,
I recognized that clay
and that color of wheat.
All the years of my life
I walked around looking for them.
I went up the stairs,
I crossed the roads,
trains carried me,
and in the skin of grapes
I thought I touched you.
The wood suddenly

Pants On Fire!

brought me your touch,
the almond announced to me
your secret softness,
until your hands
closed on my chest
and there like two wings
they ended their journey.

Pablo Neruda

From: Wylie Hymen wylie@hymenfables.com
Date: January 27, 2010
To: Ariane Altar ariane@altarpots.com
Subject: Losing it

Did I leave my swim suit there last visit? I can't find it here.

From: Wylie Hymen wylie@hymenfables.com
Date: January 27, 2010
To: Ariane Altar ariane@altarpots.com
Subject: Finding it but . . .

I found my swimsuit. But, now I can't find the red shirt you gave me. The sun is shining today, and I'm all excited about seeing you soon.

From: Ariane Altar ariane@altarpots.com
Date: January 28, 2010
To: Wylie Hymen wylie@hymenfables.com
Subject: Smoke signals

Chief Running Bare,

Did I get your smoke signals right, the ones you sent from Chicken Ridge? Pants···On···Fire! Found··· bathing··· suit. Need··· water!
My advice: Bring··· a long··· hose!

Princess Burning Bush

238

Pants On Fire!

From: Wylie Hymen wylie@hymenfables.com
Date: January 28, 2010
To: Ariane Altar ariane@altarpots.com
Subject: Re: Smoke signals

Princess Burning Bush,

    Set my blanket on fire sending those darned signals and nearly burned down the whole forest flapping it in the air! Lots of burnt chicken for dinner tonight! Ha ha!
    My hose is packed.

Chief Running Bare

From: Ariane Altar ariane@altarpots.com
Date: January 28, 2010
To: Wylie Hymen wylie@hymenfables.com
Subject: hot!

Dear Mr. Pants On Fire,

    I can no longer call you Chief Running Bare, as you must get dressed for your flight. You are probably the only person airport security will let on board carrying fireworks in your pants! I can't wait to kiss you and be in your arms.

Love, Princess Burning Bush

●

From: Ariane Altar ariane@altarpots.com
Date: February 12, 2010
To: Wylie Hymen wylie@hymenfables.com

    I am always at a loss for what to say when you leave me to return to the mainland. I suppose the fresh loss of you makes me quiet. Silent. Numb, as though paralyzed by the sad prospect of time without you.

    The desire of the moth for the star,
    Of the night for the morrow,

Pants On Fire!

The devotion to something afar,
From the sphere of our sorrow.

Percy Bysshe Shelley

I want, however, to thank you for coming and for the blissful days we shared. Every moment felt perfect (except our last night, which was pure misery). I wrote a poem, which I hope can express the incandescence of our love, and the fire it stokes, a fire that burns in my soul, our private inferno of joy.

February 12th
Burning Bed

Our sheets are scorched
Our skins scalded
And swathed in steam
We lay each other
Gently
With a sacred fluidity
Atop a pyre
Coals
At the ready
Glowing
Below

Flick a spark,
I dare you,
My incendiary,
My arsonist,
You seditionist of love
Flick a spark

Now
With your golden rod
Flick a spark

Consume us
In the final sea of flames
Hellfire and brimstone
I care not

Pants On Fire!

Shower me
Blanket me
(No, no, the blankets
Burned to cinders long ago)
Shoot
Spray me
With sparks
Ignite
St Elmo's Fire
Once more in my loins
My love

Propel us
Into
That final eclipse
And let
Our love singe
Broil and blacken
The very sun
Curl
Its shadowed edges
Toward oblivion's
Black Hole

Let your luminous plasma
Thunder through my inner storm
Fueling an incandescent ball of light
To thrust us across the electric field of night
Let white fire stream in our wake
As we hurtle semi-conscious
Across a cold and limitless cosmos

Let our pyre blaze
As meteor showers
Ignite the heavens
To sizzle the midnight spheres
A celestial conflagration
For all to see
And may our love
Roar

Pants On Fire!

Crackling
For all to hear
And may they marvel
And look to the sky
Look to the smoldering sky
And pray

Part Three

Liar, Liar

Waning Of The Moon

Postcard From Wylie to Dina
February 10, 2010
Sent from Hana, HI
Haleakala summit

Pooky,

You were wise not to come, as the altitude and harsh conditions inside the crater would have been too hard on you. But, oh, how you would have loved the views (as you can see from this postcard)! The vast moonscape of ever changing colors is awe-inspiring. I'll be home before you get this.

Aloha, my love, Wylie

From: Ariane Altar ariane@altarpots.com
Date: February 12, 2010
To: Cherry Estrella cherry@starsearch.com
Subject: Wylie's time with me in Hana

Dear Cherry,

I took Wylie back to the airport this morning after his too brief, as always, too brief visit. He is stellar, but sadly, the cancer is spreading. He says he feels fine. We are living it up while the sun shines. We whale watched at dawn, dined at seaside restaurants, and hiked the crater—awed as always by its vastness and colors. He even got to meet Ande and Kui, when we took Kui to the aquarium and Mission House. It was not only a heavenly time but also our best time yet.

He brought notebooks and filled dozens with sketches—of yours truly. My god. He amazes me with these new drawings! I can't show them to a soul as they're all nudes of me and far too flattering. On the other hand, they're absolutely gorgeous, and probably no one would guess who inspired them!

Anyway, he is sketching and painting furiously. He has made a career of his pen and ink line drawings for his children's books, but these nude drawings are quite remarkable (and not because they're me!). He loved the colors here—the many hues of orange, red, yellow, and green on a single mango, for example, coloring my form in imitation of the fruit. Everything sensual, edible, or fragrant seems to inspire him. He can't find enough time in the day or night to paint and to make love. He is truly a man on fire!

How am I taking it all? As odd as it seems, burnt out. I am feeling both let down and uneasy! Expectations and disappointments, I guess. I am a tangle of emotions! Why? I hate the long distance relationship and the toll it takes on my heart when we part. I fixed myself a tall gin and tonic tonight when I got home from taking him to the airport!

Here's the deal: I was fully expecting him to propose or to make a major commitment. It's been over a year of grand passion and professed love. With his cancer, I thought his priorities would have clarified: he would want me in this final phase of his life, you know, to go out in a blaze of glory and not be alone at the end. I thought he would, at the very least, broach living together.

We have writing projects going; we madly adore one another, we want to travel, he loves Hana, and I need to be in California to help my mom. Perfect. Or so I think. But Wylie? I am clueless.

I need your insight: why didn't he propose? Does he want to be isolated and deal with his cancer alone? Is he commitment phobic?

Wylie announced he plans to go with his adult sons to England on a "family" trip this spring, a trip I had planned for us. He told me he just learned that one of them, the doctor, Matthew, would be lecturing at Oxford. I am disappointed for myself, but understand. While he is there, I'll probably come visit you in Napa Valley, if you'll have me, and my mom in Berkeley.

From: Ariane Altar ariane@altarpots.com
Date: February 16, 2010
To: Wylie Hymen wylie@hymenfables.com
Subject: dates

Do you have dates yet for England? Don't know if this travel deal might be

helpful for your trip: try *Virgin* for cheap fares. I was planning to use it for OUR trip, if you recall. They actually give you six nights in a London hotel free!

I have an idea for you to consider: if I come to the mainland to see my mom, and if you book your London ticket with a stop in Chicago or New York, then maybe you and I could meet in one of those cities? I would love that! I am ready for a large dose of museums and theatre! Lucas says he is willing to take care of my place if I travel when he comes to guest minister at Wananalua Church in Hana.

From: Ariane Altar ariane@altarpots.com
Date: February 16, 2010
To: Juan Silver jsilver@gmail.com
Subject: Your fiancée

You really are remarkable, Juan, or are you simply stoic? How can you put your recent engagement in the past so fast? I thought you were head over heels?

From: Juan Silver jsilver@gmail.com
Date: February 16, 2010
To: Ariane Altar ariane@altarpots.com
Subject: Re: your fiancée

I don't even remember, "What's her name?" I was engaged to last fall! "Batter up!" I say!

○

From: Wylie Hymen wylie@hymenfables.com
Date: February 20, 2010
To: Ariane Altar ariane@altarpots.com
Subject: Fears and Doubts

Ariane –
[A letter was begun early yesterday morning, but when finished seemed irrelevant. Two more followed, confronting some bothersome concerns in our relationship that at first seemed crucial but now unimportant in light of all that burst into my mind over the day and last night. Perhaps I will send those letters later, but for now, I must try to focus on what is vital. I'm sorry for the abruptness and that this is fragmentary, but I hope you will soon understand, it is all that I'm capable of right now.]

Pants On Fire!

Tuesday/
Dear Ariane,

I've been up most of the night, alternately scribbling down thoughts arising from our talk and reading the *Love Letters and Poems of Wylie and Ariane* you had bound, your Valentine's gift, which I treasure. I need to write rather than talk to give us both time and space to consider what this all means. Besides, I'm just too emotionally fragile to talk on the phone. This will be a long, rambling letter, considered with great care as is everything I write to you, but especially, because at the end of it, we will each have decisions to make about nothing less than the most valued friendship and love of my entire life.

The good news: the curator for the contemporary collection at the De Young wants to see my nude series. He left a couple of messages while I was in Hana. I spoke with him yesterday, and he wants to drive up here. I guess word got out from my publishers that I was "up to no good" painting nudes instead of writing. Curiosity must have gotten the best of him. I am nervous, wary, this is such new work, and if he likes it, will I live long enough to finish the big pieces and mount an exhibition? I tremble at the very thought of culminating my career before the art world with images of beautiful you, yes, you, my love, wrapped in our poetry of love.

The sun is up now, the dark hours behind me. I tremble, too, aware of what is at stake here. I want to be holding your hand, my love, looking into your eyes.

Our talk last night unleashed a whole torrent of thoughts and was welcome for many reasons. You opened your heart to speak to me not only about love but your fears and doubts, bravely and, as always, with touching sensitivity. You took it upon yourself to begin a transition that occurs in every relationship – a necessary time out from love-blinded bliss to consider reality – sooner than most, because ours has been a breathtaking love measured not in years but a few months and we, especially me, are conscious of passing time. You and I take life in big gulps, jumping headlong into its adventures, and now both of us have taken a step back to look at one another and this love of ours more closely.

Interestingly, the feelings and concerns you expressed last night about me, I have also had about you. Here we are, come to that point of asking the two most important questions – Who is this man, really? Who is this woman? Thank you for getting us here.

[I'm breaking off from the rest of the letter, which explains what follows better, but now I'm skipping to . . .]

You wondered how many women there are in my life, and there is, and has been for many years, only one, Dina. What you fear as my secretiveness – the big one last night – I see as being discreet. I have a different (old fashioned?) sense of what's hurtful and what's appropriate. The reason you've heard little about Dina is that I find it uncomfortable and, in my world, rude, even inconsiderate, to talk about lovers, certainly never, as you do. I have been more focused on our present than on my past, because that's where I want to be with us, that's where I want to be now in life. But, you have asked.

In contrast, it's been very different with you, and me, and Juan. You have certainly been forthcoming with details of your life together and explained to me your hopes for keeping that relationship. I respect greatly your efforts to perpetuate and honor that love, because it reaffirms for me your compassionate nature (which I have tried so hard to emulate). But, I have, frankly, lived uncomfortably in a strange ménage with you two – I'm not sure we've ever had a time together when you didn't talk about him. His photo has greeted me each morning on your bureau. In my strange way of caring, I do not have photos of Dina up when you are here. Still, it also helps me explain Dina to you. You and Juan were together a long time, and it is clear, to me, at least, that a big piece of your heart remains with him and his with you.

Dina and I were lovers for ten years and friends for the past two. It's sad she can't know you. Like you, she is a brilliant, talented woman, and you are sisters in the theatre. Before you, she was my most sensitive confidante, but with a sometimes-hardened New York edge, which caused her, when we first met, to find it strange that I cried in movies and plays. Like you and Juan, Dina and I have shared many experiences, traveled the world together, and built a history. From the beginning, we crafted a relationship that respected our individual needs, especially independence and the freedom to explore my art and other friendships. Yes, she has a piece of my heart as I a piece of hers, and I continue to honor that love.

Wednesday/
Dear, dear Ariane,

I awoke crying in the dark this morning, trying to comfort myself saying your sweet name over and over. Since returning from the comfort of your arms and warm breast, I have been swept up in a maelstrom of unfathomable emotions and mood swings. Actually, it had begun before I came to you, but my days with you quieted the turmoil, and you were a gift of life and peaceful refuge from the din of voices.

I've talked about this more than I care to, but I don't want you to be fooled by my physical energy. I am emotionally very frail right now, exacerbated by the results of my recent scan (though neither Dr. Doggett, Dr. Mills, nor my son, dear Dr. Matthew Hymen, seem troubled by it).

I am only beginning to grasp the shock of this cancer and confrontation with death. If only I could explain what it is like for me, then I could calm your fears and doubts. I find myself from moment to moment in a storm of fleeting emotions and feelings, which I am unable to hold long enough to understand, feelings that take me by surprise and sadden me deeply. Just such a storm overcame me as we lay together in the dark of our last night.

I had fallen into a profound sadness, and saw for the first time that night, fear cloud your bright, glowing face, as you began to confront your own doubts and fears about us as you encountered for the first time the darkness in me, your lover. But, I was helpless to calm you, resorting to, I'm sure, ineffectual and inane explanation.

But worse, I am confronted with terrible contradictions. I want to be in your life and so much to have you in mine, but right now it is impossible for me to see how that can happen. In recent weeks, I have struggled to counter and dispel frightening forces tugging at me. Understand how terrible this is for me. As I am drawn delightfully closer and closer to you, immersed in the soothing warmth of your love, as I enjoy scenes of us being together and traveling the world, I wrestle with an opposing force pulling me back, back to the familiar, back to my life here, my comforting daily routines, my safe haven, closer to the new connections to my grown children and grand girls. Closer to the new art I am creating, albeit inspired by you and our love. At times, I can see before me, enticing visions of our joy together, inviting glimpses of what might be, but when I reach out to hold and savor them, they fade from my grasp. The only reality of you is my drawings.

If I seem vague and strange around the upcoming trip with Baron and Matthew, it is not to exclude you, but because it has taken on the feeling of a "sacred journey". It is precisely the kind of pilgrimage you made with your daughters to Italy after your Nico died. I dream of traveling with you, my Ariane, but in less troubled and desperate times. I travel with you always in my dreams.

Do not fear; I am neither giving up nor giving in, but I have to stop and pay attention to what is happening to me, hoping to emerge, if not the Wylie you know, then one wiser and more understanding of the mysteries of death and life.

You are a gift, dear Ariane, which I have treasured more than any other I have ever received. I feel blessed to have had every moment of what we have together, just thankful to be with you and, as is my way, not asking for or expecting anything more. I can only hope my love has nourished you in the way yours has nourished me.

But, your expectations are growing and are very different from mine right now, and I know that in this way I am a disappointment (there's that word again).

I don't know where all this leaves us. I am profoundly saddened, sensing that what I can offer you is not enough and knowing you deserve more. But, in all truth, my love, I am unable to offer or promise anything more than what we have now.

Your Wylie, loving you with all my heart

250

Pants On Fire!

From: Ariane Altar ariane@altarpots.com
Date: February 20, 2010
To: Wylie Hymen wylie@hymenfables.com

Wylie!

Did you just send me a "Dear John" letter? Are you telling me "goodbye"?

From: Wylie Hymen wylie@hymenfables.com
Date: February 20, 2010
To: Ariane Altar ariane@altarpots.com

No. I'll call. I'll feel better if we talk.

From: Ariane Altar ariane@altarpots.com
Date: February 21, 2010
To: Wylie Hymen wylie@hymenfables.com

What I can't understand, and what troubles me still, happened on our last night together. Why did you say those crazy things to me in the dark? Why wouldn't you be my last lover? That I would have many more after you? Ouchie! That felt hurtful and out of place. I cannot even think that way. I know you have terminal cancer, but really, talking that way unnerved me.

I'm sorry now that I left the bed, but I was being honest. I wish I had slept with you. But, since my children died, "last nights" and "goodbyes" are just too loaded for me. They are hard. Loss, loss, loss is all my mind can hear, and I can't bear it. I just didn't want to get emotional, and I knew I would, and maybe this time I wouldn't be able to contain my despair, and that is a fear that terrifies me.

I don't know when I'll see you—more cause for painful uncertainty. If I can come in March to see mom, I shall···but I don't know. I appreciate your offer to take me to your book signing on the 27th.

Then you'll go on your "sacred journey" in April. Another April without you. Like last year when you went to New York. I hate this long distance stuff. I just wish you'd get that one way ticket to Hawai'i like I have asked a thousand times and be here with me.

How about consoling me (you know, kiss the ouchie in my heart and make it all better?) by promising a short and special little trip together in May or September? Please, please, let's go to India after the monsoons! I mentioned a trip to India months ago. I would like it so.

Pants On Fire!

The conversation between Ariane and Cherry
February 22, 2010

Ariane: I need to say something that's bothering me about Wylie. I told you I really expected him to propose when he was here, and he didn't. It's not that I want to be married, but rather that after a year of being passionately in love, I think a man makes some sort of commitment, don't you? Do you think he didn't because of the cancer?

Cherry: Absolutely. When I was diagnosed with breast cancer, I thought Freddie would depart, pronto. I certainly didn't expect him to stay! I felt I had to face it on my own. But, a few days after I told him about the cancer, he said, "Well, I expect we'd better get on with the treatment. I am going to take care of you." And, he did! I was really surprised.

Ariane: And, you married him! Juan asked me to marry him every five minutes in our eight years together. Maybe it is the cancer with Wylie. I guess I don't know what it feels like to have cancer hanging over my head.

Cherry: Is he taking medication or having radiation?

Ariane: No radiation or chemo yet. He takes pills every morning, but I'm not sure what they are for. He's moody, though, crying a lot.

Cherry: I cried a lot, too.

Ariane: Say hi to Freddie for me.
Cherry: Oh dear. I hate to say anything, but Freddie is not doing too well.

Ariane: Why? What's wrong?

Cherry: We just don't know. He is down. Won't talk much. I've made a slew of doctors' appointments. He's been taking pain medication for his back for years. The moods might have something to do with that.

Letter from Wylie to Ariane
Sent February 16, 2010
From North Bay, CA
Received February 23, 2010
Hana, Hawai'i

Pants On Fire!

Valentine Letter and Heart Drawing
A (belated) bouquet of hearts for Ariane my love—Wylie
Each crimson line wraps around intertwining hearts
Memories of City
For candlelight dinners
Making love on the cool grass
Talking about books and movies
For all our delicious love making
Talk of happiness with grandchildren
Sharing stories of our lives and adventures
For our walks on the beach and splashing together in the surf
For sharing the art of your ceramics and the mysteries of glazes
Soaping your sweet body in the shower, especially all the hidden crags
Sunny breakfasts on the lanai looking over the sparkling ocean and the hills
golden in the morning sun
How I feel
When you make love to me
And hold me tightly to you in the night
Your ankles crossed over my sacrum, heels pressing my back,
Your luscious jade gates melting as they open, drawing my lotus root through,
Winging us singing and sighing to our own special heaven on earth

From: Ariane Altar ariane@altarpots.com
Date: February 23, 2010
To: Wylie Hymen wylie@hymenfables.com
Subject: sweetheart mail

Just picked up my mail and there was your beautiful, happy Valentine. It took me a long time to decipher each special heart, turning and turning, and then making certain I'd read them all, by reading them all again.

It was great to receive, because I had had a wild and fast ride down the Hana Highway with some stand-up yabbo on a motorcycle near Keanae throwing finger at me (you know which one). Your sweetness counters his sourness! I think the guy was on crystal meth and really got excited when he saw an old blonde lady he could harass. If I'd had a pitcher of estrogen handy, I'd have thrown it his way to calm his testosterone rush! It was frightening. The last thing I need is another accident! I hope your drive was saner than mine, and you have a divine time. By the way, where are you going?

Pants On Fire!

From: Wylie Hymen wylie@hymenfables.com
Date: February 23, 2010
To: Ariane Altar ariane@altarpots.com
Subject: Your gifts

Love and Renewal

Slipping into darkness so deep
I fear no return, I call to you,
and your voice from afar, strong,
calm, always reassuring,
brings me back to the light,
and fills my heart with bright images
of the delights of our days together
and the warmth of your touch.
Thank you, dear Ariane for your gift
of the most beautiful love I have known,
renewed dreams, visions of the joys to come,
and hope.

From: Ariane Altar ariane@altarpots.com
Date: February 23, 2010
To: Wylie Hymen wylie@hymenfables.com

Your long email a few days ago felt like a "Dear John" letter. I really thought you were saying "Goodbye." You haven't called or emailed in days. I've been disconsolate. Your belated Valentine arriving in the post gave me a bit of sweetness to savor.

But, I feel like I, too, went through great darkness those days after we parted. It was draining. And I, too, feel alive in and renewed by your love.

Please don't go into a dark cave again. And don't go silent. And don't push me away. Promise me. Trust me. I know you are frightened. I need to be able to be with you in those bad times as well as the good.

○

Pants On Fire!

From: Wylie Hymen wylie@hymenfables.com
Date: February 24, 2010
To: Ariane Altar ariane@altarpots.com
Subject: Trust

I have been physically ill all morning, knowing that I have done something terrible, something contrary to my values, not knowing how to make it right, worse, fearing it can never be made right again. I fear the loss of my balance and my center. I see our love as a fragile little bird that I have carelessly injured, but am at a loss as to what to do to make her whole and able to fly again.

My son leaves mid-day tomorrow. I shall call as soon as he goes.

I know you have no reason to believe me. Nothing I can say can excuse what I have done – I take full responsibility for my dreadful act – but I need to say, Ariane, that I, too, have known the deep ache of uncertainty and jealousy. Your love dispelled my fears and allowed me to put those feelings to rest some time ago, never intending to even think of them. But, once again, it's clear lives at our ages can be complicated.

I didn't intend to mention it, but I, too, have been ambushed. One morning while I was there, I awoke your computer to check my email. What appeared on the screen, and I read, was an email from a one-time lover hoping to be with you again. Who is he?

I don't want a relationship with someone I cannot trust, and I don't want to be in a relationship in which I am not trusted and under constant suspicion. I know, too, it is not a matter of putting all this out of mind; nothing less than healing and fully restoring your trust in me will do. I hope that we can find in our love what we need to make this happen.

To lose your love, Ariane, would be to lose one of the most treasured gifts I have ever received. Please talk to me about what I must do to deserve and keep it.

Wylie

From: Ariane Altar ariane@altarpots.com
Date: February 24, 2010
To: Cherry Estrella cherry@starsearch.com, Mom ednawolfeson@peoplepc.com, Lucas Dmitri lucas@unityworld.org, Juan Silver jsilver@gmail.com, Ande andeP@gmail.com

Pants On Fire!

Dear Ones,

Sad and startling news: I have broken up with Wylie!

Why? Today, on the phone, he lied to me! Big, fat, monstrous lies! Can you imagine: Mr. Sensitive Mild Mannered Professor Writer Artist Intellectual Cancer Victim turns out to be a BALD-FACED LIAR?

Angry, Angry, Angry, Ariane

From: Ariane Altar ariane@altarpots.com
Date: February 27, 2010
To: Wylie Hymen wylie@hymenfables.com
Subject: What to say, what to say, when I never, ever want to speak to you again?

The lies—your beyond boundaries of all that is sacred, lies! The lies you are telling me in all our phone conversations. Why? Even now, you are lying about the lies! Look, look at what you have done! You've ruined everything! How long has the lying been going on? From the get-go?

I wasn't born yesterday or the day before. I may be slow to catch on, but I do know a few things. One is that Baron is not with you, as you claim, nor is he ill with cancer, as you claim. That is your foulest lie of all: to say your son has cancer, and you are comforting him, when he is healthy and hundreds of miles away from you in Berkeley. My god. That lie is a sin.

What are you trying to hide? Where do you disappear so often, and, when you disappear, why is your cell phone always off?

As far as I'm concerned, truth and trust are the founding stones of love and loving relationships; without them, there is nothing. It is the first life lesson I taught my children: NEVER LIE!

Now, you and I have nothing! It is all gone. Poof. Our love burned to a crisp! Everything you were to me has gone up in smoke!

GOODBYE.

From: Cherry Estrella cherry@starsearch.com
Date: February 27, 2010
To: Ariane Altar ariane@altarpots.com
Subject: my advice to you

You sounded just awful on the phone. I am sorry about Wylie. I know you won't want to hear this, but I do think you are over-reacting. I know you, and I know you put up walls when anyone crosses one of your boundaries. I know you are fed up with liars and cheaters. But remember, you put up with your "ex" lying to you and cheating on you for years! Okay, I know you say "the new you" will not tolerate that behavior again. But, Wylie is special. Maybe you need to give him a chance to explain?

And you, I have not seen you so happy in years. He has given you zest, zip-a-dee-doo-dah, made your life happy again. Look at you: writing, giving dinner parties, going to the beach, laughing. You have spent far too many years in grief. You deserve this happiness. Not that I walk in your shoes, but I have been relieved that he came into your life and brightened your spirits. Don't throw him away just because he lied. After all, you do not know why he was lying to you. Ask.

Notes in Ariane's journal:
February 28, 2010

I am crying all the time. I am frightened by this loss, by the uncertainty of who Wylie is and of why he has been lying to me. I am frightened of the dark place where grief pulls me. I am afraid. I am afraid to go where I hid when Nico died, that bottomless pit. It has taken intense determination to pull myself out of it, not to slip, not to slip down where I might not find a foothold to get out. And then, it was even worse to have Marianna die. My identity gone, shattered: I was not a mother, I was not a wife, I was not an artist; I was lost. I fell, I slipped, I tumbled. How many nights when I couldn't sleep did I think of my own death? I imagined tempting fate, leaving my sorrows behind, a suicide just like my children. How much guilt blanketed me then? How much loneliness? I think only Juan's love and devotion saved me. And Ande's. But, she was in a terrible place herself, losing both brother and sister, and had as little to give as I.

At Nico's funeral, my grief was public; my loss, public; my vulnerability, public: there for all to see. I vowed to live my life in truth, my spirit kept as naked as it was on that sad, sad day. Yet, to be in the world, I needed protection.

How I have struggled these ten years to live, to maintain my sanity, to heal, to hide the pain, to do my best to enjoy life again. Each morning, I mentally wrap my broken heart in bandages, so I don't "bleed" all over people. Then I put on a little suit of polished silver armor, duct tape my lips, and keep my grief to myself.

What a case study in repression I am! A tin woods-woman, stiff and unyield-ing. Ironically, I know it is this very repression that allows me to function. To build a new ceramics studio and to assume a new name have given me hope for a future. My Hana home and gardens have become a paradise for me, and visitors say, an oasis for them.

Oh Lord, I didn't used to be unyielding. I was soft, malleable. In fact, soft used to be my favorite word. I liked its connotations and its sound. I wanted to be soft like a pillow for my loved ones. I created a series of clay pillows to honor the notion of softness. I thought of myself as a squishy, soft marshmallow.

But, softness worked against me in my marriage. My "ex" took advantage of my open, forgiving nature. He cheated, lied, and pushed me around. When we divorced, I vowed never to tolerate such behavior again.

Now I am mad, mad that anyone could push me toward that pit of despair and loss again. I want to punch, hit, kick Wylie for pushing me to its edge, for leading me into love only to abandon me at this place, the place of my worst nightmare: betrayal. I am so mad at him! Damn him! Damn him for hurting me, for lying to me, for not being the man I learned to love.

What do I do now? How do I live without him? I don't know what to do without our love that felt so big.

From: Wylie Hymen wylie@hymenfables.com
Date: February 28, 2010
To: Ariane Altar ariane@altarpots.com
Subject: Farewell, my love

I have never lied to you, never about our love, my faithfulness, and devotion to you, or who I am. But, it was only a matter of time before you were caught up in my craziness and the web of lies, the fictions, that have become my life: lies about my health, about my state of mind, about where I am and what I am doing, about who I am. It was only a matter of time before I could not control my life flying apart. I lie to cover up that I am lost to others and myself for hours, even whole days, now weeks. I tell you, my friends and my family I was "away" or "going away" when in fact I am here, painting, walking the woods endlessly, dissolving into uncontrollable crying, or just sitting dazed, ambushed and tormented by unimaginable fears. The only psalm I ever learned, and now understand, contained the image of the valley of the shadow of death.

Still, our love remained real for me, an oasis of warmth and caring in a strange, threatening landscape. There have been weeks when my only hold on reality has been the everyday-ness of our talks at night, hearing you laugh as you share the events of your day. I have begun hallucinating, and now realize I am losing touch with reality. I am terrified.

Too late for us, I know I need help. I've begun with a call to Mills, my physician. Please try to imagine, Ariane, even if you cannot accept or forgive, the deranged state of my mind that would bring me unwittingly to cause you such pain and such a tragic end to all we have had. I cannot believe I am capable of what I have done.

Pants On Fire!

In my craziness, I have ruined a beautiful love. I dare not hope that we can somehow transcend these devastating events. I know that in destroying your trust, I have also lost your love. I have enjoyed finding just the words to express the joy of my love for you, and I shall trouble you with it no more, for you have no reason to believe me, and I understand why. But, nothing was a lie, my love, nothing. The Wylie you've known and loved (I am trying desperately to hold on to him) was no phantom. Hopefully, he still lives at the core of this troubled Wylie.

In a way, your Wylie is no longer here. Perhaps, someday, when the pain I have caused you has subsided, you can think of me as someone you once loved and who loved you dearly. But, one day, not wanting to leave, but not wanting to hurt you any more, and though it tore our hearts to pieces, he just went away.

You will never be far from me. I have from our brief time together a lifetime of sweet memories, and you will live in my heart for the rest of my days. I will always long to hear your voice, long for your love, and laughter, all the joyous moments we shared, and all the wonderful things that are you. I continue to paint you. In every color of the rainbow.

Farewell, my dear Ariane, farewell

From: Ariane Altar ariane@altarpots.com
Date: March 1, 2010
To: Ande andeP@gmail.com
Subject: to discover duplicity

Ande, Honey,

I feel completely undone. Wylie wrote me that cloud cuckoo land "farewell" letter I read you. I think it is way over the top and a bit nutty. I have taken your advice and called his son. I told him who I was and asked him to check on his dad.

Well, it was quite a call. Baron had never heard of me! The only thing he knew about Hawai'i was that his dad had gone there once "with his hiking buddies." "Hiking buddies?" I asked. He also hadn't seen his dad in ages, saying the "family wasn't very close", had not gone skiing with him in Yosemite (as Wylie had told me), has never heard of a plan to go to England, and does not have colon cancer! Well, well, gullible me!

I feel I did the right thing by calling Baron, in case Wylie has gone completely over the edge. You know, Ande, I really don't know how Wylie could be so real to me and yet so false? Am I delusional?

Love MA

Pants On Fire!

From: Wylie Hymen wylie@hymenfables.com
Date: March 2, 2010
To: Ariane Altar ariane@altarpots.com

Sunday, A Week Ago

Sunday, a week ago, dawn,
my third night without sleep,
haggard, disquieted, by my own
turbulent runaway emotions
and fears for Baron's health. He will be fine,
but for now I want only for him to be here,
so that I can hold, comfort, and reassure him.
And though I know he is not, I feel
he is actually with me (the way you have felt
the presence of your dead son and daughter).
When the phone rings, it is your voice,
lifting me out of the darkness,
and filling my heart with joy.
        But you are not calling to comfort me
or express your love,
instead, you want to prove to yourself, you can
"catch" me at home when I said I was away,
your voice, almost triumphant,
certain I am with another woman.
I feel a blow to my chest and stomach,
as if you had struck me with all your might,
leaving me incoherent, unable to breathe,
confused, incapable of uttering any explanation.

        But, then, why did I need one?
After a thousand gestures and expressions
of how much I treasure you, and value your friendship,
opened my heart to share my most intimate thoughts,
with a truth I have never expressed to anyone else;
loved you with tenderness and passion I did not know I had;
written to you of my love in my very first poems,
created little gifts for you from my heart,
in the end, you have for me only
doubts, mistrust, suspicions, anger,
and accusations of being unfaithful.

Pants On Fire!

I feel a wrenching in my heart as the
silken bonds between us are torn away,
overcome by the sick feeling that
our relationship and all that we have been to one another,
has been suddenly and dramatically altered
– it is over, torn asunder by you.

        In but an instant, a beautiful love,
based on so many magical moments
and delightful experiences together –
the beginnings of our history, Ariane –
disappeared, poisoned by your fears,
making of two perfect lovers, strangers forever,
never again able to love the same way.
What remains, then, of Ariane and Wylie,
what is left of our love and our dreams,
why would we want to go on with something now
so much less than what we had,
after Sunday, a week ago?

From: Baron Hymen baron@classiccompany.com
Date: March 2, 2010
To: Wylie Hymen wylie@hymenfables.com
Subject: call I got from a woman in Hawai'i

Hi, Dad,

        I was contacted by Errienne (I am not sure of her name?) from Hawai'i. She
called, because she is very concerned about you, and now, so am I. Are there things
I should know about your past health and future health, beyond what you have told
me? I guess I would like to know if you are okay, both physically and mentally.
Have you had a relapse? What is going on with you?

                                                                        Baron

From: Wylie Hymen wylie@hymenfables.com
Date: March 2, 2010
To: Baron Hymen Baron@classiccompany.com, Ariane Altar ariane@altarpots.com
Subject: Re: call I got from a woman in Hawai'i

Pants On Fire!

Dear Baron,

Thanks for asking, but please don't worry. I am okay – most of the time. I've told you about Ariane, but probably not that she has become my closest confidant to whom I have been writing and talking almost daily about what I've been experiencing the past few years, entrusting her with my innermost feelings. She has reason to be concerned; sadly, our friendship has become strained by some of my craziness (some of the old craziness you might remember from when you were a kid). She has given me an opportunity to talk to you about what's going on.

I am sometimes fearful, not just the old fears, but new ones, about cancer. Matthew and my oncologist are being wonderful about keeping me up to date, explaining what's happening, encouraging me. When I asked my oncologist if I should be concerned about exercise, he said, "go climb mountains!" But, it's scary to come up against mortality. The first time I was in Nepal, I heard over and over the Buddhist idea, completely internalized there as natural as breathing, that nothing in life is permanent, something you really begin to understand in your seventies.

Given your spirit, robustness, and energy you will understand this: I do not fear death; but what I fear more than anything is being weak and ill, to lose my independence and this life I love, not to be able to walk and ski the mountains, needing the care of others, unable to enjoy people I love, unable to experience life with you and my grand girls.

Sometimes I am ambushed by fierce emotional storms. Strange, they are not anything to do with my illness or anything else that I can tell. Actually, it all began a few years ago, when I would become intensely emotional from hearing a story, or an incident in a book. Mills, my doctor and friend, suggested I try some tranquilizers or anti-anxiety drugs or even anti-depressants. I have always cried in movies and the theatre, but now I find intense emotions arising out of music and even art. They are fleeting but unpredictable; it's strange to be listening to a piece of music I've loved and listened to for years, but which now brings me to tears.

All of a sudden, I am aware of a new feeling, or emotion, or just the way my aging, cancerous body is working differently. Rather than go away, it stays with me, and I just get used to it, to the point I really don't notice it anymore – my new "normal". Sometimes all this makes me a little crazy. I'm glad you asked. I'll be sure, now, to keep the conversation going.

Love, Dad

From: Ariane Altar ariane@altarpots.com
Date: March 2, 2010
To: Ande andeP@gmail.com
Subject: Re: Re: Wylie

Thanks for listening to me go on about Wylie. I'm glad you see the break-up as a no-brainer, too. I am trying to stay focused as I disengage and not to take Wylie's behavior personally, as now I really am wondering if he is some kind of nut case. Maybe he just wanted out of our relationship and lying was part of disengaging. I can't believe any normal person would profess the kind of love he did and then walk away. Maybe I am protecting myself from grief by saying he has to be crazy to leave me! Anyway, we know he had to be crazy to love me!

I need some input from you, though. I need to visit Gramma. I am looking at late March with a stop on Kaua'i for Easter, unless you would like to have Easter in Hana. Let me know, since I need to book my airline tickets.

From: Ande andeP@gmail.com
Date: March 3, 2010
To: Mom Ariane Altar ariane@altarpots.com
Subject: Re: Re: Re: Wylie

hey moms,

hope you are still feeling good about your decision with wylie. it is sad though. he has been dishonorable and unethical, and he needs to be called on it. i think too many nice ladies like you just let the bad guy get away. have you thought about telling him he's a bona fide jerk?

From: Wylie Hymen wylie@hymenfables.com
Date: March 3, 2010
To: Ariane Altar ariane@altarpots.com

Dear Ariane,

Out of hope, out of desperation, I pen a poem for you.

Wylie

Pants On Fire!

An Awakening

I awoke this morning
feeling as though I had
emerged from some cave
of darkness and despair,
my head clear, happy,
seeing light for the first time
in days, a heavy weight
lifted from my chest,
breathing easier,
my first thoughts,
as every morning, of you.
I don't recognize the letter
I wrote to you yesterday,
but I remember picking up the phone
a hundred times to call you,
realizing, sadly, for the first time
I was afraid, not knowing what to say,
except that I love you, dear Ariane,
and cannot imagine my life without you,
and ask could you still love me?

From: Baron Hymen baron@classiccompany.com
Date: March 3, 2010
To: Ariane Altar ariane@altarpots.com
Subject: Re: your father's crazy letter that made me alert you

Hi Errienne,

I chose to delete my dad's letter, unread. It seems to me that it is relatively personal and, taken out of context, unfair to both writer and reader. I did, however, email Wylie and am satisfied with the response I have received. I believe he sent a copy to you. You are wrong about one thing. It was my dad, not my sister, who suffered delusions. He had a nervous breakdown when we were kids and was diagnosed with schizophrenia. My mom took us to England, and we didn't see much of him. After I got married, I looked for him and found him living at Indian Springs. We did some counseling sessions together to try to heal the past. I don't have a brother; there is no Dr. Matthew Hymen in our family. I see my dad occasionally, and in his way, he can enjoy his granddaughters.

Sincerely, Baron Hymen

264

Pants On Fire!

From: Wylie Hymen wylie@hymenfables.com
Date: March 4, 2010
To: Ariane Altar ariane@altarpots.com

The Blue-Green Temple

From the Blue-Green Temple
I can still hear the beating of
our two hearts and your
morning songs of love, sadly
fainter and more distant now.
They will quiet to silence
over the weeks and months,
but for me the Blue-Green Temple,
which greets me every morning
and delights me throughout my day
as you've done, dear Ariane,
will remind me of us and
hold within its graceful walls
vivid memories of
a sacred, passionate love
lasting just short of a year,
yet to remain in my heart
forever.

P.S. I know you are in pain, and I feel as though my heart and much of my soul
have been ripped from my body and seared by some devil's fiery brand. I would be
there with you in an instant if it would help you through this, but I suspect I am the
last person on earth you want to see right now.

Notes in Ariane's journal:
March 4, 2010

Numb. Just numbness. I refuse to feel. No more footsteps to the abyss. No
more nights cramped in fetal pain, nights breathing in huge gulps, swallowing
the darkness, the hours my diaphragm convulses in spasms, laying exhausted by
relentless, hiccoughing sobs as the blackness of my children's deaths and loss
enveloped me.

265

Pants On Fire!

From: Cherry Estrella cherry@starsearch.com,
Date: March 4, 2010
To: Ariane Altar ariane@altarpots.com
Subject: Re: shocking news bulletin

I just can't believe it! Wylie really was lying to you? Could it be that his illness is causing him to be confused or distressed? Keeps him from thinking clearly? What a disappointment for you. Hang in there, kiddo. You need to ask him why he kept his relationship and travels with Dina a secret. He needs to hear and understand how much his deception has hurt you. Maybe he can get help like Freddie is.

I got home late last night from Houston. Freddie is still there and has agreed to a couple of days longer while they finish up some testing and get his meds regulated. He is having trouble "processing" or something. They are doing the genetic testing for Alzheimer's today. It's difficult to diagnose mental illness, as you know. Freddie says his symptoms are gone, and he doesn't need their help. He says he will take the meds, but really doesn't think he needs them (typical of bipolar patients: when they feel a little better, they go off their meds.)

I am enclosing some drug info for you about what they've put him on to regulate his moods. In addition, my head spins just thinking about it, I have to make sure he gets regular exercise, adequate sleep, and a healthy diet. I am supposed to sign him up for talk therapy, meditation, biofeedback, hypnosis, acupuncture, and make sure he takes his *benzodiazepine* cocktail. A warning: Anxiety medication can provide temporary relief, but it doesn't treat the underlying cause of the anxiety disorder. Once Freddie stops taking the drug, the anxiety symptoms may return in full force. Scary. Of course, taking the anti-depressants has made him impotent, as though being alcoholic and sixty-eight haven't already created that little problem. Oh, my, where has my joy juice gone?

I'm trying to stay off the phone, since I'm expecting calls from doctors and insurance representatives, but will call as soon as I find a minute. We need to talk, girl!

Love, Cherry

Anti-anxiety drugs like *benzodiazepines* work by reducing brain activity. While this temporarily relieves anxiety, it can also lead to unwanted side effects. The higher the dose, the more pronounced these side effects typically are. But, some people feel sleepy, foggy, and uncoordinated even on low doses of benzodiazepines, which can cause problems with work, school, or everyday activities such as driving. Some even feel a medication hangover the next day.

Pants On Fire!

From: Ariane Altar ariane@altarpots.com
Date: March 5, 2010
To: Cherry Estrella cherry@starsearch.com,
Subject: Freddie's treatment

Poor Freddie. I never noticed mood swings. Could he be addicted to the pain-killers? And poor you, too! You are a real trouper to hang in as you are. My experience is that the hospitalization portion of diagnosing and treating mental illness just gets started at the six-week point. My daughter took five months in the hospital and treatment cost mucho dinero ($) and my sister, Melinda, years and a fortune. Oh boy. My heart goes out to you.

As to my situation: Wylie lied about everything. I saw no signs at all. Did you? It only came to light on the weekend. I heard from his son, who told me when he was a little boy, his dad had a nervous breakdown. I wonder what that was about and if it still affects him? Maybe it doesn't matter.

Out of the blue, literally, two weeks ago, it was, when I caught Wylie lying to me. The amazing part is three weeks ago I wanted to spend the rest of my life with him! All this time he has told me I am his one and only (lie), he has cancer/lymphoma (lie) and that his son was diagnosed with colon cancer (lie) and that his other son, the doctor, (who doesn't exist!) was invited to Oxford to lecture (lie) and then he added that he and his sons were going to take a "sacred journey" together to England next month (lie) and the wives were staying home (lie), which meant I had to stay home (true). My "seamless" relationship has completely unraveled! My year of great happiness is over (you know how fired up I was over him). Boo, hiss! My relationship up in flames. Crash and burn! Ashes, ashes, all fall down!

I have shed enough tears to put out any fire and am lollygagging in a sloppy pool of them now. As for my healing (what healing, I ask?), I listen to Kris Kristofferson singing *For The Good Times* over and over on my iPod. The words that resonate with me the most are "there's no need to watch the bridges that we're burning" And, pathetically "⋯ make believe you love me, one more time."

Notes in Ariane's journal:
March 6, 2010

I feel the damp approach of a storm building on my heart's horizon, clouds low and thick, pregnant with tears. I fear this storm, even if, in reality, it is only a passing squall. I fear that once the rain begins to fall, tears might decide to take up permanent residence over my heart, flooding it, washing all I have become away, washing me down the drains and gutters of my world out to the great sea, the great sea of grief where there are no shores, and I shall not return. Counting, yes, I am counting. Nico. One. I come up for air. Marianna. Two. I come up for air. Wylie. Three. Will I come up? Losses come in threes, my mother always said.

I need a life preserver.

March 7, 2010

Fear of cracking open. Of tripping, slipping, falling. Free falling into the abyss. Lost. Gone. If I crack, if I open my heart, if I accept for a moment that yet another love has left, I cannot cope.

Better to go numb. Don armor, a heavy suit of armor, fasten a thick breast-plate securely across my heart. I must protect it. Ah, how heavy. Can I stand? Yes, I can stand. But, can I move? Can I carry this new weight? And, where, o where, I wonder, my head now gusseted inside a hard silver helmet, do I go from here?

March 8, 2010

A question: is this pain worse than when Marianna died, when Nico died, when my husband left? Can pain be compared?

This, this man, this love, this loss, this betrayal, this fucking farewell. I refuse to grieve it.

One thing for certain: I was deluded.

From: Dina Cochon dinaRN@iswell.org
Date: March 8, 2010
To: Wylie Hymen wylie@hymenfables.com
Subject: Theatre tickets; photo

Macbeth at the Globe Saturday matinee: For fifty-seven pounds each, we can sit on benches, behind people standing up. Hmmm. AND, there are no evening reservations available at Zianni's in Kensington for my birthday dinner. Phooey. I am researching more restaurants.

Regarding your B&W PR photos: Number 40 is my favorite.

Has Matthew decided to go to Japan with you this summer when we get back?

Pooky

Pants On Fire!

From: Geoffrey Lord geoffrey@tukecentre.org.uk
Date: March 8, 2010
To: Wylie Hymen wylie@hymenfables.com
Subject: Re: London Spas and Therapy

Hello, Wylie,

You emailed that you are going to walk in the Cotswolds in late April as part of the program in Gloucester. You are unsure of where to stay when you arrive in London. We have affiliate facilities there, and we shall make arrangements for you. They are both in the Bloomsbury area near the British Museum, London University, and the British Library. We like the area and find it very convenient to the tube and rail stations, and within walking distance of the West End Theatre district. Give my best to Mills. I look forward to working with you again.

Regards, Geoffrey

From: Cotswolds Wellness Walks cotswoldswalks@wellness.co.uk
Date: March 9, 2010
To: Wylie Hymen wylie@hymenfables.com, Dina Cochon dinaRN@iswell.org
Subject: Cotswolds Wellness Walks

Hi, Wylie and Dina,

Many thanks, the payment has gone through, and I am forwarding all the paperwork. Please find attached your accommodation list and invoice receipt. Your walking notes will be waiting for you at the Cotswolds Wellness Centre in Gloucester. May I wish you a smooth journey to the UK?

Regards, Andrew

From: Wylie Hymen wylie@hymenfables.com
Sent: March 9, 2010
To: Geoffrey Lord geoffrey@thetukecentre.org.uk
Subject: Dinosaurs no more

Hi, Geoffrey,

I just happened to come across an earlier email in which Matthew Mills called you a dinosaur for having a dial-up modem. Well, I've had dial-up for years, until

269

my son came to visit in November. I am now on the Ethernet, and websites come up so fast, they just about knock me out of my chair.

Thanks for the London accommodations. Even Dina can be squeezed into a tiny space. Maybe you could tell us what is the best way to get from Moreton-in-Marsh in Cotswolds to your Tuke Centre in York, if Dina survives the walk, that is? Will we need to purchase train tickets in advance?

◐

From: Ariane Altar ariane@altarpots.com
Date: March 9, 2010
To: Dina Cochon dinaRN@iswell.org
Subject: Do you get letters like this from Wylie?

Dear Dina,

You do not know me or probably of me. Wylie Hymen was my high school lit teacher forty years ago. We got together in 2008, because I write children's books and needed help to get them published. We got on so well, we agreed to write a biography about my best friend's mother. Wylie had done an oral history years before of her life as a Jewish refugee.

Wylie and I fell in love. He and I had a trip tentatively planned for England this April to visit some friends until he told me he had decided to go there on "a sacred journey" to bond with his sons, as both he and Baron have cancer.

I called Baron. He does not have cancer. Nor does he have a brother. Surprise. Wylie took great care to lie to me about many facets of his life. He also told me you were in love with him, and you knew all about me, which I doubt, and that your intimate relationship has been over for years.

I am touching base in case you are as naive and trusting with Wylie as I have been. He is devious and dishonest and enjoys toying with other people's hearts.

Ariane Altar

270

From: Dina Cochon dinaRN@iswell.org
Date: March 10, 2010
To: Wylie Hymen wylie@hymenfables.com
Subject: Where do we go from here?

Where do we go from here? I do not want to discuss this attachment via email. I received it yesterday afternoon.
Call.
Me.
Now.

From: Ariane Altar ariane@altarpots.com
Date: March 10, 2010
To: Cherry Estrella cherry@starsearch.com
Subject: Dina blue

Guess who's feeling blue? Me. I hope Freddie feels better than I do. Being down IS the pits!

Thanks for the pep talk, Cherry. It hurts like hell to be tricked, have my world turned upside down. Yesterday Wylie left me a phone message and sent a poem, asking if I could still love him.

When Wylie was in Hana, he always used my computer. He left his web mail info and emails on it. I was clearing files, and I found it and his password the other day quite by accident; you know what a computer dummy I am. Well, I confess to sleuthing! Click! I took a look.

Bingo! All his correspondence! Travel info, other loves; the whole smear! He is still with Dina and traveling her to the English Cotswolds, the supposed "sacred journey" he said he was taking with his sons. He was inviting women I've never heard of to his mountain home for dinners and walks in the woods, lining up dates, even while he was with me!

Oh, I am sick, sick, sick to have fallen for an inveterate womanizer and liar extraordinaire. I am feeling low, obsessed, angry, and mean.

Confession: I did something mean spirited. I'll unburden my conscience to you and then go mum. He left me a phone message about "understanding my anger", being "sad" that I chose to go *kamikaze* in breaking up, and that he will always treasure "our journey together". What he was referring to was that I sent his letter about lies and craziness to this Dina person. I saw her photo on *Facebook* (oink oink) and got her email address. Oh my god, worse yet, she is short and fat.

You know how fascinated I am by names. I looked hers up. It means "darkness." I am sure Dina knows nothing of me, just as I knew nothing of her! At seventy-three, this guy is carrying on dual, or maybe multiple, affairs! I am hor-rified! It turns out he likes ugly fatties (god, I hope I was the exception!) as I also discovered nasty, fat women on *Facebook* who write erotic messages to him and include their photos and photos of acts so disgusting I think I'll have nightmares!

Well, today I went way off the "high road" and sent Dina a bunch of pictures of Wylie with me—I'll be blunt: naked pictures. I know it was stupid to do that; I did it just to irritate them both. That really got his goat (he is a shameless and randy old goat anyway!) and prompted his call.

In truth, I should be grateful he is out of my life. I am being quite stupid and possibly playing with fire by doing anything like sending these photos, which might infuriate him. Pray this craziness leaves me. I want my good self back!

Oh! You are going to love this: his girlfriend has a nickname: *Pooky*!

I decided to get back to work on my children's books. I was *Googling* editors and found that Wylie's favorite editor, Erica, is still at Houghton. This news sur-prised me, as Wylie told me she had left. I see now that he just didn't want to ask her to read my stories, because he really wasn't serious about them or me! Ouch!

I'll be at my mom's in Berkeley April 14 to 22. Please, let's get together. Don't we need the Carrie Bradshaw "Sex and the City" treatment: a Cosmo and a new pair of *Manolo Blahnik's*? (On my budget, I might have to settle for a pair of *Payless* knock-offs!)

From: Cherry Estrella cherry@starsearch.com
Date: Mar 10, 2010
To: Ariane Altar ariane@altarpots.com
Subject: Re: blue

Oh, Ariane. Does he not have cancer? What a horrible thing to do. And a girl-friend and⋯ and...He must be a pathological liar, and I'll bet he's always been one. I have known two men like that, and it's embarrassing to think of how I got sucked in again and again. We all have learned the hard way that some men can be shits...

I am sorry, and you know of course that this is about him and not you. This situ-ation calls for more than a couple of cosmos: how about a pitcher of margaritas? I'll tell you later about my unfortunate relationships. I'll definitely see you in Berkeley.

Wylie Hymen's phone message left on Ariane's answering machine
March 10, 2010

Hi Ariane, it's Wylie. Um. I wanted to talk. I know you don't want to talk to me, but there are things I wanted to SAY rather than write. First of all, I am kinda sad that you've sorta taken this *kamikaze* approach to the end of the relationship, and I just feel that um I know you're angry with me, and I'm a Big Boy, and I can take your anger, and what's more, I realize I deserve it, and I wish you would direct it at me. It would, uh, I think things would work out better. Dina's actually very sympathetic. She understands. She said she would feel really bad if she lost MY friendship and would be very angry.

I just want you to know that I'm honoring the memory of our time together and the spirit in which we lived it. Um, I think of the time from the moment I picked you up at the, at the bus station in San Raphael a year ago, until we, I saw you, I saw the last of you when you left me at the airport on Maui a couple of weeks ago, that for me it was a beautiful journey, and I don't, uh, I don't want, uh, I'm not, um, I am not lessening what happened at the end, but I am saying it was a beautiful journey with you, and I want you to know I don't know how much time, uh, I have left, um, I've just been actually to a counseling session, but, um, the memories of our time together will bring joy to whatever years I have left, and I just want to say I wish you wellness and, um, a life of love and beauty.

Goodbye (quavering)

Letter from Ariane to Wylie
Not sent
March 10, 2010

You lied to me! When I heard you lie, I knew the truth: Baron doesn't have cancer, you aren't taking him to England, you are taking Dina, (for God's sake, you were with Dina all along, dumb me!), to England for her annual birthday trip—like last year when you went to New York to all those plays, you rat. You dirty lying, fucking little rat! You tricked me from the beginning. Liar! Nasty ass liar! Our beautiful relationship has gone up in smoke, and I am left covered in soot. You have made everything between us filthy, filthy, and I hate you. I hate you, Wylie! I hate, hate, hate you!

From: Ariane Altar ariane@altarpots.com
Date: March 11, 2010
To: Cherry Estrella cherry@starsearch.com
Subject: Soap Opera update

Dina got the photos I sent her and forwarded them to Wylie. Have the fireworks begun?

Speaking of soaps, here is a cute photo from the last time I was on Kaua'i when I gave Kui her first bubble bath.

Love, Princess Healing Heart

From: Cherry Estrella cherry@starsearch.com,
Date: March 11, 2010
To: Ariane Altar ariane@altarpots.com
Subject: Turkey!

Guess what? We are going to Turkey this summer for our anniversary! I think I got my husband back! He is feeling much better. I am so excited! We'll be there three whole weeks in July!

As to your *Internet* sleuthing: Wow, Girlfriend! What a score: nickname and photo! She is a chunky monkey all right. Not a pudgy-wudgy, not a chub, but a genuine porker! Oink oink! Did I read that right, Pooky? Or, did you make a typo, and it's really Poopey, or Pokey, or Pukey, or Phooey, or Porky, or P-P-P-Petunia? See, I can be bitchy, too!

I promised to share my Love Saga with you: Okay, here's the short Saga of Men in Cherry's Love Life:

Marriage # 1: I was in college; he was older; don't know how, I fell into the *Corvette*, diamond ring, being wined and dined. Married at twenty, house, baby Rosie nine months later. Discovered he was a pathological liar, lied about anything and everything. Whoppers: pretending heart attacks, stealing from his mother, losing his job and pretending every day to go to work all dressed up in a suit and tie, coming home with made-up stories of the day. Stayed in that marriage for two years, then got out (lots more to it, of course). I called him a liar and more. He had a great parting shot: Me, lie? Never: unless I am seducing a woman!

Marriage #2: Wonderful man totally the opposite of the wheeler-dealer businessman; a longhaired, bearded, gentle, mountain man, woodworker beloved by all. House on a mountaintop, putting up food from the garden, wood stove, homemade bread. He adopted Rosie, we had a lovely family, home, friends, and everything was cozy perfect Maine life: house, animals, gardens, snowshoeing, pot luck dinners with friends. Strange holes appeared in the marriage, something missing, and finally a decision to move to California. When Rosie was a freshman in high school, the discovery that he had been abusing her since Maine days, and she finally told me. Police, newspaper account, counseling, courtroom. Guilt that I hadn't seen it. Horrible times. Rosie and I moved to Napa Valley. Hard times: we lost trust in men.

Interludes: Affair with a married man who would have left his wife; I discovered my conscience and sent him back to her; broke my heart, but what was I doing to another woman? If he were willing to leave her for me, wouldn't he be willing to leave me for someone else?

Sex games with a lovely man who wanted to marry me, but he wasn't athletic enough.

Play time with a co-worker, very athletic and outdoorsy and always up for adventure, but again, a pathological liar and alcoholic (how and why do I attract these men?). As Rosie said, "He'd be okay if we could cut off his head."

Freddie. The one. The right one. My equal. Honest and reliable and responsible and good; hard to live with the first few years: spoiled, set in his ways, unrelenting, his way or no way. It took a lot of years of give and take, working things out. Not easy those first years! (Never EASY, of course, but we do get along!) I am proud of him; he is proud of me; we love each other's families; we love each other's children, and we love our dog and our home and our friends. And last, but not least, we love and respect each other.

From: Ariane Altar ariane@altarpots.com
Date: March 13, 2010
To: Cherry Estrella cherry@starsearch.com

Dear Cherry,

You told me some bits before, but I didn't know about Rosie. I am delighted her baby, Maya, has come into your lives where now there is warmth, safety, and goodness. I have harrowing domestic stories of my own, which I won't go into now. Let it be said, that I understand and empathize.

Your travel schedule sounds delightful, and I am happy to hear Freddie is recovering his *joie*. I was in Turkey three times in the 1960's. Istanbul is beautiful. Its situation on the Bosporus is a bit like San Francisco's setting on the Bay. The Blue Mosque, Hagia Sophia, and Topkapi Palace are remarkable. I also recommend going south to Ephesus and the ruins along the coast. You will have a wonderful time. Of course, Wylie had the time of his life scaling Mount Ararat! Will you travel that far east?

From: Ariane Altar ariane@altarpots.com
Date: March 13, 2010
To: Mom ednawolfeson@peoplepc.com
Subject: Wylie

Dear Mom,

Can't break bad news any other way than telling it: I broke up with Wylie. He was lying to me. Not baby lies. Great big lies. Like his son had cancer, his son was visiting him in Chicken Ridge, he was taking his granddaughter to the ballet, he was skiing with his son and grandchildren. But, the truth is, he was usually with a woman named Dina. You remember the morning he came to see you on his return from Hana with the Valentine present of red heliconias from my garden? He was supposed to take some to his son and daughter-in-law in Berkeley? But, he didn't. He gave them to this Dina, flowers from my garden! I am so upset that I am not sad; sadness I am sure will come later. It's like being in a car wreck: at first, the shock protects you from the pain of your injuries. Sorry I ever brought such a person into your home. (Don't get all excited now, Madame Feminist, and think that I'll hate men, because I won't!)

Love, Ariane

From: Mom ednawolfeson@peoplepc.com
Date: March 13, 2010
To: Ariane Altar ariane@altarpots.com
Subject: Re: Wylie

Dear Emily, er Ariane,

You already emailed me that you broke up with the Fox. You are not exactly a Spring Chicken, and you should have known better. You've always had pretty bad luck with men. Or, maybe you just like losers. Get over yourself. Who needs men anyway?

Hrrumph and Grrr! Your Tiger Mama

From: Cherry Estrella cherry@starsearch.com
Date: Mar 13, 2010
To: Ariane Altar ariane@altarpots.com
Subject: Re: Soap Opera Update

Well, I do believe him about his love. I am sure that he put his soul into loving you. Maybe that love kept him sane this past year. He's damaged, and maybe there's some relief that it's in the open now. Must have been horrible to live in those lies. The "farewell" is kinda over the top. (Does he write soaps?) He should (in my oh so professional opinion) be making a plan to get better and a plea to reconsider him when he has done what he has to do to get rid of his demons.

I wonder if these lies he spins are new or if this is how his life has gone, and why he is alone in his woods? Do you think he might be schizophrenic? Maybe he is on meds and forgets to take them now and then?

From: Ariane Altar ariane@altarpots.com
Date: March 13, 2010
To: Cherry Estrella cherry@starsearch.com
Subject: Re: Re: Soap Opera Update

I think Wylie loved me. But, if he really loved me or wanted to make amends, he would not be with this other woman, would he? He would have flown right back to Maui and cleared up the situation with me!

I was somewhat repulsed by his romantic narcissism and all the melodrama about his cancer: I mean, he just went on and on. I have known a lot of people with cancer who are in far worse shape, and they don't crybaby the way he did. When he was here, I found it a bit much. I don't understand how any one who knows him hasn't gotten snagged on one of his lies and questioned his reality. I doubt that he is seeking help for his bizarre behavior. I think he rather enjoys the self-pity!

From: Ariane Altar ariane@altarpots.com
Date: March 20, 2010
To: Cherry Estrella cherry@starsearch.com

Today I found out Dina is the go-between for shipments of marijuana from Wylie and Roly to her theater friends, Iggy and Michael, in New York!

From: Cherry Estrella cherry@starsearch.com
Date: March 20, 2010
To: Ariane Altar ariane@altarpots.com
Subject: He is a rat!

Dear Ariane,

A little Destiny Humor! Wylie WAS born in the Chinese Astrological Year of the Rat! No surprise there!

Your emails have gone to my heart like arrows! They remind me of the s—t I went through at just about your age and make me grateful that I haven't met anyone to lure me into it again. I know that even now, ten years later, I could still have the stupidity to fall into that same old trap of unjustified trust. Men can con us, and we are eager to believe the con. I don't think the younger generation of women is quite so vulnerable. At least I hope not!

You might like this from Oprah's blog:

Pants On Fire!

Today's Shmuleyism:
Men who cheat do not do so, because they don't love their wives, but because they don't love themselves, and they turn to strangers to make them feel good about themselves. The salvation of the American male··· will come when men discover a moral vision of themselves··· and formulate··· a new definition of success revolving···around··· quality of relationships.

Take excellent care of yourself. I send you much love and wishes for a speedy recovery.

From: Ariane Altar ariane@altarpots.com
Date: March 22, 2010
To: Cherry Estrella cherry@starsearch.com,
Subject: this affair

The end of my affair is taking a toll. I can't sleep, and if I do, I wake at two or three or four and can't get back to sleep. I am exercising and seeing friends and working in the studio, which is fine for staying sane. But, the betrayal hurts. I am pretty wiped out.

I am ashamed of sending the intimate photos to Dina, Pooky, Poopey, or whoever she is. They're still on *Facebook* together. Knowing about me hasn't made a whit of difference to their relationship. Go figure.

Kui is an absolute doll, who loves doing the opposite of what she is supposed to, watches me carefully, and laughs and laughs! (example: bath time: scooping water in a cup, catching my eye, lifting the cup to dump the water in the tub, but quick as a flash dumping it on the floor instead, and laugh, laugh, laughing!)

From: Wylie Hymen wylie@hymenfables.com
Date: Wednesday, March 28, 2010
To: Curt Degler cdegler@ng.org
Subject: Ladakh

It's Wylie from the Ark trip to Ararat. How are you? What exotic places on the map have you filmed since our time in Turkey? Did you do the Ladakh trip you mentioned? I have been thinking about an adventure for this year, and the itinerary your colleague, Jill Forthright, sent really interests me. Let's think about the possibility of doing this together.

From: Ariane Altar ariane@altarpots.com
Date: March 28, 2010
To: Lucas Dmitri lucas@unityworld.org
Subject: still bummed

Well, I am at the four-week mark of a failed relationship and still heavy hearted. Also have a recurrence of my lung ailment, which manifests like pneumonia with lots of painful pleurisy. Let me tell you, when it hurts to cry, it REALLY hurts to cry! I remain in a state of profound shock at the extent of Wylie's lies. I have engaged the clutch and am in reverse, but it is slow going to get myself out of this sorrow. I want you to know I read *Daily Word*. I like the ideas and hopes expressed. They often lift my spirits. How about some advice from a "Man of the Cloth" like you to smooth the ruffled feathers of my soul?

From: Lucas Dmitri lucas@unityworld.org
Date: March 28, 2010
To: Ariane Altar ariane@altarpots.com
Subject: Re: still bummed

Surround yourself with people who can listen without judgment and let it out.... It's hard. Let the grief flow. You know all that, my dear. You know.

Here's a Buddhist story you might like:
A big, tough samurai once went to see a little monk. "Monk," he barked, in a voice accustomed to instant obedience, "teach me about Heaven and Hell!"

The monk looked up at the mighty warrior and replied with utter disdain, "Teach you about Heaven and Hell? I couldn't teach you about anything. You're dumb. You're dirty. You're a disgrace, an embarrassment to the samurai class. Get out of my sight. I can't stand you."

The samurai got furious. He shook, red in the face, speechless with rage. He pulled out his sword and prepared to slay the monk.

Looking straight into the samurai's eyes, the monk said softly, "That's Hell."

The samurai froze, realizing the compassion of the monk, who was risking his own life to show him Hell! He put down his sword and fell to his knees, filled with gratitude.

The monk said softly, "That is Heaven."

Pants On Fire!

Notes from Ariane's journal:
March 29, 2010

By Your Door

What if
I returned
To the us
Of us

What if
I tiptoed
To your
Door
Hesitant

What if
I waited
Breath held
For you

Would you
Know
Would you
Sense
That I was
Waiting
Just
Outside

What if
Our fragile
Little bird
The one you
Killed
What if
Our fragile
Little bird
Awoke

Pants On Fire!

I have
Heard
A bird
A mythical bird
And this bird
Could rise
This bird
Like Lazarus
Could rise from
From the dead
From the ashes
Of a terrible
Conflagration
One that destroyed
A marvelous world
Destroyed
The marvelous world
Of us

And I heard
They call
This fragile
Little bird
This rising bird
This awakening bird
They call
This rising bird
Not the Firebird
But
The phoenix

I stand
On tiptoe
Waiting
Outside
Your door
And I wonder
If this soft
Flutter
This new

This new and
Barely perceptible
Soft
O so soft
Flutter
in my heart
Could be wings

From: Ariane Altar ariane@altarpots.com
Date: April 1, 2010
To: Wylie Hymen wylie@hymenfables.com
Subject: An April Fool: me

I am writing, because I think you should know the consequences of your deceit. If you have any conscience at all, would you apologize and explain yourself? I suppose I do not expect the truth at this point, but I would appreciate it.

I came to you with an open heart and a clear agenda. I treated you with love, kindness, admiration, and generosity. You said you didn't want to disappoint or hurt me. Yet, by creating our relationship out of lies, where else were you headed except to disappoint and hurt me?

Why did you engage my affections and take a year of my life, when you were involved with Dina?

Your fabrications unraveled "seamlessly," to use a word you like. I was never suspicious. In fact, all I wanted was to spend the rest of my life with you. I loved you, and I trusted you. I know Baron was not with you on Chicken Ridge. I called him. Baron had never heard of me. He thought you had gone to Hawai'i with your "hiking buddies."

I asked when he'd seen you last. "It's been a while. We are not a close family." I asked if you'd skied together in Yosemite. "No." I asked if he had colon cancer. "Are you crazy? I'm healthy as a horse!" I asked if he was taking a "sacred journey" with you and Matthew to the UK. "What? Never! Matthew who?" You didn't tell him about your prostate cancer or Mantle Cell Lymphoma, though you told me you did. You did not have Thanksgiving with him or Matthew in Berkeley. In fact, there IS no Matthew Hymen. You even invented another son!

I now suspect that the reason you didn't tell your son, your daughter, or your friends about your cancers is because you don't have them! The cancers were a special little lie just to arouse my sympathy and to allow you to disappear for periods of time, a convenient exit strategy. To think that you are so low, you dupe real cancer survivors in the support groups you attend just to get attention!

You didn't tell your family or friends, you didn't tell anyone, about me. Were you warning me of your deception, when you wrote in one of your fables this description of the *Golden Deer* (and you gave me the original gilded illustration to hang above my fireplace):
One day there comes a deer
more beautiful than any she had ever seen,
with skin like polished gold and eyes of violet amethyst
but in death, it is not a *Golden Deer* but devilry
⋯it is an evil trick.

From: Cherry Estrella cherry@starsearch.com
Date: April 2, 2010
To: Ariane Altar ariane@altarpots.com

Relieved to know you got a clean bill of health. Also that you are feeling lighter for getting some of this off your chest. You are not an April Fool. I don't know if we should try to be our brother's keepers. But, I don't like people getting away with mistreating others, any more than I like people stealing or causing bodily harm. There is no court of law for crimes of the heart, but that doesn't mean he should just be able to walk away. Bravo to you for having the courage to clear the air.

I want to share some thoughts. We know now that Wylie is a womanizer. I wouldn't be surprised if he used the same lines on his other paramours, probably even using the same poems over and over, just changing the names and little details, like hair and eye color! By looking for old students, he was clearly trolling the waters, and you, being hungry, took his bait and got hooked.

I know I am being very cynical. He did fall in love with you, and I don't mean to belittle that. I don't think that had happened to him before! I don't think he had fallen into the well of true intimacy ever, and it happened so quickly between you, once in, he didn't know how to extricate himself. I suspect he hoped he could keep his two women separate, just as the Pacific Ocean separated you. The big problem (besides Pooky le cochon as paramour) is their connection for dope growing revenue, which I am certain is too lucrative for him to ever think of giving up.

Love yourself....enjoy being with yourself,...laugh with yourself. You have many wonderful friends, take the time to visit. Come on, you know being unhappy causes many illnesses. I look at you as having a wonderful life with a granddaughter to spoil.

Guess my good news: Rosie is expecting again in August! My mother at ninety-five is not ready to leave this earth. She is under Hospice home care and bed ridden, but that mind of hers is one of the Seven Wonders of the World. My plate is full with just her. Maybe she will still be alive to greet our next generation in the summer.

I pray you will feel better.

From: Karen Borders curator@ismuseum.org
Date: April 8, 2010
To: Wylie Hymen wylie@hymenfables.com
Subject: Shunga fantasies

Once, when we first met, you asked me what my erotic fantasies were, and I pitched you what few I have. I wish I were good at erotica, you seem to enjoy it and demand it, but I can't imagine anything more titillating or interesting than how we do, what we do, when we do, do it.

I have fantasies; they are, as you noted, quotidian. Today, they involve a quiet evening of dinner and doing simple things like reading to each other. As I am a curator in this tiny, boring, backwater of Indian Springs, I love anything to do with art. We would do all our surface talking and slide into more heart inspired communication. Maybe we could intoxicate our squeaky little minds with some decent wine. I would read you Spring Palace erotica, and you would read me Pillow Books. You would play me some music that touches you, and we would actually listen to it without touching. Oh. That's not erotic, is it?

Sometimes, in my fantasy, I sit in a corner and draw you, while you do some simple household task, like I did once when you were cooking me dinner. Then I would watch you sleep, your head resting on one of your erotic Pillow Books. Of course, somewhere in there, we would make long, sweet, gentle, blissful, perky, frenzied love, culminating in our usual explosive orgasm, which covers all of experience with the greatest, most peaceful pleasure. In the morning, Karen would go home to her husband and son, and we continue our lives with that little warm echo of happiness tucked into our nether parts as we go along disconnected until the next time we see each other.

This is part my fantasy and part reality; these things can't be cooked up, I suppose, although they can be provided with time and willingness. They flow or they don't.

My greatest desire is that, in our entire lives as friends, I bring nothing to your door but joy and delight, whatever shape that takes. You aren't shy about telling me when I don't make you happy, as you do nearly every time I call you, that's for sure. When you initiate, you are nice to me. But, watch out, if I initiate: the badger bares his teeth.

Badgers should be nice to little pussies.

Please use this email address; Don can't open it.

XXXXXXXXX Karen

Pants On Fire!

From: Karen Borders curator@ismuseum.org
Date: April 9, 2010
To: Wylie Hymen wylie@hymenfables.com
Subject: Ouch! That phone call hurt

I'm sorry I poked you, I should know better by now. I love you, little badger; stay safe and cozy in your hole, not mine. It's hard to keep my heart at home. I will make an effort to do so on Sunday at your Gala Opening, and if I can't, I'll figure out something. Your exhibition has been my project for a while, and I don't want unrelated difficult feelings to ruin my good time, especially if you bring your girlfriend, like you threaten to do. Have a wonderful life, and I will likewise.

From: Wylie Hymen wylie@hymenfables.com
Sent: April 9, 2010
To: Eli Charon elic@charontax.org
Subject: IRA Distribution

Hi, Eli,

You have some questions about my investments and dividends. The first triple digit went into two CDs at Savers Bank. I also received an annual distribution on my investment here at Indian Springs in December 09. I made a few other deposits for sales of books and art into my savings account over the year. Call, if these figures aren't clear.

You say I have taxes to pay this year? The money I deposited at Savers, apparently, did not go into an IRA account? I assumed that since I was taking annual mandatory disbursements from my IRA that I couldn't, at my age, create another. Too bad for me. I'll have to curtail my travels this year or keep my money under my mattress! Tell me the bad news of what I owe my very rich Uncle Sam.

From: Karen Borders curator@ismuseum.org
Date: April 11, 2010
To: Wylie Hymen wylie@hymenfables.com
Subject: your girlfriend

You know, I think I could like your Pooky. She has a twinkle in her eye I hadn't noticed before. Don wasn't feeling well at the Museum Gala, so I took him home. When I got back, you guys had left. Have a good trip; I know you will. I'll still be here when you get back.

From: Ariane Altar ariane@altarpots.com
Date: April 11, 2010
To: Lucas Dmitri lucas@unityworld.org
Subject: curious

Since you've decided to minister another year in the tropics, how will you and Christine work it out? Will you go to the mainland; will she venture out here? Is the long distance good/neutral/bad for the relationship? How do you cope with being alone? Lots of questions; sorry, I am curious, because I am sorting out being "alone" again, readjusting my dreams, coping with loss, hoping to rekindle a light heart.

Since I broke up with Wylie, I got quite ill with lung problems (which are for me emblematic of grief). Thankfully now I am calming down a bit. I am putting in lots of studio hours and distracting my mind with audio books and DVDs to try to get through this burnt-out period.

The worst, I think, comes from trying to understand "why": Why did he lie, why did he destroy our relationship, why did he seduce me in the first place? I learned after my children died that the question "Why?" has no answer and asking it paves a quick road to Emotional Hell. Despite this knowledge, I ask the question regarding Wylie.

His loss rattles my cage, undermining my confidence. I am hoping time and prayer will put me back together. My goal is to make my heart lighter than that proverbial feather that sits on the other side of the scales of judgment. (Guess what I've learned? A heart chopped into bits doesn't make it any lighter.) I am going on a strict fast of positive thinking/praying/meditating!

Tell me some good things.

From: Ariane Altar ariane@altarpots.com
Date: April 21, 2010
To: Cherry Estrella cherry@starsearch.com
Subject: private vs. public

Is all fair in love and war? Do you think it's fair to "tell all" now that it's over? Is it okay to joke about Wylie? We all know intimate relationships are private and, if all went well, they would stay that way, right? But, when love dies?

Okay, that was just a little preamble to announce: my gallows humor is back! You, lucky lady, are the first one to hoot at the skivvies! Let's take it from the top.

You know, when I first saw Wylie naked, I just wanted to burst out laughing. He looked like *Mr. Potato Head*! Remember that toy with the big potato body and little skinny legs? You could add body parts like oversized ears, a

Pants On Fire!

moustache, red plastic lips, a nose, and accessories like hats? Well, Wylie's
body was oblong and rounded like a potato with absolutely no butt, perched atop
two twiggy little legs. I almost whooped, but controlled myself. He also had an
itty-bitty penis and, tucked away somewhere, a pair of little, itsy bitsy, teeny
weenie balls. If he'd brought a yellow polka dot bikini, we'd have been in big,
or, rather, little trouble!

The funniest damn thing was his dick. He had confessed to years of impotency. He told me how angry he had been when—after learning of his first wife's
infidelities—he could no longer get it up. He went through decades of sex therapy
and private counseling, *Viagra,* herbal stimulants, and more, all to no avail. He
moaned that women would get angry when he could not perform, and his love life
was ruinous.

Then he discovered the Pump. It is some kind of medical device. He
would disappear into the bathroom, put two thick elastic bands around the
base of his penis, insert it into a water type apparatus, and start pumping.
He used oodles of lubricant. I could hear him pump pump pumping behind
the bathroom door, running water all the while. Then the sheer size of his
newly bulbous, purply red shaft would nearly throw him off balance as he
veered it away from the sink wheeling it around to lumber into the bedroom!
He teetered from side to side, careful not to bang a wall or door, and tottered
toward the bed, a shit eating grin on his face. To have intercourse with this
dirigible in tow, he had to prop my hips at a high angle on two stiff pillows,
aim, and "drop in" on me. He had no leverage—no steerage, I should say, to
bring his rudderless zeppelin into port!

It is funny now, in hindsight, to think of this little man disappearing into other
women's bathrooms all over the country, pumping himself like crazy for five minutes, to emerge with the *Hindenburg* in tow.

What pick up lines come to mind! (This humor might be lost on anyone under
sixty!) Picture a scene in the retirement home (at his age, there's no more hanging
out in bars to pick up chicks!): "Oh, hi, I'm Wylie, and I'm impotent," spoken
shyly to some lonely old lady shuffling down the cafeteria line in her walker. Or,
while dabbing a tender tear forming at the corner of his eye, he throws down the
gauntlet, "I haven't met a woman in years who could get me stiff···" Would his
confession elicit a stampede, wheelchairs colliding, walkers skidding, pills flying
as all the horny old ladies in the home rushed to the challenge? Or would they turn
and run the other way?

Oh, and then there was his wheezing little giggle. Imagine the sound a
naughty little rat might make, if it were trying to snigger with glee. Squealing on
the inhalation, panting on the exhalation. That was Wylie. Panting and squealing
simultaneously.

And, the rubber bands? Auschhhh! He would have to take them off after thirty minutes or his dick might atrophy or get gangrene, or something! Of course, a lot of pubic hair came off with them! Snap! Snap! Yee-ouch! He is the first man I ever met who was nearly bald down there!

Joking aside, the truth is, no matter how he got pumped up, it was marvelous!

From: Cherry Estrella cherry@starsearch.com
Date: April 22, 2010
To: Ariane Altar ariane@altarpots.com
Subject: *Mr. Potato Head*

You are awful, and you crack me up! *Mr. Potato Head*? The *Hindenburg*? I was shrieking! Here's my suggestion: buy a whole bag of colorful pony tail elastics—or better yet, softer hair scrunchies—and send them to Wylie as a parting gift from you for his future assignations! The scrunchies will be easier on his skin, and he won't lose as much pubic hair! You know, they say the *Hindenburg* went up in flames when its "skin" was touched, and this "friction" caused the hydrogen inside the skin, which kept it aloft, to explode, incinerating the passengers onboard.

Here is an article I found on the pump:

How Does A Penis Erectile Dysfunction Pump Work?

First, the user expands the penis ring over the bottom of the plastic cylinder. To promote a proper suction seal, lubricant is applied to the base of the penis, bottom of the plastic cylinder, and inside the tube to allow the penis to easily be drawn into the tube once suction is applied. Then the penis is inserted into the tube and the tube is pushed against the base of penis and body to create a proper seal. Suction is initiated by a pump. As negative pressure develops, the penis is engorged with blood and an erection is achieved. After the erection is achieved, the elastic penis ring is slipped off the tube to the base of the penis, and the erection is maintained.

I also thought you would be interested in clinical definitions of nutcases. You might get a kick out of the definition of a "primary psychopath" and an "unprincipled and amorous narcissist":

Psychopathy is a personality disorder characterized by an abnormal lack of empathy combined with strongly amoral conduct, masked by an ability to appear outwardly normal. Psychopaths use charisma, manipulation, intimidation, sexual intercourse, and violence. Lacking in conscience and empathy, they take what they want and do as they please, violating social norms and expectations without guilt or remorse.

288

Sexual narcissism is defined as an egocentric pattern of sexual behavior that involves both low self-esteem and an inflated sense of sexual entitlement. It is the erotic preoccupation with oneself as a superb lover through a desire to merge with oneself. It is most common in men and shows an inability to experience true intimacy.

What say you? Either definition fit Wylie? Here is another clue your No-Shit-Sherlock friend found: anti-depressants cause erectile dysfunction in some men!

Love, Cherry, still laughing

From: Iggy Fumer iggyf@gmail.com
Date: April 23, 2010
To: Dina Cochon dinaRN@iswell.org
Subject: Re: package

Pooky, dah-ling,

Lucky you, doing up the London Theater scene this trip. I am positively green!

Your reimbur$ement package is going out tomorrow. I tried to post it today, but the main post office is no longer open on Sundays. It used to be. Sigh. Plus c'est change! Michael will take it to the P.O. on his way to work after dropping me at the train. We are following your instructions to send the forthcoming payment to your address, not Roly's or Wylie's this time.

Lots of love to you both. Many hugs. Safe trip. I'll telephone you when I'm in the same time zone. Perchance to meet.

Love, love, love, Igg

From: Ande andeP@gmail.com
Date: April 24, 2010
To: Ariane Altar ariane@altarpots.com
Subject: your arm

moms,

hope you're feeling better. nalu said you looked pretty good after surgery. sorry I couldn't come over to help. your doggies are too rambunctious; your place is too wet and slippery. come live with us. kui would love it. you are having two too many accidents!

wuvs ande

From: Ariane Altar Ariane@altarpots.com
Date: April 26, 2010
To: Cherry Estrella cherry@starsearch.com
Subject: another accident

Rather accident-prone these days. Broke my arm—left one this time—tripping over dogs again. Another metal rod.

Wylie responded to my letter in his warped way. It was a mud bath. For now I won't expose you to any more mind-numbing boredom with my "Wylie Whine"!

From Wylie
April 19, 2010
Letter to Ariane

I picked up your letter on my way to Yosemite last week, and have had all this time to think not about what I would write to you, but if I would write at all. It was, Ariane, the meanest, most cynical, and insulting letter I have ever received. No surprise; it's completely consistent with the way you've been treating me the past few weeks; your silence above all.

But, one good outcome is that it frees me to speak my mind. Because I once loved and cared about you, I have tried to be conciliatory, considerate, to preserve something of the spirit and memory of what we once had together, hoping that I might open one of your letters some day and read words of healing. But, it's clear you care naught for me, and that you're committed to the path of retribution and revenge, and that of all your qualities, forgiveness is not one of them.

Endings are always sad and terrible. It was you who often said to enjoy love while you can, because you never know how and when it will end, almost as if you were expecting it to end.

I remember our beginning and year together as something very beautiful, and I think that's what's most important and what lives on the longest.

I have said I'm sorry in many different ways; unfortunately, we are not talking. I am sorry that I accepted the beautiful gift of your love, enjoying it, as I live, as I have to live now, one day at a time, yet unable to live up to your expectations for a future. We once talked about how unshared expectations are often the end of a relationship.

I am sorry that you have been ill. I, too, have been saddened to physical illness over what has happened. But, you really brought it on yourself. Your heart filled up with meanness when compassion was called for, and meanness is always unhealthy.

I bared my soul in a way I have never done before with anyone else, trying to explain to the woman I loved how it felt to be at the darkest, lowest emotional place in my life, scared, feeling adrift from reality, crazy is the word I used. I look back on it now as though I was in a dark cave, hallucinating, confused, unable to see clearly, certainly unable to express all that I was feeling. I had been telling you for months that I was experiencing sudden emotional storms. I told you how, while I was there with you, I had found in your presence love, peace, and protection from the pain.

Rereading that letter I'm amazed I was able to write anything at all. I wasn't the least bit afraid to write to you, because we had always shared our deepest thoughts, and I just expected that my emotional turmoil and pain would find in you if not understanding then at least forbearance. Most important, I wanted to protect you from what I was becoming and going through and, while saying farewell, to express all that you had meant to me.

For the first time in a year together, a year in which not a single harsh or unloving word passed between us, I stumbled; I fell, badly. Instead of reaching down to me with a helping hand, as I had done for you in your times of grief, you attacked me; you turned on me with a viciousness that has left me stunned to this day. You turned my words of love and devotion into weapons of hurt. I realize now there's no way that could have happened if you really loved me. You never called. Instead you set out to embarrass and discredit me, to punish me. You crashed into my son's life, expecting him to talk with you about his personal health. (He called me almost immediately and asked, "Dad, is she crazy?").

He also told me you were concerned I might be suicidal. Now let me try to understand what is wrong with this picture. It occurs to none other than Ariane Altar, or should I refer to you as Little Miss Emily Wolfeson, that her lover might be SUICIDAL, and she doesn't even call! Why does that strike me as tragic? No, amoral? Whatever, it made me realize I didn't really know you. I had always admired your compassion and impressed on me once again how little you really cared about me. I was not suicidal, while you were bent on punishment, Dina was driving from the coast to be with me. Her take on my relationship with you: "What were you thinking?" Indeed, what was I thinking?

I'm sorry that you found that year with me such a waste of time. I'm humbled; I've actually never been told that I was a waste of time. I can't imagine wasting a year in my new life where a year is worth two or three, maybe five. I've been trying to figure out why a year so meaningful to me was such a waste of time for you. Why did you stay around? Was I just okay until something better came along? All that pretending must have been trying. I'm sorry for wasting a whole year of opportunities for you to meet other men, to find more attentive, more loving lovers than I.

I'm sorry for intruding on your budding romance with Lucas. That was the first, and, for me, troubling lie of our relationship. You denied it, but how dumb or unobservant do you think I am? You went out together. You never missed a chance, even when I was along, to flirt with him. You had him over for lunch frequently, and he was with you several evenings when I called. You had pet names for one another, and he was the only man on the island (including me) to whom I saw you blow kisses when you parted. What was I to think when on the second night I was there, and we had just professed our love for one another, you announced, dramatically, "I have to tell you that my friend, Lucas, loves me."

Don't worry; as soon as he finds out Wylie's out of the picture, he will be back, if he's not already. You can cry in his arms and tell him what a shit Wylie turned out to be, and get back to your leisurely lunches, whatever's in the afternoons, candlelight dinners, watching films together on the chaise, talks late into the night, and, maybe, he'll bring you coffee and rose petals in the morning like I did. I'm no longer an obstacle keeping him from getting into your panties (though I suspect you've told him already you wear none.)

I'm sorry for keeping you from Juan who was always present in our lives; you thought of him and talked about him all the time, even when I was with you, thoughts of him coming up even in the most intimate of times. Though you said you would like to go to England to "see your pottery," I think you have been considering for a long time returning to Juan. You can cry in his arms about what a shit Wylie turned out to be. You can laugh together about how every morning when we had breakfast on the lanai, I sat in the monogrammed "Juan" chair, how I encountered his photo entering and leaving your bedroom, how you enjoyed the little frisson of seeing me naked in his or some other lover's bathrobe, and the little fashion shows of sexy underwear and dresses you had bought for his pleasure, or he bought for you. You can settle back into his castle, abbey, or whatever in England, and for days on end, resume your little game of hole-in-one.

Actually, it's been a relief to disconnect from the both of you. What you didn't know is that your continued emotional attachment to Juan and other lovers was threatening our relationship and likely to cause me to end it.

Sometime soon after we first made love here, I made a point of telling you that I was healthy, that I had regularly given blood and gotten good report cards, had many blood tests over the year, and most important, was not a sexual adventurer. You did not, however, return the courtesy. What's more, we'd been having sex for a year, and you would certainly have been feeling the effects of any infection in that time. You underwent expensive blood tests not because of concern for

292

your health, Ariane, but as an act of spite. The real joke here is that you are the sexual adventurer. If you have any positive results from your tests, you need to go through your emails, address book, and B&B guest list. You told me you don't have single men as guests, but you had at least one that I know of, you invited him to dinner and out for the evening (because "I felt sorry for him being alone".)

So, how many men over the years have stayed at your B&B, been invited in for candlelight dinners, and perhaps, as a consolation for being alone, a night or two with Ariane? Did you have blood tests after shacking up with the developer in his LA hotel? How about the "wealthy" realtor you invited over from the other side of the island to spend a weekend fucking you? (One thing I've learned is that I was an anomaly in your life; your sense of self comes largely from sleeping with rich men). And Michael? And how many others? What about the guy whose email I saw when I was there, wanting to get back into that very special thing you had going? What am I to conclude when every expensive hotel you took me to, you described as "romantic"? And you worry about my sexual health?

At first I was confused: why would you want to tell me about all these men in such intimate terms, and then I realized it was your way of putting me in my place. It made me realize that, despite what you told me, I was not any more to you than any of them. The problem with relating experiences with past lovers is it diminished our relationship and me. What was I, Ariane, number fifty-three, number seventy-five, number one hundred and two? Wow! I feel really special.

So, then, Ariane, how many men have you taken to your bed (which I once, romantic and silly, thought of as "our" bed)? How many men have you writhed under, told them they were the best fuck you ever had, counted out more orgasms than ever, complemented them on having the most beautiful dick you've ever seen, called them "my alabaster man", told them they were the love of your life? How many men have you photographed naked on your bed? Were their phalluses "golden," too?

Perhaps the one good thing that has come of your letter is that it has ended my grieving for the loss of your love and your presence in my life. I realize now that I was just one more man in your life, that the Ariane I loved never really existed, was a creation of my mind, a chimera, and I didn't really lose you, because you were never mine nor I yours. What's really cruel is that while you accused me of "toying" with your emotions, you had been performing, making me feel that I was the One, when in reality I was just another man co-starring in the Ariane lazzi of sex and loving.

The saddest thing for me right now is how quickly the memories are fading, eclipsed by your rancor and antipathy, how less and less I care. Please do not write again.

Pants On Fire!

From: Cherry Estrella cherry@starsearch.com
Date: April 24, 2010
To: Ariane Altar ariane@altarpots.com
Subject: He's no gentleman!

My heart just goes out to you. I really want you to know that Wylie's letter is awful and untrue! No one, I mean NO ONE, who's ever met you, been to your home, seen your art, eaten your cooking, known your children would EVER think you were anything less than stellar! You have such personal integrity and charisma. It's unbelievable that this cad would accuse you of—what did he say—being a sexual adventurer? Sounds to me like he is a "sexual marauder"! You are lucky to be rid of him.

What anger, vitriol, suspicion. I actually jumped into the bath after I read his letter. It was so dirty; it made me feel dirty! There's an old saying, "He who lays down with swine gets muddy!"

Okay, here's what I want to do. I want to call that fucker and give him a piece of my mind. Now I'm tempted to stalk him, drive up to that cabin, and see who's there. And then, prick his bubble. Take away his pump. Whatever. Let's get very drunk and make obscene phone calls to him!

Please don't stay sad too long. He's just not worth the tears.

Did you see the Rielle Hunter interview by Oprah? It was surreal watching her defend wrecking John Edwards' presidential aspirations, wedded life, relationship to his children with the words,

"The love in my heart was so powerful. I am a person of truth and integrity. Johnny's lies are part of his 'process' to come to the truth."!

She hasn't an ounce of conscience or remorse, justifying her actions (like no birth control and the *GQ* photo shoot) because she was following the heat in her heart! First time I've heard that excuse from a woman. Must be the equivalent of a man saying he got his brain caught in his fly. Are sociopaths ruling the world, I wonder?

By the way, did you see this review in the NY Times of Norris Church Mailer's book, *A Ticket to the Circus*, about her life with Norman? She is an artist and author, a tall, willowy, redheaded, Wilhelmina modeling beauty, twenty-six years his junior. She discovered that Mailer had been cheating on her with "a small army of women." She was Wife No. 6, yet found herself surprised that this philanderer was philandering on her

When she told him she was leaving, he went into overdrive to persuade her to stay. She was struck by how many of the women were either his age — he was near seventy then — or significantly overweight. "Sometimes I want to be the attractive one," he told her. She asked, "Why didn't I know?" He replied, "It's not

294

hard to fool somebody who loves you and trusts you." But, when you lose trust in somebody, she admitted, you never get it back.

From: Bill Partridge shipcraftsmen@verizon.net
Date: April 24, 2010
To: Wylie Hymen wylie@hymenfables.com
Subject: Re: Noah's Ark kit

I wanted to let you know that I sold the Noah's Ark kit. Took a year before the right buyer came in. Please email me your address. I'll send you a check.

From: Mom ednawolfeson@peoplepc.com
Date: April 25, 2010
To: Ariane Altar ariane@altarpots.com

Dear Dumb Daughter,

I just watched the *National Geographic* clips of Wylie's *Ark* film airing this fall. I thought the clips were beautiful. You'd never know what a jerk that randy old geezer is!

I have one comment: in the *Bible*, Noah let the animals come on in pairs: one male and one female of each species plus his wife, "Mamma" Emzara, his three sons and their wives. There is some historical writing that the old rascal snuck on board his little "love pet," Asenath. For what, I ask, a ménage a trois above the Flood? Men!

Grrr Your Tiger Mama

From: Ariane Altar ariane@altarpots.com
Date: April 25, 2010
To: Wylie Hymen wylie@hymenfables.com

The bulk of your letter was silly, and you know it.

I know you loved me. And, I loved you. For me, you were "The One," and there were no others. I can understand if, when we met and became close, you were still in a relationship with Dina. I would have thought, a point would have come when you would have let her go. You did not.

I asked why you lied. You haven't answered. It was your lies and double life that killed the beautiful love we shared.

Pants On Fire!

From: Wylie Hymen wylie@hymenfables.com
Sent: April 25, 2010
To: Fran Kroc franorg@mind.net
Subject: our old et cetera

Hi, Frannie,

I have an excuse to say hi, as I am daydreaming here, conjuring memories of our old "et cetera"! Remember the late spring snow? I want to let you know it's here (and sadly, you are not). We're having our traditional Easter Snow. I've been in a blizzard since getting home from the coast yesterday, and we may have twelve to eighteen inches of the stuff by tomorrow.

News. *Where's Noah's Ark?* was chosen as a 2010 ALA Notable Children's Book and won the Ancient Culture's Children's Book prize. Dina and I have resumed work on our theater book. *Set!* is its working title; we began thinking about this book ten years ago on our first trip to Eastern Europe. I am also painting again, nudes mainly. In May we leave for three weeks in England. Then Japan in the summer. *NG* is working out last minute details of the filmed *Where Is Noah's Ark?* which will be out this fall. Maybe you caught the preview the other night? Never did write that book on Theia.

Take care, dear friend, and know that I think of you often. When are you coming to visit me?

From: Fran Kroc franorg@mind.net
Date: April 26, 2010
To: Wylie Hymen wylie@hymenfables.com
Subject: Re: our old et cetera

Enjoy your time in England walking and inhaling culture. Know you'll love every minute! I must admit I am surprised and a bit jealous that you are still with Dina. I thought that was over. I found her a bit cold, but that was a while ago.

I still have a bit of rattlesnake grass on my kitchen windowsill to remind me of the time we (just you and I, remember? our special weekend at your cabin?) watched that falcon dive for fish near the rocks. Amazing, both the falcon and you! Wish you could be here to join me for dinner, and, later, for a taste of our old "et cetera"!

From: Karen Borders curator@ismuseum.org
Date: April 26, 2010
To: Wylie Hymen wylie@hymenfables.com
Subject: Gloating

296

Pants On Fire!

Wylie, I appreciated our conversation this morning. You didn't bite my head off! It gave me some insight why, when I write you love letters, it feels like I'm writing fiction. Of course, it IS fiction when you don't reciprocate. You pointed out that I'm terribly self-centered. And, just like you, I don't think of myself that way.

Jeez, we had so much fun that day. I can feel how close we got, how you slipped down the slippery slope into trust and care, and how I cut you off. Why did I have to fuck it up? You said some ex-girlfriend of yours was bugging you with her emotional issues. You couldn't get her to stop; you wrote her a mean letter, got it off your chest, and felt better. You felt forced to be unkind, and you felt better by making her feel worse. Did I tell you that's called gloating?

I am a dysfunctional emotional basket case. I keep wondering: why do you keep seeing me? I wish I were emotionally secure and had emotionally secure relationships. You are fine with Dina, or whoever. Like I said, I'm smitten with you. A big part of your appeal is your fierce energy for living life to the hilt. Not to mention your very kinky quirks.

Am I groveling? Yes. Do I love you? Actually, yes, for what that's worth. I would still like to bypass all these issues and just enjoy your company. But, you have told me you already have plenty of friends you "enjoy." And, I'm not all things to you. Ouch.

What do we do best? Touch. What do we do worst? Get personal. What am I hungry for? I would say a satisfying emotional relationship, but in practice, it seems to be your touch. Yum. What are you hungry for? I don't know, but my body seems to be on your menu. Often. Yum. Am I just your model? The nudes you showed me are wonderful, but none are of me. Hmmm. Who are they? Phantoms from your past or your present? When do I get to see some of me? I lay around naked for you often enough.

The new jacket cover photos or PR photos or whatever are beautiful. Much improved over the first ones you had taken!

From: Curt Degler cdegler@ng.org
Date: April 26, 2010
To: Wylie Hymen wylie@hymenfables.com
Subject: Re: Ladakh

I have a plantar wart and have re-re-tweaked an old ski injury. Right knee. It twinges a bit when I go down stairs. Going down 1,000 meters gives me pause. I don't think I'm ready for a long, high altitude hike. Mostly, I do high pressure, low altitude trips. Sometimes very high pressure. Do you know the timing (as they say in India) of Jill's trip this year? I hear she's back in the States.

Possibly, we could meet up in Manali or Leh for a drink. Or, in Pondicherry.

I'd consider that. It appears I'll be out of India from about June 1 until past August 1st due to visa requirements. If you do go to Tokyo in the summer, we could meet up there.

When do I get a signed copy of *Where is Noah's Ark?* I hear the film is finally set to air.

From: Jenn Gallway jenn.gal@yahoo.com
Date: April 26, 2010
To: Wylie Hymen wylie@hymenfables.com
Subject: ur cabin

Wylie, when did u say ur vacation is? When u'll be gone in April? As u probably gathered from my emails, I'm heavily involved in Red Cross Search & Rescue. I do want to visit u in ur mts. Trying to figure out how. When. The where-withal. And "talk" for a few sweet days. See your abode. Spring in bloom. Catch up. Hadn't heard from you since I transcribed Theia's tapes to CDs. I need to write. Too. I have opportunities now. Hope they work out. Let me know when you can take care of me, and when we can satisfy what once was our pleasure!

From: Wylie Hymen wylie@hymenfables.com
Date: Apr 26, 2010
To: Jill Forthright jforthright@ng.org
Subject: When can we meet?

Curt told me you were back. He cannot make your next trek due to a plantar's wart and a trick knee. Give me a call, and let's find a time to get together. I may want to join you on your trek. Send the revised itinerary. I've been missing you and our tent. It's been over a year! I'm off to England for a few weeks; Japan in the summer, but am yours for the fall.

From: Jill Forthright jforthright@ng.org
Date: April 26, 2010
To: Wylie Hymen wylie@hymenfables.com
Subject: Re: When can we meet?

Good to hear from you. I've written to you a few times on *Facebook*, but maybe you don't use it much. I'd love to see you. Where are you now? I live in San Francisco and work at KQED. No current work for me at *National Geographic.* I'm subletting a place until mid-May, so the other renters' voices are on the machine. You can leave a message for me. Let me know when you'll be around, or if you already are! Thanks for making contact. Hope you're well. I've thought of our special snuggle time under the tent in Turkey with much affection and glee. The *Ark* project took longer for *NG* to finish than any of us thought. I think it will air in the fall. I know some clips have been shown. Check your TV schedule! Where is Curt anyway?

From: Karen Borders curator@ismuseum.org
Date: April 27, 2010
To; Wylie Hymen wylie@hymenfables.com
Subject: poking again

I don't want you to think of me as just an immature, reactive, difficult person. I want you to think of me as a thoughtful, intelligent, willing to be constructive, immature, reactive, difficult pussy. There are two people in the whole world I can tolerate bullying from: you and my son. My son, because he is my son. You, because I refuse to see you as anything but a blessing. And, because, professionally, I am curating your next show!

From: Wylie Hymen wylie@hymenfables.com
Date: April 29, 2010
To: Ariane Altar ariane@altarpots.com
Subject: Re: your letter

I did love you, Ariane, but explicit in the letter you dismiss as "silly" is why I never could feel like "the one" – only "the next one."

The letter was not hyperbole; your friendships with men, fully aware of the discomfort they caused me, and the possible consequences to our relationship, did me in. On my very first visit to Hana, I spoke about behavior that was affecting our relationship, behavior I had experienced before, but only felt secure enough to express to you, because I knew how it had poisoned other relationships, and I really wanted nothing to intrude and disrupt the beautiful thing we had. I explained that each time it happened, it drove a wedge between us and made it harder and harder for me to reconnect, but in all respect was not asking you to change your behavior; I did not want to censure you: your reply was "I will probably keep on doing it" – which you did. In that instant, I respected you for your frankness and the clarity it brought, but also, sadly, had a clear insight into how our love might falter and eventually end.

A story, which I wouldn't bother you with except for the punch line: I have joined a remarkable twice-a-month cancer support group composed of about twelve men and women: artists, poets, writers, performing artists, a psychiatrist, all of whom are, like you, internationally known (they make me feel like an amateur). In just a couple of sessions, I have attained a much more profound and nuanced sense of what I have been experiencing over the last few months and how to move on. As Mills said, "So, Wylie, you've discovered you're human."

Among them is a famous theatre director, who is writing a book about the stage sets found in an old castle in Czechoslovakia. Some of us in the group had been talking about how we had been experiencing the same sudden, over-whelming emotions, when she began talking about her descent into madness, and I realized she was describing exactly the experience I had – the delusions, loss of center and all sense of reality, uncertain who and where she was. I must have reacted visibly. I think I began to shiver and tremble, because this kind woman took my hand in hers. She ended her story by revealing that when she finally emerged into the light once again, as I did, unable to fathom what had happened, she found she had lost her lover, who accused her of "abandoning him and lying."

I really can't tell from your repetitive letters what you want from me. I have apologized and explained a difficult and lamentable time in my life as best I can. My pain from losing you, Ariane, is no less than yours.

From: Ariane Altar ariane@altarpots.com
Date: April 29, 2010
To: Wylie Hymen wylie@hymenfables.com
Subject: Re: Re: your letter

I never deceived you. I am and was monogamous. If you looked at my emails during our time together, their constant theme was honesty. When I heard you lie to me on the phone in February, I was horrified. I never wanted to speak to you again. I felt shattered. The complete trust I'd had vanished.

Your letter about hallucinating worried me. I didn't know if you were ill or faking it. I wrestled with my feelings. I was very worried about you. I asked Ande what could I do to help you? She told me to call Baron and ask him check on you.

You don't have any photos in your house of people or places important to you. I found that odd and told you so. You called your omission being discreet; now, knowing you, I call it deception.

My conversations about friends who play a part in my life are normal! It doesn't mean I am in love with them! You are the first person to display jealousy over normal stuff. I didn't feel any jealousy of your former wives or girlfriends. I was concerned, however, about your relationship to Dina, asking about it on at least two occasions.

I can't help wondering if this sensitivity to relationships is a hot spot for you, because you were indeed leading a double life and somehow projected your duplicity on me? The other thing I wonder is when you said you were "going crazy," was it because you were trying to keep all your lies in order? I mean, if you were lying to me, were you not also lying to Dina? I can't imagine keeping all that straight! I suspect that lying is what makes you sick, crazy, hallucinatory, and, last but not least, impotent.

I have never before spoken the endearments I uttered to you. Nor have I had the fun. Nor have I played those games. That was we alone. As were the heights you took me to in our lovemaking. You made me, non-musical me, an opera star! Your betrayal of our union shocked me to my core.

From: Wylie Hymen wylie@hymenfables.com
Date: April 30, 2010
To: Ariane Altar ariane@altarpots.com
Subject: Theia's Story

I think you should return Theia's cassette tapes, because she would feel better having them in her possession. They have become key to her healing process with Selene, and, hopefully, the return of the tapes will help them reconcile. She will, by the way, be ninety this summer. You need to decide. As I've said from the beginning, the story is yours, if you want to write it. I did not make any notes of value on the historical side. I guess it wasn't meant to be. My new life has really clarified my priorities; I have other projects that interest me more, allowing more time for drawing and painting and travel. I do not want to be reminded of you or her again. You do not fit in my new world.

From: Iggy Fumer iggyf@gmail.com
Date: May 1, 2010
To: wylie@hymenfables.com, Dina Cochon dinaRN@iswell.org

Wylie and Pooky, dah-lings...I just realized you two are leaving, is it tomorrow? How is that possible with your product being worked on right now? PLUS I need you to ship one case to Jim T and a few to me. OY. Let me know if anything is possible or must it all wait until you return.

Thanks. LOVE YOU madly.

Pants On Fire!

From: Wylie Hymen wylie@hymenfables.com
Date: May 1, 2010
To: Iggy Fumer iggyf@gmail.com

Okay, five this month. Four every month until we run out. End of next week should be do-able. We leave for Cotswolds the following week.

From: Karen Borders curator@ismuseum.org
Date: May 3, 2010
To: Wylie Hymen wylie@hymenfables.com
Subject: pain relief

Oh, poor little badger! You hurt yourself. You ruptured a hernia? Were you lifting something heavy? Straining? Okay, I know you didn't hurt yourself having fun with me. Does it mean you are still playing games with your girlfriend, that Dina person, or your other "models," whoever they are? Okay, I'll help you anyway, as you have asked me to. But, you're not being very nice to me.

As far as cannabis is concerned, cannabinoids in leaf are not psychoactive and have the most pain relieving properties. There is a lot of anecdotal evidence that this works when conventional methods, such as *ibuprofen* and opiate derivatives, don't. One recommendation is to take leaves, macerate them in an inch of olive oil, and massage into the painful area. The longer they sit in the oil, the better.

The other recommendation is ingestion. Take twelve leaves blended in a smoothie, three times a day. You can also make a tincture (in alcohol) with wintergreen as a liniment. You have the "resource" right there. I hope this information helps.

I guess at this point I am only useful to you as your local curator fact checker. I would prefer to be useful as your local curator model and pain reliever. Like, want me to rub it, the cannabis oil, in? Or, better, want to light it up together? I'm also good at making smoothies. If we did all three, I am sure you'd feel better faster!

Give me a buzz, and I'll be right over to get a buzz on with you! Buzz buzz buzz sounds like a plan to me! I want to make some honey, honey, honey, honey! This little bee is buzzing all alone. She just wants honey, honey, honey. Buzz buzz buzz. I am doing my honeybee dance for you. Buzz buzz buzz buzz!

From: Iggy Fumer iggyf@gmail.com
Date: May 4, 2010
To: Wylie Hymen wylie@hymenfables.com
Subject: ruptured hernia?

Ruptured a hernia? Rushing to pack our order? Michael and I are devastated. On the bright side, chatted with my physical therapist today about you. Must be an inguinal hernia. Is it in the groin or in the balls? Either way, *ouchie*. He is suggesting that you stay with Pooky for the first month, so that she can drive you for surgery and check ups. Will you have to get physical therapy for that? Hmmm. Michael and I might be willing to help out. (Just a joke from two very bad boys to cheer you up).

Putting off Merrie Olde England a SECOND time?

From: Iggy Fumer iggyf@gmail.com
Date: May 6, 2010
To: Wylie Hymen wylie@hymenfables.com, Dina Cochon dinaRN@iswell.org
Subject: MISSING CASES

Wylie and Pook, dah-ling,

Did you get my messages from yesterday? I received two EMPTY boxes. What is with *FedEx*? We must talk! Is Wylie doing better? Trip to Cotswolds on or off? Sorry, sorry.

From: Karen Borders curator@ismuseum.org
Date: May 7, 2010
To: Wylie Hymen wylie@hymenfables.com
Subject: Re: for my book jacket cover?

That profile photo is not at all your handsome self. Was it taken after your hernia rupture? Joke. Don't use it for your book! It is kind of frightening; it gives you the appearance of a bird of prey, and it's way too dark! I'll try to turn you on and send a photo of me twenty-five years ago.

Sorry I bothered you again with my many messages. I don't like to bother you. But, email didn't work, no reply, didn't hear from you for ages. Then I called, and you took my head off. I just wanted to help. I should forget that you exist except when you decide to eventually contact me. I'm not good at that, but you have been teaching me. This is a bitter lesson. Cords, you know, or chords. Maybe what really binds us together is "chords," not "cords." The harmony or dissonance of our individual notes rarely, if ever, played together. This morning I will sing the sad,

303

unrequited love song of "I reached out for Wylie but he was busy" and go on and make my music elsewhere.

From: Ariane Altar ariane@altarpots.com
Date: May 7, 2010
To: Lucas Dmitri lucas@unityworld.org
Subject: Spreading my fingers

Glad you signed on for another year in our tropics leading your flock. It's still hard for me to imagine adhering to church doctrine as you do; possibly, it's hard for you to imagine me as a spiritual, prayerful being!

I think prayer has eased my disappointment by reminding me Not To Hold On. In trying to comprehend my losses—divorce, dead children, and so on—I've learned that you don't get things/people/situations back (you know the saying that life isn't a dress rehearsal!). I don't get my youth back; I don't get my children back; I don't get my broken dreams back.

From: Lucas Dmitri lucas@unityworld.org
Date: May 7, 2010
To: Ariane Altar ariane@altarpots.com
Subject: Ho'oponopono

You mentioned Wylie asked what he could do to make it right, to keep the silken cords of trust and love connecting you intact? Would you consider practicing the Hawai'ian custom called Ho'oponopono, the principle "to make right"? You can practice ho'oponopono alone, just by repeating the mantra. It is a process of reconciliation and forgiveness. I am sure you are familiar with it. To engage in its practice is not an attempt to reclaim the love relationship. It is rather to heal the wounds and go forward in our lives in peace, unburdened by a karmic debt.

One has to repeat constantly the mantra, "I'm sorry. Please forgive me. I love you. Thank you." It is based on the principle of 100% responsibility, taking responsibility for everyone's actions, not only for one's own.

Pacific Island peoples believe that illness usually is caused by sexual misconduct or anger. "If you are angry for two or three days, sickness will come," said one local man. The therapy that counters this sickness is confession. When the error is confessed, it no longer has power over the person.

I am not asking you to sit down with Wylie, Pooky, or Baron, to go over last year's calendar, openly detailing where you each were and with whom, correcting each lie with the truth. Instead, I am asking you to imagine taking responsibility for inviting Wylie into your life and believing his lies.

I doubt that the consequences of such a "coming to Jesus" meeting with yourself could be worse than the negativity surrounding your relationship (which may echo long into the future) unless you neutralize it.

From: Fran Kroc franorg@mind.net
Sent: May 8, 2010
To: Wylie Hymen wylie@hymenfables.com
Subject: re: Meeting

I'm glad that you and Dina have such a great trip coming up! Sounds like the Great Ash Delay may just work in your favor, weather- and convenience-wise. Will you take pictures? If so, and if you feel like sharing, I'd love to see them. I already have images in my head of beautiful spring green, early-morning mist, wildflowers, sunshine, and a good cup of tea at the end of the day. Yes, Hollywood's version of Dickens, Austen, and the Bronte's has been neatly drilled into my head. It sounds as if you'll be getting the best of Britain's city and country life. Come back to me in good health. We may yet find a time to romp without our pesky partners!

From: Wylie Hymen wylie@hymenfables.com
Date: May 9, 2010
To: Fran Kroc franorg@mind.net
Subject: Re: re: Meeting

A thought: I will return from England June 3, and will be busy much of the month. However, I shall be in San Francisco for three days teaching workshops on children's book illustration and design for the Society of Children's Book Writers & Illustrators. If you can join me, I'll find a motel close by. I'm only scheduled to teach two days. I may need to be there a third for one-on-one meetings, but I'm going to try to schedule these around my workshops.

Birth of Impressionism, Masterpieces From the Musee d'Orsay is opening at the de Young, at the Palace of the Legion of Honor a companion show, *Impressionist Paris: City of Light*; San Francisco being the only place in the world where both of these exhibitions will appear. I hope to go as many times as I can. What do you say: nice opportunity to spend some days, and nights, together?

August is out as I'll be in Tokyo working with Fuji film on some new crystal archival products for the figurative painting I have resumed.

Pants On Fire!

From: Karen Borders curator@ismuseum.org
Date: May 10, 2010
To: Wylie Hymen wylie@hymenfables.com
Subject: Your photo

I think I'm going to blow up the photo you sent and feel all moony about you. It's not the youth, it's the open, relaxed smile and the amused gaze, which I see still. I also like the gesture of your hand, like your book jacket self-portrait, which indicates contented self-possession and ease in the world. Age hasn't affected that at all! Your delight in the universe and in your life continues unabated (although I don't have the past to compare). Almost every other photo I've seen of you, even where you were younger than you are in this picture, you look uncomfortable and self-conscious. Like life is a very serious affair, and you are slightly stunned by it all. So, do you or don't you like the photo?

Go ahead! Argue with me! Give me an opportunity to practice getting into a good, floor banging, brain bending argument. Then you can hiss and spit at me, and I can "wrassel" you to the floor, and we can roll around and stuff. It would be cool if we ever took the time to actually get to know each other. I think we would still like each other. But, maybe not, and then we would spoil our perfect, ecstatic superficiality. Sometimes I like to poke you to see what's under your armor, but I just get the badger baring its teeth, and I seem to have a great fear of your displeasure. Do you play? Like a playful little kitten? Do you like to tickle and giggle? "Oh, Mrs. Hymen, can little Wylie come out and play?" Come play with me, little Wylie, you charming charmer! Or, will you nip me, bite me, sink your teeth into me, hard, like a bad, bad, bad badger?

From: Roxie Plumm roxie@Plummart.com
Date: May 10, 2010
To: Wylie Hymen wylie@hymenfables.com
Subject: seeing you!

I am touched that you remembered me last year (you said you were going through old yearbooks and trying to reconnect to students who had provoked you! Did you mean that even at my young age I was provocative?)

Glad to hear you purchased the small print I did of the *Ark*. I had no idea you had not only written a book on finding Noah's *Ark*, but you had also made a film (I caught previews on television last Tuesday). My little print is not much in comparison to your scholarly and historical approach! I just happen to love animals. The *Berggruen* people liked it, also. We made the print for my show invitation. What a surprise to see your smiling face at the opening! Little did I know I would become an illustrator, or that my teacher would become a famous writer and painter!

306

Pants On Fire!

My studio is not far from the Golden Gate Bridge at Fort Mason. Please feel free, and invited!, to drop in when you are in the Bay Area. I would love to see you again···in a role, perhaps, a little different from when you were my teacher?

Did I tell you John and I divorced this winter?

Your Provocateur

From: Wylie Hymen wylie@hymenfables.com
Date: May 10, 2010
To: Roxie Plumm roxie@Plummart.com
Subject: Re: seeing you!

It's hard to describe what seeing you again has meant to me. It may sound odd, but I have never forgotten you and your radiance since teaching at City. I knew you would make something of yourself: you had that star quality. But, seeing you again, forty years later, only confirms my earlier appraisal. You are a beautiful woman, quite unchanged from your glowing sixteen-year-old self, and so accomplished. You've reappeared in one of the more intensely introspective moments in my life; more accurately, dear Roxie, you are the cause of it all. I'll tell you more about that when we have some quiet time together. Some words I find comfort in are from a song I once heard Diana Ross sing:

Long ago, far away···Remember?
Life is just a memory···Remember?
Life is never as it seems···

I'm sorry to hear of your split with John. You seem to be doing well. If you need an ear to listen to musings on art, life, your heart, call. I would love to speak with you. Evenings are best for me. I should be back from England mid-June.

From: Cherry Estrella cherry@starsearch.com
Date: May 10, 2010
To: Ariane Altar ariane@altarpots.com
Subject: Amoral people

Read what Oprah's fans wrote to her blog site in response to her interview with John Edwards' mistress:

Rielle Hunter revealed that she exists in a moral vacuum, is self-promoting, and has circular reasoning. This thoroughly bankrupt person has the power to wound. Damage from such people is like being attacked by a rabid dog. All you really have to do is get in its way to get bitten.

I watched the interview with Rielle Hunter and found it to be very disturbing. How is it that a person can sit on National TV and claim that she made so many "MISTAKES" (like doing a GQ spread without panties!) and not take responsibility for her actions?

Oprah, you did a great job of exposing a sociopath. Rielle has a grandiose sense of self, lack of remorse, shame and guilt, poor behavior control, and a need for stimulation. Hasn't she heard the road to HELL is paved with good intentions? Rielle did us one big favor, she put an end to John Edwards' run for anything. Elizabeth can thank her lucky stars that she found out Johnny is a sociopath, too.

Rielle Hunter is such a fascinating case of human beings' ability to live in denial and delusion. We all do it to some extent, but her excessive claims to "truth," "integrity," and "authenticity" are telltale of gigantic folly. How tragic and Shakespearian, so much self-undoing. I feel embarrassed for her.

Rielle has created a kind of quicksand, the more she tries to manipulate her image to gain glory, the worse she comes off. In the end, it is comforting to know the world has such divine justice: the truth, always, comes out, and what is meant to be, will be.

Wylie's behavior, not just his but so many people's, bothers me a lot. I saw a therapist recently on television who has a reality show on sexual addiction. Imagine! I was thinking that many people in their search for love and meaning might think of themselves as having an addiction to sex: using sexual intimacy and encounters as a way to feel connected. Where do you draw the line and say "this is normal" but "that is not"?
    The reality show addicts had one thing in common: their pursuit of sex was interfering with other areas of their lives and causing disruption. For example, one woman would stalk men she'd dated. She felt compulsive and out of control. One man was a rock star who claimed he'd slept with over three thousand women, but he couldn't emotionally connect with his own wife and children. One girl was a porn star who said she tried to fill herself up by having a lot of sex, hating the feeling of emptiness she carried inside.

My thought is that Wylie is one of those sex addicts. He really cannot sustain a normal relationship. When it feels real, like your love and meeting your daughter and granddaughter, he bails. As it turns out, he was having erotic fantasies and liaisons with other women WHILE he was with you! A true sign of someone only committed to the pursuit of his own pleasure at the expense of others.

Don't cry over this little bug any longer!

Ariane's Journal
May 11, 2010

It has become apparent to me, since I broke off with Wylie, that he has a consistent pattern of luring women into his life, short term, for Wylie-style fun and games. I had it right when I emailed Dina that he "enjoyed toying with other people's hearts." He trolls for love or, better stated, he trolls for erotic titillation. It is to my great regret that I unwittingly took his bait.

In one of his first emails he wrote:

It's hard to describe what seeing you again has meant to me. It may sound odd, but I have never forgotten you and your radiance since my first year of teaching at City. I knew you would make something of yourself: you had that star quality. But, seeing you again, over forty years later, only confirms my earlier appraisal. You are a beautiful woman, quite unchanged from your glowing sixteen-year-old self, and so accomplished. You've reappeared in one of the more intensely introspective moments in my life; more accurately, dear Ariane, you are the cause of it all. I'll tell you more about that when we have some quiet time together.

When he left Hana in February, he left his email and password on my computer. One day when cleaning files, I found it. Oh my. That is how I learned of his deceptions, not just to me, but to Dina, Jill, Frannie, Karen, Lin, Jenn, Nancy, Roxie, and on *Facebook*, how many more? It is also why I wrote to alert Dina.

I suppose Dina and Jill, like some other lonely women, do not care about fidelity. They, like him, lack a moral compass. Look at Frannie and Karen, who are married and still meet him clandestinely!

I am different. I wanted it all. The love he professed felt real to me, igniting the flame in my loins and fire in my heart. I thought our love would burn through the heavens like an inextinguishable comet. My expressions of love were honest and heartfelt, unlike his.

I have destroyed his *Golden Deer*. I was hesitant at first to destroy a work of art; then I realized this was not art but rather pure trickery. I wanted it destroyed. I lit it on fire on my driveway and watched the paper curl and writhe; I watched its gold leaf turn to green flames, and I watched its ashes disappear on the wind. Never kid yourself, Ariane: Wylie treated you cruelly. He committed crimes against your heart. Do not wish him well. I hope he burns all the nudes he drew of me.

It musta been love
But it's over now
It musta been love
But it's gone like
The water flows
Like the wind blows
Leave your whisper on my pillow
Leave the winter on the floor

Roxette, from the film *Pretty Woman*

May 10, 2010
These May days have been leaden with rain increasing the heaviness of my heart. Occasionally I see the shore or a dock or boat ramp and remember that this long swim in loneliness will have its end. And, when surprised by a call or an email, it is that breath of life, of fresh air, that inflates the old life raft of my heart keeping it buoyant and afloat this wet spring season.

Longing for love, kind of like the cycles of the moon, waxing and waning, pulling me to and fro in the tidal drift. I realize I am and have always been propelled and energized by a vast loneliness deep in my soul, creating an immense itch and agitation. With age, it has morphed to a yearning: a feeling of the tide of my life going out. And, the yearning is to be loved before it's all over. Perhaps on the next wave, the tide will turn and come in. You just never know.

A Sung Dynasty poet, Chu Shu Chen, a woman, centuries ago wrote:

CVIII
PLAINT

Spring flowers, Autumn moons,
Water lilies still carry
Away my heart like a lost
Boat. As long as I am flesh
And bone I will never find
Rest. There will never come a

310

Time when I will be able
To resist my emotions.

May 24, 2010
Poem Remembering Wylie

Chimera

Was I a chimera
To you
Your fantasy
A nocturnal emission
Did you love
Me

I love
You
Still
Angry
With myself
Disturbed

Walking an edge
Between fantasy and reality
Illusion and disillusion
Or is it
Delusion

You told so many lies
Was I
One of your lies as well?

I laid down beside you
I want you
Even now
More than I have
Wanted anyone
How can I
How can I want you

Pants On Fire!

A liar
Who dishonored me
Who never planned
To live life with me
Joined as lovers
Are joined

But here I am
Siamese
Unable to function
Without my other half
My other self
You

I love you, Wylie
I can't stop myself

Why do
Passion
Joy
Surrender
Beauty
Love
Not reign
Supreme
In your heart
As they do
In mine

Unless
I was just
A nocturnal emission
Pleasurable
In the night reverie
Traversing the
Wetlands of your dreams
Vanishing
In the morning light

Tantric texts
Tell me

Pants On Fire!

Touch
Can be learned
There is no secret
To the body's alarms
Any thief can
Set them off
Were you
A robber
Who came
In the night
Hooked my soul
On desire
Snatching my heart

I am dragged
Into my days
Unbelievably
Beautiful sunlit mornings
Of birdsong and roses
Music and fragrance
On the breeze
Mountains green
Misted by passing squalls
And though I see the beauty
My heart is
Missing
A bog
Silenced
Sorrowful
Regretting
And more
Because there is
Less
Of you

Will we
Speak
Silently
In tongues
Of love
Entwined

Pants On Fire!

Yet
Apart

I loved you, Wylie
And that was
Not
A chimera

From: Ariane Altar ariane@altarpots.com
Date: May 28, 2010
To: Lucas Dmitri lucas@unityworld.org
Subject: Re: Ho'oponopono

You wrote about Ho'oponopono. I was too raw to respond. But, now I might
be ready to entertain the idea of healing or forgiving or whatever I need to do. I
think I have hit rock bottom. I am still mad, but I am willing to admit how sad I am
and to take some responsibility.

I mean, I wonder, what if I am wrong, completely wrong? What if Wylie was
telling the truth? That Dina is only a friend? What if I have jumped to conclusions
out of paranoia and suspiciousness?

I expected him to trust me completely. But, he doesn't (and he is wrong about
me and other men). Now, I don't trust him (and maybe I am wrong).

What if he wanted to hide his marijuana business from me, after I expressed
distaste about drugs and how they had ruined my family? What if Dina was only
a "business partner" and not a lover? Should I dismount from my moral rocking
horse? What if I find out that there are mitigating circumstances behind the marijuana business?

From Ariane's Journal
June 1, 2010

Set Back

Wylie, Wylie, Wylie
Why Have You Set Up Camp In My Mind?
Why do I consider
Reaching
You
Asking

314

Pants On Fire!

What happened
Asking
Do you
Want
Us
Asking
The truth
About relationships
Asking
Do you
Still love
Me
Is it just
My craziness
My usual unwillingness
To let things
Go
My need
For explanations

You lied
Hiding always
Your real reasons
For being
Away
Am I
Willing to accept
Lies
Trust
You will tell the truth
Now
This second time
Around
If there is
To be
A second

Who is this man
Really
You asked
Who is this woman

Pants On Fire!

Really
You asked

Are you, am I, are we
Ready to speak
Love
Again
O, to have you
Hold me
Your embrace
The only one
I desire
You
The one
The only

Are you dying
Do I want to lose
You
A second
Or third time
To either
A new round of lies
Or to cancer

Why am I
Clinging
Why can't I
Accept
My own decision
To end it

Notes in Ariane's journal:
A poem not sent

You wrote of spring awakening
You wrote of spring renewal
My words, I thought, were
Final
My words I thought were

Pants On Fire!

Ending

What if the numbness
What if the cold
What if my frozen
Heart
Were to thaw
What if I were
Waiting
Waiting for warmth
Waiting for
Your spring sun
A sun
Distant
Cold
Dormant above
The bleak landscape
My wintering heart
Your sun
Now
Recalled
Its heat
Nourishment
Heralding warmer days

What if I
Were to respond
Awakening
O this remembered sun
A time for planting
Time for growing
Time for life

What if I awoke
Sorry
For the winter
Sorry
For all
The long, dreary days
I froze
My heart

Pants On Fire!

From: Lucas Dmitri lucas@unityworld.org
Date: June 4, 2010
To: Ariane Altar Ariane@altarpots.com
Subject: Re: Re: Ho'oponopono

What truly belongs to us cannot be taken away. It is a law of the universe. If Wylie truly belongs in your heart, a path will open. All you can do is practice Ho'oponopono, and let go of any outcome.

Notes from Ariane's Journal
June 6, 2010

I am practicing my little ho'oponopono mantra almost every day. It goes like this: I get quiet. I look at the green mountain across the valley or up at the night sky, then I look inward. When I feel I have God's attention, I begin.

I love you, Wylie. I am sorry. Thank you for loving me. I take responsibility for myself. I am sorry. Thank you. I love you.

I was driving to Kahului the other day when I got the urge to call him. I pulled over to get a cell signal. I left this message:

"Wylie, this is Ariane. I want a healing. I love you. I am sorry. I know you have your life, and I have mine. I just want to tell you I am sorry. I want a healing. I love you."

I feel released; I feel it's over. I never thought I'd get here, to this place of freedom!

◐

From: Dina Cochon dinaRN@iswell.org
Date: June 12, 2010
To: Matthew doc@iswellness.com
Subject: Japan

Do you really think Wylie can manage alone in Japan? Can't you go? Send an itinerary ASAP. Situation worsening. Feel a bit desperate.

Pants On Fire!

From: Wylie Hymen wylie@hymenfables.com
Date: June 12, 2010
To: Dina Cochon dinaRN@iswell.org
Subject: Dying

The cancer is spreading. I think the therapy is killing me.
Come now.
I am dying.

Notes in Ariane's journal:
June 22, 2010
April Fool in June

Do you want to hear my "It should be April Fools' Day" joke? I guess it is a joke on me. Only it's not funny.

Well, I could have saved myself a lot of heartache if I had opened Theia's box of memorabilia when she sent it to me a last year! I opened it today, thinking I would check what was inside before chucking it.

There was quite a lot of great stuff: black and white photos of her arrival in Shanghai taken from the deck of the luxury liner; her family's apartment in the French Concession; Theia dressed in absolutely stunning silk cheongsams, looking like a Hollywood Heddy Lamar; side streets filled with scurrying Chinese peasants; even pictures of Madame Chiang Kai-shek and her sisters! There were some shots, too, of Theia holding Selene as a baby, and several together with her mother and father. I would have thought she would have kept those photos.

Anyway, here is the amazing part. There were lots of letters, tied into separate bundles. I couldn't read most of them, because they were in Polish or German or Russian or Chinese! But, there was one bundle, tied in a ribbon with some dried rose stems looped in the knot. These letters were in English and postmarked Berkeley. The handwriting on the envelopes was in beautiful, black calligraphic script, something you might see in a Medieval Latin manuscript. I recognized it immediately: it was Wylie's hand!

The first postmark was January 16, 1964. (Selene and I graduated from City in June of 1964). I couldn't believe it! Wylie was writing to Selene's mother back then! I untied the ribbon, pricked my finger on a thorn still deadly sharp on one of the rose stems, cursed, sucking away the blood. There were so many letters. I leafed through dozens. They had been bound in chronological order. I stopped. I knew, we always just know, don't we, when we are in the presence of something sacred? Despite my curiosity and trembling, I stopped moving. All the letters were postmarked Berkeley except the last, which was postmarked Indian Springs, November 24, 1972.

Seven years. Seven years of correspondence. Had Theia written back? I opened the first letter. It was blue, the paper, I mean. Nice heavy vellum in robin's egg blue. It was long, methodically penned as if it were a symphonic score, the record of Wylie's words, a melody of the heart, waiting to be read or played again by anyone skilled in the art of love. Wylie's words. Words of love. O my god. Wylie wrote love letters to Theia! Wylie was in love with Theia! Theia! Theia! O my god.

What I read was even more startling. Why? Almost word for word, Wylie wrote the very same poems and protestations of love to me!

I read Wylie's first letter to Theia again. Then another and another. I heard this siren, this wail. I turned my head from side to side and looked to find where this sound was coming from, as it grew louder, closer to the house. It was a cry, a high-pitched moan. My cry, my open mouthed cry, carrying the life right out of my body. It lasted until every trace of air was gone from my lungs. I collapsed and cried there on the floor like a big baby. Just wept and wailed, gasping, moaning, barking, coughing for the longest time. I must have sounded like a sea lion, bereft, left all alone on some beleaguered outcropping in the stormy sea, barking its broken heart out.

Here is a poem he sent to me this winter but which he composed for Theia in the winter of 1967:

With My Love By The Fire

Sitting by the fire into the night,
Outside the wind whispering in the trees,
You came to me from the dark,
Into the flickering light, your face
up close to mine, looking deep
into my eyes, deep into the soul of me
that loves you more than I can say.
I took your head into my hands,
thrilled by your soft, fine, raven tresses
on the back of my arms,
nuzzled my face warm against your neck,
brushed your nose and lips with mine,
and placed my lips so gently onto yours,
holding you, my hands moving, slowly
up and down your luscious body, so familiar
yet always so new, taking in deeply
your warm breath, our hearts beating together,

and I fell asleep there,
fell into a peaceful sleep,
there with you in my arms, and later,
awakening from my dream of you,
still making love in the deep, slow way we do,
You sang your purring song of love to me and
I whispered your name over and over,
Theia, dear, dear Theia, softly,
outside the wind whispering in the trees,
sitting by the fire into the night. O Theia, when will you be mine?

I have actually thrown up a couple of times. I have chicken skin. How eerie is this? How unnerving these letters? He was never in love with me. He was just re-living or re-enacting the love he felt for her, letting it come alive again. He must have been utterly obsessed for the last fifty years by the love he had for Theia!

From: Ariane Altar ariane@altarpots.com
Date: June 26, 2010
To: Ande andeP@gmail.com

Do you think you could come stay with me a couple of days? It would mean the world to me. If baby Kui was here, I know I would be distracted and feel better. We could play with the dogs, do the *hokey pokey*, and hang out at the beach. Please. Ande, please call.

Part Four

A Telephone Wire

The Gibbous Moon

Telephone Call From Ariane To Theia:
June 26, 2010

Ariane: Theia, this is Ariane. I'm calling from Hawai'i.

Theia: Oh, really? This is a surprise. How did you know I'd be at Tahoe?

Ariane: You're always at Tahoe in summer.

Theia: Your voice, it sounds so young, you know, on the phone! Before you say anything, I want to tell you, I owe you an apology.

Ariane: Oh?

Theia: The book, my story. I was supposed to sign your contract. I need to explain some things.

Ariane: Theia, I am not calling about the book.

Theia: Oh, really? This is embarrassing! I am going to say something shocking. It's been on my mind since I saw you. Let me see, where to begin? (laughs) Well, I guess the beginning is best! Is this a good time for you? Can you talk?

Ariane: I called you, Theia.

Theia: You do not really know me, Ariane. And, you do not really know Selene. This is not what a mother usually tells her daughter! Or her daughter's friend! Well, as you know, Selene has not been happy with me. You know how I annoy Selene, and she resents me. I think we need a psychiatrist before we can talk.

Pants On Fire!

Ariane: Yes, I know. I think she's always been jealous. She used to joke about being eclipsed by you.

Theia: (laughing) You are too kind. Well, let me tell you. My Selene fell in love with that Mr. Hymen. Wylie, I think his name was. The one you wanted to bring here to write the book about me.

Ariane: (gasping) What?

Theia: Yes. Him. Ariane? Are you there?

Ariane: Yes. Of course, I am here. When was this?

Theia: A very long time ago. Selene was around twenty-four, I think. She had broken off her engagement to that talented and good-looking architect, Will. You remember Will?

Ariane: Yes. We double dated at our senior prom.

Theia: Selene had moved home from New York and started grad school in Chinese Art History here at U.C. And, whom do you think she runs into on campus? Her "Mr. Hymen" from high school days.

Ariane: This is unbelievable.

Theia: When she told me she had seen him, all hell broke loose! I told her, "No, No! You cannot see that man! You cannot bring him into my life again!" "Your life!" she said, "What are you talking about?" So, of course, I had to tell her about my affair. She called me all sorts of ugly names, threw some clothes into her *MG*, remember her little red *MG*? And drove off. We did not hear from her for several weeks.

I never, never wanted Vladimir to know. I became a nervous wreck. Now I had two affairs to hide from him: Selene's and mine. I was terribly afraid. My secrets. I did not know if Selene would bring that Wylie home, here, to my house. I didn't know if she would tell Vladimir. I didn't know if I had a daughter anymore. My life was a wreck, again. Ah, (laughing) so many wrecks, but I'm still alive.

Well, I want to tell you why Selene kicked you out of her life. She was afraid, very afraid, you would bring Wylie back into our world. She had loved him. I am not sure she ever got over it. The break was sudden. She was shocked that she was sleeping, you know, sleeping with a man who had slept with her mother! Imagine!

She and I have had such an awful time, dreadful, really. And, just as she's getting married again, who calls but Wylie?

Ariane: Oh, God.

Theia: I thought you should know Wylie really didn't mean anything to me. I tried to tell Selene, but she closed the door on the subject and never, ever opened it. So, anyway, I just wanted to tell you, it was just a silly little fling. You know, something to do while Vladimir was away.

Ariane: But Wylie? He was married! He had kids.

Theia: Oh, he was such a silly boy! I would never have left Vladimir! But, Wylie kept calling and calling. He told me his wife was gone. We were free. Crazy things like that. I got rather annoyed with all the melodrama. American men are childish. He should have known me better.

Ariane: Oh. Yes, of course. He should have known you better.

Theia: Well, I was right. He whimpered and sent letter after letter. I opened very few. One day he burst into my house. It was in the late afternoon, around the time we used to meet. Well, it was unexpected.

Ariane: I can imagine.

Theia: Oh, really? Well, no, you cannot. You see, my lingerie was scattered on the stairs, my habit, and Wylie burst into my bedroom. He found me in the nude and with another man.

Ariane: Not Vladimir?

Theia: Correct. Not Vladimir. His name was Tom, a friend of Wylie's from City, Selene's art teacher.

Ariane: Oh, Theia.

Theia: Tom was painting me. Wylie tore at the canvas, at me, at Tom, screaming in a rage. He made a terrible mess. I had to have the room redecorated. After that no one heard from him. Tom told me that Wylie couldn't hold himself together at school and lost his teaching position. Then, I didn't hear from either of them for years. Eventually, it all faded away as most things do.

Ariane: Wait. I am not clear. Why did you start a relationship with Wylie? He was a young father···

Theia: Yes, well, when you and Selene were in high school, remember? Your mother and I used to teach English as a second language in the basement a few mornings a week? I got to know Wylie Hymen at that time. We would have a cup of coffee; chat a bit. Being Jewish, we talked a little about the war and Poland and my time in Shanghai. He was very attentive. One day, he asked if he could record my story. I thought it would be a good idea. Vladimir was traveling to Europe quite a lot in those days, and I had time on my hands. So, we began sessions at my house.

Ariane: I know. I have listened to over ninety hours of those sessions, Theia!

Theia: Yes. Well, that is my Poland/Shanghai story. This is the Wylie story, and I find it embarrassing! So. I was lonely, Vladimir was gone, and Wylie was so, what is the word? Enamored. Enthralled. No. Wait. Enchanted. He used to say enchanted. Anyway, head over heels, I think you say. He worked and worked on my story, or at least he said he did. Mostly we just had a few hours here, a lunch there. It fed my ego, as you say, and the attention was very pleasant. But then, Wylie wanted more.

Ariane: What do you mean he wanted more?

Theia: Well, it didn't work out. It wasn't meant to. I mean, we were both married; he had a wife and two little children. I was older, too, probably ten years or more. He was a terrible lover, like a child. And he was tiny, also like a child! For a while, I amused myself by teaching him how to, you know, give a woman pleasure. But, I was in love with my husband. For me, it was just a little fling. But, when I told Wylie it couldn't go on, he got terribly upset.

Ariane: How did he show it?

Theia: Well, at first I thought he was being a poor sport. He begged me to keep loving him. I couldn't, and I didn't. I mean, you have to understand, for me it was just something to do in the afternoon. He spied on me. I would see him behind a counter in a grocery store or casually by his car in a parking lot. I became afraid.

Ariane: Ahhhh. Uhhhh. So, that is why he never finished your book?

Pants On Fire!

Theia: No. I don't think so. He threatened to leave his wife. I didn't believe him. I am not sure what happened there, because I kind of lost track of him. But, I heard that she had run away to England with the children, married someone over there. She was a talented woman. If I remember correctly, she played concert violin. I used to see her at the symphony in San Francisco.

Ariane: Why didn't you tell me before? I've known you for nearly fifty years. But, I didn't know any of this! It is strange. He always said he was fascinated by you and abandoned your project back then, because he was feeling attracted to you, you know, it became awkward for him. He said his wife fooled around on him and broke his heart by running off to England with the children and with his best friend, another violinist. Not the other way around!

Theia: Oh, really? That is not true. I still volunteered at the school. You and Selene were away at college. I heard from the art teacher, Tom, that Wylie had a nervous breakdown.

Ariane: What?

Theia: A nervous breakdown. He had to stop teaching and was hospitalized.

Ariane: Is that how it happened?

Theia: Trust me. That is how it happened. He was being silly. School boyish. It was a crush, an infatuation, whatever. But, it scared me, because he wouldn't let go. In forty years, I never heard from him. Then I get a call in February that he wants to meet, that you and he want to write my story from the old recordings. Oh, that call, that voice, oh.

Ariane: Wylie told me you had a delightful lunch. He loved seeing you again.

Theia: Not really? I didn't have lunch with him! I wanted you to write my story, Ariane. Not him! I told him I could not have him in my life again. I told him to leave me alone. Give the tapes or CD's or whatever they are to you, give them to Ariane and to leave me alone. Vladimir knew nothing of our affair. And now he is very frail; he had a stroke a few months ago, and I am afraid Wylie will say or do something about me and the past to hurt him. I just can't risk that. And that is also why Selene destroyed your friendship. What if you had brought him to her wedding? No, we couldn't let him worm his way back into our lives through you or Selene or my story. Now do you understand?

Ariane: Not really.

Theia: Vladimir is ill. And, his heart is fragile. He has been in and out of the hospital.

Ariane: Selene mentioned it before. Look, Theia, nothing fits! I have spent a year with Wylie. I don't know why he never mentioned anything as important as an affair with you, or with Selene. A nervous breakdown. Oh.

Theia: Is there something wrong? Your voice sounds funny.

Ariane: I feel ill.

Theia: Oh?

Ariane: I, um, oh, listen, Theia. After I saw you last year and talked about writing the book, I began spending a lot of time with Wylie. I had no idea, I, um, oh god. (crying) I had no, oh, I'm sorry (sniffling). (sigh) I had no idea you and he, and he and Selene, had ever been involved. Oh jeez. I'm shocked. I mean, I am really, really shocked by all of you.

Theia: Oh, really? He never said anything?

Ariane: Never. And, neither did you! You sent me that box of memorabilia, but I never opened it. When you didn't sign our contract, I put writing your book on a back burner. I, I, god, I wanted to marry him. Theia, I haven't wanted to marry anyone in twenty years. Along comes Wylie with the Wylie intensity and whammo, I am in love. Big time. Oh god. I need to hang up.

Theia: Wait! There is more I have to tell you.

Notes in Ariane's journal:
June 24, 2010

Theia? My question is about Theia. Why? Did Theia love Wylie at all? Did Selene? They couldn't have returned his passion, breath for breath, stroke for stroke, kiss for sweet kiss, the way I did. Theia didn't write poetry about their love, long for his company, thrill and shudder beneath his touch. Wylie was simply her distraction from boredom, from housewifery, from Vladimir's absences. Did she even once consider leaving, partaking fully in the love Wylie poured out and promised her – for eternity, for god's sake? No! She cast him off with her usual disdain. And Selene?

Pants On Fire!

I suppose she lost her heart, too, with never a word to me about him. Theia. Theia. She got it all: a long life, adventure, adoration, wealth, family, love, Wylie. She got; she had; she has, my Wylie. She survived. Has that woman always been just one step ahead, like the title I chose for her story in the beginning?

From: Ariane Altar ariane@altarpots.com
Date: June 26, 2010
To: Cherry Estrella cherry@starsearch.com, Mom ednawolfeson@peoplepc.com
Ande andeP@gmail.com
Subject: The end all

I called Selene's mother, Theia. Sit down and fasten your seat belts. She told me she and Wylie had an affair when I was his student in high school! And not just that, but that he left his wife and kids for her! And not just that, but when she rejected him, he had a nervous breakdown! Are you as breathless as I am?

And that's not all! Remember when I told Selene I was coming to California for her wedding and, if there was time, hoped to meet Wylie to talk about writing her mother's story? And she freaked out and ended our friendship? I was blown away and couldn't figure out why she kicked me out of her life, and why the outrageous bridezilla behavior?

Hold on—it's going to get turbulent! Selene also had an affair with him! Not! Yes, it's true! It was about eight years after he had recovered from his nervous breakdown. She didn't have any idea her mother had had a fling with him: Selene was twenty-four, had broken off with her fiancé, Will, was going to grad school. Who does she run into on campus but Mr. Hymen! And what was he doing there? Studying Mandarin. And, why? His psychiatrist had set him on a task to focus and calm his mind. Drawing and memorizing three to four thousand sinographs or Chinese characters would help! And, what was Selene's first language? Mandarin, taught to her by her Ah-mah in Shanghai! So, they had coffee and and and···

Well, I knew nothing of this affair over the years; no one ever breathed a word. It also happened at a time I was married, living in Paris creating a theatre company of my own, practically living at the Louvre and Tuilleries soaking up the art. I knew Selene was dating and teaching second grade. But, apparently, Selene had moved back in with her parents while getting her degree. When she was going to meet Wylie one night, her mother asked whom she was seeing. "Oh, Wylie. Maybe you remember him? My teacher—Mr. Hymen. From City By The Bay?"

All hell broke loose. Theia freaked for two reasons: one that she didn't want Wylie anywhere near her or her life (she was protecting her marriage) and two, she didn't want her daughter anywhere near Wylie. Remember, Theia is a diva. She had to be the attractive one, the desired one. No way could her daughter date an

331

ex-lover! What a row ensued! Selene was ferocious, now jealous of her mother as a rival for the man she loved. To this day, I've seen that rivalry causing friction as each tries to outshine the other; I just never knew what caused it.

From: Mom ednawolfeson@peoplepc.com
Date: June 26, 2010
To: Ariane Altar ariane@altarpots.com
Subject: Re: crazy turn of events

Dear Dumb Daughter,

Duped again, I'd say. It sounds like that Theia jazzed around back then more than I remembered.

Try to find the humor, look at the irony, and count yourself lucky to have gotten out when you did. A lie is a lie is a lie. Wylie lied; Theia lied; Selene lied. And, a lie by any other name would smell the same: just plain rotten.

It's good Ande and the baby are with you. Do the *hokey pokey* and turn yourself around! That's what it's all about!

Grrr Your Mama Tiger

From: Juan Silver jsilver@gmail.com
Date: July 4, 2010
To: Ariane Altar ariane@altarpots.com
Subject: your breakup with Wylie

Cheer up, Sweetheart. Celebrate your Independence Day! I wish I could pop a bottle of *Nicholas Feuillatte* Brut and drink it with you on the lanai like we used to do. Just assume it will all come up roses. You must have something great in store, I am sure. Few women I've met can even measure up to your kneecaps! What a wonderful lady, friend, and former lover you are! You are the most intelligent lady I have met and one of the most sensitive. It's great to have you as a friend. Thank you for keeping the door open. Really fun to talk to you, even though you are a bit bruised.

Love, Juan

Pants On Fire!

Letter from Indian Springs Wellness Center
A Psychiatric Treatment Community, Indian Springs, CA
Dr. Matthew Mills to Ariane
Date: July 24, 2010

Innovators in Mental Health Residential Treatment
Indian Springs Mental Health Center is fully committed to helping you or your
loved ones recover from a mental illness

Dear Ms. Altar,

Indian Springs Wellness Center is a discreet, private, residential community, catering to the mental health needs of highly intelligent, professional, and discerning patients and their families.

This letter is written to you at the specific request of my patient, Mr. Wylie Hymen. He has signed a release of our center's evaluation of his medical condition for your information (see attached copy).

I have known Mr. Hymen since 1972 when he was admitted to Herrick Hospital in Berkeley, where I worked as a psychiatric intern. His case interested me; particularly because he was lucid, talented, yet so traumatized that he could no longer function in his career as a teacher. He had left his wife and two children to have an affair with a beautiful Jewish émigré. She, however, refused his advances. He became obsessed with her. Simultaneously, he was overwhelmed by guilt for abandoning his family.

When Indian Springs Wellness Center opened, he was one of our first residential patients. Here, we help a unique group of patients: those with brilliant minds, often autistic, overactive, or emotionally unbalanced, who can produce creative works but are not fully capable of independent living.

Indian Springs is a gated community located on an old Indian reservation called Chicken Ridge. I believe you have stayed here as a guest of Mr. Hymen's. But, you may not have known that his cabin is part of our larger therapeutic community. Our staff and patients live in individual cabins separated by ponds, waterways, and hundreds of acres of woodlands. We have created an atmosphere of normalcy and privacy within safe boundaries for our patients.

Many leave, stabilizing to return to their lives and families. Others leave for a while but find they need to come back for a "tune up." Others live here permanently. We operate like any retirement community: homes are built or leased by our patients. We offer a full range of therapy, food service, recreational facilities, and so on.

Indian Springs Wellness Center is in the forefront of the movement in California to legalize the growing of medical marijuana. The revenue generated by its sale has allows us not only to be self supporting but also profitable. Our rates are the lowest in the health care community and affordable to less affluent members of our culture. None of the patients in our program are "substance" abusers; nor are any of our patients violent or psychotic.

Mr. Hymen enjoys long periods of functionality. Shortly after moving here, he began writing children's books. He also paints and draws. We encouraged him to do pen and ink, as he has a meticulous sense of line and scale. At first all he drew were boats. When I asked why, he said he needed a boat to cross the sea to find his family (at that time, his children were with their mother in England.) Then he began drawing people. The artwork has carried him through many a dark hour. For a period of time, he experimented with color. Currently, he is focused on drawing nude figures.

Wylie responds most favorably to role-playing in group therapy. We had a drama coach on staff who was also a psychiatric RN. She and Wylie married about twelve years ago. Wylie remains living at his cabin at our facility while his wife, Dina, shares a home with her elderly father on the Mendocino coast. Wylie feels safe in her care. Together, they are able to travel, generally to specialized care facilities. This year, for example, Wylie had therapy sessions in York and in Gloucester in the UK. We believe that nature is restorative. Consequently, I also approved several solo trips for him to go to Yosemite and Hawai'i. But, several months ago, Dina noticed that Wylie was regressing, slipping into old patterns.

I regret to say that at present you, Ms. Altar, are the cause of his mental regression. Your work together on a biography of Theia Steiner rekindled his emotional arsenal and created a firestorm in his heart. You brought back to life the love that had damaged his mind and destroyed his family. Compounding this problem, he is unable to distinguish between you and Theia. Sometimes it is Theia he loves; sometimes it is you as Theia he loves; sometimes it is you he loves.

Mr. and Mrs. Hymen have requested that you not contact him in future. As his psychiatrist, I concur. We kindly request your cooperation and understanding in this matter. I feel certain you would not wish to further jeopardize his mental and emotional stability, especially now that I have revealed his history and shared our concerns with you.

I remain willing to answer any questions you may have.

Sincerely,
Matthew Mills, MD
Director, Indian Springs Wellness Center
A Psychiatric Treatment Community

ADULT INTENSIVE SERVICES

Intensive programs provide daily, specialized support to adults with a severe and persistent mental illness while maintaining ties to their family and community.

Pants On Fire!

Services incorporate case management, vocational, residential, psychiatric, and
counseling services, all of which may be used to
build and maintain recovery over a long term.
Some of the diagnoses we treat include:
o Schizophrenia
o Bipolar Disorder
o Anxiety Disorders
o Schizoaffective disorder
o Bipolar with Psychosis
o Asperger's Syndrome
o Autism Spectrum Disorders

From: Ariane Altar ariane@altarpots.com
Date: July 27, 2010
To: Cherry Estrella cherry@starsearch.com Mom ednawolfeson@peoplepc.com
Ande andeP@gmail.com
Subject: Nuts!

It's true: you've always said a man has to be crazy to fall in love with me! A
psychiatrist wrote me a cease-and-desist letter. Wylie is in therapy. He is still in
love with Theia, married to Dina, "Pooky," who is his nurse, and unstable. Ahem.
Can it get any worse? (This psychiatrist called Wylie and Dina's marriage "a win-
win" situation.)

Among many things, Dr. Mills (get this: Wylie's doctor's name is Matthew.
Wylie told me his son, Matthew, was a doctor. Well, turns out Wylie only has one
son, Baron, and the one he called Matthew is Matthew Mills, his shrink. As you
can see, there are indeed a few crossed wires in that old brain of his!) told me all
that theatre going was part of Wylie's rehabilitation! Pooky Dina took the residents
to American Conservatory Theatre productions in San Francisco, to the Ashland
Shakespeare Festival in Oregon, and to many local productions in Mendocino
County. The yearly "birthday" trips were actually vigils to specialists in New York
or Europe, where new treatments were tried. Dina makes sure the travel is stimulat-
ing, filled with museum stops and theatrical productions, whatever she can find to
bring him into the present moment and keep him there. Their goal is to make him
forget his "love."

Pooky Dina noticed Wylie slipping into old patterns several months ago and
alerted Mills: long walks alone through the hills, crying, or sitting in the window
seat in the afternoon sun looking out the window, motionless for hours. Then he
started painting. She thinks the new painting of nudes, which apparently occupies

him every waking hour, is unhealthy. The nudes are of me or Theia and not of Pooky, by the way.

Active therapy sessions resumed. Wylie calls the therapy "cancer" and complains, "The cancer is returning." Why? Mills postulates that therapy draws Wylie away from his reveries, those memories of sweet hours spent in Theia's embrace. Therapy kills those reveries, kills his love. Thus, he calls it his "cancer." He believes if therapy works, he, ever faithful to his love, will die. The "cancer" will have eaten through his heart.

Mills said Wylie's treatment over the years has followed the arc of the flavor of the month in psychiatric care: Freudian, Jungian, group, psychodrama, art therapy, role playing, hypnosis, past life regressions, in addition to a full course of anti-psychotics, anti-depressants, and more in the pharmaceutical lexicon.

Here's a sidebar of all sidebars: When Wylie lost his wife and Theia, he became-impotent. He swore to Dina that he was not impotent (I guess they've never screwed); he was merely being chaste, waiting for Theia. But, she never returned and neither did his ability to have a normal erection. Mills had put him on a regimen of anti-anxiety drugs, which exacerbated the problem of impotency. As I told you, Wylie never regained function.

Mills claims this inability makes Wylie feel insignificant and powerless around women. As he can be a very social and charming person, full of titillating stories, well read, an accomplished musician, artist, and writer, and so on, he has a retinue of female followers. He enjoys intimate dinners, afternoons at museums, and so on. He has become a regular correspondent of many ladies in the time Mills has known him. (I just couldn't bring myself to ask Mills if he had also prescribed the pump!) Mills said, "Wylie may have entertained fantasies, but he certainly could not maintain what we would call "normal relationships."

There you have it.

Ariane, Processing The Big Pill

From: Cherry Estrella cherry@starsearch.com
Date: July 27, 2010
To: Ariane Altar ariane@altarpots.com
Subject: Re: Nuts!

Listen, remember the poet, Ezra Pound, who was brilliant—probably the most influential writer of the twentieth century? He was locked up for years in an asylum. He, like Wylie, lived most of his adult life in an often-miserable ménage a trois with two women who loathed each other. Among artists and poets, Wylie isn't an anomaly! Does this bit of trivia help? I thought of you when I read this

336

poem, which I have shortened below, because Pound is talking about the "second" woman in his life.

Portrait d'Une Femme

···You have been second always. Tragical?
No. You preferred it to the usual thing:
···No! there is nothing! In the whole and all,
Nothing that's quite your own.
Yet this is you.

From: Ariane Altar ariane@altarpots.com
Date: July 27, 2010
To: Cherry Estrella cherry@starsearch.com
Subject: Sloppy seconds···

Like the Pound poem says: second always. Seems to be me. Second Hand Rose.

From: Ariane Altar ariane@altarpots.com
Date: August 8, 2010
To: Lucas Dmitri lucas@unityworld.org
Subject: Feeling lighter!

Hello, hello! Home from Kaua'i with a much lighter heart. Can belly laugh about my crazy ex-love now! What's more, I also learned he had an affair with my best friend and her mother! (As a point of interest, last April when I got so unsettled and talked to you, wondering if Wylie was traveling with Dina, the answer is yes, he was. Lesson learned: Trust my instincts!)

From: Lucas Dmitri lucas@unityworld.org
Date: August 8, 2010
To: Ariane Altar ariane@altarpots.com
Subject: Re: Feeling lighter!

Are you celebrating, my dear? I am glad you are feeling lighter. It has taken quite a while. A big love will do that.

L'affaire Wylie raises some questions for me. Judging by your descriptions, it was, to borrow a gross quote from the movie, "Basic Instinct": the fuck of the century. The question, not answered by the psychics or the astrologers or we, the clergy, is where can we turn to know what is real and what is not? How do we create that epic relationship that has it all? Or, is it a cosmic joke, and there really is no such thing, only moments, fleeting moments, during an otherwise disappointing, and often anguished, journey?

What did work unfailingly, as you point out, was your gut feeling. Lesson: Trust in yourself.

Maybe the trick is to want and need no-thing? Then, whatever comes along is a gift, and whatever leaves, leaves, because that is in the nature of things.

Lately, I've been watching the flowers and plants bloom and leaf in cycles: a rose comes and it goes, and new roses come and in turn go. This may be the nature of life, and as you suggested, all you can do is keep your heart open, take love when it comes, bid farewell when it leaves, and rest serene in the knowledge that this is the nature of life. And, we, too, as a part of nature, briefly bloom only to die; and some mystics say, bloom and die, over and over again. Of course, this may just be a lot of high-sounding, re-played spiritual gobbledygook.

I'm thinking in images: you, Selene, and Theia are blossoms; Wylie is the little bee, just doing his job, pollinating!

Au revoir, I'm on my way back in time to Delphi to seek the Oracle. Or, maybe I'm off to Jerusalem to the Temple. A nap under the Bodhi tree sounds good, too.

From: Wylie Hymen wylie@hymenfables.com
Date: August 16, 2010
To: Selene Steiner laluna@gmail.com
Subject: getting together?

Dearest Selene,

Ever since I called you a couple of years ago, I have been hoping we'd get together and add the second "parenthesis" to our relationship hiatus these forty years.

I am planning a trip down to Berkeley. I want to see you. I have been engaged in some deep therapy sessions. I sense you and your mother have never healed the rift between you. I hope I might be able to help. If you wish to see me, might Theia join us?

My conversation with Theia the other night took an odd turn, putting me in the rather peculiar position of being the one to invite you to have lunch with us. The sense I get is that she feels I'm more likely to be successful getting you there than she would be! If I've learned anything over the years, it is not to wonder about – to say nothing of getting involved in – the dynamics of families. The fact that I've agreed at all to participate in this charade attests to how much I value our friendship and reflects my interest in seeing you again.

So, here's what's happening. I'm meeting Theia for lunch at noon on Sunday. Theia's hope, and mine, is that you can be there, too. I would like to be part of your healing. If that doesn't work, and you would like some other way for us to get together, that would be fine, too. Whatever happens, I remain your friend.

Enchanted by you, as always, Wylie

From: Selene Steiner laluna@gmail.com
Date: August 17, 2010
To: Wylie Hymen wylie@hymenfables.com
Subject: Re: getting together?

I will not, let me repeat, I will not EVER join you or see you.

From: Wylie Hymen wylie@hymenfables.com
Date: August 18, 2010
To: Roxie Plumm roxie@plummart.com

Your call this morning was a delightful surprise – direct, candid, and open, accepting. But then, I shouldn't be surprised; your thoughtful comments just reaffirmed my immediate impression of you that first morning we met – a bright, strong, sensitive woman to whom life has taught compassion. What a beginning for a new/old friendship.

From: Roxie Plumm roxie@plummart.com
Date: August 18, 2010
To: Wylie Hymen wylie@hymenfables.com
Subject: talking

That's a lovely thing you called me, "a tall glass of water on a long dusty trail." Thank you. Guess I was thirsty, too. It was easy to talk with you. You are so alive, and I am feeling energized by our connection. Looking forward to knowing you better.

From: Wylie Hymen wylie@hymenfables.com
Date: August 24, 2010
To: Roxie Plumm roxie@plummart.com

For Roxie

Breakfast, an unseasonably cool summer morning,
from across the table your warm, assured smile

Pants On Fire!

that turns so readily into laughter, reveals
a lifetime of joys, adventures, and secrets
that make me even more curious. We talked
so easily, words flowing as between old friends
perhaps, in some other life, lovers. Suddenly,
I was caught up in the blue blue of your eyes
(but why hadn't I seen them before?)
and forgot what I was going to say next,
enchanted, losing my whole train of thought,
I decided I would much rather enter
into the blue blueness than think.

Then, walking behind you in the cool mist
on the flowery, brambly trail, below
the swash and white froth of the surf,
I wanted to encircle you in my arms –
Too soon! a rational voice from within warned,
too soon! – and bury my face in the softness of your auburn hair.

What a delight, walking a foggy day with you,
and another surprise; you tell me you write poems.
I would be honored if you would read your favorites to me
someday, so that I might not only enjoy your poetry
in your own voice, but enter again, as many times as I wish,
into the deep blue, blueness of your eyes
and the warmth of your smile.

From: Roxie Plumm roxie@plummart.com
Date: August 25, 2010
To: Wylie Hymen wylie@hymenfables.com

Reading this made me feel smiling glowy soft. Thank you. I would like
to be able to respond with a poem but find I am not ready to do so, because
I really don't know where to take it and, I guess feel a little shy? Cautious?
Uncertain? Maybe downright scared, if I tell the truth. Right now I am just
breathing. For one thing, I think a bit of emotional housecleaning from my
split with John is in order. It's not such a big deal; nothing dramatic. I'm
really long over it and everything; it's kind of like some residue, which I need
to sweep out.

Anyway, you are brave and sweet, and I'll be brave, too, and maybe we'll get together and hang out toward the end of this month. I'm looking forward to it. I am imagining coming there and just taking it easy walking, talking, whatever. I'll bet it is peaceful there, and we could have easy quiet or alone time as well. I have a feeling you are someone with whom it would be comfortable to be alone/together. Hmmm that's a nice thing. Hope it doesn't sound like a weird thing to say. I also imagine we can talk for hours.

I am sitting here and watching a movie about Rumi and going into a realm of ecstasy. Now it is I thinking of you. I am noticing that several times in the last couple of weeks when I was experiencing some kind of ecstasy and joy I thought of you and wanted to share some of it with you. I am thinking that it shows me we are connected in a deep place. Think I will call you.

From: Dina Cochon dinaRN@iswell.org
Date: August 29, 2010
To: Wylie Hymen wylie@hymenfables.com
Subject: WHERE ARE YOU?

Call me already

From: Wylie Hymen wylie@hymenfables.com
Date: September 7, 2010
To: Roxie Plumm roxie@plummart.com

I cried when I returned to the house and realized you had really gone. I am responding the old fashioned way, by mail which you should have when you get home . . . unless you plan to stay longer in the East Bay. Let's stay in touch by cell phone; I promise to keep mine on and check messages regularly.

I'm driving down Sunday morning, having lunch with friends in Berkeley. I want to tell you about Selene and Theia some day. I plan to stay at least through Monday, but that depends on your plans.

You are in my heart, dear Roxie and I've thought of nothing else except our time together.

Your Wylie

From: Roxie Plumm roxie@plummart.com
Date: September 8, 2010
To: Wylie Hymen wylie@hymenfables.com

Pants On Fire!

Wylie, I love what we are sharing. It just gets deeper, more comfortable and exciting every time. I am still awash in the feeling of pleasure. How could I be so lucky to encounter an initiate into the realms of sensual and sexual ecstasy and be loved to such a state of such surrender? The more we talk and share the more it clarifies as a soul level connection. I love you already. What a sweet, comfortable, and erotic couple of days. Parts of me, my body, are awake and abuzz, and it is deliciously welcome. I'm glad we spent this time together. It felt familiar as well as very pleasant. It seems so easy for each of us to understand the other. You and images of the last few days keep rising in my mind. Now I must be patient and wait for days to read your letter, but I am enjoying that suspense, and I will write a letter back. Such a good idea.

From: Ariane Altar ariane@altarpots.com
Date: September 8, 2010
To: Cherry Estrella cherry@starsearch.com
Subject: The Sound of Pumping

I have to share a ha-ha: I had a dream in the wee morning hours. I could hear the rhythmic pump pump pumping of you-know-who's you-know-what. Not in my bathroom, thank god! But in some other woman's bathroom, in fact in many women's bathrooms, all over the continent. I could see his tired little member slowly inflate, that incorrigible dirigible rising for yet another joy ride in some other bed. It would float up, quite unattached to his heart and soul. In fact, it detached completely from his body (did you ever hear that crazy song, *Detachable Penis*? If you haven't had the pleasure, I've included the lyrics below). In my dream, I watched Wylie's bloated penis float out of the bedroom window and hover over the city, whose lights twinkled far below. It was a blimp, a penis blimp, traveling aloft on the night's sultry breath, fueled by the heated and panting sighs from the paramours' bellowing lungs below. On it flew, and on, and on. Oh well. Maybe it's only funny to me, as I used to howl at this song by King Missile:

Detachable Penis

I woke up this morning···
And my penis was missing again.
This happens all the time.
It's detachable.

This comes in handy a lot of the time.
I can leave it home, when I think it's gonna get me in trouble,

342

or I can rent it out, when I don't need it.
But now and then···
I can't for the life of me
remember what I did with it.
First I looked around my apartment, and I couldn't find it.
I was starting to get desperate.
I really don't like being without my penis for too long.
It makes me feel like less of a man,
People sometimes tell me I should get it permanently attached,
but I don't know.
Even though sometimes it's a pain in the ass,
I like having a detachable penis.

From: Cherry Estrella cherry@starsearch.com
Date: September 8. 2010
To: Ariane Altar ariane@altarpots.com
Subject: the detachable penis

 Where's my detachable vagina?

Notes in Ariane's journal:
September 18, 2010

 Your love didn't belong to me, Wylie. It was meant for another. I got it on loan.
Borrowed it from your love library, an edition fifty years old, when you lost yourself,
a time when the world and all its conceits fell away, when you encapsulated moments
of eternal bliss and seared them into memory. It was for you true love, if true love
lives beyond the constraints of time and place. But, that love was not requited.

 I loved you. You responded, I think, sometimes, yes, sometimes you responded
to me, but also to that old bound and frayed edition of your love. You loved the
artist in me and the poetess and the eternal feminine. I loved the artist in you and
the poet. Mainly, I loved you, the man. You loved Theia, neither an artist nor a
poet, simply a woman. And Selene, o Selene the moon, you wanted only for the
reflected light of her mother.

 Your piercing stare, that amethyst fire in your eyes, I saw as the flame of our
love, but it was not directed at me. It was looking inward. You were peering at a
memory, the memory of another woman, another love. Your first, and only, love.
I think you were haunted by a special power only Theia, the Titan, possessed: the
gift of inner light to illuminate our world: light which emits from our own eye onto
an object, thus lighting it for us to see. And when you lost her, you sought her

343

daughter, Selene. You, a lover of darkness, used that tiny sliver of silver reflected by her crescent to illumine your way back in time.

I understand now your cavalier treatment of my heart and the hearts of too many others. You have been on a quest to find Theia, to reunite with her, and re-experience the brilliance of rapture. Your heart was true, though hers was not, never returning your ardor or loyalty. Unable in the real world to share this love, you made her an obsession, the object of your inner eye, the muse for your paintings and poems.

I rekindled in you a memory long repressed, when its intensity threatened your sanity. I inadvertently allowed you to come alive again, to love once more only because I reminded you of Theia. In the flesh, the flesh of your seventh decade, you loved one, last, luminescent time. That love was returned by me. Together, our smoldering hearts burst with an incandescent fire.

One last time, Wylie, before our bodies fail and fade away, as they soon will, as we age and die, before our flesh is burned away and our bones purified, as they will be, scattered, ashes to ashes, over the crust of our molten orb and onto the winds circling the spheres, we have loved. Yes, these, our well beloved bodies will die. But, love, my love, our love, your love, your loves, will not die.

You have convinced me that love, any love, so true, so profound, so relished an experience, cannot be extinguished. It burns, beaming outward from our souls, lighting the journey through eternity. Perhaps our love began before time began. For me, it existed before and during and after all moments in time. And our time together will continue to exist, even if, somehow, the universe and time itself were to cease.

Don't you suppose a pure and faithful love becomes one of the countless points of light in the night sky? I think our torch will still fly high in the heavens, freed from time and earthly bonds. And, seen from afar, our love's brilliance no longer burns me with such deadly heat.

I loved you, believing your words, believing your touch, trusting our love was mutual and true. Now I know it was not. You saw light beckon through the open doorway of my heart, and it led you back to Theia. Ha! And, all along, I thought I was blind. When our love star burned close, I was indeed blinded by its light, incinerated by its flame. But, it was you who couldn't see me!

Our love was an illusion. No different from the light we see cast by now dead stars. Perhaps our star burned out billions of light years ago, like countless others, long before becoming visible in our galaxy. Does that lapse of time make it any less real?

It is a point of light, after all, an oasis in the night sky, a star, once afire, a love, an illusion, to remember.

Pants On Fire!

Letter from Ariane to Dr. Mills
September 20, 2010

Dear Dr. Mills,

You wrote me months ago concerning your patient, Wylie Hymen. Your letter came as a shock. I did not know Wylie was living in a mental health treatment center, that he did not have cancer, or that he was married.

If there is anything I could take as positive from your letter, it is that you continue to encourage Wylie to paint, draw, and write. Creating art and poetry was a large part of the love we shared and of who he is.

I have a last request of my own. I would like you to give him a note, which I am enclosing. I ask that you deliver it to him unopened.

Thank you.

Ariane Altar

For Wylie, My True and False Love
The Last Poem

The Mirage and the Oasis

I saw you
I thought I saw you
Across the rolling desert of my dreams
A speck of hope
On a sea of shifting sands
And lost travelers
I saw you
Shimmering in the heat
Arising
An oasis
You
An oasis
Upon an arid landscape
Affording a balm
Perchance
To slake
My thirst

And how did I come
To the oasis

Pants On Fire!

Did I arrive
Guided
On camels bearing gifts
Did I stagger
Parched
Lost
On foot
Did I crawl
Exhausted
Upon my belly
To you

Your shade beckoned
Its promise looked real
You drew me to you
You drew
Didn't you
From your well
And trickled its waters
Over my parted lips
A sip o just a sip
Poured
Your waters
Down my parched throat
Washed them
Over my hot skin
Quenching the desert
Fire
Water
Waters from your well

The night began its dance of cooling
An occasional star lit the darkness
A slight breeze
Stirred
You
Me
Once inside
You ignited
A burning lantern
Called desire

Pants On Fire!

I ask
What did I give you
In return
In return for
Reviving me
Refreshing me
In return for
Your water
For
My life

I lay
In your arms
Naked
Bearing nothing
You cleansed me
Baring everything
You cleansed me
Bearing nothing
You cleansed me

I offered nothing
Nothing in return
You
Took
My heart

O the desert and its mirages
O I saw what was
Not there
And what was
Or so it seemed
And you

You held for a time
Me
You nourished
For a time
Me
You gave
Love and devotion

Pants On Fire!

Me
For a time
Filled all
My longings
And more
I hadn't
Yet
Imagined

You held others
At your oasis
You held her
At your oasis
And when you held
Me
You held her
She who came first
To your oasis
And drank
And drank
And drank
Laughing
All the water from your well
Leaving only dribbles
Behind
Her
Tiny
But still sweet
Dribbles
For the next traveler
To sip

I came
To that well
I know not how
And you
Saved me
With a few
Tiny
Dribbles
Sweet

Pants On Fire!

Water
From your well
And I cried
And I was happy to
Drink
And you gave me
More
My tears

Choking
Choking
I am choking

And you collected
My tears
On canvas
Saved them to
Fill
Your well
And with them
My tears
You wiped
Away
You painted
You erased
A tiny part
Of my soul

I loved you
Well

●

Afterward

Total Eclipse

From: Cherry Estrella cherry@starsearch.com
Date: October 12, 2012
To: Ande andeP@gmail.com
Subject: Your Mom and an Art Exhibition

Dearest Ande,

As you are living on Kaua'i, I know you don't read the mainland newspapers. I thought you would want to know about this upcoming exhibition.

Figures and Faces, Painted Poetry of Wylie Hymen: A Body of Love
Palace of the Legion of Honor and the de Young Museum
San Francisco

A Body of Love

Mark your calendars: This December the de Young is proud to present at two of its venues the recent work, both exquisite and erotic, of renowned California illustrator and author, Wylie Hymen. Tickets should be purchased in advance for timed viewings. Hymen's nudes are composed not of pen or brush strokes but rather of a unique fusion of drawings and poems. Lines of words lyrically intertwine, wrapping his figures, lovers locked in eternal embraces reminiscent of those in Rodin's *The Kiss*. Poetry is a key part of Hymen's art, having been written originally to his female muses, whom he depicts at dawn, again in the spring, on beds of roses, and more.

I hope I do not offend or upset you by sending you this announcement. I thought you should know about it rather than getting ambushed later.

Pants On Fire!

I think of you and your darling family every day and wish only the best for you. Goldie and Beauty are adjusting well. I hope to return for a happier visit next time.

Much love, "Auntie" Cherry

From: Ande andeP@gmail.com
Date: October 16, 2012
To: Cherry Estrella cherry@starsearch.com

dearest "auntie" cherry,

how can we thank you for everything you do for us? you are ever present, supportive, and helpful.
thanks for telling me about wylie's show.
i knew mom loved wylie (i met him once) and felt utterly betrayed by him and his lying. i didn't care for him in the brief time we shared, but then, i often didn't like the men my mother chose. we plan go to his exhibition (how could we not?).
i don't know what to say.
we'll see you then. you are in our hearts.

ande, nalu, and kui

From: Cherry Estrella cherry@starsearch.com
Date: December 1, 2012
To: Ande andeP@gmail.com
Subject: Re: Your Mom and an Art Exhibition

Dear Ande,

Wylie's exhibit opened, and I am sending you the review from the Sunday paper. Apparently, there are a lot of paintings in the show of your mother.

Love, "Auntie" Cherry

Art Week Sunday Supplement *San Francisco Herald*
Figures and Faces, Painted Poetry: A Body of Love
Curated by Tom Jensen
Palace of the Legion of Honor and the de Young Museum

PAINTED POETRY: HYMEN CAPTURES A BODY OF LOVE
Review by Corinna Bugliosi

Pants On Fire!

It is no wonder, art lovers, that Wylie Hymen's *Painted Poetry: A Body of Love: Figures and Faces*, the current exhibition at the Palace of the Legion of Honor in San Francisco, with a concurrent print and text show at the de Young Museum, is proving wildly popular, and the timed tickets are nearly sold out. His lush line drawings of poetry, in luminous script on crisp, crystal archived mica impregnated parchment, reveal the very incarnation of human emotions — ecstasy, anguish, awakening, shame, despair, downfall, erotic yearning, contemplation.

This new work glows, as though lit from within. And with it, Hymen is rapidly achieving an international reputation. You, the viewer, may decide if his appeal lies solely in the realm of erotica, or if his figures allow us to rise with them to glimpse sublime possibilities in the sphere of eternal love and timeless art.

Hymen is unique in contemporary Bay Area art circles for elevating a cult of pleasure in erotic poetry and painting. Like the ecstatic joy, which *fin de siecle* Viennese artist Gustav Klimt hoped to find in beauty, Hymen sees the world "in female form." Klimt's fame rests on his reputation as one of the greatest sensual painters and graphic artists of his time. In particular, his drawings, which have been widely admired for their artistic excellence, are dominated by the portrayal of seductive women. The difference between the two artists is that Hymen's erotic vision is overshadowed by death.

Elegant gold or colored decoration, spirals and swirls often distinguish Klimt's work, and phallic shapes are used to conceal the more erotic positions of the drawings upon which many of his paintings are based. This can be seen in *Judith I* (1901), in *The Kiss* (1907 – 1908), and especially in *Danaë* (1907). One of the most common themes Klimt used was that of the dominant woman, the "femme fatale."

It is a duo, Theia-Ariane, who plays the "femme fatale" in Hymen's poetic lexicon. Hymen frees the female body from all inhibition. Naked sexuality for him appears to be a natural, crucial part of existence. One thinks of Japanese Shunga or Chinese Spring Palace erotica. He draws women in many different moods, departing from artificial poses. His spontaneous pen captures gestures that you feel are almost divine.

One of his most explicit portraits, *Theia*, possibly inspired by the Elgin Marbles seen by Hymen on a visit in 2010 to the British Museum, is erotic and feral, her raven tresses cascade down her back as we glimpse her from behind. A little background in mythology tells us Theia was the Titan goddess of sight (theia) and the shining light of the clear blue sky (aithre), the goddess who endowed gold, silver and gems with their brilliance and intrinsic value. According to the Greeks, Theia married Hyperion, the Titan-god of light, and bore him three children—Helios, the Sun, Eos, the Dawn, and Selene, the

Moon. An all too human Theia was also Hymen's great love, an unrequited love, which drove him to madness while in his early thirties.

Hymen's poetic line work and choice of provocative postures also reminds the viewer of classical Greek statuary, from the marble caryatids and statues of Pallas Athena on the Acropolis to bronze replicas of the goddesses and muses. This mimicry further adds to their power as modern myth. Hymen has infused the Classical and Renaissance heritage of figure depiction with a modern sense of urgency.

Much has been made of Hymen's serial intimacy with his muses, Theia, Ariane, Selene, and a full cast of female associates. Hymen's women are not only passive objects of desire but, more often, lustful Amazons, imbued with their own sexual prowess. Do note that in each portrait, Theia is depicted with eyes open but Ariane is drawn with eyes closed as though blind or asleep.

Ariane Altar, the sculptress, was the second great love of Hymen's life, invigorating his seventies, the final years. While their relationship was tragically fraught, he clearly has not forgotten her in this exhibition. Look at his *Ariane Awakening* and *Ariane at Dawn,* and you will see a distillation of love and longing lift from the sensuous drape of his former lover across their bed. Her bodylines are composed of poetry he had written her at the height of his passion.

The mythical Ariane, meaning "pure" in Greek, became the wife of Dionysos, the ancient Greek god of wine, theater, agriculture, and fertility. Dionysos, or Bacchus as the Romans called him, was the god who inspired ritual madness, ecstasy, and the epiphany. He was "the god that comes and the frenzy he induces." It is arguable that the real Ariane might have been fated for madness. She fell despondent on learning Hymen's love for her was false, triggered by an obsessive memory of his lost Theia.

Hymen takes us on a journey from the expansive to the intimate. Some canvases are so large, we must stand as far back as the gallery will allow in order not to be engulfed by them. For example, the most magnificent piece in the exhibition, a "must see," is *Burning Bed.* It is a luminescent canvas, a full forty feet long and fifteen feet high, filling an entire gallery wall. The image is of an inferno. On closer viewing, a pyre emerges from within the conflagration where you can see two swathed bodies burning. The entire canvas is made of words, presumably the love poems written by Hymen and Ariane to each other over the passionate course of their ill-fated affair. It is consuming, blinding and heart rending.

For this exhibition, Hymen spent time in Japan at paper making factories and with the Fujii film company. He was intrigued by the new photographic papers being produced, which could reflect light almost like the stars against the backdrop of the night sky. He had a special formula made by Fujii; the paper fibers were soaked in mica before being pressed into massive deckle edged parchment sheets. The mica is responsible for this unique refractory phenomenon with a thin layer of porcelain coating to deepen the colors. Hymen added strontium aluminate pigment to his inks and paints, which make them glow with phosphorescence. These technical advances work seamlessly to make his new work literally "on fire"!

Michelangelo's *Dying Slave* inspires *Ariane Lost*. The piece evokes a similar drama and tension, even a softness in the sway of the hips. Autumnal hues of amber and rust underscore the waning of love. Then Hymen takes us a step further into winter tones of gray and black with its companion piece, *Theia Lost*.

The poet, Rainer Maria Rilke, one of the most thoughtful interpreters of Auguste Rodin's art, described how the pain expressed in man's face is re-played in the body itself – "every part was a mouth that spoke a language of its own." Also true are the writhing lines of Hymen's figures expres-sive of the emotions of love, loss, desire, ecstasy, and beyond. Few, if any, can match Rodin in his sensuously expressive way of recreating the human body, not simply to tell a story, but also to redefine what it is to be human.

Hymen makes an admirable challenge. Male and female bodies float, writhe, and tumble in a mass of poems, lines can be read as figures converge, emerge, and disappear into a solid mass of the color and light. There is a suc-cession of confines and release, of imprisonment and freedom, inhalation and expiration, of positives and negatives; a constant inverting of the idea of inside and out, of exterior and interior. As Rilke succinctly phrased it, 'surroundings must be found within'.

And, within Hymen takes us. He employs a late style of realism, modern-izing it, as he uses poetry as line, an intriguing twist. To see the words, you must approach the paintings intimately, almost pressing against them. Such intimacy is necessary, for the paintings revel in the most intimate aspects of love. Most of the words are so tiny that they require a magnifying glass to be read. Fortunately, curator Tom Jensen places the full text of each poem next to its drawing.

The most touching piece is small and unassuming: *Ariane on the Blue-Green Temple*. Done in blue, this piece is prescient, predicting the tragic turn her life took. In it, the nude Ariane is draped over the broken shards of a large ceramic temple, which emerges from a silvery, moonlit pool. You cannot tell if it is a waterfall pool, a pool of her tears, or a pool of blood. On closer inspec-tion, you see that she is impaled on the broken temple shards, pierced through the heart by the words of the poem, "Blue-Green Temple." She bleeds navy blue ink into the night's watery shadows.

One of the techniques Hymen uses to draw us in to inspect each line ever closer is to write poems which spiral from large to small or small to large. In *Theia in Blue*, for example, the words circle outward from the tip of her nipple, shading and filling the areola in heavenly azure tones from sky blue to a deep cerulean of the sea.

Likewise, look at *Ariane Reclining*, an exquisite study in gold leaf, inset with black ink. Her pubic mound forms an inverted triangle for the poem, "Sing Me Your Little Song of Spring Dawning." Its last word, "me" sits astride what we presume to be an erogenous zone.

Hymen's lovers embracing is inspired, like Rodin's before him, by Francesca da Rimini and her husband's brother, Paolo Malatesta, the adulterous and tragic lovers from Dante's *Inferno* in *The Divine Comedy*. In Dante's story, the couple grows close while reading the tale of Lancelot and Guinevere. Thus, on Rodin's statue, *The Kiss*, it is Paolo who clutches Dante's book in his hand. *The Kiss* was intended to be part of a bronze door commission, the entry to Dante's *Inferno*, called the *Gates of Hell*.

In the story, Francesca's father arranged for her to be married to Gianciotto in a political union to end a war between Malatesta and Rimini. Gianciotto's younger brother, Paolo, was sent as emissary. Upon meeting Francesca, he fell in love. Tricked into the marriage with Gianciotto, Francesca remained true to Paolo. One day, the furious Gianciotto found them in an embrace, thrust a rapier right through Paolo and into Francesca's bosom. In sharing a grave, these lovers became eternal. Artists have frequently found inspiration in such fatal love.

Although the *Gates of Hell* was never completed, some of Rodin's most famous and memorable pieces were originally done for it, including *The Thinker, Adam, Eve,* and *The Kiss*. The sculptor recreated these same lovers, caught in that eternal moment many times over and from different angles. Hymen uses Rodin's works as inspiration for his drawings of the same names.

In Hymen's *Kiss*, the tragic lovers (Paolo and Francesca or are they Wylie and Ariane, you may well ask?) are depicted moments before their murder. He captures the tenderness of their eternal kiss in an individual line drawing, a delicious whirling of words written in ever deepening tones of red, from pale rose to deep crimson to darkest maroon against a globular and scarlet setting sun.

This comprehensive show celebrates the erotic and immortalizes the sublime. See it!

Of note in the catalogue:

As to Hymen and his muses: Hymen remains an active resident of Indian Springs Wellness Center; Theia Steiner enjoys good health in her ninth decade and was recently honored at the museum's Trustee Circle Dinner; the sculptress Ariane Altar died tragically, found floating in a waterfall pool near her Maui home last year. Her untimely death remains shrouded in mystery. Had she slipped by accident or by design into what

Pants On Fire!

Hymen painted as her "pool of tears"? Despite speculation to the contrary, her death was ruled accidental.

A particularly nice touch at the de Young is Stravinsky's *Firebird*, reputed to be one of Hymen's favorite scores, played as background music in the galleries.

The Palace of the Legion of Honor and the de Young Museum's Curator Tom Jensen, Curator Karen Borders of Indian Springs Museum, Dina Cochon Hymen, and Dr. Matthew Mills are to be congratulated on the cataloging and sensitive mounting of the exhibition which continues through February 14th.

Full color catalogues and bound copies of *Love Letters and Poems of Wylie and Ariane* are available for purchase in the museum gift shop. Giclee prints of the art and audiocassettes of the poetry are available through the de Young Museum.

○

Letter from Ande to Cherry Estrella
December 16, 2012

dearest "auntie" cherry,

glad we had special time with you
it means so much to us now
i still don't know how to thank you for all you did for my moms service and now for our visit with you
except to say we love you
you have a special place in our lives
as you witnessed first hand, nalu and i remain devastated and the thought of kui growing up without her beloved gramma breaks our hearts
thank you for being my mom's "bestest" friend and for helping grandma edna with the news and looking after her when you can
know that i am particularly grateful to you for sharing with me moms state of mind before her death
wylies exhibition...
again, i don't know what to say
it was pretty hard to see those paintings
it is hard if not impossible to think of my mother as someones lover
yet there she is naked before the world

not my mother but some old artists muse
maybe the blackness she fell into after my brother and sister died overtook her
maybe her fall was one of her accidents
she always said hana was not a place for sissies
we tried to get her to move but she loved it there
if she had wanted to kill herself she would have left a note
she liked to write, remember
i am glad i have her beautiful ceramic pieces
perhaps one day i shall have the courage to read her journals
perhaps
i love you "auntie" cherry
thank you for taking such good care of beauty and the doggies
come see us on kaua'i
you are in our hearts

ande, nalu, and kui

From: Cherry Estrella cherry@starsearch.com
Date: December 23, 2012
To: Ande andeP@gmail.com

Dearest Ande,

You may not realize it now, as the pain of your mother's loss is fresh, but as I reflect, I think having her sculptures and knowing Wylie's paintings exist brings a little chunk of stardust right here to earth, a bit of immortality. Imagine, little Kui will have those pieces of art to hold on to and to know at least a fragment of who her Gramma was··· that she loved and was loved···creating beauty wherever she went.

Look to the night sky. Imagine her twinkling there.

Big Hugs, "Auntie" Cherry

The End

Notes

LIAR, LIAR

"*Liar, liar pants on fire / Hanging from a telephone wire.*" is a paraphrased version of the 1810 poem The Liar by William Blake, reprinted here in full. Blake, a romantic, settled the question of whether or not honesty is the best policy.

Deceiver, dissembler
Your trousers are alight
From what pole or gallows
Shall they dangle in the night?

When I asked of your career
Why did you have to kick my rear
With that stinking lie of thine
Proclaiming that you owned a mine?

When you asked to borrow my stallion
To visit a nearby moored galleon
How could I ever know that you
Intended to turn him into glue?

What red devil of mendacity
Grips your soul with such tenacity?
Will one you cruelly shower with lies
Put a pistol ball between your eyes?
What internal serpent
Has lent you his forked tongue?
From what pit of foul deceit
Are all these whoppers sprung?

Deceiver, dissembler
Your trousers are alight
From what pole or gallows
Do they dangle in the night?

Pants On Fire!

HALEAKALĂ

Haleakală ("house of the sun") is a shield volcano forming more than 75% of the Hawai'ian Island of Maui. From the rim at 10,000 feet, a massive depression opens seven miles long and two miles wide, dropping nearly 2,600 feet. The walls of the crater are steep and the interior barren.

According to Hawai'ian legend, Maui's grandmother helped him capture the sun and force it to slow its journey across the sky in order to lengthen the day.

GERTRUDE BELL

Gertrude Bell: Queen of the Desert, Shaper of Nations
Biography by Regina Howell

Gertrude Bell (1868 – 1926), "the most famous British traveler of her day" was also a "poet, scholar, historian, mountaineer, photographer, archaeologist, gardener, cartographer, linguist and distinguished servant of the state." Gertrude was something of a phenomenon as the only daughter of a supremely rich English industrialist. She was presented at court, like other girls of her class; but rather than pursue a husband, she established her reputation as a fearless mountaineer, climbing unscaled Alpine peaks in her underwear. A visit to Tehran awakened her interest in the Middle East, and within two years, she had not only mastered classical Persian but also published a translation of the poetry of Hafiz. She learned Arabic next by traveling in well-equipped expeditions into the Arabian Desert, meeting with Bedouin, surveying archaeological sites. She amassed an extraordinary knowledge of the politics and personalities of the Arab world, which made her briefly indispensable to the British government after the outbreak of World War I. Faisal went out of his way to curry her favor, and so she found him a kingdom: Iraq, which was strung together out of the most unlikely constituents.

BLACK ROBE

Director: Bruce Beresford

Black Robe is brutal saga of redemption and salvation. In 1634 a young, aristocratic French Jesuit missionary is assigned to trek 1,500 miles through the New France wilderness to a mission settled in Huron Indian country. *Black Robe* chronicles the journey of Father Laforgue as he leaves his Jesuit brothers and, with the aid of a young translator and guide and eight canoes of Algonquin Indians, moves into the uncompromising Canadian northern territory on a mission to convert the natives. It is a restless tale of Laforgue's conflicted faith juxtaposed against the sublime spiritual harmony with the land that the Huron and Algonquin already hold. *Black Robe* is tuned into the precarious balance between nature's mystery and spirit and the strident, unyielding religious ethic.

FITZCARRALDO

Director: Werner Herzog

Iquitos is a town isolated in the middle of the Peruvian jungle at the turn of the century. On the outskirts a few shacks are rotting in the mud. In the center are the splendid houses of the nouveaux-riches rubber barons. Fitzcarraldo is an avid opera lover and rubber baron who dreams of building an opera house in the Peruvian jungle. He determines to reach an isolated patch of rubber trees to make his fortune. But, these trees are not directly accessible by river because of dangerous rapids. Fitzcarraldo enlists the aid of the native Peruvians to drag his ship over a mountain. But, the natives seem to have their own agenda. The results manage to both mock and affirm the dreams of Fitzcarraldo, making absurdity out of the stuff of human endeavor without negating the beauty of that effort. The image of Fitzcarraldo's ship being pulled up the mountain with cables and pulleys is awe-inspiring as is that of the ship resting in mid-ascent in the thick morning fog of the jungle.

LUST/CAUTION
Directed by Ang Lee

Set in China during the Japanese occupation of early World War II, the underlying plot concerns the story of young Wong Chia Chi, an actress and member of a small group of student resistors planning to infiltrate the home of Mr. Yee, a high-ranking collaborationist government official, in order to kill him for his role in the torture and executions of Chinese resistance fighters.

The story of their love is told through their sexual relationship, which starts out violently. This is lust with a capital L; the film's sex scenes have become famous for their frankness and acrobatic portrayals, but they are never prurient. The nature of the sexual relationship, and not the sex itself, is the point, which shows the difficulty of being essentially human in an inhumane world.

MIT DIE SCHLAGSAHNE with whipping cream

TAROT

The Major Arcana are intended to trace the 'process of initiation leading to enlightenment'. It is an analogy to the occult path, the life of the quester.

0 - The Fool is the 'soul before enlightenment', meaning the quester (or the 'initiate') before ascending the occult mountain to the final state of gnosis. The Fool is the starting position, point zero.

I - The Magus signifies the magical force or power, that energy which the quester uses to propel him or herself ever-forward on the quest.

II - The High Priestess is the 'other' energy. One energy (Magus) seeks the other (Priestess). When found there is supposed to be spiritual unity, the state of the human soul. Envisage the Fool as the soul before birth, and conceive the Magus and Priestess as the inherent powers the soul has, the dual opposing forces of nature the possession of which is intrinsic to the soul.

III - The Empress is supposed to portray the person's biological mother.

IV - The Emperor symbolizes the father, but also 'rules and their official enforcers', the civil and social laws to adhere to.

V - The Hierophant stands for education in all its many forms, the indoctrination of the individual.

VI - The Lovers is the card of rebellion outside the family and education. You can't choose your family but you choose your friends. It is that sedition, that moment in life where for the first time there is thought to be something outside the structures.

VII - The Chariot pioneers forward.

VIII - Adjustment is thoughtful reflection, the quester discovering the unfairness of life, and the need to 'adjust accordingly', to think out personal methods of settling conflicts in as just and fair a way as possible.

IX - The Hermit, card nine, expresses contemplation: introspection and the will to withdraw from participating in active life.

X - The Wheel of Fortune brings the quester back into the world. The circular form of the wheel of Fortune shows how events come in cycles.

XI - Lust is a vigorous and healthy engagement with life.

XII - The Hanged Man is a painful, self-imposed contemplation. This card holds the concept of sacrifice - going through physical suffering in order to gain illumination.

XIII - Death is the thirteenth card, and renders 'total change' or resurrection. The Hanged Man has been through the agony, and now there is rebirth; the redemption, the salvation, the change has come to pass. Death is the ultimate operative of the natural cycle, destruction being the force in nature that paves way for the new. Change occurs in life, whether desired or not. This has to be met with acceptance.

XIV - Art is creation out of the preceding card's destruction.

XV - The Devil, card fifteen, is means materiality and entrapment.

XVI - The Tower brings a mocking light that reveals the meaninglessness of structures, the emptiness of every aspect of ordered life. The individual is not only down, but kicked by the knowledge that his or her life is worthless and that to pretend it was significant would be a terrible act of bad faith. The Tower is destructive in that it attacks the substance of the person's life, each and every compartment of it. The Tower overcomes the Devil because the Devil is materiality. The experience of the Tower makes the quester put no faith in the material world.

XVII - The Star is safety.

XVIII - The Moon is the card heralding the transformation to come.

XIX - The Sun is a release from the Moon-trial, and preparation for the final test. The Sun is the heart of the Tree of Life.

XX - The Aeon is that ultimate test or Judgment.

XXI - The Universe is the ascension. Oneness of being. As the Fool is zero, it can come either at the beginning or the end, signifying perhaps that all-knowledge is akin to madness. The occult quest is accomplished.

SCHEHERAZADE

Scheherazade is a legendary Persian queen and the storyteller of *One Thousand and One Nights*. The king had been betrayed by his first wife and was unable to trust love or women. By the time he was introduced to Scheherazade, his vizier's daughter and the last beauty in his kingdom, he had killed three thousand beautiful women, whom he had married and had killed the next morning.

Against her father's protestations, Scheherazade volunteered to spend one night with the King. Once in the King's chambers, Scheherazade asked if she might bid one last fare-well to her beloved sister, Dinazade, who had secretly been prepared to ask Scheherazade to tell a story during the long night. The King lay awake and listened with awe as Scheherazade told her first story. The night whiled away, and Scheherazade stopped in the middle of the story. The King asked her to finish, but Scheherazade said there was not time, as dawn was breaking. And so, the King kept Scheherazade alive day by day, as he eagerly anticipated the finishing of last night's story. At the end of one thousand and one nights, and one thousand stories, Scheherazade told the King that she had no more tales to tell him. During these one thousand and one nights, the King had fallen in love with Scheherazade, and had three sons with her. Therefore, having been made a wiser and kinder man by Scheherazade and her tales, he spared her life, and made her his Queen.

MAGELLAN

Over the Edge of the World: Magellan's Terrifying Circumnavigation of the Globe
By Laurence Bergreen

Ferdinand Magellan was the first captain to circumnavigate the globe. He spent years trying to win the favor of the king of Portugal and then swore loyalty to the Spanish crown

Pants On Fire!

in order to receive Spain's backing for a trip. His obsessive 16th-century quest to find the Spice Islands was an ill-fated journey that altered Europe's perception of the planet: "It was a dream as old as the imagination: a voyage to the ends of the earth.... Mariners feared they could literally sail over the edge of the world." Magellan's mission for Spain was to find a water route to the fabled Spice Islands, and in 1519, the Armada de Molucca (five ships and some 260 sailors) set sail. Many misfortunes befell the expedition, including the brutal killing of Magellan in the Philippines. Three years later, one weather-beaten ship, "a vessel of desolation and anguish," returned to Spain with a skeleton crew of 18, yet "what a story those few survivors had to tell-a tale of mutiny, of orgies on distant shores, and of the exploration of the entire globe," providing proof that the world was round.

Once Magellan embarked, he had to contend with violent storms, mutinous crewmembers, and hostile natives. Bergreen tells a well-rounded story of Magellan, not just that of a hero but also that of Magellan's darker side. The book puts the voyage into historical context, what was known of the world and charted seas at the time, the rivalry between Portugal and Spain, and the church's attempt to divide up the New World between the two countries.

MARCO POLO
Marco Polo: From Venice to Xanadu
By Laurence Bergreen

In writing of his journey begun at age fifteen to the Chinese court of Kublai Khan, 13th-century travel writer Marco Polo was mocked for his tales of gem-encrusted clothes, nude temple dancing girls, screaming tarantulas. This book follows Polo's commentary on everything from Chinese tax policy to asbestos manufacturing, crocodile hunting and Asian sexual mores, one of which was the practice of sharing one's wife with passing travelers. Polo ended his days back in Venice as a greedy and litigious merchant. Yet, the result is a long, strange, illuminating trip.

RAMAYANA

The Ramayana is a luminous saga of abduction, battle, and love played out in a universe of deities and demons. The Sanskrit original was composed around the fourth century B.C. Countless versions can be found in different cultures and different languages. The Ramayana can be enjoyed for its spiritual wisdom, or as a thrilling tale of ancient conflict.

RAMA AND SITA

Rama won his bride, Sita, by a physical feat. Rama was the oldest son and heir apparent to Dasaratha. In response to a promise the king had made to Rama's stepmother Kaikeyi, Rama was sent into exile for 14 years and her son made heir to the throne. The king died. Meanwhile, Rama and Sita lived in the forest until Ravana, evil king of Lanka, kidnapped Sita, luring her away from safety disguised as a golden deer. Rama renounced Sita as unfaithful. When an ordeal by fire proved Sita faithful, Sita returned to Rama to live happily ever after. It is perhaps surprising that Rama is considered the one enduring the tragic fate, rather than Sita.

THE *HINDENBURG* DISASTER

The *Hindenburg* disaster occurred on May 6, 1937 at Lakehurst Naval Air Station in Manchester Township, New Jersey when a zeppelin airship en route from Frankfurt, Germany exploded just before landing. Thirty-six passengers and crew died. The actual cause of the fire remains unknown, although a variety of theories, including friction, have been put forward for both the cause of ignition and the initial fuel for the ensuing fire.

Some witnesses reported the fabric ahead of the upper fin fluttered as if gas were leaking. Blue light—possibly static electricity—flashed moments before mushroom shaped flames appeared. When the *Hindenburg*'s tail crashed into the ground, a burst of flame came out of the nose, killing nine of the 12 crewmembers in the bow.

Herbert Morrison's broadcast on WLS radio remains one of the most famous in history. "···It's a terrific crash, ladies and gentlemen. It's smoke, and it's in flames now; and the frame is crashing to the ground, not quite to the mooring mast. Oh, the humanity!"

Hydrogen fires are notable for being less destructive to immediate surroundings than gasoline explosions because of the buoyancy of H2, which causes heat of combustion to be released upwards more than circumferentially. The hydrogen in the *Hindenburg* burned out within about 90 seconds.

Sabotage was commonly put forward as the cause of the fire, initially by Hugo Eckener, former head of the Zeppelin Company and the "old man" of German airships, who later endorsed the static spark theory. He concluded the presence of aluminum and iron oxide in the airship's coating may have been a factor in the disaster and that the fire was caused by the ignition of hydrogen by a static spark:

"I believe that the fire was not caused by an electrical spark, but by a static spark. A thunderstorm front had passed before the landing maneuver. However, if one observes more closely, one can see that this was followed by a smaller storm front. This created conditions suitable for static sparks to occur. I believe a spark had ignited gas in the rear of the ship."

An observer in 1937, Professor Mark Heald of Princeton, New Jersey, saw St. Elmo's Fire flickering along the airship's back a good minute before the fire broke out. Standing outside the main gate to the Naval Air Station, he watched, together with his wife and son, as the Zeppelin approached the mast, dropping the bowlines. Mr. Heald then noticed a dim "blue flame" flickering along the backbone girder about one-quarter the length abaft the bow to the tail. "Oh, heavens, the thing is afire," he cried to his wife. Then, there was a big burst of flaming hydrogen from a point he estimated to be about one-third the ship's length from the stern. Professor Heald's view of the starboard side of the ship against a backdrop of the darkening eastern sky would have made the dim blue light of a static discharge (or burning hydrogen) atop the ship easily visible.

A variant of the static spark theory, presented by Addison Bain, is that a spark between inadequately grounded fabric cover segments of the *Hindenburg* itself started the fire, and that the spark had ignited the "highly flammable" outer skin. The *Hindenburg* had a cotton skin covered with a finish known as "dope" or plasticized lacquer that provides stiffness, protection, and a lightweight, airtight seal to woven fabrics. Proponents of this theory claim that when the mooring line touched the ground, a resulting spark could have ignited the dope in the skin.

Proponents of both the incendiary paint theory and the hydrogen theory agree that the fabric coatings were probably responsible for the rapid spread of the fire. The combustion of hydrogen is not usually visible to the human eye in daylight, because most of its radiation is not in the visible portion of the spectrum but rather infrared. Thus, what can be seen burning in the photographs cannot be hydrogen. However, black and white photographic film of the era had a different light sensitivity spectrum than the human eye, and was sensitive farther out into the infrared and ultraviolet region than the human eye. In addition, while hydrogen tends to burn invisibly, the materials around it, if combustible, would change the color of the fire.

Pants On Fire!

The loss of lift at the rear caused the airship to nose up suddenly and the back to break in half (the airship was still in one piece). At that time, the primary mode for the fire to spread was along the axial gangway, which acted as a chimney, conducting the fire. It burst out the nose as the airship's tail touched the ground, as seen in one of the most famous pictures of the disaster taken by Murray Becker for AP.

GENGHIS KHAN
Genghis Khan or the Emperor of All Men
By Harold Lamb

Eight hundred years ago, Genghis Khan, Emperor of All Men, born as Temujin in 1162, almost conquered the earth. He made himself master of half the known world and inspired humankind with a fear that lasted for generations. Genghis Khan cannot be measured by ordinary standards. When he marched with his army, it was by degrees of latitude and longitude instead of miles; cities in his path were often obliterated and rivers diverted from their courses; deserts were populated with the fleeing and dying, and after he had passed, wolves and ravens were often the sole living things in a once populous area.

Genghis Khan achieved his notoriety by uniting many different nomadic tribes that had previously been at war with each other. Together they came to be known as the Mongols and were perhaps the most ferocious, ruthless and relentless group of "barbarians" the world has known.

Under the brilliant generalship of Genghis Khan (and later his descendants), the Mongols conquered all of Asia and came close to dominating Europe as well. They won battles not only by their courage and ferocity but also by utilizing sophisticated military techniques and trickery. They were, of course, expert horsemen and archers. They completely destroyed the Chinese and Persian empires. The Mongols, probably more so than the Christian crusaders, prevented Islam from becoming the dominant force in the world. Genghis Khan was a practical ruler, caring little for politics or religion, and using them only as tools. For example, he expressed a belief in one God, but allowed Christians, Buddhists, and Moslems alike (along with the older shamanistic nomads) to worship as they pleased, as long as they submitted to his rule. His grandson, Kublai Khan, was made famous in the West by Marco Polo.

Historically, like Alexander the Great and the Roman Empire, the Mongols were instrumental in opening up and connecting different regions of the world. They created a vast system of communication across Asia.

BROKEN EMBRACES
Directed by Pedro Almodovar

A blind screenwriter in the present day reminisces about his favorite leading lady. He had cast her in a screwball comedy and fell in love, and their passionate off-screen affair began.

MARCEL PROUST
A La Recherche Du Temps Perdu
Swann's Way: In Search of Lost Time, Vol. 1 (Penguin Classics Deluxe Edition)

Remembrance of Things Past is Marcel Proust's novel about memory and the senses, describing time passing and its effect on memory.

The largest section of the novel is not about the narrator, but rather about Swann, a friend of his family. Fifteen years before the events described in the first part, Swann fell in love with Odette, a woman with a terrible reputation. And, his love affair affects the rest of his life.

Pants On Fire!

Proust took a deep interest in literature and the visual arts. His main character's relationship to his mother echoes Sophocles' *Oedipus Rex*. With a caldron of references and allusions, particularly to works of Monet and Botticelli, Proust created one of the most respected literary works of the twentieth century.

SHOAH
Directed by Claude Lanzmann

Shoah is a nine-hour film completed in 1985 about the Holocaust (or *Shoah*). Though *Shoah* is conventionally classified as a documentary film, director Lanzmann considers it to fall outside of that genre, as, unlike most historical documentaries, the film does not feature reenactments or historical footage; instead it consists of interviews with people who were involved in various ways in the Holocaust, and visits to different places they discuss. The film is concerned mainly with four topics: Chelmno, where gas vans were first used to exterminate Jews; the death camps of Treblinka and Auschwitz-Birkenau; and the Warsaw Ghetto, with testimonies from survivors, witnesses, and perpetrators.

Lanzmann divides his witnesses into three distinct archetypes: survivor, bystander, and perpetrator. Lanzmann makes an effort to represent each archetype quite differently.

Survivors are those who directly experienced the persecution and horror of the Holocaust, and survived to tell their story.

Bystanders are those who were present during the events of the Holocaust without directly being part of it. Some were peripherally involved while others were witnesses.

Perpetrators are those who were directly involved in orchestrating the Holocaust. All of the perpetrators whom Lanzmann interviews are German. From these perpetrators, Lanzmann establishes a historical narrative. They give detailed, detached accounts of the workings of the Holocaust.

SEPTEMBER SONG
Lyrics Maxwell Anderson and Music by Kurt Weill from *Knickerbocker Holiday*

PUNT
To the ancient Egyptians, the land of Punt, with its reed, beehive shaped houses raised on stilts above water, was the most exotic and mysterious of places to visit, and from which to receive visitors, for more than once the Royalty of Punt came to the court of the Pharaoh in Egypt. It seems to have been considered by them a most unique haven, an emporium of goods for both king and gods, and gradually acquired an air of fantasy, like that of an Eldorado or Atlantis. For this reason, it was sometimes featured in narrative tales such as the Tale of the Shipwrecked Sailor.

IRIS MURDOCH
Iris Murdoch DBE (15 July 1919 – 8 February 1999) was an Irish-born British author and philosopher, best known for her novels about political and moral questions of good and evil, sexual relationships, morality, and the power of the unconscious. Her first published novel, Under the Net, was selected in 2001 by the editorial board of the American Modern Library as one of the 100 best English-language novels of the 20th century.

LOSING JULIA
By Jonathan Hull

WWI vet Patrick Delaney's diary layers two stories with scenes from the nursing home where he is dying in alternating sections which merge into the larger work, a story of love and death. "Our lives – all our lives – are a struggle between love and loss," Julia

Pants On Fire!

tells Patrick in Paris, where their affair unfolds over one week in 1928. Hull seamlessly incorporates period detail, referencing the toiletries the enlistees received in their trench kits and how the weather affected the roads at the Battle of Verdun. Equally honest and effective are the unsparing descriptions of the loneliness, physical decrepitude and indignities of old age.

NPR National Public Radio

PBS Public Broadcasting Service

WINGS OF THE DOVE
Directed by Iain Softley
The Wings Of The Dove is a provocative tale of passion, temptation, and greed.

FOUR FEATHERS
Directed by Shekhar Kapur
Set in the 1880s, a promising soldier resigns on the eve of battle in Britain's Sudanese campaign and is labeled a coward by his fiancée and his three friends, who send him the titular feathers representative of cowardice. He redeems himself by posing as a Muslim warrior to rescue his best friend from certain death in the desert.

UNCLE WIGGILY LONGEARS
By Howard Garis
Uncle Wiggily Longears, the distinguished elderly rabbit, first appeared on January 10, 1910 in the *Newark News*, and was created by Howard Garis. *Uncle Wiggily* was an instant success, and over 15,000 stories appeared in the newspaper over the next thirty years. Uncle Wiggily books were the most popular children's stories in the early 20th century.
Uncle Wiggily thrives on helping others and thinks nothing of self-sacrifice. He is very ingenious at building things in his effort to help or rescue those in need, even those like Woozy Wolf and Skillery Skallery who try to do him harm. Uncle Wiggily drives a *Model T* roadster and flies an "airship" as well. His housekeeper, Nurse Jane Fuzzy Wuzzy, a muskrat who is always cooking up savory dishes to eat, plays a significant role in the stories. He exudes self-confidence and poise as he goes about his days with a spring in his step and a song in his heart.

SHUNGA: Erotic Prints Of Japan
Shunga, literally translated as "Spring Pictures," are a genre of woodblock prints that depict the entire gamut of sensual and sexual pleasures.
To fully understand the unabashed nature of shunga, it is helpful to understand the society that inspired and nurtured it: a pleasure bent culture of Edo, a fabulous city of eroticism unmatched by any in the West. Within the confines of its sumptuous quarters, courtesans of stunning beauty and exquisite sensibility elevated the gratification of physical desire to an art. The shunga print was both the natural outgrowth and the fullest expression of this hedonism, and as such, mirrored an endless range of physical passions. Yet, although shunga fulfilled a major purpose in the Yoshiwara, its illustrations often serving to train inexperienced courtesans as well as to arouse prospective clients, it also played a central role in the education of newlyweds. In many families, it was the custom to give brides shunga albums, or "pillow books" that were treasured by each generation and often passed down from mother to

371

daughter. Aside from its practical usefulness, Japanese erotica was also valued for its beauty. The shunga print is technically and historically an integral part of ukiyo-e. Virtually all the great masters of ukiyo-e felt that designing good shunga was vital to their artistic careers.

Sex. Mere mention of the topic provokes within us intensely diverse emotional reactions, yet few subjects are as universally understood and as instrumental in forming our identities as adult human beings. Sexuality has been a consistent topic throughout the history of visual art in various cultures. Japanese artists of the Edo period (1615-1868), including the most revered designers of ukiyo-e prints, were involved in the production of erotica known as shunga (literally "spring pictures") as well as more restrained depictions of sexuality. Exploring the genre of shunga offers us a much richer understanding of ukiyo-e printmaking as well as the general attitudes about sexuality and gender that were prevalent in Edo society.

SPRING PALACE PAINTINGS: Chinese Erotic Art
Erotic Chinese art in letters and pictures was a tradition that spanned from antiquity until its apex in the Late Ming Dynasty (early 17th Century). Not just produced for stimulation, Chinese erotica was layered in ideals of feminine beauty, narratives on imperial and vernacular life and most importantly, humor, tenderness and love. However, after the last dynasty and between the two republics (1912 and 1949), Chinese sexual art was suppressed by modern Confucius followers and Western missionaries, resulting in the destruction of many pieces.

The word "Spring" refers to the archaic springtime rituals during which girls and boys separated by a brook sang love-songs to each other. Later, when lovemaking became part of refined imperial court culture, the word 'palace' was added as an allusion to the emperor's residence. Erotic fiction in China spun tales of the misbehavior of rulers and their consorts. Fervid imaginings of what happened behind the walls of the Forbidden City and the pleasures one might enjoy if in the possession of absolute power were irresistible to novelists, painters, and the audiences for whom they were created. Erotic art developed concurrently with the rise of the rich mercantile cities of southern China from the 10th century on.

In China, the tradition of erotic literature called pillow books, ranges from poetry and novels to instructional manuals. Like spring palace paintings, erotic poetry typically embodied attributes of humor and flirtation. However, novels often blurred the line between fiction and non-fiction, integrating a mixture of historical figures and narratives that are themselves factually questionable.

Chinese erotic art can be found on inlaid boxes, porcelain figurines, silk or rice paper paintings, and even on the soles of ceramic shoes. The album (a series of paintings loosely bound in book form), however, was the preferred form of erotic art.

Snuff Bottles are another medium where sensual scenes can be found either through reverse painting or through the craftsmanship of the glass. Reverse painting on snuff bottles is just as it sounds, executed from the inside of the bottle facing out. Tobacco was believed to have medicinal benefits in China and was consumed both in the imperial court and in the larger population. It is only natural to find snuff bottles and erotica paired.

Although clothing, hair, and even the scenes for seduction can vary (gardens, brothels, palaces, bedrooms, and boats) there are a few visual hallmarks that are recurring in spring palace paintings such as sweet-faced lovers wearing softly folding fabrics. Foot binding was widespread in China until the twentieth century and – not surprisingly – feet play an important part in Chinese erotic art and literature. Small feet in China were analogous to ample breasts in the West.

About the Author

Arabella Ark lives in the Hawaiian Islands. She received a Master's degree in Directing from University of California at Berkeley and worked in theatre, film and news journalism. A serendipitous career as an international clay artist came unexpectedly through the back door of her life forty years ago. In just the same way, love often arrived, uninvited.